NIGHTWORLD

Suddenly the sack was dragged along the floor and pulled through a gap in the corrugated iron wall of the shed. The man smell, seamed with a sweetness like flower scent, filled Hawscrag's nostrils. She was bundled into something hard and taken on another jolting ride that left her bruised and shaken. But after a long while she smelt the turf of the clifftops and the breeze lifting off the sea. The sack was opened and she rolled out, baring her teeth and expecting the dogs. The boy and girl clapped their hands and the sow shook her head, snorting away the crumbs of dried blood from her muzzle. The grass held the faint reek of sheep and the morning flashed and winked with a brightness she found alarming. Above the shoulder of the down, where land and sea met in high, dark-shadowed cliffs, the sun shone. Hawscrag trotted through the bracken towards the light and found herself shaking off the fear.

NIGHTWORLD

Brian Carter

THE SHERIDAN
BOOK COMPANY

This edition published in 1994 by
The Sheridan Book Company

First published in Great Britain by Century 1987
Random House, 20 Vauxhall Bridge Road, London SW1V 2SA
Arrow edition 1988

© Brian Carter 1987

Printed and bound in Great Britain by
Cox & Wyman Ltd, Reading, Berkshire

ISBN 1-85501-681-8

Contents

Author's Foreword

The illegal and excessively cruel 'sport' of badger baiting is still with us despite the efforts of the RSPCA and other animal welfare groups.

Badgers are dug out and either killed on the spot or taken elsewhere to be savaged to death by dogs. The South Devon gangs I knew as a boy used Jack Russells not only to locate the badger underground, but also in the actual baiting. Normally, then as now, larger dogs like the Fox Terrier were unleashed to do the killing, yet during by boyhood in the late 1940s I attended baitings exclusive to Jack Russells. The barbarism persists and baiters operating today use Staffordshire Bull Terriers, betting on the performance of their animals. Ruth Murray, a world authority on the badger, told me of occasions when Jack Russells and even smaller dogs were expected to provide the 'entertainment'. The choice of dog depends on what the men involved can afford. One thing is certain – victim and attackers suffer terribly throughout. This book is dedicated to all those fighting on behalf of the badger – Britain's most persecuted wild creature.

Brian Carter

Chapter 1

Moonborn

Clenching on fur and flesh the heavy iron tongs dragged the badger sow from her underground chamber. The metal jaws were clamped to the side of her neck and as the man at the end of the long handles lifted her body weight, muscle and hide were pierced and torn. In a contortion of panic she twisted and savaged the tongs but already they were hoisting her clear of the sett. Then the clamp opened and she rolled free on to hard mud. The spasm of pain corkscrewed and she staggered and tried to turn her head and lick it but the dogs had begun to go about their business. Five terriers swarmed over her, slashing at her hindquarters with their teeth. A bolder one attacked her face and bit her snout. The sow sneezed blood.

The clifftops were giddy with daylight and colour. Smells whirlpooled at the centre of her confusion, smells that had not risen from the living world. All the nuances of the man smell soaked her being – sweat, boot polish, tobacco smoke, dental decay, cider fumes, damp overalls and something else, dark and chilling, that the badger could only guess at. The dog smells were stronger and less unpleasant but the collective stink of the giant figures was sickening. She had smelt it before and detested it.

Bewilderment subsided under another jolt of pain. The dogs were relentless but she bristled and snarled, swinging her head from side to side and occasionally striking the target. Startled yelps rose above the chorus of growls and whines. She was fighting mad and ready for anything.

'Call them off,' said a voice. 'Tap her on the nose and put her in the bag.'

So the nightmare pursued its familiar course. There was the sharp blow, dizziness and life draining from her limbs. Then the bumping and rattling, the persistent growl and vibration, the reek of men and petrol and terriers while the darkness enclosed her like a skin. She tried to read it with her snout but the texture was coarse and smelt only of damp grain.

Presently the noise and violent movement stopped and still in the sack she was thrown into a shed and the door was bolted. After a moment the world beyond her darkness came alive again. Men were laughing and shouting and from the babble of noise lifted a sound that cut to the core of her being. It was a boar's cry of despair and misery. Hawscrag settled on her helplessness and waited.

Suddenly the sack was dragged along the floor and pulled through a gap in the corrugated iron wall of the shed. The man smell, seamed with a sweetness like flower scent, filled Hawscrag's nostrils. She was bundled into something hard and taken on another jolting ride that left her bruised and shaken. But after a long while she smelt the turf of the clifftops and the breeze lifting off the sea. The sack was opened and she rolled out, baring her teeth and expecting the dogs. The boy and girl clapped their hands and the sow shook her head, snorting away the crumbs of dried blood from her muzzle. The grass held the faint reek of sheep and the morning flashed and winked with a brightness she found alarming. Above the shoulder of the down, where land and sea met in high, dark-shadowed cliffs, the sun shone. Hawscrag trotted through the bracken towards the light and found herself shaking off the fear.

The landscape blurred and darkened to become the lovely night of underearth. A voice was calling her out of sleep and opening her eyes she ran her snout over the blackness that was heavy with the essence of badger living.

'It was the bad dream?' the voice enquired.

'Yes,' Hawscrag sighed. 'Always the death smell and the cry.'

'And do you think,' the voice continued, 'the Baiting awaits us all?'

'Some of us,' the old sow grunted. 'Men are death. Their smell clings to the gins and snares. They can make death leap from a loud noise. They have dogs which kill our kind and they have the Baiting. It is the way of the world.'

Her tone softened. 'I didn't know the boar who died but my heart still hurts when I think of him.'

'Humans released you?' said another voice. The constant re-telling of the story had not blunted the listeners' amazement.

'Yes,' said Hawscrag.

'But you are Moonborn,' said the voice of Aspen the young sow and daughter of Hawscrag.

'I'm sure that was of little consequence,' Hawscrag murmured, drowsily scratching her belly.

The badgers considered the notion and slept again.

Three maiden sows shared the sleeping chamber with Hawscrag. Aspen's companions were her sisters Guelder and a timid little creature who stuttered and was called Birdcherry. Dug at two levels Big Sett was vast and ancient. Sixteen holes provided access to an underground labyrinth of tunnels and galleries which linked family chambers, rest chambers and the sleeping quarters of the boars and sows. Two families were in almost permanent residence although neighbours and relatives occasionally visited and the vixen, Cowtail, had moved in as a lodger the previous winter.

No sett on the South Devon coast had a finer or safer

situation. It had been excavated from earth and sand on the great, well-drained steeps of Froward Point below a copse of Monterey pines where the bunkers of old gun emplacements stood empty. The paths running to the entrance holes wriggled through a sprawling tangle of rusty barbed wire into a thicket of scrub blackthorn and gorse. The seaward side was protected by vertical crags.

The dense undergrowth on the steeps had so far thwarted the attempts of badger diggers to take animals for sport but all the other clifftop setts from St Mary's Head to the estuary of the Marl, a distance of roughly seven miles, had been opened at one time or other. The Froward badgers often used these smaller dens at the end of forage with dawn threatening. Hawscrag had been dug out of the sett above Blackbottle Cove three autumns ago to become the only member of the clifftop tribe that had survived a baiting.

The paradox of the old sow's capture and release puzzled Aspen whenever she turned things over in her mind. It was like an itch she could not scratch. Man was the shadow that fell across animals and left them lifeless; but where did life come from and where did it go? She stirred and sighed, feeling the approach of dusk which badgers call dimpsey. Hawscrag insisted the mystery was enough and knowing all the answers would take the edge off living. Birth was a mystery but birth was a happiness and death a sorrow. Why was it necessary to cross all the nights between the two running the hazard of traps and snares, guns and dogs? Why had the world been made that way?

Sitting back against the side of the chamber Aspen raked her chest with a forepaw and the fleas fled to another part of her body. All badgers knew Earth Mother was waiting behind the final breath to guide them into an eternity of summer nights free of danger. When she was very young Aspen had this mental picture of a benign sow presiding over a countryside pitted with setts amongst forage that ran in all directions forever. And there was no man smell on the wind,

4

no danger, just a starry hush and the cries of cubs and the contented murmur of feeding sows and boars.

Birdcherry yawned and stretched, digging her back feet into Guelder. Aspen stood up and shuffled from the chamber down the tunnel which smelt of soil and roots, past Cowtail's vacant lair towards the chamber occupied by the boars, Bullenspur, Ashblacken and Furzebright. Silently to herself she sang: 'Earth Mother is the smell of the living world. She is sunset and moonrise. Her love is the Now of life and only the Now of life is important.' Aspen sighed. Help me understand your silence. Help me understand the journey I'm taking. The living is now but I believe in what lies beyond nose and ears and eyes.

'Yes, I do,' Aspen whispered, feeling the presence of the great sow badger whose breath was the scent of Nightworld.

She was conscious of badgers thumping along the other tunnels towards the main holes. A couple of hours after dimpsey the entire sett was awake and heading for the surface, for badgers do not feed underground. Even Hawscrag's mate, the ancient boar Cragbriar, who was blind and barely capable of climbing the steeps joined the exodus.

Aspen was first at the entrance that overlooked a wild lawn and the moonlit sea through a tracery of brambles and thorn twigs. To the right was a heap of soiled bedding thrown out of the sett by the badgers. On the other side was the stump of an elderberry tree which served as a scratching post. Aspen sniffed the darkness, decoding the smells and rounding her nostrils to the chill that took the fullness out of the night. It was late autumn. The breeze had the dead bracken and thorns ticking and the withered thrift whispering. Above the line of the horizon the sky was enormous and full of stars. Birdcherry and Guelder joined her, lifting slender white faces with the distinctive vertical black stripes which ran from the white-tipped ears almost to the snout. The stripes were so black it was difficult to see the animals' little round eyes. Wearing expressions of good humour as they were swung slowly from side to side the faces held much of the night's stark beauty.

The sows enjoyed a spell of mutual grooming with the emphasis on scratching. They were dwarfed by the sky that stood up and curved over the sea in a starry arc. An aeroplane droned by and from below came the rumble and lisp of waves. Coolness flowed around Aspen as she led the way to the stratching-tree. Then it was necessary to stand on hindlegs, stretch up, extend the forelegs and drag down her claws. Guelder bowled her over and ragged her in one of those scuffles the other sett-dwellers found irresisitible; but the romp did not last long.

In single file behind Aspen the sows climbed the steeps under the thorns. Random scents filtered through the vast web of smells covering Froward Point. The dead bracken was odourless and the moonlight breath of fungi a faint suggestion among the wealth of leaf humus. Here and there the broken ceiling of thorn branches was hung with more distinctive smells clinging to wisps of sheep wool or fox hair and the mutes of songbirds.

Halfway up the steeps and partly hidden by thorn and gorse was a drystone wall holding the scent of sea winds and rain which comes off the sea. Sows and boars scrambled through the gap, testing the air continuously. Gorse gesticulated as the wind rose and gusted and slackened again to a murmur among the undergrowth. The cries of gulls drifted a quarter of a mile across the Rips from Dragon Rock. Twigs scraped on stone and the wind spilled its scents and made the Monterey pines roar. The moon gave enough light to lift the rocks of the Point out of silhouette into solid form. Although the night was not bright enough to disturb the badgers they were more wary than usual.

Taking a separate path the boars led by Bullenspur left the thorn scrub before the sows and cubs, negotiated the barbed-wire tangle and paused on the turf before the pines. The sea wind swept their fur back the wrong way and made it difficult to assess the darkness ahead. One by one the sows joined them.

6

The heads swung to and fro with something close to urgency. Aspen's nose caught the pleasant resinous scent of the pines.

'Aren't the trees n-noisy,' Birdcherry whispered. Her fixed, friendly expression failed to conceal her anxiety. Aspen rubbed her snout against her sister's chin.

'I d-don't like the coming out to f-forage. I wish it was cloudy.'

'You're trembling,' Aspen said. 'There's nothing to be afraid of. The trees won't hurt you.'

'It's H-hawscrag's dream,' said Birdcherry. 'Every time she speaks about it I s-s-see awful things, t-t-terrible –' and she became tongue-tied in a spasm of stammering.

'Don't be ridiculous,' Aspen said briskly. 'You'll know more autumns than you've got claws, and you'll pass away peacefully in your sleep like old Ironpate did last winter. He was never in a wire or a gin and he must have crossed these clifftops as many times as there are spikes on that thorn. You worry too much.'

'I know but I c-can feel it. There's a sort of ache in her w-words as if she's only speaking to m-me. Sometimes I'm so frightened I d-don't want to leave the sett.'

'Life is a walk through the unknown,' said Aspen.

'I w-wish it wasn't,' Birdcherry sighed.

Hawscrag trotted up behind them with heavy footfalls and butted Birdcherry's rump.

'Move on,' she said playfully. 'D'you want the boars to grab all the best forage?'

'B-B-But –'

'No b-buts,' Hawscrag grunted, shouldering Birdcherry aside. 'Follow my rumbling gut.'

'I'm always scared st-stiff,' Birdcherry said, lifting her eyes to Aspen.

'Try not to be,' Aspen said in her low, kind voice which the other young sows loved. 'Nightworld is good to us.'

'Oh dear! what's that?' Birdcherry gasped, glimpsing something under the pines.

7

'Moonlight running away on the wind,' Guelder laughed. 'Shadows haven't got teeth, Birdcherry. Hurry up or Hawscrag will get angry.'

Short, powerful legs carried the badgers into the trees where they drifted apart and went in search of forage. Breaking through the foliage the moonlight gleamed on their grey bodies, sparking on the tips of the guard hairs and lending a dull gleam to their ivory-coloured tails. Now and then Aspen and her sisters stopped and raised their muzzles to the sky or scent-marked the ground with a rolling of rumps. The paths running in all directions among the trees, pill-boxes and concrete bunkers, had been compacted by generations of badger paws.

The constant shift of light and shadows was not to the sows' liking. They preferred dark, still nights when it was impossible to tell where sky and land ended or began. Several thousand acres of coastland were roamed by the Froward tribe. Some of the smaller setts on the steeps elsewhere were used by communes of bachelor boars with yearlings occupying lairs on the frontiers of the tribe's territory.

Beyond the Monterey pines to the north the coast undulated in great sweeps of down scored by broad coombes and indented with coves or dropping abruptly to the sea in crags. Behind the steeps of bracken, gorse and thorn was hilly farmland covered in high-hedged fields. The stink of sheep was waiting for Aspen as she emerged from the copse to tread the first zigzags of the main badger highway. It crossed a wilderness of bracken to a clump of sycamores above Wrangle Bay then continued among the gone-over thrift down to Spaniard's Point. The steeps yielded earthworms and beetles and the sows fed noisily, conscious of Bullenspur's oil on the half-dark. The young boar had left evidence of his masculinity on the bracken stabs and turf. He was a fighter many of the older boars respected but he was also gentle and protective.

Grubbing about in the soil Aspen gradually drifted away from her companions but Birdcherry's scent pursued her. She pushed her snout into the dew and drank the odours of decay which only an autumn night could provide. Rabbits scattered with a flash of white scuts. Their departure had left a broken circle of fairy-ring toadstools.

'I c-could come with you, Aspen,' said Birdcherry's voice. 'W-we could go to the wild apple tree the other s-side of the wooded coombe.'

'I'd like that,' Aspen said warmly.

'Then there are the b-blackberries on the wall on top of the cliff where the r-ravens nest.'

'And corn to be gleaned in the field by white owl barn,' said Aspen.

'You really d-don't mind me coming with you?'

Birdcherry's breath smelt of earthworms. Her coat was dew-spiked. Aspen shook her head and led the way at the trot. On the reefs below they could hear the gurgling advance of the tide.

'Do you suppose,' Birdcherry said presently, 'Hawscrag's d-dream is really j-just that – a dream?'

'Perhaps,' Aspen said. 'Sometimes it's difficult to tell what's dream and what's actually happening.'

'Yes!' Birdcherry exclaimed. 'That's exactly how I f-feel.'

But Aspen knew Hawscrag could see into things and stare through the night into nights yet to come. Her wisdom came from Earth Mother.

At the top of the steeps the young sows sat awhile and contemplated the moon through the dizzy descent of sycamore spinners. The path was carpeted with dead sycamore leaves that stirred and rustled. The chill wind filmed the sisters' eyes and brought a tingle to their snouts and a whiff of guano from the cormorant ledges on the cliffs below. The quiver of moonlight on the sea blurred to a knife-blade glare.

Up at Effords Farm, the collies began to bark and were answered by a couple of terriers. The terriers pranced and leapt to yap their challenges. Tugging at their leashes the man smiled and said: 'Hold still, you little rascals. It's just they old work dogs up over. Leave 'em, Gritt. Lie down, Jimmy. It idn' badgers and that's for sure. But you wish it was, don't you?'

9

The Jack Russells stood up and placed their front paws on his legs, whining for attention.

'There, there,' the man crooned. 'You're a pair of rascals, yes you are, you are.'

He patted their heads and stared about him before turning and retracing his steps. Scrambling up the bank Bullenspur came through the hedge and slithered into the lane. The stink of the man and the dogs filled his nostrils and he crossed the rutted mud with surprising speed for a creature of his bulk. But the Jack Russells caught his scent and were barking and whining again in their eagerness to get at him. The man stooped to calm them and the collies locked in the outhouse went crazy.

'Chard ought to put a bullet in those boneheads,' the man said softly.

Bullenspur ambled over the stubble, pausing to gobble up grains of oats. All his senses were alert and the hair on his spine bristled. Cowtail the fox approached him gingerly looking elegant and cat-like beside the badger. She was a bold cheerful animal who had lost all the hair off her brush in a swaling fire. It had grown again only at the tip – hence her name.

'Stupid snap-happy dogs,' she said in a high-pitched, nasal voice. 'Thick, yappy man things. There's more sense in a dead sheep. 'Ere, were they bothering you? Were they?'

'Not in the least,' came the amiable reply. 'I'm more than a match for any yap-dog that fancies his chances.'

'Of course you've never run before the hounds,' Cowtail said, suppressing a shudder. 'Hounds is different. Hounds don't mess about. They're straight in and chomp! 'Ere,' the fox added. 'Don't let me keep you from your grub. I've eaten. Have you eaten? No, you haven't, have you? It's them yap-dogs.'

A light came on in the farm outhouse and the barking stopped. The cries of the terriers grew fainter and Bullenspur sniffed the breeze, aware of Cowtail's departure and the swift rustle of voles. Then he dropped his head and sent his snout quivering through the stubble.

10

Chapter 2

Sea Mist

The badgers slept. Dawn light crisped to clarity. Long, slow swells were sweeping in from the English Channel with a lift and run of darkness across the gleam. The tide had turned and was boiling white over the mussel reefs of Dragon Rock. A buzzard skirled and the sun blinked through gulls' wings. Feathers fanned the sky above Cowtail and she narrowed her eyes and curled the tip of her tongue over her nose. The steeps were alive with movement and scent as the wind strengthened and odours of the loomeries and gulleries wafted off the cliffs.

Cowtail crinkled her nose. She was kennelled snugly in the grass and bracken of Spaniard Point. Above the Point women were picking potatoes on the farmland of Backways in the field where the sixty-foot day mark beacon stood. Known locally as King Arthur's Tower the beacon was a hollow roofless cone of tight stonework on eight slender stone legs. From the sea it was visible for miles.

Between gusts of wind inoffensive farmyard smells drifted to Cowtail's nostrils: the dung of sheep and cattle, swedes gnawed by livestock, wood smoke. The fox yawned. On the rocks at the foot of the cliffs the great black-backed gulls

11

boomed and oystercatchers fluted. A crab boat chugged through the Rips in the lee of Dragon Rock. Cowtail yawned again and looked up quickly as the starling flock passed overhead with a rush. Daws jangled by, skirmishing in mid-air, and higher up the sky herring gulls hung on the wind and a solitary buzzard traced its circles.

Some of the easterly's coldness had glazed the cloudless morning. Then the kestrel tiercel of Wrangle Bay rode the updraught to quarter the steeps, registering as a series of flashes in Cowtail's vision; but the vixen had fed on sheep carrion and was content to lie quietly with her chin on her forepaws. Throughout the morning scents and sounds sprinkled her cat-nap, and shortly before noon she heard men's voices. Her head shot up, her ears pricked and her nostrils dilated. The men and dogs were following the wire fence along the top of the steeps on the edge of the plough. Breathing slowly Cowtail mastered her tension but was prepared for instant flight.

Once or twice during the next few days the smell of men and dogs was waiting for the badgers when they left the Froward thorn scrub; but it was never strong enough to send them running for the sett.

'Something's up,' Cowtail said, addressing no one in particular. Birdcherry eyed her nervously. The fox and badgers had met on the sloping lawn of grass and thrift at the end of the Point. Aspen lowered her hindquarters to the ground and began to scratch. Watching her Hawscrag and Cowtail soon felt itchy and followed suit but Birdcherry continued to stand sniffing the air. It seemed to hold an unfathomable loneliness and the little sow sighed.

'Men have come here before,' said Hawscrag.

'Men are everywhere,' Cowtail sniffed. 'But something's up.'

'Like w-what?' Birdcherry enquired.

'Like . . . plenty of bother for us. Like . . . digging and snap-happy yap-happies doing us a mischief. Like...'

'Go and eat earth,' Hawscrag growled and she glared at the fox. 'We've got work to do.'

''Ere,' Cowtail said. 'You know me. No offence intended.'

'And none taken,' breathed the old sow, heavily sarcastic, and she turned her back on the vixen. 'Leave us, now – go and stink out another sett.'

'Well, something is definitely up,' Cowtail insisted as she vanished into the undergrowth.

Birdcherry swallowed hard several times and Hawscrag looked at her. Dimpsey was darkening to night. The wind had swung to the west but it was hardly strong enough to ruffle a discarded feather. The sky was clear. Stimulating scents were fuming down from the fields and Nightworld settled into unsteady focus for the badgers' eyesight was not good.

Before forage there was fresh bedding to collect for the chambers. Sows and boars were busy on the horseshoe-shaped lawn between the thorn scrub. Bullenspur had shown an interest in Aspen but was not possessive as yet. Guelder and Ashblacken were also on the threshold of pairing. So the atmosphere as they all worked together was cheerful. Grass and bracken were scraped into bundles which could be tucked under the chin and held there with the forelegs while the badgers shuffled rapidly backwards towards the main holes. Every so often they checked, listened and lifted their muzzles before continuing. At the hole there was another stop while the animals re-orientated, then they vanished underground with their loads.

'It will rain soon,' Hawscrag grunted, trampling down the bracken on the floor of the sows' chamber. 'Birdcherry,' she added tartly, 'you're shaking. This will not do.'

'S-sorry, mother. I c-can't help it.'

'Stop thinking about yourself,' said the old sow, and she waited for an evasive reply; but Birdcherry remained silent.

Forage was late. When Aspen and Birdcherry stood together at the edge of the pines a silver light came creeping across the hills. Soon there was enough radiance to bring the badgers' heads up in wonder. They breathed quietly and deeply. The first thrushes from the high latitudes were crossing the stars. The thin double notes of redwings rang through the air as the flock swept inland. The hush returned, a barn owl screamed, a curlew cried, seabirds murmured, and the newly risen moon wore a halo.

The badgers walked with haunches rolling, dipping their heads to sniff interesting objects or jerking up their muzzles to scent danger. They padded noisily through the leaf litter under the sycamores to the hazels at the top of Spaniard's Point. The hazel nuts tasted good and the plough yielded earthworms. Slowly the animals walked and ate their way along the edge of the farmland to the trees of the Warren Fishacre estate. Oak, ash, sycamore and alder covered the slopes down to the stream and Old Spanish Cove. The badgers drank and crossed the coombe between brambles and salt-browned foxgloves and trotted down the tunnel of gorse to the wild apple tree. Here they discovered the yearling sow, Dogrose, munching the over-ripe windfalls. After the elaborate sniffing and scenting the animals settled to the forage unaware of the darkness rolling in off the sea.

More flocks of migrant thrushes spilled along the coast to wing swiftly over the fields. Fieldfares chacked their contact cries and descended on the pasture. Glassy-eyed sheep stared through the moonlight where the downs curved to meet the bracken and one world ended and another began.

Aspen and Birdcherry left the furze and padded along beneath a shimmering ceiling of spider spin which had been spread on the tips of the bracken in separate threads. Now and then a strand would lift and wave and catch the light.

The path brought the badgers to the steeps of Hellweather Point and the grubbing for roots. A little to the north was Garrowcombe Head and its tiny clifftop copse of elms and sycamores standing above precipices. Sometimes the sows were brought up sharp by a scent that was so impelling it had them waggling their muzzles. They were dew-drenched and muddy. At either hand the small leaves of nettles were covered in gull droppings, and the hoof-scarred soil held cattle odours. In the field above, bullocks grazed with swift, wrenching tugs of the jaws and the odd stamp and snort. Rabbits rattled off among the dead hogweed.

Birdcherry followed Aspen over the matted ivy and through the bramble mounds to the copse. Woodbine, bryony and old man's beard trailed over the undergrowth. A remarkable stillness held the coastland in a trance and the sea mist wreathed the badgers. They sniffed at it unconcerned while the stars disappeared and the sky darkened. The mouldy reek of the sea enveloped all the other scents of Nightworld. Briefly Aspen put her nose to the honey tuft fungus on the tree stump. Minute beads of moisture clung to her whiskers and body hair. She came out of the trees and turned to Birdcherry.

'How do you feel now?'

'N-nervous,' Birdcherry replied with a little laugh.

'Come dawn we'll use the sett above the beach near the old quarry,' Aspen said. 'There are blackberries in the hedge by the stream in the bottom of the coombe.'

'You know I l-love blackberries,' Birdcherry said.

By now the mist was an opaque greyness from which objects materialized: a solitary hawthorn tree, a wall, the pebble banks beside the stream, barbed wire clustered with brambles and blackberries. Rising on her hindlegs Birdcherry greedied the fruit.

Later, in the small sett on the steeps that fell abruptly through thick undergrowth to the grit and shingle of Runnage Sands, the two sows tried to sleep. Perhaps dawn had broken although it was difficult to tell with the mist hiding everything. Birdcherry was dozing off when she suddenly realized she was alone in the cold breeding chamber.

'Aspen,' she cried, scrabbling up the tunnel and out of the hole. 'Aspen, what's h-happened?'

'Be quiet and listen,' Aspen said. She was sitting among the

15

thrift close to the entrance trying to decode the mist with ears and nose. The vapour was becoming luminous as daylight strengthened.

'I heard dogs barking – yap-dogs, not farm dogs.'

'Dear oh dear,' Birdcherry whispered. 'I d-don't think we should go back underearth. I have a feeling about this place. It has a nasty smell as if s-something's died in it.'

'We'll return to Big Sett,' Aspen said firmly. 'If we stick to the clifftops we'll be all right.'

A contradiction of instincts overcame the badgers. They were inclined by nature to retreat underground yet the sett behind them was rank with peril.

'Follow me,' Aspen said, her mind made up. 'And don't dawdle.'

'T-towards the dogs?' Birdcherry said.

'Would you prefer to stay here?'

'No, no, of course not. Only, I d-don't understand.'

There was no time to comfort the oddling. Aspen ran down the side of the coombe, slipping on the shale path and startling the sheep which were uncomfortable in the mist. The stream was forded and the flanks of Garrowcombe Head ascended with a speed that left the sows breathless. The mist was thinning on Hellweather Point but the downs were still invisible.

They ran low under briars and brambles which stood higher than a sheep. The yapping seemed very close and Birdcherry confirmed that Aspen was actually running towards it. She was also certain every dog for miles would come looking for her. Then the men would put her in a sack and – and – she let her mind go blank.

The badger path meandered up the slopes to the fields of Downend and came with the fence to the top of Shippen Cove. Here another path dropped to the promontory. From the mist below lofted the yelping of dogs and the cries of men and the sound of metal crunching into soil.

'They are at Dogrose's sett,' Aspen whispered. Through the

16

crumbling greyness the sows gazed at each other and Birdcherry shook her head, too full of heartache to speak.

Then a giant figure stepped from the mist above them and fired a gun. The pain in Aspen's right hindleg went almost unnoticed as the sisters came stumbling and gasping into the furze south of the cove and lay pressed to the ground.

'There are only r-rabbit holes in here,' Birdcherry panted.

'Lie still,' Aspen said. 'We're safe enough. They'll go away.'

'Dogs c-can get at us.'

'Please, Birdcherry,' Aspen said. Twisting her head and lifting her wounded leg she tried to winkle out the pellet.

'I'll do that,' Birdcherry said but her offer was rejected.

The mist thinned until the steeps and part of the sea were visible. Aspen cleaned the wound with her tongue and listened to the terrible din rising from the sett. At last she could bear it no longer and crawled to the edge of the gorse thicket.

'They'll see you,' Birdcherry whispered.

Sitting back on her haunches and staring through the screen of bracken Aspen could look onto the promontory. A moment or so later Birdcherry joined her, fearfully scenting the air. Wreaths of mist continued to curl up over the clifftops and another dense mass was advancing slowly from the Channel. The men at the sett crowded round a seething mass of terriers and the man with the shotgun joined them. A pick was swung repeatedly at the soil beneath some stunted elders. Then there was a pause and the men retreated and formed a rough circle enclosing the dogs and something else, a ripple of greyness among the white and tan terriers.

'Dogrose,' Aspen breathed.

The black and white face lifted to mouth a silent cry that left Birdcherry whimpering with her muzzle in her chest fur. But Dogrose was gone, buried under the snarling scrum. At length a harsh voice called off the Jack Russells and a man crouched to swing an iron bar. Now the terriers were whining. Matches flared and cigarettes were lit. Rolling in a cloud the mist crept over the shallows and climbed the shillet slabs at the base of

17

the promontory. Someone laughed and lifted Dogrose's body by the tail. Up after it went the terriers in leaps of curiosity and excitement, eager to worry the carcass back to life and continue the game. Mist swirled around them and over them, and the promontory vanished.

Birdcherry was weeping silently. Tears crept down her face to bead her muzzle and Aspen rubbed her snout against her sister's chest while sadness lapped over them colder than the mist.

'Poor Dogrose,' Birdcherry choked.

A lark was singing up on the downs. Nothing had changed except Dogrose was no longer part of the morning. A rawness closed round Aspen's heart.

'We can't stay here,' she said, rising and stretching and rounding her nostrils to the smells coming off the mist. 'Big Sett is the only safe place and we must reach it before this lifts.'

'C-can't the men smell us?'

'I don't know. Men aren't animals.'

'What are they, Aspen?'

'Death, Hawscrag says, and she's rarely wrong.' Her tongue lapped slowly at the pellet wound.

'But didn't s-some men save her from the dogs?'

'Yes,' Aspen said. 'Unless it was just one of her dreams.'

Chapter 3

Dogrose's Journey

'Everything living comes from the earth,' said Hawscrag.

Sows and boars sat on the lawn at Froward looking out over the sea and grieving for Dogrose.

'Earth Mother breathes into things and they come into being – bluebells, primroses, grasses, trees, animals. And we all return to earth when we die but the deathless part of us goes to Earth Mother.'

'To the big Nightworld,' Furzebright breathed, raising his soil-stained muzzle. 'To the spirit life.'

'The spirit life of the wind and moonlight,' Hawscrag said.

'B-but what of the perfect s-summer night and the p-perfect forage?' said Birdcherry, watching the gulls drifting around the jagged pinnacles of Dragon Rock.

'That as well,' Hawscrag continued. 'Earth Mother is the everything of life Man can't touch. She is the seasons, a feeling as well as a place and a sunrise and a sunset. We must make sure Dogrose begins her journey into that happiness.'

'Is there a corner of all this good news for me?' Cowtail whispered.

'I hope not,' Hawscrag yawned and the badgers laughed.

'Why don't the d-dogs come to Big Sett?' asked Birdcherry.

'Dogs and men work together,' said Cragbriar. 'And the thorns keep the men away. Do you remember, Hawscrag, dogs were put in five or six summers ago?'

'Yes,' said Hawscrag with a hardening of the voice. 'The boars killed two of them. They trapped them in a dead-end, mauled them and pulled the roof down. No dogs have come near us since.'

Cowtail grinned nervously but was ignored. The day brightened to a lurid vividness that warned of impending rain. The fox wondered why the sett-dwellers weren't underground, asleep. They were a strange tribe, she mused, running her green elliptical pupils over them. Always in a dream. Always elsewhere, inside their heads.

After a while Bullenspur addressed Aspen towards whom he had become increasingly attentive.

'We'd better be going,' he said.

'Have the men g-gone now,' said Birdcherry.

'We hope so,' said Hawscrag.

Birdcherry seemed determined to voice her fears but Aspen nudged her hard with her snout and silenced her. Then Bullenspur led the sows up the steeps.

Lark song crept off Downend and the man laughed quietly to himself. The sun was warm on his face and the sky was everywhere, even at his feet. Never before had outward life been so full of colour and texture. Again David Garrison laughed, feeling much younger than his fifty years. He was tall and well built with blue eyes, fair hair streaked with grey and a lazy smile. His corduroys, faded navy blue fisherman's sweater and reefer jacket had a well-worn look about them, and his boots had gone a long time without dubbin.

He sat on a rock overlooking Shippen Cove sketching the landscape. The steeps glided down to the clifftops and space, and beyond the last of the scrub thorn lay the sea. Then her image edged unexpectedly onto the scene. Lifting his eyes from the drawing he saw her standing in the bracken but as she vanished the pain grew. Maybe he was searching for a time-suspended world. It was an odd notion. Garrison set aside the sketch-book and lit a cigarette. Ann was lying in bed in the Swiss sanatorium fighting the tuberculosis that had nearly killed her. Every time he visited her he was conscious of the stoicism holding back the misery. Losing Neil in the war might have been a big enough cross for any couple to bear. To have an only child snatched from you in the last months of that nightmare! Garrison drew a deep breath and crushed the cigarette under his heel. Maybe Ann had wanted to die, but he dismissed the thought before it could hollow his guts. The lark continued to sing. He picked up a sycamore leaf and studied it for a moment before writing on the bottom of the sketch: 'Kestrel-coloured slopes, patched with grey-green.'

The day had a supernatural calm. In the distance was the mica glitter of Froward Point. His eyes strayed back to the promontory with its strange little humps and wind-angled elderberry. The sketch was part of his effort to make a visual catalogue of the entire coast from St Mary's Head to the Marl estuary. A Spitfire droned low across the sea, skimming Dragon Rock and looping up to buzz inland. Hitler's War had been over for three years but Garrison kept seeing Neil walking up the road away from the house in Exeter at the end of his last leave. All that cheerfulness and optimism snuffed out.

'Oh Christ,' he murmured. 'Christ.'

Along the top of the steeps the starling flocks were falling, rising and falling again only to rise, dilate and depart. 'The purpose of life is to create more life,' Garrison laughed wryly. He had been one of the best war artists, quarrying something beautiful and dramatic out of bleak moments of violence like the Normandy landing. From barbarism and heroism to wildlife art seemed a logical step. From a requiem for the human race to a celebration of the natural world. Now he had a growing reputation but nothing mattered except getting it down in paint as if each picture was an affirmation of the fundamental principle: Out of life, more life – that and money for Ann's treatment.

Taking Coastguard Cottage had helped. Ann would love it when she came home. It was a whitewashed building, long and squat with dumpy chimneys and a dark tiled roof. 'You step out of the front door,' he wrote to his wife, 'walk across a bit of rough lawn flanked by tamarisks and you're on top of a cliff with the sea and sky before you.'

'When you come home,' Garrison whispered, lifting his field-glasses.

The south-westerly had begun to rock the ash trees on the skyline, shaking free the remaining 'keys'. The sycamores were swaying, but down on the steeps the hush prevailed. The first clouds appeared and the sun went out for a moment. Jackdaws flew by at his level, veering away when they caught sight of him. How huge and blue was the sky. He was putting down the binoculars to pick up the pad again when a badger coughed. Garrison looked down the steeps to the gorse thicket. One by one the sows followed Bullenspur across the turf into the bracken. Garrison sucked in his breath and held it as he focused the glasses. Then he had a close-up of grey backs and black and white faces in the binocular window.

Bullenspur crinkled his nose disdainfully and drew it away from the ink cap toadstool. A magpie chattered.

'What's upset that b-bird?' whispered Birdcherry.

'Us, probably,' said Hawscrag. 'All you do is ask stupid questions, like a cub. Even Earth Mother couldn't answer some of them.'

'S-sorry, Hawscrag.' Birdcherry retracted her whiskers until they were pressed to her muzzle.

'Yes, you're always sorry and always worried and always worrying everyone else. Just be quiet.'

Steadying his bulk sideways to the angle of the slope Bullenspur read the air.

'She's over there,' he grunted.

Guelder's head drooped and she gave a faint cry. Her sisters stared blindly down at the grass.

'She's waiting,' Bullenspur continued and lumbered out onto the open turf.

Dogrose's body lay among the dead sea pinks and bracken husks. She wore a snarl of defiance but the light had gone from her eyes. Blowing down the steeps the wind ruffled her fur and Aspen's heart swelled. One by one the sows advanced and gently nudged Dogrose with their snouts, moaning and shaking their heads while Bullenspur and Furzebright released tremulous cries of mourning which Hawscrag took up.

Out towards the tip of the promontory rabbits had been digging in a small hollow. Bullenspur completed the excavation to the badgers' satisfaction and by the time the job was finished the sky had clouded over. The chill greyness seemed to emanate from the animals. Lowering their heads until their snouts touched the ground the sows shuffled towards the boar whose head was also bowed. His keening went unanswered but every two or three steps the sows paused and swung their muzzles from side to side. Bullenspur met them halfway and they turned back towards Dogrose. Eventually Hawscrag and Guelder took hold of a hindleg in their jaws and dragged Dogrose to the grave and rolled her in. Without further ceremony Bullenspur and Furzebright began to rake earth over the body and the sows shuttled back and forth carrying bracken, grass and leaves.

Despite their ceaseless toil it was late afternoon before the funeral ended.

'Back to Earth Mother now; back to life,' Hawscrag chanted.

'Back to life,' chorused the badgers. Their tears were spent, for Dogrose had begun her journey.

23

The dispassionate, watchful gulls settled on the slabs below and it began to rain. Large drops smacked into the bracken husks and Hawscrag turned and led her companions back to the gorse thicket.

'Dear God,' Garrison said in an awed whisper.

He dropped the binoculars and sketch-book in his rucksack. Drifts of rain masked Froward Point and oystercatchers were calling across the mussel reefs. Shouldering the rucksack Garrison stepped quickly down the slope to the burial mound. Then he crouched and dug deep enough to expose Dogrose's head. The dirt could not hide the wounds on her muzzle and the gash left on her snout by the iron bar. Whoever had killed the animal had known his job, Garrison thought. There was a crest of bone running from front to back along the skull called the interparietal ridge. It could deflect a hard blow so the experienced badger digger always went for the snout or the spine.

Garrison covered the body once more and stood up. The rain was driving into him, running down his face and neck. Dusk was spreading grey off the sea, but the gulls and waders were still ready to give it a voice.

'What about the fundamental principle?' Garrison said bitterly.

He climbed the steeps and meeting the full force of the wind at Downend wondered if he could cope with the loneliness without alcohol.

'David Garrison's seascapes and scenes of British wildlife in natural settings have an authenticity and a haunting beauty,' wrote the reviewer in the quality newspaper. 'Lyricism lifts them above the mere photographic. In his watercolours especially we have access to a remarkable empathy.'

Ever since his boyhood he had been searching for something that walking, running and climbing in wilderness places had come halfway to providing. What the hell was it? he thought, striding over Garrowcombe Head, the wind and rain at his back. Between squalls there was dusk blurring the

24

landscape and summoning up visions of Ann; but soon the memory of the badgers burying one of their own kind eclipsed everything. He came up onto Woodash Down through a blustery gloom. The worst of the rain was racing out to sea and the far bulk of Firebeacon Point was visible against the distant flare of St Mary's Head light.

'Ann,' he groaned as the sheep broke and ran and ravens climbed the wind off the pasture.

At last the flooded marsh, the beach and Coastguard Cottage were in view. Slithering down off the hillside the sight of the broken tile left Garrison undismayed. He came to the stone wall and followed it around past the tamarisks to the garden. Another squall swept off Woodash Down and the shutters on the kitchen window flapped and banged.

Garrison took off his boots and jacket in the porch and went into the living room and lit the fire. Before long a cosy brightness puddled the ceiling and he was reluctant to light the lamp. The driftwood fire burnt with a spit and crackle and the hiss of salt bubbles. He crouched over it, soaking up the warmth while his trousers steamed. Then he grilled the kippers, poured the Guinness and put on the adagio from Bach's Concerto for Violin and Strings in E, and cranked the gramophone waiting for Ann to take possession of the moment. The nearness of Christmas heightened his longing.

Why kill a badger? He stared into the flames and ate the kippers and brown bread. The latch with its loose hasp rattled in the draught and the music eddied around him. Somewhere along the cliffs the badgers would be coming out. Setting aside the empty plate he put on the record for the fourth time and went to the front door. Dusk was deepening under the rain's percussion. Out to sea ships' lights were dimly visible. He closed the door and brought the lamp to his studio. Among the collection of stuffed birds in glass cases, feathers and animal skulls was a badger's skull he had picked out of the soil at one of the clifftop setts. The interparietal ridge stood up in sharp definition. Garrison sighed and put the skull back and glanced morosely around the room. Unframed oils stood against a chest of drawers and on the easel was a large watercolour of a seascape he had yet to complete. Tomorrow he would paint badgers, badgers at dawn on December Point, sparking life.

The music had ended. He came back to the fireside and piled on the logs. The need to write to Ann was unbearable so he sat with the pad resting on his thigh and began to tell his wife about the badger's funeral.

Chapter 4

Encounters

The last of autumn's gales deluged Froward Point and, coming out to forage, Aspen walked into the roar of the Monterey pines. The rains had flooded one of the chambers on the top level but it had been unoccupied and no harm was done. Walking into noise night after night made the badgers uneasy. All that movement and chaos of scents kept them close to the Point.

The floods had washed potatoes down onto the steeps below the field at Backways. Here the tribe congregated to eat the tubers as well as worms and woodlice. Ashblacken and Guelder were always in each other's company but Bullenspur was less assertive despite his status as sett-master. The animals were heavy from the summer feasting but continued to add to their body fat. Meanwhile wet dimpseys closing dark on rain-lashed days kept the men and dogs elsewhere, and before long even Birdcherry's fears had faded.

The badgers sometimes chose to leave Big Sett by day if the rain ceased. At the entrance holes they exercised maximum caution, reading the air with repeated swings of the muzzle and staring about themselves to detect unusual movement. Often, after satisfying herself, Aspen sat in the hole scratching while her ears confirmed the things her nose and eyes had suggested. When the lawn and thorn scrub, sea, rock and sky had settled into the familiar she would emerge and use the latrine pits beyond the spoil heap. Then Birdcherry would join her at the scratching tree and deposit the mud of the night's underground digging in long, brown claw marks. The wind coming off the land suited them and to find it free of man's taint left the sows confident.

Cowtail returning from her scavenging would also bring news of Nightworld. The vixen had been screaming for a mate all round Warren Fishacre and told of the fierce dogs which had come rushing down from Efforts to hunt her.

''Ere,' she said, narrowing her eyes. 'It was touch and go. I could feel them breathing on me tail and hear their jaws snapping – snap-snap-snap! Lucky I got underground sharpish. Them farm crazies chopped a fox up over a couple of nights ago. An old dog, he was,' she added wistfully. 'They caught him nappin'' and –' she stopped and sniffed before murmuring: 'There's an animal in the first sett up towards the wooded coombe. I think it's sick.'

'An animal?' Aspen's small eyes rounded.

'Stinky old animal with a funny smell,' Cowtail grinned.

'Like the stinky old fox?' Aspen asked.

'This fox ain't stinky. This fox is just foxy and dog foxes like that.'

'P-perhaps it's a dog,' said Birdcherry.

'No,' Cowtail shook her head. 'Dogs don't smell like pee-soaked earth.'

'We'd better have a look at this mysterious creature,' said Aspen.

'M-must we?' Birdcherry sighed.

'You needn't. I'll forage over that way alone.'

The late afternoon was grey enough to suit the sow. Seabirds rose quickly from the rocks along the shore to flicker

28

against the precipices. On rigid wings the fulmars glided back and forth across the rock buttresses where they would breed in the spring. The tidal drift of bird life was slack with the winter yet to come and the auks still at sea.

Aspen trod over the brown 'pin cushions' of thrift and pushed through the mallow where the steeps levelled to tables of clifftop turf. Bits of storm debris and broken crab shells littered the grass, and rock doves clattered away. Then the peregrine tiercel appeared over Froward to agitate the gulls and panic the woodpigeons. The hunter soared on a quick beat of the wings. His name was Skyhook and he had fed and was merely taking the air. The gleam of the sea contracted to tension below him. He noted the movements of birds and saw the badger trotting along the edge of the cliffs towards the sett at Ramsons Dip. It was his last flight of the day and before the light finally faded he would be roosting on the crag in Old Spanish Cove. Turning in a wide loop Skyhook also saw the man and the two small dogs standing motionless in the field by King Arthur's Tower. They were staring out to sea but before his turn was completed Skyhook had lost interest.

Aspen's back brushed against the ceiling of blackthorn and she came to the goyal of willow and sallow that was divided by a brook. The sett was among the bracken above the cliff where shags nested. Aspen approached slowly after a careful examination of the air. Her nostrils quivered.

'Cat,' she breathed, smiling to herself.

She entered the largest hole and faint movements told her the chamber was occupied.

'Are you hurt?' she said, addressing the darkness.

A moment's silence was followed by a gravelly sigh.

'Ill,' said a voice hoarse with some sort of throat infection. 'I'm afraid I'm too weak to search for food. My body's on fire and I keep coughing.'

'Are you a man-thing?' Aspen asked.

'A pet?' from a wheezy laugh. 'No. I'm wild born of a gone-wild mother. I come from places around the town. Lived on

29

scraps at the fish market and scrounged from houses and fields. I don't know what brought me here. Maybe this is where I'll find death.'

Again the gravelly indrawn breath that melted Aspen's heart.

'Could you eat something?' she said.

'I could eat anything,' replied the tom-cat.

'What's your name?'

'Fingo. And yours?'

'Aspen of the Big Sett tribe.'

'I knew an old boar badger once called Cragbriar,' said the cat. 'We met on the clifftops near the flashing light and I warned him about the gin traps men had set for him and his lot. He was from the Big Sett tribe. Is he still alive?'

'Blind and lame but still living,' Aspen said. 'Are you dry down there?'

The cat said he was and Aspen told him to sleep while she foraged for him.

'May Earth Mother watch over you,' Fingo whispered.

'Over us all,' said Aspen. 'What sort of forage can I bring you?'

'Anything with meat on it – a bit of rabbit, a bird, fish, a mouse even. I'm not fussy.'

In the hedge-bank beside the root field on Effords land the farm labourer had tilled gins and Aspen nosed along the trapline. Only one had been sprung and, caught by the front paws, the young rabbit had died an hour or so earlier. Aspen chewed free the carcass and carried it to the sett and waited while Fingo fed.

'You are welcome to remain here,' she said, 'although there is plenty of dry cover under the pines on the point should you prefer something more open. You won't be disturbed and my sisters and I can bring you scavenge until you're well enough to forage for yourself. Cowtail will help.'

'The Fellowship of Nightworld,' Fingo said.

'Yes,' the badger smiled.

30

It was darkfall. Rain swished down in straight lines and Aspen was reluctant to lift her snout and decipher the wind. The plaint of oystercatchers and the dunlin's high flight notes lent a poignancy to evening.

'I feel better already,' Fingo said. 'A couple more nights and I'll be out mousing.'

Aspen scratched behind an ear. The hawthorn on the clifftop was rattling and the cool, stony fragrance of the rain was rising off the steeps.

'Bloody rain,' the man said softly, leaning against one of the legs of King Arthur's Tower. 'We don't like rain do we, you little rascals?' he added, addressing his dogs.

Then he cupped his hands and lit a cigarette and loosed smoke from his nostrils. The Jack Russells gazed up at him in adoration while the daws in the top of the roofless tower shifted on their ledges. Tugging the collar of his raincoat up round his ears the man wondered if the badgers would be leaving their setts to grub for food. The old brocks didn't like the wet any more than he did. Maybe it was time to shake up a few over Runnage and December Point. There was the Boxing Day baiting to consider. Three animals were the traditional requirement of the Mary's Haven Badger Club. That loud-mouth Stoneman from Lansworthy was supposed to have a pair of really gutsy dogs, long-haired tan-and-whites like his Gritt and Jimmy. He licked his lips. They'd need animals in prime condition to test the terriers, and good weather if the business was to be a success.

'Bloody rain,' he murmured.

One dawn Bullenspur failed to return from forage and after two nights of searching the tribe were forced to think the worst.

Aspen went through the rituals of survival, acquainting her spirit with the inevitable as the grief ebbed and the Now of life filled her emptiness. Waves crashing against the Point announced a change in weather. The wind came off the sea in

31

strong gusts that scattered the flocks of small birds from the haws and dog hips. The easterly which brought blue skies and the cold wailed and whistled in grass, furze and wire. Then the badgers leaving the sett heard the boom of breakers hitting the seaward side of Dragon Rock to rise in a surge of foam and spray and subside with an oomph!

Aspen loved the feel of the wind stroking her fur. She had enjoyed a long dig and a scratch and was ready to forage. Uttering happy cries she padded into the copse where the ground below the pines was heaving and falling. A sickle moon and starry sky provided the sort of conditions she liked. Across the steeps the tribe dispersed. The last of the blackthorn leaves had fallen and the trees stood bare and spiky, their tracery dotted with withered sloes.

From beneath one of these solitary thorns a small black shape rose, arched its back and stretched as Aspen approached.

'Fingo,' smiled the badger.

Trotting up behind her sister, Birdcherry said: 'Wh-who?' like a nervous owl.

'The cat. Please calm down and don't blunder about.'

Fingo chuckled.

'Good scavenge?' Aspen continued, staggering a little as Birdcherry barged against her.

'Excellent,' the cat purred.

'Have you seen Bullenspur?' said Aspen.

'No. Why? Is he missing?'

'Gone,' Aspen said simply and Fingo nodded.

'You've left the sett?' Aspen went on.

'Yes, I'm in your copse, in one of the stone huts on the hillside. A girl at the big house in the wooded coombe puts out good scavenge for me – fish, bread and milk, scraps of meat. So does the man in the cottage by the beach.'

Silence suddenly came between them.

'I know what you're thinking,' the cat said. 'I don't understand it either. Some of them can fire a gun at you or trap

32

you or end things like they did for Dogrose. Others can put out scavenge and welcome you at their fireside.'

'Perhaps it's different for cats.'

'Perhaps. Men aren't animals so we shouldn't expect anything except the unexpected – my mother's words and she lived with man.'

'Look, Birdcherry,' Aspen said when the sows were alone. 'I want to forage by myself. Go back with Hawscrag or help Cragbriar. Please,' she insisted as Birdcherry hesitated. But the yearling wore such a pitiful expression Aspen relented.

'Oh come on, then,' she said. 'No chatter, though. Just the rooting.'

'If there are k-kind men,' Birdcherry blurted, unable to restrain herself, 'why d-did Fingo's mother go wild?'

'I don't know,' Aspen said sharply, and noting her sister's real irritation Birdcherry spoke no more.

The following morning the badger diggers met on December Point not far from Coastguard Cottage. Standing on his lawn looking out to sea Garrison saw men and dogs trailing up the hillside to the clifftops but the significance failed to register. It was just another gang out ferreting. He had fed his stray cat and done the chores. The downs were shafted with sunlight. Cloud shadows raced over green flanks and the buzzards had soared to become mere specks against the blue. All it needed was Ann to round everything to perfection.

Garrison returned to the studio and looked at the badgers. The larger animal was almost finished. He would touch up the ears and snout and add the whiskers. Sometimes he forgot the whiskers and once or twice a picture had been sent to the London gallery with whiskerless foxes or whiskerless hares.

'Hairless hares,' he laughed, selecting a fine brush.

It was difficult to believe the bear-like creatures were mustelids, related to stoats and otters. The sow's gaze was gentle and Garrison felt a warm ache of achievement as he returned it. Satisfied with his work he walked out to the porch.

The waves stood up and exploded on Hard Sands and a boy and girl were running along the tideline, dodging the aprons of foam which were advancing and retreating over the shingle. They came past the old lime kiln and climbed the track between the tamarisks. Stepping from the doorway Garrison caught them on his lawn. Something in their white, desperate little faces stripped the grumpiness from his voice. Instead of bawling them out he said: 'What's the hurry?'

They were primary school age with the pinched, under-nourished look of back street living. The boy was short and wiry. He had hair like towrope and pale blue eyes. The girl was taller but just as skinny with a hardness about the mouth and mousy hair cut short. The pair stood defiantly watching him, hands buried in the pockets of their overcoats.

'Are you a new member of the bleddy badger club, mister?' the boy said.

'I'm not a member of any club,' Garrison replied.

'Well,' the boy continued, 'Strawberry Rapson and his lot are digging badgers up on the Point.'

'Are they now,' Garrison said. 'Hang on a minute and I'll get my coat.'

'We ain't got a lot of time,' the girl said. After the boy's soft Devonshire her cockney accent grated.

'Do you think you can stop those men by yourselves?' Garrison said.

'Dunno. Only it's certain we won't do it jawin' down here.'

'Shut up, Sheena,' the boy said. 'Are you goin' to help us, mister?'

'Yes. Just give me a moment.'

'He don't look as if he could knock the skin off a rice puddin',' the girl mumbled, fixing her eyes on Garrison.

'Sheena!' The boy glared at her. 'Shut your mouth. I mean it.'

Garrison was still buttoning his reefer jacket as they scrambled up the hillside. God, I'm out of condition, he thought. There was a definite need to burn off the alcohol and the consequences of all the static hours before the easel. It registered in his knees and loose stomach muscles. The morning smelt good – sea and wet grass and the sky on the move. The boy raced ahead as if gravity had no hold on his thin legs.

'Billy,' the girl cried. 'Don't you go and do nuffin' daft.' The scent of Devon Violets perfume was wafting off her body warmth. 'Billy!'

The wind whisked her cry away, and Garrison rested, hands on knees, body doubled, sucking in big gulps of air. Sweat dripped off his nose and chin.

'Come on, mister.'

At the clifftops December Point dropped to the sea in undulations of slate, shale and bracken. A rusty strand of barbed wire separated the slopes from the pasture. Less than twenty yards down the first slope half a dozen men and perhaps twice that number of dogs had gathered round the sett. The wind was a solid wall. Pieces of bracken and grass whirled past his head.

'Bloody Strawberry,' Billy growled, fishing out his catapult.

'That won't be much use,' Garrison smiled. The girl's blank gaze was disconcerting. He stooped under the wire and waded down through the bracken. Faces turned in his direction but the pick continued to swing and the shovels cut into the soil. The wind was a deep, droning whine.

'Hello,' Garrison shouted. 'What's this then?'

They came and stood above the diggers.

'Mind your own bloody business, mate,' one of the men grunted.

'It is my business. This is my land.'

The men rested and exchanged glances.

'Since when?'

'Since a fortnight ago,' Garrison roared. 'Now, if that's the end of your impertinence I want you gone.'

'What?'

'You heard.'

Then a man who had been standing apart from the others walked over to Garrison with a couple of Jack Russells at his heels. The smile on his cupid's bow lips made Garrison squirm but the warmth seemed genuine enough.

Practically covering the entire left side of his face was a strawberry-coloured birthmark.

'You're Mr Garrison from Coastguard Cottage, aren't you, sir?' he said, extending his hand. 'Frank Rapson, Chairman of the Mary's Haven Badger Club.'

Garrison frowned at the hand until it was replaced in Rapson's pocket but the dapper little man continued to beam and run the tip of his tongue over the curiously feminine mouth that was so conspicuous in the red and white pug face. His fingers rolled and teased a cigarette and he half turned away from Garrison to hide his disfigurement.

'We thought this was still Warren Fishacre land. Mr Chard, the farm bailiff up Effords, said we could dig here. We did'n mean to give offence.'

'Well, you have,' Garrison said. 'Get off my land, now, and don't come back with your dogs and spades.'

'A badger lover,' someone sneered.

'Better than a badger killer,' Billy cried.

'You don't want to listen to back alley rubbish like him, sir,' said Rapson, and Garrison wondered if he slept with the smile on his face. 'Him and that girl are always in and out of trouble – thieving, lying, trespassing.'

The wind set the dark brown curls dancing on Rapson's head. The humour had vanished from his smile.

'Badgers are pests. Ask the steers up Woodash, ask any farmer. These cliffs are crawlin' with brocks and foxes. You got chickens, sir?'

'No.' Garrison folded his arms and glanced at his wrist-watch. 'You have five minutes to get off my land. Then I'm calling the police.'

'There idn' a phone at Coastguard,' said a voice but Strawberry lifted a hand.

'Pack up, boys,' he said. 'We'll go back Efforts way. The gennelman can do what he likes on his own property.'

'That shot you up the bum, didn't it, mate?' Sheena crowed.

'There's an awful lot of vermin about,' Strawberry said pointedly. 'You got to keep it down.'

The birthmark exaggerated the pallor of the rest of his face. Garrison and the children watched his departure.

'How much of this is yours, mister?' Billy said. The wind flattened his hair to his head and muffled his voice.

'The cottage down there, the lawn and the hedge and the bit of beach under the cliff,' Garrison said.

'Not this here? Not the blimmin' Point or anyfin' else?' Sheena said. Garrison shook his head.

'Then you was lying?' Billy chuckled.

'And on Sunday, too,' said Garrison.

The stoniness had gone out of Sheena's gaze and she was laughing.

'Strawberry won't forget it,' she said. 'Him and his lot are meaner than ferrets. You put one over on him. Crikey! – that'll really stir things.'

'Want to come back to the cottage for a cup of tea and a bite to eat?'

Billy nodded.

'You can tell me all about this badger club,' Garrison added, ducking once more under the wire.

Angling their wings, the buzzards rode the gale. Peaceful co-existence, Garrison reflected. The war years had been a dark tunnel leading back to nature, back to all this. Sinking his hands in his pockets he clenched his fists and let the ache for Ann flood his stomach.

Chapter 5

The Badger Club

But how often the absence of humans lent eloquence to a landscape. It was difficult to think of an All-loving, All-merciful God after Belsen; and Ann's illness had left what remained of his belief in tatters. God moving in mysterious ways was the threadbare excuse for the inexcusable. How hard it was to bear the suffering of someone you loved.

The stink of seaweed was stronger than the smell of wood-smoke. It was the iodine smell of casualty wards. Maybe we shouldn't harbour such enormous self-esteem, Ann had said on his last visit when Garrison had voiced his doubts. 'Maybe God cares equally for everything – dung beetles, dandelions, saints. A wild flower must be very attractive, after all it never sins.' Somehow it was a sanatorium conversation edged with unreality and desperation. Anyway, he reflected, as the kettle began to purr on the Aga, gratitude for life should make saints of us all.

Billy and Sheena sat at the fireside eating 'doorsteps' of bread and jam. They spoke about the baiting in Rapson's scrapyard.

'They bet money on their dogs,' Billy said.

'Or how long the badger will last,' Sheena added. 'It's horrible, mister. There's all this blood and noise and them blokes bawlin' and shoutin'. It didn' oughta be allowed. The dogs get it almost as bad as the badgers.'

She cleared her throat and glared at the fire.

'We saved a badger once,' Billy said giving Garrison a quick birdlike glance. 'They was busy at the baiting and me and Sheena prised a couple of sheets of corrugated off the side of the shed where they kept the animals. Then we dragged out this sack with a sow badger in it and put it in the basket on the front of Colin Law's butcher's bike. Col lends us the bike sometimes.'

'Billy borrows it, he means – only Col don't know.' Sheena hugged her knees to her chin and grinned.

'We wheeled it all the way to Firebeacon Point and let the poor thing go. Crikey!' she exclaimed. 'It didn' half shift. I never knew badgers could travel that fast.'

'Do they always bait the animals at Rapson's Yard?' asked Garrison.

'No,' Billy said. 'It idn' always a big do. Most of the time they just dig 'em out and kill 'em on the spot for the farmer.'

'They're supposed to be pests,' Sheena sneered. 'Supposed to roll in the corn to get at the grains and Strawberry reckons they kill chickens and lambs.'

'Bleedin' rot,' Billy said. 'It's just an excuse for that lot to kill them. Why do they do it, mister? Baiting's worse than trapping or shooting or anything else.'

'I don't know, Billy.'

The boy got to his feet and fished something out of a pocket in the overcoat crumpled beside him. It was a battered volume on British animals.

'Look,' he said, choking on his indignation and flicking through the pages. 'Here and here and here, wherever there's a predator it says: "Only enemy, man." That's us, mister. It's always us.'

39

'Strawberry's lot make you sick,' Sheena said.

'Has this badger club got a meeting place other than the yard?' Garrison said.

'The upstairs room at the Ship in Mary's Haven,' Billy said. 'They have their club supper there and get-togethers and things.'

'You seem to know a lot about them.'

'We go to school with the youngest Rapson, bleedin' Tony,' Sheena said. 'He never stops showin' off about his dad and big brother and the club. I hate the little rat but he don't know how to keep his mouth shut.'

Garrison nodded. 'How old are you Sheena?'

'Ten – same as Billy. I was an evacuee from Islington. My dad didn' want me back.'

There was no self-pity in her voice.

'Why on earth not?' Garrison said.

'I s'pose I reminded him of me mum. She run off wiv another bloke. I live with the Rowdens now. They're gettin' on a bit.'

'My dad didn' come home from the war,' Billy offered. 'He died in a Jap PoW camp.'

'I'm sorry,' Garrison said, feeling his own problems paling.

'I was little when he went away.'

Garrison decided the situation needed rescuing.

'Could you two eat some kippers?' he smiled.

'I could eat an elephant,' Billy cried.

'Same here,' Sheena said.

'Do you know all the badgers' setts on the cliffs?' Garrison shouted from the kitchen.

'Most of 'em.'

'Will you show me? – this afternoon if possible.'

'Any time you like, mister.'

'Don't you go to school?'

'Not always,' Billy said. 'Sometimes we mitch. What do you do for a living?'

'I paint animals and birds and landscapes.'

40

'For money?' Sheena said. 'Can we have a look, mister?'

'Go in the studio, but don't touch anything.'

That evening after an exhausting afternoon tramping the clifftops Garrison missed his cigarette case. He was not a heavy smoker but enjoyed the occasional Players. It was the silver case with his initials on the lid. Ann had given it him before her departure for Switzerland. He recalled leaving it on the table beside the jam jar full of brushes. Reluctantly he concluded that one of the children must have stolen it.

'Now that's a pity,' he murmured.

The wind came off the sea in a gust and boomed in the chimney. Smoke puffed across the hearth. Garrison's rocking chair clacked gently and rhythmically and memories of the afternoon lifted on the flicker of the flames.

'I know you care, mister,' Billy said, his face screwed up with emotion. 'But you eat animals, don't you? – sheep, pigs, cows, bits of 'em anyway. There's a slaughter-house in Mary's Haven. It's an awful place. Awful.' And his voice had sunk to a whisper. Then the vision of a street full of jostling, lowing cattle had blotted out the beauty of the sea and sky.

'What a pity,' Garrison sighed again, and he reached for his whisky bottle. The cat was mewing at the door but wouldn't come in, so he fed it on the lawn.

For Bullenspur the nightmare could not have had more mundane beginnings. He was sharing one of the outlying setts with two juveniles that had left Froward in the late summer.

Forage had been lean and he was bad tempered but despite the youngster's nervousness he had curled into sleep. At first he thought he was dreaming the dog. It was yelping in the back of his mind and he woke up growling irritably to the realization that there was a dog in the sett. It was in a passage outside and the cubs were scrambling over him to bolt up another tunnel. He followed hastily but the youngsters' whimpering told him it was a dead-end. There was just

41

enough room for him to turn and wedge his hulk in the burrow.

The dog came to an abrupt halt and kept up its ear-splitting din. Bullenspur snarled and firmed the muscles in his hindlegs, pressing them against the tunnel walls. Then he heard the pick biting into the soil above. Before long half the roof collapsed and daylight poured in. Spades widened the hole and he smelt men and dogs. Fluffed out to fighting size Bullenspur leapt at the terrier but the clamp closed on his rump and he turned and bit at the metal until his teeth grated. Strawberry dragged him clear of the sett and he was kicked into a heavy meal bag which was instantly tied at the neck.

Throughout the journey to the scrapyard Bullenspur lay quivering in a daze of disbelief. Fragments of Hawscrag's story kept scratching at his mind. He would wake up soon within the beloved confines of Big Sett. All he wished was to breathe the rooty, damp scent of underearth and luxuriate in the warm odours emitted by the other animals. Hawscrag, Aspen, Birdcherry, Cragbriar, Ashblacken: the names pattered across his misery.

They released him from the sack and dumped him in the shed. After a futile attempt to break free he settled in a corner on the bare stone floor. A moment passed to the thumping of his own heart then a small frightened voice said: 'What will happen to us?'

It was a badger sow named Sloeberry. Raising his muzzle Bullenspur scented another animal lying beside her.

'Firethorn,' Sloeberry replied to his enquiry. 'They broke his lower jaw and he can't speak. Please – what will they do to us?'

'I don't know,' Bullenspur lied.

'Something . . . bad?'

'It's best not to think about it. Earth Mother will look after us.'

There was a short silence until Sloeberry whispered: 'I'm so frightened. I have been ever since the men took us from the

42

sett. I've tried to dig but the ground is solid. My claws hurt.'

'Go to sleep,' Bullenspur said gently and as he drowsed he wondered what had become of the cubs. Eventually his mind shrank from his predicament.

The big boar from Runnage was the toast of the Mary's Haven Badger Club when it met for the Christmas Eve supper at the Ship Inn.

'He'll give your dogs a hard time, Archie,' Strawberry smiled and ran his tongue over his lips.

'I hope you'm foolish enough to bet on that, Frank,' Archie Stoneman said. 'I got three dogs capable of seein' off a lion.'

The men drank and grinned at each other over the rims of their sleevers. Strawberry's head was turned slightly to the right to present the unblemished side of his face.

'Five quid my Gritt and Jimmy stay longer at the job than your animals,' he said.

'And another fiver on your boar not givin' 'em much trouble,' said Stoneman.

'You're on,' said Strawberry, and they shook hands.

'But the brock will fight un-wired,' said Stoneman firmly. 'Over Lansworthy us don't tie up their back legs. It idn' sport.'

'Are your dogs up to it, Arch?'

'Don't worry about them, mate,' Stoneman said, nettled. 'Yours are as lean as racin' snakes but I don't suppose they'm pure bred like mine. Gritt's a bit long in the leg and Jimmy's got funny ears.'

But Strawberry would not bite. It was Christmas Eve and he was happy so he draped an arm round Stoneman's shoulders and escorted him upstairs to the club room. Twelve men of various ages sat at the table before the fire. Stoneman knew most of them – Stike, Small, Eric Rapson, fat Charlie Dunning who never bought a round, old Hill the retired market gardener, three or four trawler-men. On the wall over the mantelpiece a badger's mask was prominently displayed.

'Gentlemen,' Strawberry beamed, and he unbuttoned his sports jacket. 'Archie Stoneman, our guest from Lansworthy, idn' a stranger and I know you'll make him feel at home, especially as he's in a hurry to part with his cash. Come Boxing Day I'm going to help him out so no matter how much grub he puts away tomorrow by Boxing Day evening he'll be several pounds lighter. Meantime let's get on with supper and have a few wets. Merry Christmas to you all.'

Then the landlady and the barmaid ferried in the rabbit stew, the bread, the ale and the port wine. The fire was built up and Strawberry blew softly onto the savoury mess in the bowl before him. He had that glow of well-being which self-esteem can produce. His son Eric caught his eye and winked. Looking up Strawberry saw the firelight gleaming red on the badger's teeth.

Chapter 6

Part of the Light

Bullenspur lay in the half-dark of the shed listening to Firethorn's gurgling indraw of breath. Throughout the ebb and flow of light Sloeberry had woken to dig in a frenzy until her claws bled. Pressed to the cold stone floor Bullenspur could offer no words of comfort, and after a while Sloeberry, too, curled into quiet acceptance. The wind blew, gulls wailed and the bells of nearby St Mary's Church rang out; and when darkness deepened night conjured up those invisible things which instinct recognized but could not label.

Struggling out of a bad dream into a worse one Sloeberry gave a cry and there was a flurry of claws raking concrete. Bullenspur waited for the panic to pass while his nostrils sifted through the smells in Rapson's yard – oil, grease, rust, bruised metal, dog excrement. He pressed his snout between his forepaws and waited for sleep to cancel out misery.

Through the end of a cat-nap he heard men's voices and a squirt of fear brought him to his feet. Involuntairly Sloeberry dribbled scats. The little sow had already shrank back against a wall when the door swung open and the glare of daylight was

45

suddenly full of man-shapes. Laying back his upper lip Bullenspur showed his teeth in a snarl. A torch shone in his eyes and he blinked and recoiled.

'We'll have the one with the broke jaw first,' said Strawberry, and Firethorn was taken.

'A bit of practice for your mongrels, Archie.'

The door crashed shut and the bolt rasped. Sloeberry pressed her shivering body against Bullenspur.

'What is happening?' she whispered.

'Firethorn is going to Earth Mother,' said Bullenspur.

'Are we to follow him?'

'Yes, Sloeberry.'

'But how? I mean – what –'

'Close your mind to it. You will go to sleep and wake up with Earth Mother.'

'Must I go alone?'

'That journey is always taken alone.'

The terriers were snarling and yelping and the men's voices were raised. Whenever the din subsided the badgers could hear Firethorn grunting and snorting. Bullenspur closed his eyes and saw Aspen. She was coming down the hedge-bank of bare red soil under the ash saplings.

Again the door opened with a bang that made Sloeberry jump. She tried to burrow under Bullenspur and all at once his terror was gone and he was angry. He flew at the nearest leg and would have savaged it if a boot had not caught him on the side of the head. Through the dizziness he saw Sloeberry gripped by the tail, hanging limp in the man's fist. The door closed and the whining yelps blurred to a single snarl of excitement.

Sloeberry took longer to die and by the time her grunting had ceased Bullenspur was in a white-hot rage. He paced up and down the shed, hackles raised and rippling in a wave along his spine. His body ached for action. As soon as the door opened he charged out into the morning and the men and dogs retreated. Then he was gripped in the tongs and flung into the

46

pen. Beyond the low corrugated walls enclosing the pen were heaps of scrap metal. Overhead a grey sky was racing westwards.

'Just Archie's dogs and mine,' Strawberry said.

On rigid, quivering legs the Jack Russells strained at their leashes. Their killing lust was inflamed by the sight of the swining black and white striped head. They whined and yelped from blood-frothed mouths and followed Bullenspur's every move. Stike prodded him with a stick and the badger snapped at it and growled. He was dauntless and the men recognized in him something formidable.

The five terriers were unleashed and dropped into the pen to swarm around Bullenspur but he was sure-footed and nimble. A quick jerk of the head brought his jaws into immediate contact with Stoneman's smooth-haired bitch. Teeth met through the crack of shattered bone and the terrier's yelp became a prolonged howl of pain. Stoneman winced as she limped away to be hauled out of the pen by Stike who was blowing little bubbles of spit and humming to himself. Strawberry had stopped smiling. Once more the black and white head flashed and a yelp told the onlookers the badger was still on target. Gritt staggered from the mêlée pawing a wounded ear. The side of her face glistened red but not as red as Strawberry's, Stoneman thought.

'That old brock knows his job,' he said, and Strawberry switched on a smile for the audience's benefit. Gritt pawed at her head a couple of times then snarled and rejoined the scrum.

'You gutsy little rascal,' Strawberry murmured.

Stoneman glanced at him. Gulls were leaving the rooftops in a yodelling mass but Bullenspur's world was all noise and pain. The morning had become a fever-dream. Jimmy and Stoneman's rough-haired dog, Joey, had succeeded in laying bare his snout and cutting him badly about the face while the other terriers concentrated on his haunches despite his efforts to place his rump to the corrugated. Every so often a dog got

47

on his back and he rolled over to dislodge it and thus became vulnerable to the attacks of Jimmy and Joey. They always went for the muzzle in defiance of the badger's awful bite. The air rang with the snap of teeth and the cries of the animals, but the spectators had fallen silent. Joey trotted out of the action carrying the broad gashes left by Bullenspur's claws on his belly. Stoneman swore as he nursed the bitch, knowing his money was lost and she would have to be destroyed. He hated the way Strawberry's tongue crawled over the full lower lip, like he was polishing his smile.

Unexpectedly Bullenspur shook off his assailants and staggered free. He was wet and spiky and the once beautiful face was dark with grime and blood. Lifting his muzzle he read the morning. Everything was dissolving into pain yet he still deployed an amazing, destructive violence. Joey somehow came out of his own pain to fling himself at the badger's hindlegs, but a flash of teeth produced some more yelping. Rolling clear the Jack Russell tried to lick his torn shoulder but Bullenspur was coming at him hard and only the intervention of Gritt and Jimmy saved him. The badger's grunts rose to a scream of fury, but his strength was failing at last and he began to make mistakes as exhaustion brought heaviness. Finally, with Gritt and Jimmy hanging off his muzzle, his forelegs collapsed and his head flopped down on the ground. Bewilderment swelled and he struggled to rise as the pain faded to numbness. His snout was in the dirt but it might have been resting on a cushion of sun-washed thrift for Bullenspur was beyond suffering. He did not feel the blow that released his spirit.

Strawberry called off the dogs.

'That was a heller,' Stike said. His maggot face of ill-health had taken on an uncharacteristic flush. 'A real heller. He destroyed Archie's dogs.'

Pursing his lips he blew a perfect bubble of saliva.

'Badgers don't feel anything,' Stoneman rasped. 'They'm all muscle and bone.'

'He took nearly an hour to die,' someone said in an awed voice.

'We'll have the mask,' said Strawberry. His fingers closed on the five-pound note Stoneman held aloft.

'Leash your dogs, Arch, or there'll be nothing left to put on display.'

It was customary to rake over the finer points of the baiting in minute detail, recalling some small demonstration of courage by a terrier or an unusually savage act of defiance from the badger. Mrs Rapson brought out the sausage rolls and mince pies on a tray and Strawberry opened a couple of gallon jars of rough cider. Bullenspur's body was put in the shed and the men gathered round the blood-splattered Gritt and Jimmy. Even Stoneman grudgingly admitted they had more than their share of guts. Despite the prospect of his top bitch being put down he had to agree it had been the best morning's sport for years.

Strawberry could not stop smiling. Old man Hill, who had dug and baited badgers for well over half a century, gave him a cigar.

'That Runnage boar was a marvel, Frank. You get his head on the wall, boy, and I'll pay for it. They sea cliff buries breed good fightin' stock, yes sir. The Lansworthy lot couldn't believe it was happening. Their faces was pictures.'

The slow spiral through darkness ended in deeper darkness and silence that held something exciting. It was not dead, unknowing sleep but Bullenspur felt curiously weightless and shapeless, more a breath of mist than badger. There was no seeing or hearing or smelling or touching, only a knowledge of being part of a sensation rather than experiencing it. Like looking outwards from a light.

'Yes,' said Dogrose's voice, again from the inside, like a thought. 'Part of the light, part of everything.'

'And you?' his thought-voice murmured. 'It is my voice, isn't it?' he added.

'I understand you,' Dogrose said.

'What are we now, Dogrose?'

'Anything you wish. We are all life, the light that never goes out.'

'I would like us to be boar and sow in Nightworld.'

'It is usually the wish of badgers.' Dogrose's voice had a smile in it. 'But there's no Nightworld, Bullenspur. Nightworld was the dream.'

Around them the summer morning assembled. Hills and coombes ran to the shore and a sea full of the sun's incredible brightness. Dogrose and Bullenspur touched snouts. Beneath the dewy grass were bluebell bulbs and the wild bees' nests hung in the hedges smelling of honeycombs.

'We are more than badgers, aren't we?' Bullenspur whispered.

'Yes,' said Dogrose. 'We are Forever. We are the life magic that lifts grass and flowers and holds birds in the sky and conjures the young out she creatures. We are sunrise and the seasons.'

'Could we be birds? Kestrels? Just for a little while.'

'There is only now, Bullenspur. Now we are hawks.'

'But the flying feeling is no different than the walking feeling,' said Bullenspur.

They sailed across the sky where butterflies danced and birds sang.

'Shall we be badgers again?' Dogrose asked.

And they were badgers among many badgers under the sun that never set. Ambling through the radiance towards them came Sloeberry and Firethorn.

Chapter 7

Snares

Aspen left the soil-scented comfort of underneath and found a still night waiting for her. Lights were coming on in the sky and the moist, mild air held scent in pockets. The sun had set on a day of mist and clear skies and it had been dark for some time when she joined Ashblacken and Guelder at the scratching tree. The pair had only recently returned from the sett at Parson's Cove. They were well-mated and happy in each other's company with Guelder preparing to cub within a month or so. Cragbriar, Furzebright and Birdcherry were soon above ground and there was much nose touching and the rubbing together of bodies between the scratching and mutual grooming. Seabirds cried and a seal splashed about among the reefs. Dark, soft-textured night settled on their knowing and every so often Ashblacken swung his head, sniffing and listening for other boars or any sort of danger. He was thick-necked and proud of the power and ferociousness his black and white striped face advertised. Then he gently circled Guelder on the clifftop lawn and led her off to forage.

Aspen sat back and groomed her forefeet which were like

powerful hands designed for digging. Birdcherry lay close by, running her teeth like clippers through her chest fur.

'I dreamt of Bullenspur,' said Hawscrag. 'It was a good dream.' She spoke in a low, purring voice as if she were addressing cubs. Aspen plucked a piece of bracken from her mother's back and smiled.

'Bullenspur is happier than we are,' Hawscrag continued and Birdcherry licked her lips and swallowed half a dozen times in quick succession. Why then are we born? she wondered.

'Happy, I said,' the old sow repeated, dropping her head to peer into Birdcherry's face.

'Birdcherry was born with the jitters,' chuckled Cragbriar.

Guelder returned to the sett and vanished underground. She was widening a new breeding chamber although she had determined to deliver her cubs elsewhere.

'W-what's up with her?' Birdcherry said.

'Cub-restless,' said Hawscrag. 'She'll be out again soon.'

A crackling of the undergrowth announced the return of Ashblacken. He was followed by Fingo.

'Trouble,' the boar grated and Hawscrag asked him to explain but he preferred to leave it to the cat.

'This morning men came to the pine copse,' Fingo said quietly. 'I was lying up in the round house and could watch them from one of the windows. They went to all the badger paths leading into the thorns and hammered in big heavy stakes and prepared the snares. Those wires could hold a bullock.'

'But not a badger,' said Hawscrag. 'How many snares are there, Fingo?'

The cat lifted a paw and Hawscrag counted his toes and nodded.

'Then we'd better get busy,' she said, 'before someone from an outlying sett comes visiting and ends up in trouble.'

'I'm going back to sleep,' Cragbriar observed grumpily. 'I'm too old for these capers.'

Guelder emerged and joined the sows who were filing along behind Ashblacken, Furzebright and Fingo up the main path. The wire was invisible against the dark slope but Aspen could smell the bruised ash wood stake and the noose. Ashblacken pushed his snout under the wire and dragged his hulk clear. The others joined him.

'Now what?' said Fingo.

'We dig,' Ashblacken grinned. 'Guelder and I'll see to this stake while the others split up and deal with the others. It shouldn't take long. As soon as you uproot them,' he added, addressing his fellow badgers, 'hide them in the thorn thicket.'

Throughout the early part of the night the sett-dwellers worked until the stakes were loosened and dragged from the soil. Winter moths fluttered about the animals' heads and the barn owls of Effords glided among the Monterey pines. Nightworld dripped and ticked and rustled, and Aspen and her companions walked through it with haunches rolling. Soon their large molars were crunching foot fibres on the steeps under the reek of kale. The winter lambing had begun and in the pens on the pasture ewes were in labour. Trotting between the hurdles Aspen found the low grunting of the sheep strangely badger-like. Now the darkness was heavy with the scent of newborn animals. Up on the hill the shepherd's lantern bobbed and Birdcherry smacked her lips nervously. Hawscrag had gone her own way along the steeps, stopping every once in a while to deliver a high soft call like a moorhen.

'She's content,' Aspen laughed.

'H-how does she manage it?' said Birdcherry.

'The night is beautiful. It provides everything she requires. She could ask for nothing more.'

'Earth Mother will be angry with m-me when I go to her, w-won't she, Aspen? I'm always w-worried about something.'

'It's not your fault,' said Aspen, and seeing Birdcherry's head droop she laid her muzzle on her sister's shoulder.

'I remember the d-days when men didn't come to B-Big Sett country very often.'

A light breeze rattled the sycamore spinners as the sows returned to the steeps. The dog fox loping by ignored them. He carried himself with a self-conscious alertness which the badgers found amusing. They paused and giggled. Silence returned and the Rips could be heard churning between Froward Point and Dragon Rock.

'Like Cragbriar's stomach,' Birdcherry said. 'Slosh-slosh.'

'Don't let Hawscrag hear you,' Aspen snorted and the sisters leaned on each other, chests heaving, laughing helplessly.

'Slosh-slosh-slosh,' Birdcherry gasped. 'H-heavy indigestion.'

Several nights later a storm beat against the Point and the steeps were shrouded with surf-vapour. Aspen and Birdcherry felt secure enough to lie up in the sett at Hellweather Point. After dimpsey they discovered the wind threshing Nightworld to send it flying through their senses. Before long caution gave way to jubilation. Up on the downs they ambled among the sheep and lambs under a cloudy sky. The storm had made way for another spell of mild weather and the pastures were dotted with rabbits. In the kale on the north flank of Garrowcombe Ashblacken and Guelder were eating earthworms. There was a brief silent exchange of scent before the animals settled to forage.

The constant coming and going of sheep and cattle had turned the path to a gruel of hoof-mashed mud. Chard's collie stared through rheumy eyes at the scene. Bunched together against the stile the ewes and lambs regarded him with alarm but he was watching the raven. It was the old cockbird Murdo, a lover of storms and carrion. He stood on the drystone wall and bowed to the sun. Then, totally ignoring the dog he hopped down and began to waggle his bill in what looked like a small bundle of wool and bones. Lowering his head the collie trotted on along the edge of the downs and the sheep ran for the open ground away from the fence and the great bracken-covered landslip overlooking Runnage Sands. The wind whistled through massed thorn twigs and set the clifftop ash swaying. Birds were forever moving across the countryside. The immense congregations of starlings were almost rivalled by flocks of woodpigeons whose numbers had been swelled by birds from the continent. They fed on the green ivy berries before joining the black-headed gulls on the plough.

Emerging from the Hellweather sett earlier than usual Aspen and Birdcherry were surprised by the number of small birds coming and going through the dimpsey. Flocks of greenfinches, linnets and yellowhammers were skirmishing for roosting sites along the hedges. Above Down End a golden moon shone across the hilltops, leaving the coombes deep in shadow. The badgers trotted up Garrowcombe Head to the gap in the hawthorn hedge that led into the turnip field. In the nearby oak the starlings were screaming.

Aspen placed her nose to the green cow parsley leaves at her feet and unravelled the scents left by voles, shrews and wrens. The sisters' eyes met and they smiled. Rabbits feeding far out into the field meant the absence of danger. Then a black and white face was lifted clear of the turnip leaves for a moment and turned towards them.

'A stranger,' Birdcherry murmured but Aspen had bitten into a root and was chewing a mouthful of succulent pulp.

Chapter 8

Raw Weather

Somehow he was not surprised to discover the cigarette case prominently displayed in the window of the second-hand shop in Mary's Haven. The little old man with the bright brown eyes and trembling hands wanted two pounds for it but accepted a pound note when Garrison gave him the facts in a voice that suggested a total unwillingness to compromise. Then Garrison saw the children in Woolworth's but they ran off before he could collar them. A few casual enquiries confirmed what he suspected. Up at Woodash where he got his milk and eggs the farmer's wife had nothing good to say about Billy or Sheena. Apparently they had been before the bench for stealing milk money off doorsteps and robbing crab pots. Billy had even stolen from the poor box in St Mary's Church. Farmer Steer was less inclined to write off the children.

'They ran away together once,' he said. 'Got as far as Wales on foot before they were caught. That Billy is a prapper little heller like his dead dad. If Harold Drew had come home from the war I reckon he would've took the boy in hand. As 'tis he's

56

run wild. His mother idn' a lot of cop. They say her's drawing public assistance and working at the same time.'

'Bad blood,' said Mrs Steer.

Peter Cox from Garrison's London gallery called to collect half a dozen new paintings and leave the sort of cheque that takes the sting out of bitterness.

'Give my love to Ann, David,' was his parting remark.

A clear, frosty sky produced a beautiful sunset but Garrison's evening walk was soured by the discovery of four dead rooks hanging from a barbed-wire fence on Woodash Down.

'Poor old black tops,' he murmured.

Down on Garrowcombe Sands a bonfire was burning. Approaching cautiously he surprised Billy and Sheena who were sitting facing the sea, smoking tea leaves in clay bubble-pipes.

'I s'pose you'll go to the cops,' Sheena said when he had unloaded his anger.

'And why shouldn't I?'

She shrugged and lowered her eyes.

'Do you always take what you want? Doesn't it matter if you hurt people in the process?'

'No one does anything for us, mister,' Billy said. 'They'd have me on the keeper's gibbet given half a chance.'

'That's it,' Garrison said. 'All you can do is feel sorry for yourselves once you get nabbed. You're the big brave outlaws until that knock on the door. Then you start looking for excuses. Why don't you pull yourselves together?'

'It's goin' to snow,' Sheena said coldly.

'Look,' Garrison went on, crouching in front of them. 'I've got to go away for a fortnight. I'll give you five bob a week to watch out for the badgers and keep an eye on my place.'

'Five bob each?' said Billy.

'Between you – every week from now on. All you've got to do is promise on your word of honour not to lift anymore milk money or get into trouble down the market.'

'Why are you doin' this, mister?' Sheena asked.

'Because I'm soft in the head,' Garrison grinned.

'We idn' goin' to Sunday school or nothing daft like that,' said Billy.

'Do I look like a missionary?' Garrison said.

'Well, there's usually a catch,' said Sheena. 'People don't do nuffin' for nuffin'.'

'Maybe we can work together to mess things up for the Badger Club.'

'They killed three animals on Boxing Day,' Billy said, relighting his pipe and coughing. 'You ain't got no real tobacco have you, mister?'

'Back at the cottage. Can you handle it?'

'We ain't wet,' Sheena sneered.

'I had to go over Lansworthy to my gran's for Christmas,' Billy said, 'and Sheena was at Totnes with the Rowdens.'

'Bleedin' boring,' said the girl. 'All them old fogies noddin' off wiv their mouths open.'

'Tony Rapson says his dad and the others killed a sow and two boars,' Billy said. 'One of the boars took an hour to die.'

'That's awful,' Garrison whispered.

'What did you do at Christmas, mister?'

'Got drunk.'

'My dad was good at that,' Billy grinned. 'My dad was the best fighter in the world.'

'He sounds as if he was a good man,' said Garrison.

Billy nodded, his eyes sparkling in the firelight. Then he cleared his throat and growled: 'When I grow up I'm goin' to kill Japs. Crool little yellow bleeders.'

Back at Coastguard Cottage they sat smoking the tobacco he had bought for the own-rolls he could never bring himself to make.

'What do we do if we catch the club at one of the setts?' Billy said.

'Crikey, Bill,' said Sheena. 'He don't have to draw you a picture. Where you goin', anyway, mister?'

58

'To see my wife. She's ill in a sort of rest home in Switzerland.'

'TB?'

'Yes,' Garrison nodded, startled to hear the expression on her lips.

'I had an auntie who died of that.'

'Ann isn't dying,' he said. 'She's on the mend.'

But the child's words haunted him all the way on the train to the ferry, and the journey across France seemed particularly slow and tiring.

The raw weather kept the older badgers underground. The wind was raking the Channel, lifting waves to peaks that dissolved in foam. Light snow on the hills faded to green where it met the cliffs. But the cock pheasant rising from the bracken on Garrowcombe Head loosed all the colours of the spent autumn in a firework explosion of wings. Despite the wintry tingle in the air a chaffinch sang from the furze and a storm cock was also raising its voice against the cold which could not mask the smell of cattle.

Snow lay on the steep ascent to the downs. Beside the fence were the tracks of two foxes running together downhill. The shoulder of Woodash Down was streaked with a whiteness patterned by the feet of small birds, rabbits and voles. The sea raced to Garrowcombe Head and on to the horizon in blinding brilliance. Solitude swelled around Cowtail. Shrubs and trees were alive and singing as she came to a hanging copse of oak, ash, thorn and gorse halfway along the landslips of Runnage. Across the undergrowth were glimpses of shale cliffs aslant like slabs of ham. Chest-deep snowdrifts lay at the top of the steeps and clouds were massing above the far hills to deliver fresh falls. The white countryside inland was braided with dark hedges. Sheep bleated.

Cowtail had become separated from her mate when some poachers had fired at them just before dawn near Firebeacon Point. The vixen had ranged about for a while then ran for

Froward, disliking the snow which balled to ice between her toes. Out of the wind melt-water was pouring down the steeps in a stream. Glancing over her shoulder Cowtail saw the yaffle dip into the copse and loose its manic cry.

'Stupid bird,' the fox murmured. She snaked under a strand of barbed wire and bounded through the bracken and stumps of dead mallow. The sky was clouding over rapidly and snow fell on Down End and the air darkened. Flakes whirled around Cowtail and the full force of the squall hit her and the snow became a giddy chaos of white scribbles. Distances were erased and the wind howled in the thorns. Behind the noise was the faint piping of oystercatchers. The world had shrank but already some brightness was showing over Woodash.

Yet the ache in the air was not due entirely to the weather. Cowtail's pace slowed and she repeatedly rounded her nostrils to what the morning had to offer. Her ears were pricked and she checked often to swing her head. The snow had gone with a flurry and the day was bright and wind-washed. From the direction of Froward Point came the faint 'chock' of metal cutting into timber. The sound beat across the cliffs and the fox halted. More than one sharp edge was biting into wood. Then dogs began to yelp as they did when they were fighting. Others joined in until men shouted and the animals fell quiet. Something was happening at Big Sett, Cowtail decided, and she took to the earth at Blackbottle Cove where Aspen and Birdcherry were curled up asleep. The fox thought it wise to leave them undisturbed.

Strawberry mewed to his dogs and joined the others under the pines while the snow flailed down. Stike was acting the fool and the others were encouraging him. The idea of clearing a path through the thorn scrub was a pub strategy born of a common desire to 'shake up' the Froward animals. The sett had never been dug and over the years its occupants had achieved weights and sizes tailored by pub mythology. There was even beer-talk of a giant white boar but the thorn thicket had always deterred the diggers and segregated fiction from fact. An abundance of badgers elsewhere had not shaken Strawberry's belief that Froward was a personal challenge. Chard had warned him to look out for the old lady from Fishacre who regarded the steeps as a bird sanctuary; but she spent a lot of time in the Caribbean. Strawberry's upper lip curled. What did the gentry know about brock? They had fox-hunting and hare coursing but the mysteries and pleasures of the baiting were unknown to those people. Maybe some even looked down on it and Chard said old Mrs Ordish from the big house wasn't even remotely interested in blood sports. No wonder her land was crawling with vermin – foxes, badgers, the lot. He ran a thumb down the edge of his grass hook. A fleet of steam trawlers came butting down the Channel. It would take hours to reach the sett but he was patient and the club members were keen, especially his boy, Eric.

The Monterey pines were roaring. Lighting a cigarette Strawberry wondered if it had really been badgers that had dug up his snares. Stike was talking about spiders, punctuating his monologue with little bubbles of spit and braying laughter.

'You ought to be on the wireless, Ern,' said Eric Rapson.

'Or the stage,' someone said, less kindly. 'The last stage out of town.'

Strawberry smiled and sent his tongue flickering across his lower lip. The squall had passed and the sun was out.

'Us better get on with it, I suppose,' he sighed and the terriers backed away from him with quivers of expectancy. A mistlethrush sang from the brambles which shrouded the biggest of the four concrete bunkers among the trees, and Fingo, who was lying on the roof no more than half a dozen cat lengths from the bird, chattered his teeth in an agony of killing lust. Then he caught the sound of human voices on the path leading down from King Arthur's Tower and flattened himself to the concrete. The thrush sang on.

61

Despite their assortment of hand scythes, billhooks, saws and cleavers the work party's progress was slow. Getting through the barbed wire had been difficult enough and it was only Strawberry's unflagging cheerfulness that kept them going. The blackthorn scrub was remarkably tough and pliable and the angle of the steeps offered little purchase to smooth-soled wellingtons.

Resting after a prolonged attack on a great tangle of furze Strawberry reflected on the tenacity of the Mary's Haven Club. Surely it made them superior to the other South Devon clubs. Choosing to use Jack Russell's instead of larger terriers for the baiting set them apart. They were the embodiment of Churchill's bulldog spirit. Good dogs and good men had that spirit. Glancing up through his sweat he saw the woman, the teenage girl and Billy Drew step out of the trees. The terriers were charging up the slopes to meet them.

'What are you doing?' the woman said, ignoring the dogs and slithering down over the turf to confront the diggers. She was an elderly, fiery-looking old lady with smiling eyes and a sharp tongue who carried herself with immense confidence. Strawberry saw the shabby tweeds and down-at-heel veldtschoen as the uniform of authority. He tried to explain but was silenced by an impatient wave of the hand. 'Trespassing and destroying property,' Mrs Ordish observed. She had the refined voice Strawberry hated. It reminded him of certain high-handed young officers in the war, who had never seemed put out. Attempting to salvage the remains of his pride he mentioned Chard but the woman's face hardened.

'I leave these slopes to the birds and animals,' she said. 'Chard has instructions to see off people like you. Badger club, indeed! Take your tools and dogs and get off my land now and never come back unless you want to deal directly with the police.'

'But badgers are pests, ma'am,' Stike said.

'And so are you,' Mrs Ordish replied. 'I'll not tolerate riff-raff coming onto the estate and tearing it up. No more of your

62

impertinence. Just make yourselves scarce – at once.'

The 'at once' was barked and it stuck in Strawberry's craw but he helped put the tools in the sacks and called his dogs to heel. Briefly he caught the eye of the girl standing with her arms folded beside Mrs Ordish. She was smooth-faced, slim and pretty despite a fixed expression of contempt. Bloody toffs, he thought. There should be mutual respect among sports people. Taking badgers with dogs was no different than them hunting foxes with hounds. The injustice galled but he never stopped smiling as he led the retreat.

Passing Billy he said: 'I won't forget this, Drew.'

'One day, grandmother,' the girl said when the men were gone, 'you'll find yourself in hot water if you go around bullying ruffians.'

'Nonsense, Lucy,' Mrs Ordish laughed. 'Look what they've done to my lovely blackthorn. What a dreadful man with his awful leer.'

'And strawberry and vanilla face,' Billy grinned.

'I've a good mind to give Chard his notice,' Mrs Ordish continued. 'I've never liked him.'

Lucy smiled, finding beauty in the older woman's aquiline noise, stubborn mouth and the ruts and wrinkles. Billy stood before them with his hands in his overcoat pockets.

'You saw 'em off, missis,' he beamed.

'Yes, I did, didn't I, Billy,' said Mrs Ordish. 'Thank you for warning us.'

'You and old Garrison are a right pair.'

'This Mr Garrison likes badgers?'

'He paints 'em,' said the boy. 'He's got stacks of badger's skulls and stuff in his studio. He's like you, missis. He don't want to kill things. Mr Garrison reckons most wild animals live under siege – whatever that is.'

'I wonder if it's David Garrison, the wildlife artist,' Lucy said.

'Yeah – that's him!' Billy exclaimed. 'He's famous, but he idn' around at the moment. He's in Switzerland 'cos his wife's in one of them chest places. She's got TB.'

He began heaving the cut branches back in the gap left by the badger diggers.

'Do you still want to go with me to Barbados?' Mrs Ordish said, wrapping an arm round her grand-daughter's shoulders.

'No,' the girl smiled. 'I was wrong about Fishacre. It's a fabulous place.' She planted a kiss on the old lady's nose.

'You thought so as a child and your father loved it – God rest his soul.'

Snow fell again. Sunlight came and went in gasps and the wind borrowed its shape from the things it touched and enfolded. Skyhook the peregrine rode it above the cove and hung at his station. Shading his eyes Strawberry looked up at the bird before giving Froward Point a long backward glance.

Chapter 9

Animal Unity

Slow wing-beats carried the barn owls up the coombe to the wall where they made pellets containing feathers, insect carapaces and the fur of small animals. Aspen and Birdcherry soon lost interest in the birds. Moonrise swiftly firmed to an orb and light leapt across the Rips. Aspen sighed. The sea was transformed into a prairie of silver fire.

'C-cowtail saw the stranger again this evening,' said Birdcherry.

'A b-boar,' she added, hoping Aspen would bite.

Her companion nodded and tugged off a mouthful of grass.

'Animals come and go,' Aspen said. 'It's not unusual. There are many setts between ours and the Flashing Light.'

Birdcherry was thinking of the snares and the cutting of the scrub thorn. Her world had become fraught with danger and every breath flooded her being with anxiety. Sometimes she woke in the middle of the dog-nightmare surrounded by snarling mouths and pointed teeth, her haunches wedged between the walls of some underground cul-de-sac.

'Birdcherry,' Aspen said gently and she licked her sister's snout.

The owls took wing again and a crackle of bracken betrayed the passing of badgers. Hawscrag was leading Cragbriar to forage. Higher up the steeps Ashblacken and Guelder had met three yearling boars from the sett at Hellweather Point. The night rang with high, soft contact calls.

Aspen went to the stream and drank. The tranquillity of the goyal pleased her. It offered almost everything Big Sett could supply except the solid security of chamber and tunnel and the warm rooty smell of underearth. The yearling boars hoped to take up residence in Big Sett and Ashblacken did not object. The newcomers were friendly, playful animals who loved to romp around Aspen and Birdcherry and tease Hawscrag. Only Cragbriar with his indigestion problems and short temper took umbrage, and despite his age the yearlings were wary of his bite. Fluffed out with anger he could still be an imposing creature and even Ashblacken and Furzebright trod carefully when the old boar was moving about the sett. Witnessing what seemed to be Ashblacken's timidity on several occasions Aspen began to wonder if he really was the great fighter Guelder boasted about.

Once or twice the stranger came near the tribe at forage and answered their greetings in a low, friendly voice. As soon as he had gone Ashblacken and Furzebright would lift their hackles and strut around the sows. Then Aspen and Birdcherry would look at each other and try to swallow their laughter.

'Boars can be more than a little bit daft,' said Hawscrag one evening when Ashblacken was fluffing up for no apparent reason. 'They're very self-conscious.'

She buried her snout in the clean-smelling bracken bundled at the main entrance. Deepening twilight had reduced Dragon Rock to black silhouette. The wave-break on the Rips registered as little blinks of light. Much of the countryside's scent was masked under frost and the remains of snow showers. Leaving the thorns to forage the badgers found the stranger waiting beneath the pines. He proved to be a boar of four winters who had come from the woods on the other side

66

of the headland of the Flashing Light.

'One of my sister's whelps,' said Hawscrag.

'Men dug out the sett,' he said simply. 'They took my mate and two maiden sows.'

'May Earth Mother provide all they require,' said Hawscrag and Ashblacken nodded.

'May they enjoy the forage of Nightworld and lasting peace,' chanted the sows.

'Yes,' said the boar whose name was Greybob, 'but how do you get rid of the heartache.'

'Heartache shared is a light burden,' said Hawscrag and the sows gathered about Greybob and rubbed their muzzles against his shoulders.

'I killed a dog,' he said absently. 'The men could not reach my chamber. It was too deep. They put in a yap-dog and it made a mistake.'

Aspen met his gaze with eyes full of compassion.

'Hawscrag's ḏ-dream is becoming the r-real thing,' Birdcherry whispered. 'It's touching everyone. One day it will happen to you and me, Aspen – the d-dogs, the digging, the – the –'

Greybob stared at them blankly. The wind furrowed his coat and whistled faintly in his whiskers. He was a sleek, handsome creature testing the air with a nose that was covered in a mesh of scars.

'You are welcome to use our sett,' said Ashblacken.

'Yes,' said Aspen. Snow powdered down and turned to jewels on her fur.

Yet she chose to forage alone wandering through the maze of blackthorn, bramble and bracken, content to receive all the night had to offer. Above the bleating of lambs were the owl cries. Poking her head clear of the undergrowth Aspen saw the luminescent water racing towards Dragon Rock and heard the seal bark. The floodtide ran behind the light easterly wind. She pushed her snout into the coldness and turned over the leaf mould where the first aconites were uncurling. Above her

67

on the steeps the yearlings gambolled. Higher still the stars flared away to the edge of something so vast her mind faltered. Night saturated her being. She dug out and munched roots, loving the darkness and all its sounds. Then she stood beneath a little hawthorn tree and leaned hard against it to rub the itch from her sides and back.

The hazels in the goyal of Ramsons Dip shook out yellowing catkins and a mistlethrush competed with the lark that was singing over the winter wheat. After several nights away Aspen returned to Froward Point, dropping her muzzle to read the taint of man in the mud. It was strong enough to crinkle her nose and lend an unpleasant edge to the morning. The rush of passing starlings jerked her head up but she was usually too late to see the flocks. Ravens cronked, black-backed gulls boomed and Hebog the buzzard skirled his cat-calls. Dark-etched against grey Skyhook cruised and watched the coming and going of wild fowl at the marsh behind Coastguard Cottage. Rock doves beat across gulfs of shadow and the tiercel came to agitate them and the waders. He soared on a quick beat of the wings and glided into an upward loop, unhurried and unconcerned. He had fed and was merely taking the air. His raw, thin cry lifted the oytsercatchers off the mussel reefs and kept the pigeons in the treetops of Fishacre.

Aspen walked under bramble and thorn leaving the odd wisp of fur on the hooks and spikes. Lapwings were flinging themselves off the frost-bound pasture and the air was painfully keen. A dozen or so rabbits broke cover and clattered off down the steeps. Catching a whiff of Fingo Aspen turned and stopped. Something black separated itself from the shadows beneath the gorse and became a cat. There was a brief touching of noses before Fingo and Aspen walked together. Coming up the zigzags onto Froward they met Cowtail.

''Ere – what's wrong?' said the fox.

'Nothing's wrong,' Aspen smiled.

68

'That stranger don't like me,' Cowtail went on, sniffing first the badger then the cat. 'He growled at me when we met underground.'

'Perhaps he's not used to you.'

'Maybe, maybe. The big boar badger's got nasty teeth and a nasty glint in his eye. He could do this vixen a mischief.'

'You'd better stick to the round houses in the pines,' said Fingo.

'They're not safe for cubs,' Cowtail said. 'And I'll have my cubs underground.'

'Then you'd better be polite to Greybob,' said Aspen.

'Yes – polite to Greybob and Ashblacken and old sore-arse Cragbriar and Hawscrag. Life in Big Sett can be very boring.'

'But safe for foxes,' Aspen said.

Cowtail trotted after them. 'You go and speak with the stranger, hey, Aspen?' she said. 'Tell him Cowtail is a good fox. Tell him I'm a good friend of the badgers.'

'Why should he listen to me?'

'You're his sow. Everyone can see that, can't they, Fingo? Hey?'

'Perhaps,' the cat murmured, unwilling to say anything which might upset his friend.

''Ere, come on, now, come on,' Cowtail urged. 'Are you blind or something? Greybob's always giving Aspen the glad eye.'

The cat blinked. Snow was falling and the pines were shaking out their darkness. The beauty of the living world united the animals in silence. The wind held the resinous scent of the trees, the sea murmured and the peregrine tiercel shrilled his wild cries. Sadly Aspen thought of Bullenspur. Death came to the beautiful ones, to those so full of life the world stood still and bowed as they passed. Death took them all. She sighed and the cat and the fox glanced at each other. They could feel the splendour that took them beyond the boundaries of breath. They tried to read it with their noses – the things singing in their blood, but mystery deepened. From a bright haze the pines crumbled black into the air and the sky descended to catch the gleam of water. The wave built to break but never fell and the gull hung in flight but never called. The animals stood in a trance where the wind spoke and the stones sang. Something nameless was stalking them. Breathing gently Aspen felt her hackles lift in expectation. There was a light all around her and her coat shone. Snow drove down from the north, snuffing out the brightness. Crags and steeps stepped in and out of a white smoke and the pines began to roar. Flakes whirled around the animals and all the waders on the reefs of Dragon Rock began to cry. Twigs and boughs were screaming and the world had shrank. Then Froward was emerging from vagueness and hardening to its familiar browns and blacks. Cloud-tops caught the sun and the storm faded to a few flakes. But the wind had a cold bite to it. It ran through Aspen's fur and she brought the smell of it into the sett.

All the badgers were assembled in the great chamber close to the largest entrance hole. Their warmth created a most pleasant atmosphere and Aspen found it easy to settle and listen to Hawscrag's incantation.

'Where have you b-been?' Birdcherry whispered and Aspen felt Greybob's snout creeping over her face.

'We've been worried.'

The three yearling boars pressed close with something more than curiosity and Greybob growled a warning. Cragbriar's cackle of mirth brought Hawscrag to a halt and she showed her disapproval with a little cough. The kin group waited in polite silence for her to continue.

'So many fidgets,' the old sow grunted. 'If you must scratch or chatter go outside.'

'S-sorry, Hawscrag.'

'Yes, you're always sorry,' came the grumpy reply.

'Oh get on with it,' said Cragbriar and he broke wind.

The muffled explosion of laughter was the final straw as far as Hawscrag was concerned and she went thumping off to her chamber muttering to herself.

70

'Now perhaps we can all get some rest,' said Ashblacken. 'I shall,' said Cragbriar.

Aspen and Birdcherry curled up together in a chamber on the lower level while the boars remained in the bachelor chamber.

'Hawscrag was difficult to understand th-this time,' said Birdcherry. 'She kept on about drifting towards the quiet s-sunset. "The slow s-silent drift towards Earth Mother," she said. "Breath by breath"; and she said our n-names were there among the stars. Why can't I s-see these things or hear the v-v-voices she hears and you hear? Sometimes I hear Dogrose sobbing in the d-dark. Then I feel so lonely.'

'In the Nightworld beyond Nightworld Dogrose and Bullenspur are happy.'

'But I keep seeing the sharp dog teeth.'

'You'll turn into a rabbit one day,' Aspen smiled. 'I keep seeing the Bluebell Radiance and the shine of summer grass. Life is the great gift and to live in fear is wrong. We are Earth Mother's children.'

'The Moonborn?' Birdcherry whispered.

'She-creatures carrying the destiny of our kind as the earth holds the life of things to come – grasses, flowers, fruits, everything. We are tomorrow, Earth Mother, spring, rebirth, hope.'

'Yours is a c-clearer vision than Hawscrag's.'

'Age has made her a mystic,' said Aspen. 'She feels things in the blood and there's no easy way of putting them into words. She is close to something more remarkable than Nightworld living.'

Chapter 10

The Awful Sound

Guelder was spring cleaning despite the fact that winter was
not even half-done. Feeling the cubs kick she hastened to
bundle clean bedding into her chamber while the other
badgers showed a reluctance to venture any further than the
latrines. They had sufficient body fat to carry them through
bitter spells when forage was a penance. Greybob and Aspen
were constant companions although Birdcherry usually
dragged along. The approach of cub time affected the entire
sett and the boars became very protective, leaving the
entrance holes first only after a lengthy nosing of the air.
Forage was not easy to find especially under frost and snow,
but confinement underground pleased the badgers. Packed
into the communal chamber they could listen to Hawscrag's
revelations or Cragbriar's earthier tales. Even the yearling
boars had something to contribute to the story telling but
behind all the monologues was the enduring vision of dogs and
digging tools and the going down into pain.

'And why must it be so?' Ashblacken demanded angrily.

'Perhaps there is a greater force than Earth Mother,' said
Cragbriar.

'Perhaps she also lives in the shadow of man.'

'No,' said Hawscrag. 'She is life and man is death.'

'And death always wins,' the old boar said drily.

'Appears to win, as winter appears to win,' Hawscrag said. The other badgers grunted their approval.

'Perhaps without the baiting and digging, the shooting, trapping and snaring,' said Guelder, 'there would be too many of us. Then something terrible would happen to claim us all.'

'There have been seasons of great sickness,' Hawscrag said. 'Perhaps man is to us what foxes are to rabbits.'

'It is the great mystery,' said Cragbriar.

'But life is the thing,' said Aspen. 'The mystery is at the beginning and end. Between the two mysteries are all the seasons.'

'Yes,' said Greybob. 'Nightworld is now.'

Following them up through the Monterey pines onto the pasture Birdcherry ached to pursue the matter but sensing their happiness she held her tongue. Leaving the potato field the other side of King Arthur's Tower the badgers rolled in the grass in the stillness of the cloudy night, nipping each other playfully and embracing in bear hugs. The smell of sheep came in a cloying breath. Lifting their heads the animals saw the trees aslant on the skyline and plodded up towards the lesser darkness of the horizon. Aspen suddenly halted and tested the air. Diesel and oil had leaked from a tractor. It offended her nostrils and made her screw up her eyes. A grubby rag fluttered on the barbed-wire fence. The badger sniffed at it and turned away, glad to see rabbits' scuts vanishing into darkness. The sky was clearing and stars were mirrored in Greybob's eyes. Aspen gazed at him for a moment then swung away and ambled off. He pursued her at the trot but Birdcherry retraced her steps.

Wordlessly the boar and sow walked down through the oaks of Warren Fishacre into the coombe, exploring the shadows with their snouts. Occasionally he brushed against her and groomed her. The warmth of his breath was on her muzzle

73

and the eyes she had closed. Flattening her stomach to the ground she eased under the elephant rhubarb, jumped the stream and scrabbled up the slope beneath the laurels and rhododendrons. He seemed fascinated by the water and followed it down to the falls.

On the edge of the gorse thicket she waited but he did not appear so she continued alone, happy in her own company. Scents and sounds lapped around her. As always on calm nights there was the sea breaking over rocks and the saltiness mingling with the smell of gull droppings. A long descent of Down End brought her to Garrowcombe Head and a leisurely forage for rhizomes under the trees. Out on the Channel the lights of cargo vessels and fishing boats were larger than the stars and their movement fascinated Aspen. She sat and groomed herself then took the badger path to Runnage steeps. The land above was dotted with sheep and rabbits. A ewe was pawing the ground in a field corner. Her forelegs were buckled and she was heaving and panting. Then the lamb was dropped and as she licked it a faint bleating was added to the other sounds.

Along the shore seabirds and waders occasionally loosed a cry. The moonless night was full of the familiar things which put Aspen at peace with herself. Her muzzle pushed through the wet grass and she sneezed. Climbing the slope beneath the bracken close to the gorse where the buzzards nested she passed over Woodash Down and saw a light in Coastguard Cottage. Wriggling under the lowest strand of barbed wire she ran at the hedge-bank, shouldered aside the bramble snarls and skidded down the other side where the gin trap was waiting. Her left hindfoot thumped hard on the plate and the serrated metal jaws closed with an awful sound, chewing through flesh to clamp to the bone. Aspen gave a wavering scream and collapsed. Twisting in pain she bit at the gin and the iron chain and the iron stake, but the pain swelled hot in her leg and she licked the wound. It was a heavy fox gin, tilled securely. Low, eerie cries came from Aspen but she lay

74

crookedly beside the stake and began to dig.

'They're more machines than animals,' Strawberry said, smiling. The beer on his mouth emphasized its shape. Slowly and delicately the tip of his tongue trailed along the lower lip and the fishermen watched fascinated. The birthmark was dark in the firelight.

'God made them to sort out the good dogs from the bad buggers. A terrier's pedigree is measured by the way he handles himself and brock, and Old Brock soon separates the men from the boys.'

Again a pause to lick his lips.

'Everything about badgers is designed to inflict injury. They're all muscle and bone from head to tail. You can't kill 'em by banging 'em on the head, no sir. You have to catch 'em smartish on the snout with a bar and that idn' easy. Their back feet can disembowel a dog and the claws on their forefeet can rip out a dog's eyes. What makes it worse is they haven't got no feelings like dogs or cats. Even when they're badly wounded all they want to do is kill. Let 'em loose in a hen house and see what they'll do. I'm tellin' you there idn' no fiercer creature in Britain and it takes a dog with the heart of a lion to drop that sort of opposition.'

He fondled the ears of his terriers and they gazed up at him in adoration. Their faces carried the scars left by badgers' claws and teeth.

'Gritt and Jimmy have seen off more brocks than I've had hot dinners. It's in their blood. Dogs like this don't grow on trees.'

'That old boy you had at Christmas was a heller, wasn't he, Frank?' someone said.

'Iron-headed,' Strawberry smiled. 'Less feeling than a stone. He murdered one of Archie Stoneman's dogs. A brock like that takes a long time to die. No feeling, you see. Dogs don't like pain but Old Brock don't know what pain is. He's tougher than leather and idn' ever afraid. When you idn' scared and you can't feel pain you're a bundle of bloody trouble for a dog. That's why baiting is just about the tops as sport. There's no harder test for a terrier. Old Brock can see 'em off in job lots. I've knowed heavy boars with their back legs chained put the finest and bravest dogs out of action. It took half a dozen blows with the spade to kill one old boy us had Easter '46 at the first club do since the war.'

He drank and moistened his lips, half-turning away. The terriers whined softly.

'Sows don't provide the same sort of sport but even they can mess up a good dog. Their jaws sort of lock and you have to break 'em to get the dog free. Even with broke jaws they have a go and their feet which are strong as hell from all the digging can really open up an animal. Sometimes six dogs idn' enough to get the better of a badger and I've seen crowbars bend on that skull. I got a record of all the kills us have dug and baited.'

'What about foxes, Frank?'

Strawberry's upper lip curled. 'Them that chases foxes don't know what they're missing. The dog's aren't tested. Fox-hunting idn' about courage like the baiting. Baiting is all about blood and guts and it idn' cruel because as I've said, Old Brock don't know the meaning of pain. But they can dish it out. If you got a terrier that'll stand up to a forty-pound boar you got a good dog. I reckon God made badgers to test dogs just like he made rabbits to fill pies.'

The fishermen laughed and Eric Rapson poked his head in the back door and called his father outside.

'We got the lead,' the young man said quietly and Strawberry smiled and nodded.

'Put it with the rest of the stuff against the wall by the shed,' he said. 'Make sure no one can see it. Any trouble?'

'None,' Eric grinned.

'Good. When you've done come back and I'll buy you a pint.'

For most of the night Aspen dug around the stake but it had been driven deep into mud and shillet and her efforts were in

76

vain. Then despite the agony she tried to prise open the jaws of the gin but the metal was unyielding. The hair on her back lifted all the way to her neck in wave-like ripples. By dawn she was exhausted and slept with her chin on her forepaws letting the numbness spread through her hindquarters. At first light Fingo found her and his heart turned to ice.

'There are men with sacks and dogs in the copse on the big headland,' he said. 'And they're coming this way.'

'What are you doing here?' Aspen said groggily.

'The cottage is good for scrounge. The man always puts out fish and other scraps.'

Aspen nodded and licked her torn leg.

'Even if you could get to Big Sett and bring Greybob and Ashblacken to dig it would be too late,' she said. 'I'm well and truly caught this time.'

Fingo sat and thought. The light was on in Coastguard Cottage and he heard the clink of the tin dish being put out. Smoke rose from the chimney.

'Maybe things aren't so grim after all,' said the cat and he bounded off down the field towards the building.

'Where are you going?' Aspen called.

'Trust me,' said Fingo.

Lifting her head Aspen saw the raven in the hedgerow ash and bared her teeth. It was a fine morning with a sunrise that held the sheep spellbound. Golden light crept across the field to warm Aspen but far off she caught the clamour of dogs and was frightened.

Down at Coastguard Cottage Garrison stood in the doorway and waited for the cat to come to the food he had put on the slate step. The smoke from his cigarette curled away on the lightest of sea breezes. If he raised his eyes he was staring into the sun. Already the morning had a spring-like warmth and Garrison was in a good mood. Ann had looked no worse and the doctors had assured him she was on the mend. Priding himself on being an intuitive person he had recognized their sincerity. So he had left the sanatorium in an optimistic mood, swallowing his dislike of the wealthy neutrals and the way they had ridden out the war in comfort. At Basle, waiting for his train, he had found himself thinking of the badgers and the sea cliffs. Men like Rapson could open a door onto the Dark Ages. He exhaled smoke and saw the cat gliding over the drystone wall into the garden. It came up to him and threaded through his legs. Unused to any demonstration of affection from the creature Garrison crouched to stroke it but Fingo broke away. Garrison grinned and pushed the dish of kipper scraps towards the animal with his foot, but Fingo mewed and advanced and retreated, gazing first at the man then in the direction of the side of the coombe.

'You're in a playful mood, little fella,' Garrison murmured. 'Aren't you hungry? Come on – no one's going to hurt you.'

Once again Fingo rubbed against his legs but darted back as soon as Garrison stooped to stroke him. There was an urgency about the cat which puzzled him. Mewing and purring Fingo walked up and sidled away, never taking his eyes off him. Garrison unhooked his reefer jacket off the back of the door and slung it on. Fingo leapt onto the wall and cried out.

'OK, I'm coming,' Garrison said. 'Lead on.'

They went up the coombe to the fence above the steeps of December Point, Fingo leading but returning to the man time after time in little darting runs, ears flattened to his head and tail erect. Somewhere in the distance dogs were barking.

Eventually Fingo trotted to the hedge and did not return. Garrison found the cat sitting beside the badger and the full pathos of the scene had him clenching his teeth.

'Oh Christ,' he breathed.

Aspen had gone crazy in the gin. Her muzzle was caked with mud and her claws were broken and bleeding. She had dug a pit eighteen inches deep and lay half in it, her head bowed and the metal jaws clamped to the exposed white bone. She was barely conscious but he felt her eyes on him as the emotion balled to a lump in his throat.

78

Garrison took off his jacket and threw it over her but he needn't have bothered. She was incapable of resistance and made no effort to struggle free even after he had put his weight on the spring and released her foot. She lay quietly in his arms and Fingo watched from eyes round with concern.

'It's all right,' Garrison said. 'No one's going to hurt her. We'll soon patch her up.'

He brushed some of the mud of Aspen's muzzle and she closed her eyes.

'Don't give up on me,' Garrison whispered.

The yelping clamour of the dogs was getting closer but Garrison came swiftly down the hillside and was in his garden when the men and terriers appeared. They would see the trap and put two and two together. Despite himself Garrison smiled. Fingo sat on the threshold but would not enter the cottage.

Garrison laid Aspen on a blanket before the fire, closed the door and fetched a bowl of warm water. Aspen stirred feebly as the wound was bathed.

'No bones broken,' Garrison breathed and the badger lay on her side staring into the flames. The first sharp stabs of fear screwing through her exhaustion had been dulled by the passive acceptance characteristic of her kind when death seems inevitable. She was at the mercy of the great enemy and suddenly felt very close to Earth Mother. But the kindness of this human was undeniable. His touch was as gentle as his voice and the fire made her drowsy. The pain in her leg had become a tolerable ache. Aspen sighed and slept.

Throughout the day Garrison continued to bathe the wound and with the return of her strength Aspen snapped at the hand holding the wet cotton wool; but the voice crooned to her and soon she was content to lie in the warmth grooming herself and licking the wound. Then she slept once more for a long time and woke feeling hungry. Beside her was a bowl of porridge covered with honey which she wolfed. Fish scraps and cornflakes were also gobbled up before she drank the milk left in Fingo's bowl. Finally she went all round the room sniffing at the furniture and investigating every corner. Garrison grinned and she came over to him and put her snout to his boots; but when he stroked her she shuffled swiftly away, backwards, showing her teeth.

The following morning after a night spent trying to dig by the front door she allowed him to touch her while she ate. Outside she heard the wind knocking against the building and could smell the sea. Lifting her muzzle she gave a cry, like the chirping of a bird, and ranged restlessly up and down before the fire.

'Time for you to go, little lady,' Garrison said with a note of sadness in his voice. 'Your friend the cat is outside.'

The latch clicked and the door swung wide. Aspen trotted to the step and swung her head to read the air. Then she ran with the cat, jumped onto the wall and was gone. Garrison fetched his binoculars and saw the animals climbing the side of the coombe to vanish onto the steeps.

It was something to tell Ann. Balling his fists he brought them together and laughed. Wildfowl and waders were leaving the flooded marsh and the air was full of wings and sunlight.

Chapter 11

On the Steeps

'Maybe some men are animals after all,' said Fingo.

The cat and badger were kennelled at Runnage. The sett was cold and smelled of terriers.

'He puts good scrounge out for me,' Fingo continued. 'And his voice had no threat in it.'

'It's different for cats,' said Aspen working on the wound with her tongue. 'Most cats are man-things.'

'How can you say that after what he did for you?'

Yes, it was stupid. I'm sorry, Fingo. It's just that I can't understand but I really am grateful. You're a good friend.'

The cat curled against her and began to lick the injured limb. Above ground light was fading and they could hear the muffled jangle of daws. When they emerged a little later a sickle moon showed through thin cloud. Sheep and their lambs stood motionless in the pastures. All about them grass, ash whips and brambles ticked and whispered in the wind. Down near the sea the shale was turning into slabs of light. Underfoot the sudden surprise of moss brought down Aspen's snout. Then it was raining. Drops pattered on bracken. The air was full of it and it streamed down the face to drip off the muzzle. Soon the grass was drenched and all about the animals water gurgled and hissed. But the wind was a soft south-westerly and no penance to walk into.

Coming onto the farmland they discovered a dog fox hanging head downwards from the barbed-wire fence. He was stiff, rain-washed and lifeless. For a moment all Aspen's senses focused on the animal but a high-flying curlew delivered its double note to break the spell. Standing on hindlegs Fingo gingerly ran his nose over the body before following his friend over the turf. The pair paused to sniff the empty cartridge cases scattered among the sheep droppings, crinkling their nostrils at the acrid smell. Now the cloud cover was thinning and parting and stars appeared in wonderful clarity.

Aspen had shaken off her slight limp and was rejoicing in her strength and vigour. Behind the glow of her muscles was a craving for something that expressed itself in life but still her lungs heaved with the memory of the gin trap. All the ghost forms of Nightworld could not blot out the memory. The abrupt division of grass and stone, the mirage of crag and water fed her craving. She was following the ancient paths of her kind, aware of the night in every fibre and secure in the calmness of animal society.

So they traversed the steeps, chesting the beds of bracken stems and scrambling over rocks and stone walls. Often they were roofed in by brambles beaded with raindrops. Starshine glittered on the bracken and the fingernail moon hung low over the fields. Scent was washed from everything living.

The badger and the cat held some of the universe's magic in their minds as they walked. The gleam of the coastland played on their senses. Then there was a darkening and rain fell again. Among the pines Cowtail was waiting and Aspen told her of the dead dog fox.

'Old Taggo,' she said in a cold voice. 'He was a good old boy, a good mate, a good fox. I wondered what had become of him.'

She sniffed and the tears slid down her muzzle.

'I am full of his cubs.'

'You'll find another mate,' said Fingo.

'But I want him,' Cowtail whispered. 'It ain't fair. Bang! and all the life goes out of you. Why? Why? I don't care if Earth Mother understands. I don't and even if I did it wouldn't bring the light back into Taggo's eyes.'

Aspen licked the vixen's face and for a long moment the animals stood with bowed heads.

In the sett Greybob was quietly attentive and Birdcherry as talkative as ever. Ashblacken had moved to the small sett at Hellweather Point and Hawscrag seemed irritated by everything, even Aspen's mishap. She plodded up and down the galleries pursued by Cragbriar's tart remarks, and Aspen wondered why the old sow chose to sit in judgement on the younger animals. Perhaps life had lost its relevance for her and she waiting to die. Perhaps she had truly seen something desirable beyond Nightworld. Again Aspen was confused. Her leg had begun to hurt again so she went to a chamber on the first level and spent the next three days sleeping and cat-napping. During this healing period Aspen had a dream in which she was wandering through one of those gentle sea mists which are not dense enough totally to hide the stars. The hillside was steep and crowded with badgers. Somewhere close at hand a bird sang and the stars were dancing now. Against the sky something waited. Then she stopped and the other badgers were also suddenly quite still.

'Things change but everything is changeless,' said the voice. Was it the voice of Hawscrag or Earth Mother?

Aspen's pupils were fixed on the darkness, staring through it to the mist-shrouded hillside. The animals climbed to the top and gathered to look down into the vale that spread through the sunshine of early summer to vast distances. It was watered by streams which wound through meadows choked with flowers and studded with copses of summer-leafing trees. Gazing in rapture across the vale whose horizons were another dream away Aspen felt it was the synthesis of all her emotions. The creatures of Nightworld were there but it was Sunworld, for Nightworld was the secret place animals had been forced into by man.

Aspen walked slowly down into the deep, sweet-smelling grass. Ahead, sitting on a low mound was a badger, no larger than any sow but very sleek and beautiful. Beyond her was brilliance within brilliance radiating an intensity of love. Glancing about her Aspen saw all the other badgers shining like stars.

Transfigured, her companions stood motionless – boar, sow and cub – aware of the mystery behind the light and the hosts of other creatures approaching it from every corner of the vale. Then Aspen knew she carried the glory within her and had done so since birth. She came before Earth Mother and looked into the kind face.

'Walk on, my child, into the light, for you are the light. You are the love.'

'Yes,' Aspen murmured lifting her head and opening her eyes, 'The love.'

Birdcherry was beside her in the warmth of underearth.

'You've b-been dreaming,' she said.

'Oh Birdcherry, it was such a wonderful dream.'

But she could not put the dream into words although Hawscrag questioned her later in the Meeting Chamber. Ever since Aspen could remember the age-silvered sow had posed the riddles which the tribe considered unanswerable, for they were part of Hawscrag's power and the mystery of life.

'What is softer than spiderspin?' she said from the darkness and Aspen answered: 'Earth Mother's touch.'

The gasp of indrawn breath from the assembled badgers seemed to affect Hawscrag and she cleared her throat before continuing.

'What is darker than the crow's wing?'

'Man's shadow, which is long.'

'What is warmer than sunlight?'

'Honesty between friends.'

'What is colder than the white frost?'

'Ingratitude.'

'What is deeper than the deepest sett?'

'Earth Mother's wisdom.'

'What is brighter than the morning dew?'

'The love of a sow for her young.'

'Good,' Hawscrag whispered and she shuffled across to stand before her daughter so that her breath was warm on Aspen's eyes.

'In the Beginning how many moonborn dwelt in Nightworld?'

'Two,' Aspen said without hesitation. 'A boar and a sow.'

'How many setts are there in Sunworld?'

'One. That which is lived in.'

'Ah!' breathed Hawscrag. 'I see you have been on the journey few take in this life. And what was your forage?'

'Mystery, mother. I was in Sunworld.'

'I have been there, my daughter. Now I know you truly share the vision.'

'D-doesn't it frighten you, Aspen?' said Birdcherry.

'No. It's like seeing with the heart.'

'Will you forage now?' said Greybob.

'Yes. I'm hungry.'

'We'll go to the turnip clamp by the gate near the old linhay,' said the boar.

'A good idea,' Birdcherry said.

'You can come with me,' grunted Hawscrag. 'It needs two to feed old Cragbriar.'

The yearlings chuckled.

'Time you gadabouts got mates,' said Hawscrag. 'There are maiden sows north of the wooded coombe.'

'Plenty of time for that,' Cragbriar cackled. 'Come midsummer and you won't see their rumps for dust. Would it be too much bother to get me to the scratching tree?'

The ancient many-branched ash tree halfway up the side of

85

Woodash Down had shed the last of its keys. Against the blue sky it stood motionless. Billy stroked the bark.

'He earnt his half-dollars when you was away, mister,' said Sheena. 'Look at his face. He's still a bit grey and yellow round the right eye.'

'Who did it?' asked Garrison.

'Strawberry's son, Eric – the nasty sod. He give Billy a hiding on the way home from school.'

'Then I went round their house after dark,' Billy said, 'and biffed a brick through the back window while they was having supper.'

'If you don't watch it,' Garrison chuckled, 'you'll end up on Devil's Island.'

'Old Strawberry didn' like me gabbing to Mrs Ordish,' Billy said. 'He told Eric to do me.'

'And that bleeder Chard!' Sheena fumed. ''Im and 'is traps. It was 'im who put down the gin what caught the badger. He's as bad as Strawberry. I don't know why old muvver Ordish puts up wiv him.'

'Old muvver Ordish,' Garrison thought. It was hardly the way to address a member of one of the most respected county families in the area. And she sounded a remarkable lady, one of a dying breed whose toughness and integrity he had always admired.

'Does everyone call Rapson, Strawberry?' he asked.

'Behind his back,' Billy grinned. 'Sheena told him he looked like the Phantom of the Opera.'

'And what did he do?'

'Gave her a big ear.'

They walked on among the sheep and lambs towards the sett at Runnage. A bomber flew low along the coast with a loud drone of propellers and just for an instant Garrison was back on the Normandy beach. The ache for Ann cancelled out the sudden emptiness of loss that firmed to an image of Neil. He let his eyes fall on Billy and Sheena. They skipped along before him, totally self-absorbed. Billy was pulling the sorrel between forefinger and thumb to loose the brown seeds. Garrison smiled, remembering how he had done it as a boy. Winter could never win despite the killing winds and the frost and snow. There were the little round green leaves of pennywort on the drystone wall and the larger leaves of cow parsley along the margins of the steeps. Leaves, too, were tufting the bramble feelers and the lambs also struck the right note. Optimism and resurrection, Garrison thought – yes! that was it. The flocks of finches and fieldfares feeding on the pasture with the lapwings in the sunlight that strengthened day by day lifted his spirit as much as the lark song.

Angling their wings to the sea breeze the buzzards cruised over the downs to quarter Garrowcombe. Their pinion feathers buckled at the tips and their mewling spread across the silence. Slowly they circled on the thermals and again and again the hush of noon was slashed by their cat-calls. Wool spiked on barbed-wire fluttered like the scuts of departing rabbits and winter's coldness filmed the hawk's eyes and made them ache. The pulse of life in the coombe only faltered when Garrison and the children intruded. Laying their wings on the breeze the hawks sailed in a wide glide out over the sea. Their pale breasts caught some of the day's luminosity and the tips of their primaries opened like fingers.

'They old 'awks,' Billy said.

Together the buzzards wheeled until a final circle brought them to the warrens pitting the bank under the copse. They cried joyfully to each other and shuttled between the gutting-post and the coney runs. The larks sang unaware of the world beyond their own needs and desires. A blackbird raised its voice from the thorns while the sun climbed the sky and the first cloud shadows glided up the hillside.

Chapter 12

Snow

The north-east wind brought Siberia to South Devon. Snow fell in gritty flakes which became larger as night closed and the temperature dropped. Great waves broke against Dragon Rock and the spray carried into the Monterey pines of Froward Point. The cold was intense – a 'killing cold' the countrymen called it, breaking the ice on the cattle troughs in the fields. The sea roared continuously and the ground hardened beneath the drifts the wind was piling up against walls and hedges. Underground the badgers slept.

For Garrison it was a blizzard of awesome violence. He stood on the top of the low crag in front of Coastguard Cottage, leaning against the wind. Spindrift scattered off the combers and December Point kept vanishing and materializing as the spray broke and swept inland. Yet the seabirds rode the wind effortlessly.

Garrison glanced at the downs. Except for the margins bordering the steeps the fields were white. Then a huge wave climbed the crag at his feet and slid back again but not before its crest had swept over him in a grey ice-cold sheet of spray.

The little stream falling down the cliff face was blowing back on itself. Snow had drifted against the front of the house but the lawns were clear. Garrison worked loose the bird table on its pole and re-assembled it round the side of the building out of the wind's full blast. Lapwings, golden plover, fieldfares and redwings were dipping their beaks into the lawns. The redwings seemed to suffer most and one actually died in his hands.

The sea was one vast chaos of storm water and the marsh was crowded with wildfowl. It was a new reality divorced from rationing, austerity and politics and Coastguard Cottage was a symbol of other-worldliness. It faced the sunrise, turning its back on the muddle of man's world.

He walked the beach and found a dead gannet on the shore close to a couple of oiled guillemots which were also lifeless. It put him in mind of all the shipping the war had claimed in the Channel. Then he was thinking of Neil and the snow squalls were tearing out of the greyness which had once been the horizon. Dunlin and turnstones retreated in large groups before the tide. Further up the beach were more winter thrushes looking for food. The wind smelled of kelp. Absently Garrison wondered why the turnstones were always in a hurry, always racing up and down the wave-break with a blur of legs. He grinned, knowing Ann would have been amused.

Duck left the marsh and were cuffed inland on a roar of salty air. Ravens and a couple of crows picked over the carcasses of seabirds. Garrison turned and skirted the cottage to climb onto the down. Redshank came flighting to the flood water, throwing their cries to the wind. Snow creaked underfoot but behind the second shoulder of the hill the noise of the gale was suddenly muted. Near the top Garrison looked north towards Dartmoor and saw Hay Tor white above snowy hills. Squalls continued to race in from the continent and all at once he disliked his loneliness. His head ached from the night's alcohol and he wanted Ann. The calls of the lapwings overhead were beautiful and melancholy, and his loneliness thrived on the sound although it was barely audible above the surf thunder.

He turned his binoculars on the beach. A lot of the foreign thrushes were hopping about in the dulce still searching for food, and it occurred to him that he hadn't put out anything on the bird table. Coming awkwardly down the snow-covered ice of the sheep-walks he was surprised by the yellow gorse. It looked so incongruous.

Garrison chopped up the bacon and apple, crumbled the bread and broke the suet into reasonable chunks. Tits, robins and wrens had gathered near the bird table but he scattered the apple on the lawns before dispensing the rest of the feast. A flock of goldfinches landed in the tamarisks and he returned to the cottage. From the studio window he could see redwings and fieldfares swarming around the apple pieces. Then the birds took flight and he hurried to the front door. The cat was on the bird table eating bacon scraps. It jumped down mewing and fixed him with its gentle gaze.

'Where's your friend the badger?' Garrison smiled, stepping aside and inviting the animal to come to the fireside, but it would not be persuaded so he brought out half his supper and Fingo gobbled up the haddock and loped off. Soon the thrushes returned and Garrison began work on the large seascape. After the sky was finished to his satisfaction he roughed-in the peregrine tiercel.

'Brings it to life,' he grunted. 'A nice wild sea, plenty of wind and movement and the slate-blue bird.'

He paused to have another look at the thrushes. Tomorrow he would buy more food. He had enough coupons. Garrison lit a cigarette and was puzzled to see the birds fly off again. Across the snow came Billy and Sheena in their rubber boots, overcoats and balaclavas.

'Come in,' Garrison shouted giving the picture a final, critical squint and shuffling back to the living room fire.

The door was flung open and Billy cried: 'They digging badgers at Hellweather Point, mister – Strawberry and his lot. We followed 'em.'

'In this weather?' Garrison said.

'Yes, it's perfect for what them rats are up to,' Billy gasped.

'Calm down, son,' Garrison said. Both children were quivering. 'Go to Fishacre and get Mrs Ordish, then meet Sheena and me at the sett.'

'Mrs Ordish idn' there. She's in Barbados. There's only Miss Lucy.'

'Is she OK?' Garrison buttoned himself into his coat and threw some logs on the fire.

'Good as gold. She's got bags of pluck.'

'So go and get her. And don't worry, Billy. Rapson won't kill any badgers today.'

'Can we have our half-dollars, Mister Garrison?' Sheena said.

He took some loose change off the mantelpiece and pressed a half-crown into each grubby outstretched hand.

'Now get a move on,' he said. 'Fishacre in record time.'

'What you goin' to do, mister?' Sheena panted as they hurried up the hill. 'Strawberry ain't soft and he's got three or four blokes wiv 'im.'

He puffed out his cheeks and blew into the wind. It was snowing again.

'Have you got a bully at your school, Sheena?' he asked.

'More than one,' she said.

'Then why don't you get together with the other kids and give them a bad time?'

She sucked in the side of her face and bit it and shook her head.

'It's not that easy is it? Someone's got to risk a punch in the eye. We've got our little gang – you, me and Billy, Mrs Ordish and Lucy. And we've got Rapson. I think we've got to show him he can't get away with what he's doing.'

'Are you goin' to duff him up, mister?'

'I hope it won't come to that, but I'll have a go if I have to.'

She socked a finger in her nose and looked sideways at him. 'Do you understand, Sheena?'

'Yeah, it's a good idea. Let's hope Strawberry gets the

91

message. Blokes like 'im don't take fings lyin' down. You don't get rid of a Rapson by breakin' a bottle on his head. Stoppin' a rat like him ain't like gettin' someone out at cricket. He'll hit you on the back of the nut wiv his bat when you're not expectin' it. The Rapsons don't play by the rules.'

'We'll see,' Garrison said, but the girl's unexpected insight took some of the bounce out of him.

Woodash Down rose in two heaves of hill to a height of four hundred feet directly from Hard Sands. Against the hedge at the top were high wind-sculpted snowdrifts. Garrison stopped and drew breath. Snow smoked away on the wind.

'I'm blowing like a carthorse,' he said.

Sheena stared past him across the white and black landscape. She suddenly looked very small and skinny and vulnerable. White scales of snow sheathed her balaclava and her old topcoat flapped and cracked in the wind. All the hardness had gone from her face.

'I'm a mistake, ain't I, mister.'

Garrison drew down his eyebrows. 'I don't understand.'

'A bleedin' mistake as big as the sea,' Sheena said.

'No you're not, love,' he said, wrapping an arm round her shoulders. Her body was rigid.

'Even if the bomb hadn't flattened our house,' she said, 'and even if mum hadn't gone off wiv another man they wouldn't have wanted me back. They was always up the pub or dancin'. I was about as popular as a pimple on Deanna Durbin's nose.'

He laughed and gave her a squeeze and Sheena smiled.

'Why's it men who like killin' badgers?' she asked. 'Why don't women do it?'

'I don't know,' he said. 'Women hunt foxes and otters and stags – and they course hares which is pretty damn cruel.'

'I don't understand.'

'It's all about class, Sheena. Some cruelties are socially acceptable. Others aren't.'

'I still don't understand.'

'Don't worry about it. We've got to stop Strawberry, haven't we?'

92

'Yes,' she said. 'He's got it coming to him.'

Strawberry Rapson blew on his fingertips and down into his mittens. The terriers sat on a sack watching him intently. The dogs of Stike, fat Charlie Dunning and Wilf Short were too unruly to let off the leash and they resented being tied to the sycamore where the snow was flying like buckshot. Despite the cold and patches of fallen snow on the steeps there was fresh dung in the latrine pits and the tracks of several animals around the main entrance of the sett. So Strawberry breathed some life back into his fingers and smiled to himself. There were badgers underground. The tip of his tongue slid slowly across his lower lip and teased the cold sore that was swelling in the corner of his mouth. Stike tipped the pick, grasshooks, spades and bars out of the sack.

'Tez frosty, Frank,' he sniffed, stamping a foot and frowning at the soil.

Strawberry sucked the loose mucus from his nose into his throat and spat into the wind.

'The pick will soon put that right,' he said.

Down on the rocks the cormorants shifted uneasily and the great black-backed gulls barked.

'Best set to, then,' said Dunning. 'I'm bleddy freezin'.'

Strawberry pursed his lips and made a strange kissing sound which brought Gritt and Jimmy to his side.

'Go on in, Gritt,' Rapson said, turning his head from the shotgun blast of snow. Obediently Jimmy sat and watched his brother vanish down the badger hole; but the other dogs went wild, leaping the full length of their leashes to choke off the barking and whining into coughs and gurgles.

'Shut up, you noisy hellers,' roared Short and he lifted a spade like a weapon. The terriers cringed and snarled and barked even louder.

'They kin smell badger,' said Stike, stuffing his hands in the pockets of his old army greatcoat and kneeling to listen at the hole.

Underground Ashblacken and Guelder lay together in the

93

breeding chamber, their snouts pressed into the fresh bedding. The adjacent chamber was occupied by the maiden sows, Briarfrost and Thornsong.

'Yap-dog,' Ashblacken growled, the hair stiffening and running in waves along his spine.

'And men?' said Guelder.

'Yes, men. Men and many yap-dogs,' Ashblacken replied.

Waddling out of the chamber he stationed himself in the gallery where the main tunnel ascended to a higher level with the help of a natural step of rock. The muscles of his haunches bunched and he wedged himself firmly and waited for the dog. In the darkness the two animals could smell each other. Gritt had a rank, man-soured body odour; the badger scent was a pleasant mixture of root, soil and night-cool freshness.

Gritt let a prolonged growl worry the back of his throat as he belly-hugged the ground and settled to assess the situation. Ashblacken grunted and showed his teeth. Then Gritt began to deliver a yelping bark that hurt the badger's ears and made him wrinkle his snout in a snarl of irritation.

'Come on, man-things, come on,' he rumbled, but Gritt, like all dogs did not understand the language of Nightworld, for being a man-thing he had no language of his own.

Stike gestured wildly and Strawberry jumped onto the mound of clay and shillet and stamped his foot.

'Here,' he said. 'Smack away, Charlie. Let's give them bleddy brocks a headache.'

The first blow of the pick registered as a distinct thud above Gritt but the terrier understood and pretended to attack the badger. Ashblacken growled and swung his head and Gritt retreated behind a series of excited barks. The maiden sows emerged from their chamber leaking terror. Ashblacken could smell it and feel it. 'Go back and be still,' he said sharply, and there was a shuffling and a scrabbling of claws.

Springing forward Ashblacken nearly caught Gritt but the dog backed off and at that moment a blow from the pick

94

brought earth showering down. Guelder whimpered and Ashblacken returned to his station. Drugged with cold it was difficult to pull himself together.

The pick broke through the roof of the tunnel and a little light stood between dog and badger. The next blow widened the gap and the two animals could see each other. In the confined space the boar looked enormous with his hackles raised. His face was a stark snarl of ferocity and despite all his experience Gritt quailed, unaware that Ashblacken was sick with fear. Now men were using the iron bars and more debris crashed into the tunnel. Ashblacken closed his eyes and shuddered. Then he shuffled backwards into the chamber and hid his muzzle in Guelder's fur.

'What is happening?' she whispered.

Beneath his snout the unborn cubs kicked inside Guelder's body and he was unable to speak.

Whenever the wind slackened Garrison heard the whispered squeak of his cord trousers rubbing together as he walked. The downs were deserted for the sheep and lambs had been folded in the root field beside Woodash farmhouse. Even the sky was empty, save for the swirling snow.

On Garrowcombe Head Sheena picked up the body of a lapwing that had been killed and decapitated by the peregrine tiercel. She took some of the feathers.

'I like the green shine,' she said, stuffing the feathers in her pocket. 'You see it on a mallard drake's head.'

Standing at the top of the badger path on Hellweather Point they saw the figures at the sett and heard the crunch of the pick.

'Old Strawberry's busy,' the girl said in the cold little voice she used when she was upset. Then she looked at him.

The life had left Garrison's limbs. He came heavy-legged to the headland.

'You should've brought a gun, mister,' Sheena said and he knew she wasn't joking.

Halfway down the slope to the sett he was seen and the digging stopped.

'Here,' Stike said sarcastically, blowing a perfect bubble of saliva, 'Idn' that Squire Garrison, the big landowner?'

Dunning laughed and Strawberry's smile broadened.

'Looking for a bit of sport, Mr Garrison?' he said.

'Aw, go and play wiv your dollies,' Sheena said and Garrison wondered why he could never deliver a witty retort. He was on the mound a few paces from Dunning, Small and Stike. Strawberry straddled the main entrance hole.

'Mrs Ordish and the police will be here in a moment,' Garrison said.

'Now idn' that amazing,' Strawberry smiled. 'At breakfast time she was in Barbados. Norman Chard spoke to her on the phone. What did she do, Mr Garrison, come by rocket?'

Garrison felt he had lost the initiative. He also felt Sheena's eyes on him. Most of his adult life he had tried to reason with mediocrities. He took a swift step forward, snatched the pick from Dunning's hand and sent it spinning through the air into the sea. Then he crouched and grabbed an iron bar.

Sheena whistled softly to herself.

'That pick cost money,' Strawberry said, still smiling through the falling snow. 'I'd put that bar down if I was you, mate.'

'And leave you to kill the badgers, you sick little man,' Garrison said.

'Clear off, you bloody fool,' Dunning grated and he picked up a spade. 'Any more of your lip and I'll wrap this round your head.'

There was a medieaval twist to the confrontation, something bizarre which brought Garrison close to laughter. He considered the situation for a moment and let the bar slip from his hands.

'Stupid move,' Sheena muttered. She had no time for heroics. 'Remember what I said about the cricket bat.'

'If you want to dig badgers you'll have to shift me first,'

Garrison said. 'Swing that spade and you'll go up the line for a long time.'

'You don't need no weapons, Charlie,' said Stike and Dunning tossed the spade aside. He was a really big man and the bulky navy-blue overcoat made him appear even bigger. Garrison's stomach dropped. Dunning had blue jowls, a three-day stubble and small, dark-rimmed eyes. His khaki balaclava gave him a pugnacious and bullet-headed appearance. He gazed at Garrison with malevolent curiosity and lurched at him, arms outstretched. Garrison swung a right hook and caught the fat man on the chin. The punch was packed with manic desperation and the curiosity in Dunning's eyes clouded instantly to a blank. His arms flapped and he sat down heavily on the mound. Garrison stared at his knuckles and slowly unclenched his fist.

'Bleedin' heck!' Sheena whispered and when Garrison turned to smile at her Small kicked him hard under the left knee.

Garrison fell face downwards. The bracken stabbed his cheek and he groaned and rolled over. The next kick numbed his shoulder but he managed to stand up only to fall again with a 'dead' leg.

Then Stike knelt on his chest and slammed half a dozen punches to the face until Sheena got her fingers into the man's hair. Stike squealed and Garrison tried to grip him by the throat.

'Bleedin' little coward,' the girl hissed and Small grabbed her under the arms and wrenched her off her feet.

'You rotten bleedin' pigs,' she protested.

'Shut your mouth,' Small said. His face was white and taut. 'Shut it or I'll drop you off the sodding cliff.'

'You do, rat breath, and you'll swing,' Sheena screamed.

'Let Mr Garrison get up, Ern,' Rapson said. 'It was foolish of him to attack Charlie like that but I dare say he's learnt something today: If you poke your nose in other people's business you run the risk of gettin' it broke.'

Sheena was sobbing out her anger and frustration but Small seemed loathe to release her until Strawberry nodded at him.

'You wait,' she said. 'You bleedin' wait, Strawberry. Some of my cousins are comin' down from London next week. They'll have your guts for garters.'

Strawberry ignored her.

'Mrs Ordish will have the law on you,' the girl bawled and Small smacked her across the back of the head.

'You hit that child again,' Garrison said, 'and I'll come after you with a gun.'

'Pack up the gear, Charlie,' said Strawberry.

'But we're into the tunnel, Frank,' Stike said.

'Do as I say,' from a bleak smile.

Garrison bent and placed his hands on his knees and retched. His nose was bleeding and Sheena climbed onto the mound to give him a handkerchief.

'Take it,' she insisted. 'It ain't snotty.'

Garrison grinned despite his aching, swollen face. They sat together in the bracken above the sett while the diggers departed and the snow whirled around them.

'You copped a good one, mister,' Sheena said, spitting on the handkerchief and dabbing it on Garrison's nose and cheek. 'But what a mug you was.'

'I thought I did reasonably well considering I haven't hit anyone in anger since I left school,' he said.

'You had the iron bar in your hands,' she said. 'They wouldn't have tried nuffin' if you hadn't come the toff. You forgot all about the cricket bat, didn't you? I told you, blokes like Strawberry and Co. don't play by the rules.'

'You really think I should have hit that man with the iron bar?'

'No – but as long as he wasn't sure fings was OK.'

'You'll make a fine politician one day, Sheena.'

'Leave off!' she laughed. 'I ain't posh enough.'

Garrison looked into her plain little face and saw the innocence behind the worldly mask.

The snow stopped but the wind was whipping off the sea. The bracken above them crackled.

''Ere's the cavalry,' Sheena said, rolling her eyes up at the steeps. 'Like in them daft cowboy films, always too bleedin' late. Where's Miss Lucy?'

'She wadn' there,' Billy said. 'I looked all over – even went up Effords. Chardie set his dogs on me and told me to – to –' He glanced at Garrison, 'to sort of go away – only that wasn't how he put it.'

The boy jumped onto the mound, stuffed his hands in his pockets and stared out to sea.

'Did they get the badgers, mister? I saw 'em go up over.'

'No, Billy.'

'But they got 'im,' Sheena said. 'They got Mr Garrison and he got fat Charlie. Nearly knocked his bleedin' head off.'

'Help me fill in the hole they dug,' Garrison said, 'or the draught will give the badgers a cold.'

'I should've been here,' Billy said, unwilling to turn and face them.

'Oh yeah,' Sheena scoffed. 'Wot would you have done, you little squirt, had a go at Dunning's kneecaps wiv your teeth?'

Billy shrugged and his misery reached out to Garrison.

'They really believed you'd come back with Miss Ordish and the police, Billy,' he said. 'If it hadn't been for you they would have used me as a punch bag.'

'OK, then,' said Billy, taking out his clay pipe. 'OK, maybe we ought to fill in that hole and clear off. Them badgers can't be very happy, not after all this.'

The hours passed. Underground the badgers measured the approach of dimpsey by the fade away of light in the main entrance hole. Ashblacken and Guelder and the two maiden sows had remained curled up together in their chambers throughout the attempt to open the sett. Afterwards had followed the long unfriendly silence and apprehension which left the animals dry-mouthed and queasy. Guelder's head bobbed every time she swallowed and her breath came in quick painful gasps. Laying his muzzle on her shoulder Ashblacken tried to remain calm and presently the sow stopped shivering but her distress lifted from her body in a sour musk.

Dimpsey closed and the wind softened to a breeze. Then a muffled bumping along the tunnel announced the arrival of a badger.

'Guelder?' Aspen called, undecided in the blackness. The tunnel branched to the left and right and the scent of badger was overpowering.

'Have they gone?' Ashblacken demanded gruffly.

'Yes,' Aspen said, for the smell of men and dogs clung to the air all round the sett and she needed no telling.

'They began to dig,' Guelder sighed. 'Then they stopped. It was terrible.'

The young sows padded down the passage and the leading animal, Thornsong, advanced respectfully and rubbed snouts with Aspen. The cool fragrance of night broke from her coat.

'It's stopped snowing,' she said in her deep gentle voice. 'There's good forage above the steeps by the barn. Greybob has opened the potato clamp.'

'You go,' said Ashblacken. 'Guelder and I will try the sett near the wooded coombe.'

'It's a good sett,' said Aspen. 'The tunnels run deep.'

'And everything is fine at Big Sett?' Ashblacken went on, pretending he had never been afraid. It was totally acceptable boar behaviour.

'Apart from the intruder,' said Aspen. 'Fingo and Cowtail met an odd boar in the pine copse.'

'Odd?' said Ashblacken.

'Apparently he's a big unfriendly animal from somewhere over by the river. He chased Cowtail and she really believes he would have killed her if he'd had the chance.'

'That vixen!' Guelder laughed.

'Fingo also thought this boar was unpleasant,' Aspen said.

The immediate past had been swept away as if it had never happened. All the animals were relieved and the maiden sows could hardly wait to get outside. At the scratching tree they found Birdcherry. Thornsong and Briarfoot paid their respects to Aspen's sister and there was prolonged scratching and mutual grooming before the sows moved off.

The night above them was dark and starless. The cold nettled their snouts and made their eyes and teeth ache; but the wind and salt had kept the steeps clear of snow. Through the flat bracken the badger paths led from sett to sett and up onto the farmland. The animals climbed in single file with Aspen leading. At the fence she raised her muzzle and deciphered the darkness lying on the snow-field. A solitary hare loped across the white downs and was gone.

The four sows ranged over the empty sheep pasture, rounding their nostrils to the coldness that had no scent. Nightworld was dead to the nose.

Chapter 13

Raised Hackles

There was a temporary respite from the wind. The sun shone and two fine days were followed as usual by fog spreading inland off the Channel. On a night of grey stillness Aspen and Greybob heard a lorry in the lane above Warren Fishacre but the sound meant nothing to the badgers. None of their tribe had been road victims and apart from the tractors at Effords and Woodash the farm machinery and carts were horse-drawn. The next morning Lucy Ordish returned from London to find the garden shed had been broken into and most of the equipment gone including two motor mowers and half a dozen lead animals and figurines which had been destined for the terrace gardens. It was a curious robbery and neither the girl nor the police could understand why the thieves hadn't entered the house. The Ordish plate and valuable eighteenth-century tapestries had been there for the taking.

The wind had risen again and powder snow had blurred the footprints on the lawns and obscured the tyre tracks in the lane at the top of the drive. When Billy and Sheena called with news of Garrison's fight they were told of the break-in.

'Lawn-mowers!' Sheena said.

'Worth quite a lot of money,' said Lucy, pushing her fingers up through her hair which was shoulder length and chestnut brown. 'All they had to do was knock off the rusty old padlock and wheel them out. But with the house at their mercy it does seem odd. The police are baffled. It's a bit like forcing your way into Tiffany's and stealing the lead off the roof.'

'There's them didakais down at Greenaway,' Sheena said. 'They nick anyfing they find lyin' around.'

'The police thought of them straight away,' Lucy said. 'Although it really isn't fair. Those people work hard in the fields lifting swedes and potatoes and helping out with the harvests. You can't just storm into their lives and make things difficult for them.'

Life is difficult for them, Sheena thought, gazing round the big clean kitchen and sipping her tea. Her eyes met Billy's and were instantly lowered because she knew he was close to laughter.

They talked about Garrison and the badger diggers while Lucy provided Dundee cake in impressive wedges and brewed a second pot of tea. She sat on a stool near the Aga in her jodhpurs, swinging her legs and gesturing with her hands to emphasize some point she was making. She was very attractive, pleasant and youthful.

'Surely badgers are hibernating at this time of year?' she said. 'If my grandmother didn't go to Barbados she'd hibernate for certain when the weather turns nasty.'

'Badgers don't hibernate, miss,' said Billy. 'Least, not down here in Devon. I know it says they do in all the books but they're wrong. You go to any of the setts now and you'll see paw marks in the snow and tracks coming and going on the hillside. Then there's the beddin' in the holes and fresh dung in their lavatory pits. When the weather's really rough they stay underground for a few nights but all this stuff about sleeping through the winter idn' true.'

103

'You really know your animals, don't you, Billy?' Lucy smiled. She had a broad mouth and white teeth. 'And I really think it's time the police warned Rapson and the rest of them to stay off Ordish land.'

'Old Strawberry won't be too upset,' said Sheena. 'And Mary's Haven ain't got the world's brightest rozzers.'

'But it will show them we mean business.'

'This is Strawberry's territory,' Billy said.

'The Strawberry patch,' Sheena giggled.

'There's more setts between Firebeacon Point and Froward than anywhere else around for miles,' Billy went on. 'And they idn' that far apart. If Strawberry's stopped coming here he'll have to trespass somewhere else that he don't know. Maybe he'd even have to go into the territory of the Lansworthy Badger Club.'

'You mean there's another gang of baiters a few miles away!' Lucy exclaimed.

The boy nodded and stuffed his mouth full of cake.

'The poor animals haven't got much of a chance, have they,' Lucy said sadly and from that moment Sheena decided she liked her.

'You ain't nicked nuffin', have you?' She frowned at Billy as they crunched over the frozen snow on their way home.

''Course not,' he said but the colour in his cheeks had not been put there by the wind and cold.

'Wot you got?' Sheena said, barring his way.

'Only an old penknife,' he said. 'It was in a basket on one of the stools.'

'Let's have it,' she said, extending a hand.

'Aw, come on, Sheen – they idn' goin' to miss an old knife.'

'Billy,' in a hard little voice.

'It's got an antler horn handle,' he said, reluctantly placing the knife in her palm.

'This goes back the next time we call,' Sheena said. 'No more nickin' from friends.'

'OK, OK,' he growled, kicking up the snow.

'Want a tanner?' she said.

'Where d'you get it?'

'There was 1s. 3d. on Strawberry's doorstep in the tin Old Muvver Rapson puts out for the milkman. I beat 'im to it this morning.'

'You cheeky bleeder,' he laughed and the sixpenny bit was pushed down inside his glove.

'Billy the Kid,' Sheena said and he drew a couple of imaginary pistols from imaginary holsters and shot her through the heart. Sheena gave a yell and collapsed.

'Do you still love me, Bill?' she whispered, rising in white resurrection from the snow.

'Yeah,' he grinned. 'Lots.'

'More than wot?'

'More than Tarzan loves Cheetah. More than Roy Rogers loves Trigger. More than –' and he thought a moment. 'More than a horn-handled penknife.'

Arm in arm they walked down the lane, wading wherever possible through the snowdrifts towards the toll house and the Greenaway–Mary's Haven Road.

'What do you think about the garden stuff gettin' lifted?' Sheena said out of the blue.

'Funny, idn' it,' he said. 'I still reckon it was them didakais. My mum says it was they who stole the lead off the Methodist chapel down Greenaway.'

'Maybe,' Sheena said, looking up at the sky. 'It's goin' to snow like hell,' she added gleefully.

'But not like last winter,' Billy said.

Towards dusk the rooks were still noisy in the snow-smoke above Froward Point. Cowtail came into the communal chamber of Big Sett with flakes melting on her fur and found the badgers had decided to give forage a miss.

'That wind,' said the fox. 'It bites into your bones.'

The chamber was crowded with drowsy animals. The three yearling boars, Scragtangle, Bramblebriar and Brackenzeal

105

lay in a heap in the corner while Briarfrost and Thornsong groomed Hawscrag, and Cragbriar snored in his own recess. Greybob, Aspen and Birdcherry sat together near the entrance.

It was claustrophobic and the air was powerfully laced with badger smells. Badger everywhere, Cowtail thought, but the warmth pleased the vixen and the tribe displayed no animosity. They were sett-drugged and more than content. Hawscrag and Cragbriar had told the old stories and the kin group waited for Aspen to speak of the world she saw behind her eyes. A strange lot, Cowtail decided, but nice strange. She found a space and curled up with her chin on her forepaws.

''Ere,' she said all of a sudden, recalling something. 'Who's the badger prowling around in the pine copse? He came in me kennel and would have had me if I hadn't gone out the window sharpish. He's a funny old pale badger – and big! Cor! He's as big as a donkey. I hope he don't come down here.'

'He won't,' said Greybob and Cragbriar chuckled.

'I mean it,' Greybob said, gently menacing.

Furzebright growled agreement.

'You ain't seen that old boar,' said Cowtail. 'He's big and nasty, a killer, I'd say. You ask Fingo.'

'And he's there now?' Greybob demanded.

'I felt him close by,' Cowtail shuddered. 'Darkness in darkness – a lurking old nasty.'

'Sounds more dog than badger,' said Cragbriar.

'Well, we'll soon find out. Come with me,' said Greybob.

'I'm staying put,' Cragbriar grumbled. 'I've seen it all before, sett-master and challenger, blood and fur flying.'

Furzebright and the yearling boars pressed forward eagerly but the sows showed little enthusiasm.

'M-my nose is dry and hot,' Birdcherry whispered in Aspen's ear. 'And I don't feel well.'

'Stay in the sett,' Aspen said. 'Go to the maiden sows' chamber and sleep. You don't have to come with us.'

'You're sure?'

'Yes. Go and sleep.'

106

Greybob led the tribe out of the thorn thicket and up into the pine trees which were roaring in the wind. Caught on the slope by the blast of the gale the younger animals staggered. The ground between the pines was bucking and falling as the trees swayed and their roots lifted. A flurry of snow powdered the badgers' coats. They lurched and bumped into each other whenever the soil and pine needles rose in swells beneath them. Fingo stepped from the shadows with his hair stiff and eyes staring.

'He's up on the top path,' said the cat. 'Rooting round and growling and charging at everything that moves.'

'Perhaps he's sick,' said Hawscrag.

'Sick in the head,' Fingo hissed. 'He's been lying-up in the sett under the slope of wild garlic. I thought I'd kennel there for a bit but I never dreamed a badger would give me such a reception. He tore into me like a crazy dog and I just got down a rabbit hole in time. Then he saw me sneaking out of another hole and chased me as far as the pines. What's wrong with him?'

'He's a boar,' Hawscrag said flatly and the maiden sows lowered their snouts to hide their smiles.

Greybob glared at them. His hackles were up and he was growling. From the trees into the snowlight stepped the unknown badger. He too was fluffed out to fighting size and strutted rather than walked, quivering from head to toe. His nostrils were dilated and his eyes stood out in his face. His coat had a silvery sheen.

'Who are you?' Greybob asked.

'Who are you?' the stranger answered mockingly, showing his canine teeth in a self-confident snarl which faded to a groan.

Greybob gave him his name but received only a grunt in return. Then Aspen saw not a badger but something darker than night, dripping darkness. Its teeth clanged together like the jaws of a gin trap. The grinding and scraping was of steel on steel.

The two animals rose and fell with the movement of the

107

ground. The earth is breathing, Aspen thought. Greybob's shambling looseness advanced and from his mouth burst a flash of fangs. The wind rasped across the scrub thorn and barbed-wire, rocking the treetops and shaking darkness out of darkness. The snow fumed about the badgers and they were finding it increasingly difficult to keep their feet on the constant rise, fall and lurch of soil and roots. Yet somehow the boars crashed together, slashing with their teeth. Great strings of saliva trailed from their jaws. They were face to face and snarling, and the newcomer looked bulkier than Greybob yet it was Greybob who raked his opponent with two sets of claws. The boars' teeth gleamed and the wind ran through their fur and each shift of the world sent them staggering. Beneath the roaring pines the ground undulated or stood up abruptly to fall back again.

The animals circled each other, proclaiming their ferocity and stumbling but somehow managing to hold their heads erect.

The growling crescendoed to a solid scream of fury but only Greybob had blood-foam on his lips. His heart pounded. The smells and sounds were real enough although his opponent had become a dim shape. He grappled with it and the boars twisted and kicked in their tangle. Breath erupted and was whipped away. Soon it became apparent to the onlookers that the challenger had a wounded hindleg and was swaying slightly to the left whenever he lunged. The tang of warm, damp bodies lifted in a musk which the sows found exciting, but they were dismayed when Greybob rolled over three times before climbing to his feet and sneezing. Bracing himself he took the next charge squarely on the head and there was a crack of skulls. His anger escaped in a war cry and he came stumbling up the incline unaware of the young sows' amazement and concern. The stranger's forelegs buckled, his head tilted and his mouth gaped; but like Greybob he was strength and stubborness personified.

The boars met and melted together in a ball of rage, flesh

prickling under the hide. There was a staccato suck and snort of breath and an exchange of gruff barks. The snow flickered around them and a sudden surge of energy brought a high-pitched scream from Greybob. The stranger was sagging but still looked enormous and shadowy. His stink filled the air and mingled with the smell of blood. In the dim light Aspen saw an owl sail between the trees, circle the boars, turn and vanish. She shivered. The earth was alive and running away in every direction through the darkness. Closing her eyes she saw the giant entrance hole of the sett open in a scream.

The boars collided, snarl to snarl, with a clack of teeth. Greybob's pain and growing exhaustion were forgotten in a frenzy that bewildered the maiden sows. But Aspen recognized the chaos which had assumed the boar shape and she was chilled. This was the violence that was absent from her vision of Sunworld. Bright teeth gleamed from the arc of the swinging head and behind the frantic leg movements came the grunts and squeals which were badger yet appeared to emanate from something beyond animal life.

Greybob threw himself at his opponent who reeled under the impact, rose on a hump of ground and sank once more, still seeking to dodge and twist and bite. Flurries of snow blurred the assailants and made them even more remote from the half-circle of onlookers. Then Greybob felt the stranger squirming under him and the lust for the extremes of violence silted his veins. Dark dribbles splashed from the scratches on his muzzle but the ground was going mad and he staggered sideways. Powerful forefeet worked on his belly, threatening to spill out his tripes.

Aspen found it difficult to breathe. A black fire burnt around the boars. They were sheathed in night's flames. Then, as her senses focused to clarity Greybob was struggling to deliver a terrible wound to the stranger's head. The bleakness of the moment reached out to all those watching. Slowly the two shadows absorbed each other and were one and the mouth of the sett expanded to become an enormous black void.

But it wasn't quite finished. The boars met in another off-balance collision with the fallen snow conjuring up its own light and tiny flakes descending to rise again and whirl into the gloom. Greybob's breath streamed away in deep gasps. Then the stranger tried to charge but his momentum was destroyed by the heavy ground swell of the copse. His head jerked up and wordlessly and slowly he shuffled backwards into the trees, leaving some of his blood, a dribble of scats and his smell to remind the sows of the fight.

Greybob retired to the slope above the blackthorn thicket, scent-marked a prominent tussock and did some repair work to his wounds. The young boars and sows were led past him respectfully by Hawscrag but Aspen remained to lay the healing properties of her tongue on his cuts and bruises.

'Aspen,' he whispered, lifting his head to meet her gaze. 'Was that creature badger?'

'Yes,' she answered. 'And something else.'

'Explain,' he murmured. 'I don't understand.'

'I can't explain,' Aspen said and she licked his snout. 'Let's go to forage by the stream in the goyal of willows.'

'In this weather?' he smiled.

'Unless you are too tired.'

He rose and shook himself and Furzebright stood aside to let him pass.

Sheep often strayed into the small hanging valley and their hooves had opened the soil beneath the carpet of fibrous bracken stems. Aspen sat and dug rapidly to uncover the bluebell bulbs with their fuses of succulent pale yellow shoots. Then the badgers drank from the stream.

The snow had practically ignored the goyal and near the top almost against the drystone wall the soil yielded worms. Absently Greybob stood on his hindlegs and sniffed along the wall beneath the protruding stones until he found a cluster of snails slime-sealed within their shells against the cold. He shared them with Aspen and they crunched noisily and it was some time before they realized they had company. Ashblacken

110

and Guelder sat watching them a little way up the sheep path.

'Greybob fought and beat the boar who has no name,' Aspen said when greetings had been exchanged.

Ashblacken nodded, unable to bring himself to acknowledge Greybob's courage and strength. The sett in Ramsons Dip among the broom and thorn on the clifftop pleased him. It was cunningly tucked under a great sycamore-hackled mound. After a little while the pairs went their separate ways.

'Ashblacken isn't very gracious,' Aspen said.

They had come to the great tangle of furze covering the steeps above Old Spanish Cove. The thicket sang and shook in the wind but during a lull Aspen caught the sound of rapid footfalls and the suggestion of a familiar scent.

'Birdcherry,' she smiled. 'I thought you were ill.'

'I am,' came the faint reply. 'I can't keep down my food.'

The sows nuzzled each other with a gentleness that amused Greybob. He turned abruptly and trotted on through the half-darkness out onto the down. Each animal left clear five-toed prints in the snow. Near the sheep trough by the gate in the hedge above Parson's Cove they nosed out a couple of dead lapwings whose breast meat and heads Greybob devoured.

Snow-smoke curled around them and they were cold when they arrived at the sett which although small was very old. It had been excavated long before the Romans came to the South-Western peninsula and harassed the Celtic Dumnonii. Its shafts plunged into the slopes of a hollow between two rocks on the north side of the cove. Over the main hole grew an elderberry tree with a bole scarred by badger claws.

The animals visited the latrine pits and made droppings before going underground. Here they discovered three chambers and fresh bedding but no occupants. They settled to scratch and groom in the luxury of shared body heat.

Chapter 14

Small Griefs

The sun climbed red out of sea mist. Woodash Down was alive with rabbits determined, it seemed, to remain on the grassland after the thaw despite Garrison's presence on the beach below. He had bought a small dinghy and was dragging it into one of those flat calms which still managed to roll wavelets onto the shore. Once afloat he dipped the oars and began to row ineptly out towards December Point thinking of a trip to Dragon Rock. Once clear of the shelter of the Point he encountered the push of the incoming tide but found it was not sufficient to deter him although he was already wondering if Dragon Rock was not an over-ambitious goal. Yet the rowing was rewarding. Across his thoughts rippled the piping of oystercatchers. Then he 'caught a crab', lost his balance and nearly lost an oar; and all at once another time and another place clicked into focus.

Posting the Valentine's card to Ann the afternoon before had started him thinking of their time together in Paris before the war, before Neil was born. He had persuaded her to sit in the stern of the skiff while he showed off his prowess as an oarsman with the inevitable comic result. The missed stroke had left him on his back with his legs in the air and the oar floating down river. Recollection of her laughter brought a smile to his face. The sea and the cliffs vanished and she came through the doorway in a cotton frock, the dark shape of her body defined against the sunlight that reduced the thin fabric to luminous transparency. Faure's 'Requiem' was on the wireless.

They had felt it important to immerse themselves in the romance of the city because their love was lending an aura to the outside world. The Pont Neuf, the Tuileries, La Madeleine – another wet spring afternoon and a stroll through the cemetery Pierre Lachaise among the greened bronze statues. After the intimate conversation in the brasserie they went to the Jardin des Champs Elysees. And she came out laughing from the charcuterie on the corner where the down-and-outs lingered to stare in the window.

The dream was fading and he tried desperately to retain it. The Seine, the galleries, the bars, Ann. Garrison stood up in the boat, clenching his fists. 'Ann' – the cry caught in his throat and he closed his eyes but the tears spilt from his lashes. The dinghy swung sideways to the current and the morning returned on a din of gulls. But she was getting better. Dr Reidlinger, the sanatorium director, said she could come home in three or four months. Ann was on the mend.

He sat down and began to row again until his lack of fitness made him shake his head and turn back towards December Point, blowing hard. Out to sea a couple of trawlers were laying their smoke along the horizon. Then his mind flew ahead of him to the watercolour in progress – Froward Point on one of those blowy winter days which always made his heart beat faster.

Midway through the morning Billy said: 'Why don't you get a dog or a cat, mister?'

'Why aren't you at school?' Garrison countered.

The boy shrugged. 'It's too nice to be indoors.'

Garrison grinned. 'I don't keep pets because they'd distract me from wild animals and exercising a dog might become a duty, even a chore. Anyway,' he added cheerfully, 'I've got a cat. He's a wild little chap who comes here most days to be fed. Himself I call him.'

Billy opened his mouth to speak but closed it again. His eyes were red and puffy.

'Is anything wrong, Billy?' Garrison asked.

The boy shook his head.

The morning's calm had given way to bluster and greyness lit by flashes of sunlight. The brambly steeps were quivering under the wind. A flight of mute swans joined the ducks and waders on the marsh. Along the side of Woodash Down jackdaws stood on the backs of sheep winkling out ticks. The black birds and their sudden blue sheen were startling.

Halfway through the afternoon Garrison had found himself alone, aching to work but forced to abandon the picture in the failing light. He had slung on his jacket and walked onto the down. Really I should be running, he thought with the effort of climbing the hill leaving him breathless. Near the top the mounds of a huge warren were pitted with holes. Then the ache for his wife hollowed his stomach and he turned from the cliffs and the sea. At the head of the valley Woodash farmhouse was silhouetted on the skyline among cider apple trees, horse chestnuts and pines. A cluster of grey outbuildings, straw ricks and haystacks stood below it on the hillside and Garrison decided he needed mature human company. He strolled over the pasture until a copse of oaks turned him down into the lane. Under the hedges were the flowers of coltsfoot, and hazel catkins were already a dusty off-yellow. Near the top of the lane muscovy ducks were bathing in the puddles. Garrison looked back into the valley. A horse was grazing the field below the byre among the cattle. Big heavy South Devons and some Jerseys were munching the grass beside the stream. Seaward the sky was clearing to blue.

He came to the wall and looked down into the bullock yard.

114

A cow gazed back at him over the half-door of the byre and hens scuffed through the straw litter. Sunlight glinted on liquid excrement and golden brown pools of urine. It was an earthy, strangely moving scene. Then he saw the row of fox pads and stoats' tails nailed to the lintel above the byre door and he lit a cigarette. Someone was working in the loft above the barn but Garrison no longer felt lonely. The smell of hay scented the air and he dropped the cigarette and ground it under his heel.

'Wot a waste,' said Sheena's voice, and he turned to find her large expressionless eyes on him. Billy was grinning.

'We could've shot you, mister,' he said.

'Why would you want to do that, Billy?'

The boy coloured. 'It's just a joke. We come up like a couple of redskins. You didn' hear us, did you?'

Garrison shook his head and smiled.

'What have you got behind your back, Sheena?' he prompted, and she held out a little bunch of snowdrops.

'For you, mister.'

'They're beautiful,' he said.

'We got 'em from the churchyard.'

'Not off one of the graves,' Billy added, seeing the look on Garrison's face. 'There's hundreds of 'em growing under the trees.'

'It was a nice thought, thank you,' Garrison said and he cleared his throat and blew his nose.

Billy stood on tiptoe and peered down into the yard.

'Only an old cow,' he said from mild disappointment. 'Is that all you was lookin' at, mister?'

'I was thinking,' said Garrison.

'Anyway, I like cows,' said Sheena. 'When I lived in London I never knew the Sunday joint was once a part of a cow or a sheep.'

'Want to come down and have tea?' Garrison said, already knowing the answer.

'The school inspector was after us early on,' said Sheena.

115

'We give him the slip 'cos we're fitter than the butcher's dog. He came up Billy's home, though.'

'Mum'll belt me tonight,' the boy said glumly. Then he screwed up his face and frowned at Garrison. 'Are you growing a beard, mister?' he asked as they walked down the lane.

'Maybe, or maybe I'm just too lazy to shave. I'm turning into a bit of a hermit and I'm sick to death of respectable people.'

'We knew an old tramp who was an 'ermit,' said Sheena. 'He used to live in the lime kiln down on your beach and sometimes he got so lonely he used to draw signs on stones in the lane for other tramps to see. But no tramps came that way and he upped and went. I don't fink he really wanted to be an 'ermit.'

'He was a dirty old bleeder,' Billy said. 'Ponged like a ferret.'

Garrison held the snowdrops to the sky and the children watched him.

'Have you heard the story of Eve and the snowdrops?' he said. They shook their heads.

'Well, when Eve was sent out of the Garden of Eden it snowed and she began to cry – not because she felt sorry for herself but was sad for the flowers the snow was covering. Looking down from the sky an angel pitied her. So he caught a snowflake in his hand and it turned into a tiny white flower. Then he flew down and gave the flower to Eve. After she had wiped her tears she saw thousands and thousands of snowdrops springing from the ground all around her.'

'I like that,' said Sheena. Her hands were in the pockets of a faded navy-blue gabardine and she was staring down at her feet.

'Why did God kick Eve out of Eden, mister?' said Billy.

'Oh you know why!' Sheena said angrily, glaring at him. 'She took off her clothes and acted rude in front of Adam.'

Billy grinned and winked.

116

On the lawn at the cottage the boy said: 'Idn' you going to grow vegetables?'

'No,' said Garrison. 'I'm not a gardener. I like grass. So I'm going to let it grow long for the wind to run through.'

'A good idea, mister,' Sheena said and she crouched by the porch.

'Crocuses,' Billy said as the girl pulled the grass to one side and revealed the purple and orange flowers.

'I never saw them there,' Garrison confessed. 'I'm always looking at the sea or the sky. I've got to learn to use my eyes.'

He brought the children into the kitchen and sat them before the stove until the living room fire was roaring up the chimney and they could draw up their chairs in front of it. The snowdrops were put in a glass in the studio.

'Wild flowers look sad indoors,' Billy said dreamily.

'They did his rabbits,' Sheena blurted without warning. 'Tony Rapson let both of 'em out of the hutch the other night. The cat got one and the other's still missing. They was called Titch and Thumper.'

The heat of the room lifted a strong whiff of Devon Violets perfume off her face and neck.

'But why?' Garrison said.

'What's a rabbit to that little sod,' Sheena said. 'Anyfing to hurt Billy. Strawberry won't let him off the hook.'

'I'd no idea it would go this far,' Garrison said. 'Look – tell me where you live, Billy.'

'Why?'

'I may need to get in touch with you quickly about the badgers or something.'

After they had gone he tried to read Wordsworth but the night was starry and the wind had slackened. Opening the front door he gazed up at the sky and kneaded the spare flesh on his middle. Tomorrow he would walk hard to Froward Point and back and sweat off a few ounces of flab. It would be nice for Ann to see his old trim self.

The white owls were screaming up on Woodash Down and

he wondered if she was asleep or if there were owls in Switzerland.

Chapter 15

Dark and Light

Aspen dug through the dark humus to unearth the bluebell bulb. The owl screeched and was answered by its mate. A flicker of scuts advertised the hurried departure of rabbits. Aspen ran her snout over the tiny leaves on the honeysuckle vine and left her scent on the wild arum. The other sett-dwellers were emerging from the thorn thicket to read the night wind as it flowed softly over Froward. From the far distance of Start Bay the light on the point flashed three times every five seconds. Now the wind was coining a response from the pines and sycamores and shaking the gorse. Swooping over the farmland above, the white owl said 'ee-yick, ee-yick' but received no answer.

'I think I'll g-go back underground,' Birdcherry said in a hoarse whisper.

'Aren't you hungry?' said Aspen.

'N-no, just tired and seedy. My throat's on fire and m-my ears ache.'

She had tonsillitis and Hawscrag was worried because throat infections were often fatal.

'Keep warm and sleep,' said the old sow. 'Go and curl up beside Cragbriar. That's about all he's good for.'

Birdcherry nodded and shuffled off along a path worn hard and smooth by the feet of many generations of badgers.

'Is it throat-burn?' said Briarfrost.

'Yes,' Hawscrag replied. 'But it's not too bad – not enough to send her to Earth Mother. We must look after her and make sure she has plenty of peace and quiet.'

'My mother died of throat-burn,' Briarfrost said.

'Forage and go below and help keep her warm,' said Hawscrag. She swung her head and stared at Aspen.

'Where is Greybob?'

'Gone,' Aspen said. 'He spoke of living away from Big Sett for a while.'

Hawscrag grunted. 'He will be looking for the other boar.'

'Perhaps,' said Aspen.

'Have you mated? Furzebright is beginning to show an interest in you.'

'No, but I think I shall pair with Greybob.'

Beneath the pines were cones which the squirrels had gnawed to get at the seeds. Aspen ranged among the trees pausing to sniff at interesting things or to lift her muzzle skyward as she read the darkness. Beyond the copse Nightworld presented its broader stratas of scent. The bony steeps were soaked in the smell of the sea and Aspen walked alone through the wetness of grass and bracken until her grey coat was soaked. Then it rained and she hurried up to the field of winter wheat and waited for the earthworms to surface. With the passing of the shower the field gleamed palely under starshine. Far off now, the barn owls called. Raising her head from the wallow of brown scents Aspen looked down over the field and the trees of Fishacre to the steeps above Old Spanish Cove. Then she caught sight of torches and heard the high yelp of a dog. Men with lurchers were out lamping rabbits.

Trotting up the muddy track Aspen came to Effords Farm and the mangel clamp by the Shippen. Whisperings in the straw announced the frantic departure of mice. Aspen barged through the hedge under sprays of old-man's-beard dislodging the feathered awns and carrying some of them off on her back. She nosed around the clamp but made no attempt to quarry into it. The taint of man and dogs was heavy on the farmyard air but stronger still was the smell of rotting kale. She turned and retraced her steps.

Another shower fell, blotting out the stars. In the field to her left she could hear the thump of running rabbits and instantly questioned the air. Beneath the hedge-bank was a ditch that would have to do if she were attacked. The sides were steep and slippery and she rolled over in her efforts to keep her balance, but once planted in the mud she lifted her muzzle ready for battle. The rain stopped and silence returned, broken by the patter of drops falling through massed twigs. Aspen's nostrils dilated but failed to capture the dog smell. Instead she nosed out the powerful scent of badger. Standing on hindlegs she looked through the nettles, grass and cuckoo pint leaves to see the boar Greybob had fought, scent-marking the wayside opposite. Starlight was catching his rain-spiked fur, sheathing him in silvery radiance. The swinging face was like an element of a ghostly dance and the creature's silence belonged entirely to Nightworld. Although he laid his feet down heavily there was no sound or so it seemed to Aspen. The blood was thrumming in the base of her skull and she breathed quickly and softly. Again there was the sensation of being in a presence that had nothing to do with life.

Down came the rain once more and she shook the drops from her eyes and felt the outside world leap back to possess her.

The boar had gone, leaving his footprints in the mud just like any other badger, but Aspen had no desire to follow them. Her snout sifted badger scent from the other smells webbing the lane, yet she remained full of anxiety. It was only while crossing the field above King Arthur's Tower that two realities dovetailed. She stopped and raised her muzzle. The

121

darkness was reaching out to take Birdcherry. Aspen shook herself and dashed down towards the pines with the rain chasing her.

She arrived at Big Sett to find Hawscrag and the maiden sows at the scratching tree.

'Birdcherry is very ill,' said Hawscrag. 'It isn't so much throat-burn as her readiness to give up. She's such a weak-willed little oddling.'

'I'll go to her,' said Aspen.

'She cried out for you a short while ago,' said Hawscrag, setting her teeth to the claws of a forefoot. 'Then I realized she was letting herself sink. The chamber went cold and the darkness was suddenly frightening.'

Cowtail made a brief appearance but she was chased off by Furzebright. At the entrance hole Aspen had one final shake from snout to tail before going underground. Soon she sniffed out Birdcherry and Cragbriar in one of the small rest chambers.

'The poor scrap's stopped shivering,' the old boar whispered. 'But her nose is dry and warm. I hope – I hope –' He could not bring himself to complete the sentence.

'Go and forage,' Aspen said kindly. 'I'll look after her.'

'I have a soft spot for her,' Cragbriar grunted, heaving his bulk out of the chamber. 'I remember her as a cub. She was not the least bit playful but we all loved her.'

Aspen located Birdcherry's face with her snout and proceeded to lick it all over. Birdcherry sighed but did not stir. Still Aspen persisted, pressing her warmth against her sister's body, feeding the sick spirit with her own strong life force. Quietly she began to speak.

'Though we may forget her she never forgets us. She is waiting beyond the last breath but our going to her will not stop the sunrise or make the stars go out forever. She speaks to us through the scent of Nightworld though we may fail to understand her silence. All paths run to Sunworld, to the rapture that never fades. Do you believe, Birdcherry?'

122

The little sow stretched and drew a deep breath.

'Yes, Aspen,' she whispered. 'I believe in the moon and stars and the grass and the smell of the sea. I believe in all the life under darkness and the life that lies beyond nose and ears and eyes. I believe in the deathless part of me and what the heart can see.'

She yawned and pressed her nose against Aspen's face.

'Do you realize,' Aspen smiled, 'you never stammered.'

'B-because it didn't seem to be m-me speaking,' Birdcherry said. 'I was in the m-middle of a dream and spoke f-from the dream.'

'Could you manage some forage?'

'No. I'd just like to sleep; but I feel much better.'

'You won't give up again without a fight, will you?'

'I don't think so. Thanks for h-helping me.'

'I didn't,' Aspen said. 'You helped yourself. Go to sleep now.'

Like all animals Aspen had placed her trust in the seasons that came and went. The earth spoke to her. The stars were a music in her head. The ocean breathed as she breathed. In the end all sorrow became song as all darkness became light and she desired above everything tranquillity and liberty shared in the fellowship of her own kind.

'I needn't ask if Birdcherry's all right,' said Hawscrag.

The sun had risen and the old sow was lost against the brilliance of the sea. Her silveriness was spectral and Aspen hesitated a moment in the entrance hole.

'Is it really morning?' she gasped in a dazed voice. 'I'm not dreaming am I?'

Her eyes were round and bright in the vertical black stripes.

'The throat-burn?' Hawscrag coaxed.

'Almost gone,' Aspen said, rising to drag her claws down the bole of the elderberry. 'You were right, mother. She was giving herself to darkness that was cold and lifeless.'

Cragbriar vanished underground mumbling: 'Cub-fears, cub-fears. Boars know. They don't say a lot but they know.

123

Sows dream and windbag. Boars act.'

'Old fool,' Hawscrag growled. 'What good could he have done Birdcherry?'

'He loves her,' Aspen said.

'Love!' Hawscrag snorted.

The maiden sows giggled.

In the stunted willow of Ramsons Dip a chaffinch sang against the double note of a great tit; but the cattle coming down the track from Effords still wore their shaggy winter coats. Many dark cold days lay between the first celandines on the steeps and spring. None of the badgers were deceived. Birdcherry and Aspen had foraged late by the barn at Garrowcombe. Drowsily they had watched dawn break and pricked their ears to the bird calls. The lark song was as intense as anything spring could offer, and the sky seemed full of it.

The sows trotted along the contour of the hillside following a sheep path and scattering rabbits. Below, the stream threaded through reeds and dead flags under an overgrown hedge of ash and elm. The reek of carted dung was everywhere.

They came to the landslips of Runnage and sniffed around the small sett buried in brambles and bracken. Greybob had drenched the place in his musk and there were fresh droppings in the pits. Entering the sett they encountered the scent of a young sow and knew Greybob had taken a mate, but he permitted them to use the vacant chamber.

'I thought y-you were his mate,' Birdcherry whispered.

'It's often the way,' Aspen said bravely.

'Perhaps it's because you're H-Hawscrag's daughter and moonborn.'

'Don't worry,' Aspen said. 'Mates will find us soon enough.'

She began to scratch and let her mind go blank.

Returning to Big Sett the following night they learnt that Guelder had cubbed in the sett at Ramsons Dip.

'Twins,' said Hawscrag. 'A boar and a sow.'

The wheat field was yielding earthworms in the mild spell. Badgers slowly worked their way up the field at the forage. The news of the birth brought an ache to Aspen's heart. Sharp-nosed, the sows decoded the darkness, drinking its faint spices. Higher up the slope Furzebright was skirmishing playfully with Thornsong. Their purring cries annoyed Aspen but she quickly laid aside her bitterness.

'To think that was Cragbriar and I not so many winters ago,' said Hawscrag. 'He was sett-master then, with a voice like the pines in a storm.'

'Why d-do we grow old, mother?' Birdcherry asked.

'Why do leaves wither and fall?' Hawscrag said in a tone that was acid rather than cryptic.

The sky to the east above the sea was growing lighter as they returned to Froward Point. Hawscrag went underground immediately but the others remained for a while on the lawn scratching and grooming. The wailing cry lifted the hair on their backs. Aspen ran to the main entrance of the sett and found the old sow standing there keening, her muzzle raised and eyes closed.

'Mother,' Aspen said softly. 'What is wrong?'

'Cragbriar is dead,' came the reply in a sob-quaked voice.

'B-but how?' said Birdcherry and the kin group looked at each other.

'Oh don't worry,' Hawscrag gulped. 'There's nothing to be afraid of. He died in his sleep.'

'Ah,' chorused the badgers, for it was the desirable death.

'Shall we attend to him?' Furzebright said.

'Please. Take one of the boars and do it well,' said Hawscrag.

Then the sows went back to the lawn and sat in a half-circle gazing towards the brightening east. The star-dance had paled and the sea around Dragon Rock was calm. One by one the gulls took flight, rising silently into the sky. The winter dawn was hushed and still.

Underground Furzebright and his companion dug until the cavity in the side of the chamber was large enough to hold the body. Working together the boars pushed Cragbriar into the soil and walled him in. Afterwards they crouched and lowered their snouts and mourned.

'It's done,' Furzebright told Hawscrag and the old sow nodded.

'I wonder,' she whispered, 'what Earth Mother will make of the grumpy old creature.'

But she was distressed and did not try to hide it. Her muzzle was raised and her eyes closed while her head swung slowly from side to side. Beyond her grief the sun rose.

Looking out over the sea Aspen thought of the warm new life in Guelder's sett, and of the old badger tucked up in the earth close by. The mystery deepened and the beauty of the morning crept through the sett-dwellers. Then a lark began to sing.

Chapter 16

In Mary's Haven

The waterfall at Garrowcombe Sands ghosted down through its own rainbow onto the beach and poured on over the pebbles into the sea. Long, lazy swells were collapsing, rasping up the shingle and sliding back with a swish and a rattle. The tide was ebbing. Wet pebbles and rocks caught the sun. Strawberry Rapson blew on the red tip of his cigarette, licked his lips and smiled. Gritt and Jimmy raced together up and down the water's edge, barking at the waves. After a little while they came to him and lay panting at his feet, occasionally casting an eye up at him while their tongues lolled and their flanks heaved.

Strawberry was happy. Life was on the move again. Where the headland stood dark against the sky the fulmars' flicker was like a conjurer's trick but Strawberry thought the birds with their tube noses and rigid wings were gulls. His curiosity rarely reached beyond his passion for dogs and badger baiting. The old brocks had been digging on the steep, north-facing side of the coombe. Despite the sun the twin barrels of his twelve bore remained cold. He laid the gun across his thighs and settled back against the rock. Shuffling on his belly through the shell-crumble Gritt managed to thrust his head onto Strawberry's lap and the man laughed and made a fuss of the animal.

'Idn' you the little champion,' he murmured. 'You could see off the world's biggest brock. You idn' afraid of anything.'

Kicking up the steeps to Hellweather Point he lurched into lark song. The slope beyond Garrowcombe Head was bright with celandines but Strawberry's mind was elsewhere. The lark song was irritating. He called his dogs to heel only to find them there. The Froward Sett couldn't be an insoluble problem. Christ, he thought, it must be full of badgers. It was warm and the larks seemed tireless, yet the clarity foretold rain. Cloud shadows drifted across the sea and a trawler furrowed the sun-dazzle.

Coming onto the Point he paused a moment and gulped air. Finches broke from the hedge. Then the first clouds of morning crept over the sky and soon the small white ones were gone and large grey ones were gathering westwards. Rain stood dark above Woodash but the sea was blue and green.

Beneath his feet the ground was yielding. He had reached the neglected drystone wall with its pennywort and dwarf blackthorn. The stream tumbled down the steeps ahead and fell over the crag in a white vapour. Strawberry looked across his right shoulder. Beyond the approaching shower was a gulf of clear sky. Left of him the cliffs descended in slabs and buttresses to the sea. Towards the horizon was an endless parade of shipping.

Rain beat down and became hail. Blue sky was at either hand and before him but the shower was slow in passing. Shaking the drops from her feathers the raven rolled sideways and took the sun on her breast in her dive towards the Point. Then out of sheer joy she tumbled and croaked and at that moment Strawberry shot her. The shift from vivid light into utter darkness was instant. Lifeless she fell to the steeps and was lost among the bracken.

128

Strawberry drew his sleeve across his nose and eased out the cartridge case to reload. From the belt of his raincoat dangled a brace of rabbits. Gritt and Jimmy whined their excitement but he ignored them to plod heavily up through the celandine glitter to the edge of the pasture. Behind him Mort the male raven was crying his bewilderment. Strawberry glanced back but the old bird was out of range, flying back and forth across the scrub where his mate had fallen.

Fingo loped away from the shooting unmoved. He had heard the bang, laid his ears to his head, pressed his belly to the ground and slowly raised himself, alert to what the morning might hold. Stepping gingerly over the tussocks of grass he sniffed the dead raven's body but Mort drove him off with his great bill and loud calls. The rocket ascent of a cock pheasant did nothing to calm Fingo's nerves. Crowing its staccato complaint the bird made a vertical, tail-quivering take-off to whirr away on the wind. Narrowing his eyes to knife slits Fingo released his frustration in a soft almost peevish chatter of the teeth and a moaning cry.

Among the bleached tussocks were wind-burnt primroses and here and there lay bundles of odourless bones and feathers which had once been gulls. Cowtail's tribe had been busy all winter taking roosting birds; but the cat paced on into lark song, stopping to read the invisible parts of morning with his nose. There were so many larks in the air above the plough, the sheep pasture and fields of swedes. Fingo was content. He had received his scrounge at Coastguard Cottage, cleaned himself and decided to return to Froward. Behind him Mort was soaring to croak his misery, but the cries of the lapwings were sweet. The black and white birds rose and fell above the downs while the cockerels of Woodash sang out.

Fingo mewed and flopped down to roll on the bracken. Then he watered a gorse stump and trotted on with marvellous suppleness. All along the drystone wall above Spaniard's Point the blackthorn was beginning to show its blossom buds. On one of the gnarled boles Cowtail had left her musk. When Fingo put his nose to it the stink made him sneeze.

For Strawberry it was a special Saturday. His son Tony was eleven and the badger club was preparing to celebrate its twenty-fifth anniversary. Strawberry's father had been the first master back in the bad years after the Great War. The old boy had been a good father, Strawberry recalled with a glide of the tongue across his lips. Family was everything – family and dogs.

He went into the front room where his wife and her sisters were preparing for the party. Tony was still in his pyjamas, unwrapping his presents. The house smelt of dogs.

'Come here, son,' Strawberry smiled and he caught the boy in his arms and lifted him up to kiss the top of his head. The four-year-old twins Doreen and Mary rushed down the stairs and chivvied their father for kisses. For a moment chaos reigned but Mrs Rapson's sharp call for order restored peace.

'My present's in the hall,' Strawberry continued.

'What is it, dad?'

'Go and see.'

Tony knelt and lifted the lid of the large cardboard box.

'A Hornby set!' he cried. 'Is it mine, dad? Is it really mine?'

The girls joined him as he wound up the engine.

Strawberry nodded and his smile broadened to a beam of pleasure. 'It's got the lot,' he said. 'Bridges, signals, stations, everything. It's no use runnin' the engine on the lino. Fix the track together – the girls will help you. Go on, in the front room.'

He consulted his pocket watch. 'Me and Eric will have to be away shortly, Rene. We got the club photo in a couple of hours.'

'I pressed your best bags, love,' Mrs Rapson said. She was a smart little woman just beginning to go to seed with a loosening of the flesh.

'And my club tie?' Strawberry smiled. 'The blue one.' Blue was the club colour.

'What do you think?' she answered.

Strawberry stripped to the waist and went into the kitchen to shave. Gritt and Jimmy remained quivering under the front room table as Tony's railway engine and three GWR coaches whizzed around the track.

St Mary's church clock was gonging twelve when Strawberry and his elder son walked self-consciously in their best clothes through the fish market to the Ship Inn. Stike, Dunning and the other members were already tilting their elbows in the public bar.

'Here comes the bloody master,' Dunning said sarcastically under his breath and Stike nodded and piped: 'The photographic bloke's waiting, Frank. It's all set up. What you havin', boy?'

'A light split and Eric's on best bitter.'

'Perhaps we ought to take our drinks out the back,' Dunning said. 'The photographer's been here since half-eleven. He'll be chargin' overtime if us don't watch it.'

In the whitewashed yard the landlady liked to call the 'beer garden' the tables and chairs had been pulled to one side but before the members took their places in front of the camera Dunning produced a large flat parcel wrapped in brown paper.

'A bit of hush, gentlemen, please,' he said, clearing his throat and tapping his mouth lightly with his fist. Strawberry eyed him curiously from a smile. 'Frank,' Dunning went on, 'we all know the Mary's Haven Badger Club would be a pretty poor effort without you. As 'tis our twenty-fifth anniversary the members have all chipped in to get you something as a token of our respect.'

Strawberry's face was suddenly a uniform scarlet. His fingers fumbled the paper and he smiled when the navy-blue jacket with its silver badger's head buttons was uncovered.

'Your missus gave us the measurements,' Stike chuckled.

131

'Put it on, Frank. The Master's got to look smart for the snap.'

The photographer stared up at the gulls which were peering down from the rooftops.

'The committee thought it appropriate,' Dunning concluded, shaking Strawberry's hand.

The Master nodded and did up the buttons.

'I'll thank you all afterwards in the upstairs room,' he beamed. 'And anyone who isn't on shorts can leave the club. I don't want no one sober when Mrs Whidden calls time.'

'Are you ready?' the photographer enquired without enthusiasm. He was a tall, lanky young man in a cravat and hound's-tooth sports jacket.

Stiff and unsmiling the Mary's Haven Badger Club posed against the whitewashed wall.

'Everyone's ordered at least two copies,' Dunning confided as he and Strawberry strolled around the trestle table admiring the spread.

'The boys reckon we ought to do something special to celebrate, Frank,' Dunning continued.

'Like what?' Strawberry said.

'A charabanc trip to Ilfracombe or something.'

'Why on earth Ilfracombe?' Strawberry asked in genuine amazement.

'Sid Proctor says it's got some good pubs.'

'Christ!' Rapson breathed and he juggled a piece of hot potato round his mouth with his tongue. 'Listen, Charlie, 1948 will go down as a great year for the club but it won't kick off with a bloody trip to Ilfracombe.'

'What then?'

'I'll think of something. We're a badger club. Maybe we'll dig out that old sett at Froward.'

His companion nodded and rested his dark eyes on Rapson. Then Strawberry realized who Dunning resembled. It was the heavy villain who tossed gas stoves out the window and dropped coppers by the job lot in those Charlie Chaplin films. For a moment he choked on his potato and the badger's mask

132

over the mantelpiece grinned down at him from its eternal snarl.

That afternoon Garrison walked over the cliffs to St Mary's Head and down into the port past rows of small houses set alongside the narrow road above the outer and inner harbour. On his back he carried a rucksack for his provisions but the excursion was really just an excuse to be among people again. It was good to see women gossiping on the pavements outside shops and the men congregating in small groups on the quay for the same purpose. A herring gull stood on the head of the statue of William Prince of Orange and crooned as Garrison paused to read the inscription. Straightening again he saw Billy and Sheena entering Washbrook's secondhand shop across the way.

'Oh no!' he breathed.

The doorbell tinkled and the children turned guilty faces in his direction. Behind them the little man lidded his eyes and smoothed the cat curled up on the counter.

Billy's hand closed on something Garrison could not identify and vanished into his pocket.

'What is it this time, Billy?'

'Nuffin',' said Sheena and the shopkeeper's fingers beat a soft tattoo on the countertop.

'Billy,' Garrison persisted but the boy just shook his head and stood staring down at the floor.

'Come outside and tell me.'

'It's none of your business,' Billy said but he let Sheena push him out the door onto the pavement. For a moment the little old man in his unbuttoned waistcoat watched them from the window, then he put up the 'Closed' sign.

'Show 'im, Billy,' Sheena said, nudging the boy with her elbow. Reluctantly Billy's hand emerged from his pocket and the fist slowly opened to reveal a necklace of freshwater pearls.

'He didn't nick it,' Sheena went on. 'It's his muvver's.'

'And she asked him to sell it for her?'

Billy looked up at him and said coldly. 'One of them Yanks gave it her. One of them 'uncles' she used to bring home on Friday and Saturday nights. She's always wearin' it and strokin' it like it's – it's –'

He shrugged, too full of emotion to risk any more words.

'It's her property, Billy,' Garrison said. 'Why don't you go and put it back? Your dad wouldn't approve of you stealing off your own mother.'

'He would have sorted out them bleedin' Yanks,' said Sheena.

'My dad was a hero,' Billy said. 'But he couldn't afford to give her posh things.'

'In the end, Billy, the things don't count. It's what comes from the heart.'

'I hate her,' the boy hissed, and he turned and stalked away with an aggressive and defiant roll of the shoulders.

'He's in a mood, mister,' Sheena said. 'You won't tell her, will you?'

'Of course not but try to make sure the necklace goes back.'

Sheena caught up with Billy by the fish and chip shop and they strode on in silence for a while until she said: 'Are you sulking?'

He shook his head.

'What you goin' to do wiv the pearls?'

'This,' he said, standing over the drain and letting the necklace slip through his fingers. Striking the metal grill the pearls came apart and some scattered in the gutter. Slowly and deliberately Billy crushed them under his heel.

Sheena sniffed and waited for him to finish.

'Let's get some chips and go to Garrowcombe sands,' she said. 'I'll buy.'

'Old Garrison's a funny bloke, idn' he?' Billy said.

'He's OK,' she grinned. 'A bit wet behind the ears but OK.'

Three streets away Garrison went in the pet shop and ten minutes later came out with a couple of rabbits in a box. After a lot of asking he found the street where Billy lived and climbed the steps to the glass-panelled door of number 3.

'I thought you was the police,' Mrs Drew said, ushering him breezily into the hall and lighting a cigarette. 'Plain clothes. The little sod's always in trouble. He's got sticky fingers but I blame most of that on Sheena Nelson. Her's a proper little crook. Most of them cockneys are.'

She was well-fleshed with heavy features and blonde hair pushed up under a turban. Fashionably dressed she lacked any sort of style and had that washed-out, unhappy look of a woman going nowhere except into middle age. Maybe it was her awful perfume, Garrison reflected. It overwhelmed him almost to the point of nausea. When she smiled and folded her arms under her bosom he felt revulsion give way to embarrassment. The cigarette was held between forefinger and index finger with all the exaggeration of an American film star.

'I've brought Billy a pair of rabbits to replace the others,' he managed.

'He needs a good hiding not more animals to stink out the yard,' she said. 'Pity his dad idn' here. He'd sort him out, the little sod.'

Garrison nodded helplessly.

'I suppose they'd better go in the hutch out the back,' she said, dismissing him as a do-gooder who would never stand a girl a drink.

Trying to ignore the yard's squalor Garrison deposited the rabbits and beat a hasty retreat under her contemptuous gaze.

'I don't want him mitchin' school with that little tart,' was her parting shot. 'And don't encourage him to come down your place when he ought to be learnin' his lessons.'

'Maybe you should try speaking to him,' Garrison said. 'He seems in need of a bit of encouragement.'

'Maybe you ought to mind your own bloody business,' and the door was slammed in his face.

Leaving Mary's Haven Garrison took the coastal path home, walking hard as part of his fitness programme. Striding along he let Ann back into his thoughts on a rise of love-sickness. But he would be with her on Monday evening. Five days in Switzerland would help lessen the ache.

The mild afternoon of late February had opened some of the blackthorn blossom in the hedge at Firebeacon Point and the sight of its whiteness warmed his heart. Next year he and Ann would look for that confirmation of winter coming to an end. It had been a long winter without her. Up on Bullen Down he heard the cawing of rooks and saw the peregrine tiercel cruising through the smoky sunlight. On the edge of the marsh golden plover had joined the lapwings. Garrison selected a dry tussock of grass and sat down and lit a cigarette. Christ, it's beautiful, he thought. Finches filled the air around him and came in swooping flight to the hazels of Woodash Lane. Wildfowl arrived and departed on a whistle of wings. The flood water gleamed and the sea was the colour of the peregrine's back. He searched the sky for the tiercel but although the raw familiar cry carried down the valley he failed to locate the bird. Immediately overhead a raven spoke and he saw the solitary black shape beating high towards Woodash Down, uttering deep cronks. Garrison settled on his elbows, closed his eyes and took the sun warm on his face. Then the cigarette began to burn his fingers and screwing it into the turf he saw three primroses among the dead bracken beside him.

Back at the cottage there was a note caught in the letter-box.

'Dear Mr Garrison,' it read. 'I called after lunch but you were out. I thought you might like to know Chard, our bailiff, has got the sack. I caught him and another man putting terriers in the sett near our cove at the bottom of the woods yesterday evening. He said he was after foxes but of course I didn't believe him, so he's on a month's notice. Grandmother confirmed it on the telephone. I think he'll be gone quite soon. He really is an unpleasant man. May I call on you to discuss some sort of campaign to stop all this badger digging on our land? Perhaps you'd let me know when it's convenient.'

It was signed 'Lucy Ordish'.

Garrison promised himself he would get in touch with the girl as soon as he returned from Switzerland. He glanced at his wristwatch. The taxi would be at Woodash Farm at six but all he had to do was bath and change. His bag was packed.

Chapter 17

Sett Life

Sunrise sent light leaping across the water. The din of seabirds rose from crags and reefs. Where the land ended in jagged walls of rock gulls swung close to the precipices, riding up-draughts of air. For millennia guillemots had held their water ceremonies on the sea below Garrowcombe Head, dancing and diving with remarkable synchronization. The courtship ritual continued in the sky with the flocks wheeling, soaring and descending. Sometimes birds buzzed across the loomeries only to be ignored by the mated couples displaying on the ledges. There was perpetual movement against the shadowy crags.

The water was a sheet of trembling light which Skyhook round irritating. Out towards the horizon cloud was massing. Rock doves shuttled between gulleys and buttresses on clapping wings, as if unaware of the danger. The tiercel and his mate alarmed the auks and fulmars and disturbed even the great black-backed gulls. Many seabirds plunked down on the water but the falcon had selected her target. Turning on quick wing-beats she bonded to a rock dove from behind to conclude an almost casual assault. The tiercel soared to his station above Hellweather Point and hovered. When he stooped the waders scattered at wave level and escaped his talons. Crying repeatedly he joined the falcon and perched close to her on an outcrop while she plucked the dove's breast and tore at the flesh with her hooked upper mandible. Then peace returned to the loomeries and the birds on the guillemot ledges bowed and pointed their beaks skywards according to the mysteries of the courtship display. They were entirely engrossed in each other.

Still nursing his grief Mort the raven flew over the point half-expecting to see his mate flapping towards him. The sun was warm. Skyhook gathered it on his feathers as he stood at look-out on a flake of slate. He was motionless and watchful in a way peculiar to raptors.

Narrowing her eyes Cowtail followed the badger path across the steeps to the goyal that was choked with blackthorn blossom. Approaching Ramsons Dip she met Fingo.

'Ashblacken's gone,' said the cat.

'No he ain't,' Cowtail said, her breath stinking of sheep carrion. 'He's up in the sett way over towards Flashing Light.'

Fingo licked a paw. 'Guelder will be pleased. She's been fretting.'

'It's the whelps,' said Cowtail knowingly. 'Whelps put a mother on edge.'

The cat and the fox strolled back to Froward Point together, enjoying each other's silence. Under the Monterey pines there was a final exchange of gossip.

'They were screaming last night,' Cowtail said and Fingo waited for her to elaborate.

'Ashblacken and that big old boar Greybob saw off. I thought there would be another fight but nothing happened.'

'Greybob's back in Big Sett,' said the cat.

'One goes, another returns,' Cowtail said. 'Cragbriar was a right old sore-arse. He always made me feel uncomfortable and unwelcome.'

'Setts are for sett-dwellers,' Fingo said.

'A hole's a hole if you're a fox,' Cowtail grated. 'That Hawscrag thinks she's – she's –'

'Earth Mother?' Fingo prompted.

'No – Earth Mother's a fox, every animal knows that.'

Fingo smiled and retired to the ivy-covered bunker whose empty gun port faced the sea.

Below ground, less than a hundred yards from Fingo's lair, Greybob and Aspen were curled up together in their own chamber. Birdcherry was forced to bed down with the other maiden sows. Waking every so often she heard Hawscrag crying out in her sleep. A vision of the snarling dog faces grew out of darkness and the little sow whimpered and hid her head between her paws. But the animal warmth was comforting. All around her flanks gently rose and fell in the rhythm of rest. Drifting back into sleep she was partly aware of the moans and sighs of the slumbering animals. Going to sleep was such a strange business, like a journey. Perhaps death was like that, but not death under the fangs of the terriers. She buried her snout in the harsh-textured coat next to her and a sow stirred and grumbled. Fleas became active then settled before it became necessary for her to scratch. She dozed fitfully, turning this way and that, until her mind went blank. Then she was awake again, listening to the small-talk of her companions and participating in the grooming. Dimpsey had become night. The sett was alive once more and she heard Aspen's voice and ambled off along the passage.

Greybob had visited the scratching tree and gone to forage before the sisters were reunited outside the main entrance. Aspen's nose was questioning the night whose fabric was melting and tingling in her nostrils. The Rips were noisy with the tide ready to turn and flood. Half a moon was shining on the thorns and grass. Sirius twinkled and the night was open and receptive to her nose and ears. It oozed scents and held small furtive sounds. Somewhere close by a rabbit screamed under a stoat and a roosting bird flapped its wings.

140

The badgers had rid themselves of excess body fat and were much leaner.

'Has he claimed you?' Birdcherry asked.

'Not yet,' said Aspen.

'Do you s-suppose I'll ever find a boar who w-wants me?'

'Of course you will,' and Aspen licked her sister's muzzle.

Other sett-dwellers pushed past them to the forage. Aspen and Birdcherry raised their heads to the sky before setting off up the path with its tangled vaulting of twigs and branches.

A forage of roots in Ramsons Dip left them refreshed. Clouds drifted across the moon and light faded. Then an animal blundered up through the bracken to the nearest willow, and their noses told them it was Guelder. Aspen and Birdcherry ambled over to join her.

'Has Ashblacken returned?' said Aspen.

Guelder shook her muzzle emphatically and scent-marked the grass beside the path. Then a piercing long drawn out cry rang down the hillside to lift the sows' hair. On the skyline against the stars was the silhouette of a large boar. He was up on his hindlegs leaning against the middle wire of the fence, his face turned towards the moon. Again the cry broke from his throat and northwards another boar responded, but trotting into the dip Furzebright could only growl half-heartedly.

'Is it that n-nasty stranger?' said Birdcherry.

'Yes, it's him,' Aspen sighed.

'What's wrong?' Birdcherry whispered.

The cry ended and the stranger was gone.

'He doesn't scare me any more,' Aspen said. 'He just seems sad and a bit lost.'

'He's crazy,' Furzebright rumbled. 'You stay away from him. He's worm-brained.'

'Hark at the great sett-master,' Guelder said sarcastically, turning her hindquarters on him. 'He only has to waggle his snout and every boar this side of Flashing Light starts running.'

'Just remember what I said,' Furzebright muttered, climbing the side of the goyal with short, powerful steps which failed to conceal his embarrassment.

'Ashblacken would have answered the challenge,' Guelder said when the three sows assembled on the edge of the field to scent-mark.

'It didn't sound like a challenge,' Aspen said.

'I think you're r-right, Aspen,' said Birdcherry. 'It was m-more like a cry for help.'

'Help from what?' Guelder grunted as she ate earthworms before digging out swedes.

'I don't know,' Aspen confessed.

'You are the moonborn,' Guelder said, her mouth full of swede. 'You are supposed to know.'

'Very well,' Aspen said. 'I feel in my blood that he is unhappy and would like to make his life with us.'

'By killing all our boars?' Guelder scoffed and Aspen reluctantly accepted she had never really liked the self-opinionated sow with her abrasive tongue; but if Ashblacken was missing she would need friends.

'Greybob was admitted to the k-kin group,' said Birdcherry.

'Because he has the blood,' Guelder said, pushing her snout into the mud and plucking out worms. 'Hawscrag's line have all been fertile sows. The stranger may win a place in the sett by force if he isn't badly mauled in the process by Greybob or Ashblacken or even old wind-and-pee Furzebright.'

That description could also fit Ashblacken, Aspen thought, but she said: 'There is a sadness about him.'

'You've too much heart,' said Guelder.

'That's why she's the moonborn' said Birdcherry.

'Yes, well, I've got cubs to feed,' Guelder growled, as unwilling as ever to concede anything in an argument.

'May we visit them?' Aspen asked, melting before Guelder's motherhood.

'Please do,' Guelder said in a softer tone. She lifted her

142

round, puzzled eyes to look at Aspen.

No sow with a family absents herself for very long from the sett. When she had eaten her fill Guelder slithered down the steeps of Ramsons Dip, between the willows and alders beside the stream to her den on the clifftops. The sows left muddy scats in the latrine pits before going underground to the nursery chamber. Here Guelder had made a large nest of grass and bracken which she constantly changed. From the centre of the bedding came the squeak of her whelps. Creeping forward Guelder answered them with a soft, purring cry before settling to suckle. Then Aspen and Birdcherry were permitted to approach the cubs. Very gently Aspen ran her snout over the nearest little body, delighting in its smell and fluffiness. The twins had yet to open their eyes. Each weighed less than half a pound and lacked the distinctive vertically striped face of an adult. Now they struggled through the sow's warmth to get at the teats. Oblivious to Aspen's and Birdcherry's presence Guelder gave a groggy twist of the head to snap at her fleas. Quietly the visitors retreated.

'By the end of next winter,' Aspen said outside, 'you'll have cubs of your own, Birdcherry.'

'Will I? H-have you really seen that?'

'Yes,' Aspen said. 'You'll have three cubs and know the great happiness.'

'What great h-happiness?'

'Making life,' Aspen replied.

On the headland beyond Old Spanish Cove a boar cried and they knew it was Ashblacken. Together they walked up the banks of the stream to the fence again into the stranger's musk. Out of the shadows beneath the blackthorns stepped Greybob. He was grinning but Birdcherry felt excluded from his friendliness. She glanced at Aspen, noting with something close to jealousy, the joy on her face. She turned and plodded across the field towards Warren Fishacre, uncertain once more and empty despite the forage.

*

The first, small, bronze-coloured tufts of new leaf had appeared on the bramble feelers in the hollows along the top of the steeps. The neighbouring field lay under the odours of muck-spreading and the music of larks. The sunny spell ended on a fresh north wind that sent the blackthorn blossom flying and had the early primroses shivering on the banks above Garrowcombe sands. Close to the setts the elderberry was also leafing but the return of cold weather suddenly put the spring which had been so close out of reach.

Hunting the air above Hard Sands marsh Skyhook killed a lapwing which he then passed to his mate in flight. Over the downs the buzzards mewled. Clouds piled up in the north, the day darkened and it snowed.

Chapter 18

In at the Kill

Over the whiteness came the badger diggers preceded by their dogs. Cocks were crowing at Woodash but the Sunday morning was still too early for church bells. The terriers and Dunning's two lurcher bitches cast about, pausing every so often to urinate. Snow-smothered distance ended in the grey of sea and sky. To the north-east St Mary's Light was a flickering glow behind Bullen Down. With a rush of wings the starling flock swept down Garrowcombe.

Half a dozen men and twice as many dogs had walked down the lane from the parked vans to the old stone barn and onto the pasture. The snow had abated but threatened to come strong again. In the field corner lambs lay against their mothers. A coal tit sang from the hedge-bottom among primroses and dandelions which were partly covered in snow so white it made the gulls look dirty. The wind swept off Dartmoor filling the sky with birds.

'I hope it idn' goin' to be like last winter,' Stike said. He tried to pull his mittens over the freezing fingers clenched on the long handles of the badger tongs he was carrying.

Strawberry smiled and licked his lips. The lapwings in the bottom of the coombe were crying and snow fell in a stinging shower and passed on out to sea. Each of the men carried an implement essential to the digging: mattock, pick, iron bars, spade, shovel. All save Strawberry wore ex-war department balaclavas, khaki greatcoats and rubber boots with soles so worn they gave little purchase in the wet snow. Strawberry's cloth cap was almost a mark of distinction.

The gang stumbled and slipped down the hillside to the stream and walked on to the three large elms in the goyal above the waterfall. The shafts of the sett had been sunk between roots and shale. The largest chamber was occupied by a young bachelor boar who had pneumonia and had chosen an isolated sett as his last resting place after wandering South of St Mary's Head.

'See the tracks, Frank?' Dunning said. 'And there's dung in the pits.'

'I'm gaspin' for a fag,' Strawberry smiled and he accepted a Woodbine from Short's tin.

Stike took the thermos flask from his pocket and filled the cup with hot, sweet cocoa.

'My breakfast,' Eric Rapson sniffed and he blew on the tip of his cigarette and held it up.

'No wonder you'm lean as a racing snake, boy,' Dunning chuckled.

'The bugger eats like an elephant and drinks like a fish,' said Strawberry.

'Then how do 'ee keep so trim?' Dunning said.

'Worry,' said Eric. 'Work and worry.'

'If you was married to my missus you'd have something to worry about,' Dunning snorted. 'Her never stops nagging. Nag, nag, nag, bloody nag – day and night, even when her's asleep.'

'Why don't you leave her?' Small said, genuinely baffled. He had divorced his wife and was enjoying a pampered life with his mother.

'Because I couldn't cope with all that happiness,' Dunning said, poker-faced, and the men laughed.

'I'm buggered if you idn' a born comedian, Charlie,' Stike chuckled.

Strawberry sent his cigarette end flaring away and said, 'If you're ready I'll put in Gritt.'

The clouds were scudding out to sea and some yellow had crept into the grey above the horizon but another snow shower came hissing down the coombe. The goyal was out of the wind and the hush closing in behind the shower was ruffled by the sound of the waves on the beach and the low, urgent whining of the terriers.

Gritt was sent down the main hole and the men waited for him to find. Presently his muffled barking presented Dunning with the information he required and he swung the pick. Like a military operation, Strawberry mused on a surge of self-satisfaction. One day when he had time he would write a book on the art of digging and baiting badgers. *The Badger Baiter's Bible* by Francis Harold Rapson. He smiled at the notion. The Badminton series was incomplete. And why not? He had the notebooks and a list of all the club kills since he had become master. The pick crunched through his daydream and his pug face lit up with joy.

Sheena woke Billy with the bad news and they held a whispered conversation in his kitchen while he dressed.

'I saw 'em leave Rapson's yard,' she said. 'Two vans, Strawberry, Stike, Dunning, Small – the bleedin' lot. I was in the doorway of Pottinger's gettin' our paper. Eric Rapson was on the corner talking to Small. He let it drop. They're going to Woodash.'

'Could be any of the setts above Runnage or Garrowcombe,' Billy grunted, tying his bootlaces.

'The snow'll help,' Sheena said and he looked at her questioningly. 'We can track them, bird brain.'

'OK,' he said. 'You fetch Garrison and I'll find out where they're diggin'.'

'Don't do nuffin' brave.'

They ran out of Mary's Haven to Hard Sands Lane where they separated. Billy crossed the fields by Raddicombe to Forders and Woodash but found no tyre marks in the snow. So he ran towards the crossroads. Less than a hundred yards from the farmhouse the vans were parked on some waste ground tight to the hedge. Billy let down the tyres, giggling as the rubber slowly crumpled.

The trail of footprints led him along the lane to Garrowcombe Barn and down the great hillside towards the waterfall and Garrowcombe Sands. Patches of blue sky were appearing and the last of the snow showers seemed to have fallen. Then the yelping of the terriers had the coldness churning in his stomach. It was Sunday. Why didn't God help? Why did God always let bad things happen? Why did God let his dad die? The sob caught in his throat. He slipped and fell but rolled back onto his feet in the same movement. That bleedin' Steer at Woodash must have known about the digging. He rode to hounds and shot anything unlucky enough to wear fur or feather. Maybe old Garrison could do something about it. He was rich and famous but so was the bleedin' King and he let bad things happen.

He flung himself over the fence into the goyal and came crab-wise across the steeps above the sett and the men. For a moment he was too breathless to speak. Strawberry turned and smiled up at him. The red birthmark was livid against the snow glare.

'This is becoming a habit,' he said.

Stike and Small ignored Billy and began to dig. The sound of the metal cutting into the stony soil made the boy wince.

'You bloody stop that,' he gasped, pointing a finger at Strawberry. 'You bloody stop it.'

Eric Rapson laughed. 'Or you'll do what?'

'Miss Ordish knows you'm here', Billy managed, 'and

Sheena's gone for Mr Garrison. They'll bring the police.'

'Bullshit,' Eric Rapson said. 'Old Mother Ordish is still abroad and the girl's gone to Bath for the weekend.'

'And did that bumhead Chard tell you Sheena's gone to Hard Sands? Garrison will sort you out.'

'Garrison's in Switzerland,' said Strawberry. 'Perce Steer up at Woodash knows the score.'

'He's one of the Ordish tenants,' Billy said. 'Mrs Ordish'll roast his arse when she gets home.'

'Not if her's got any sense,' said Strawberry. 'Steer's a good farmer. Look,' and his voice became pleasant. 'Why don't you stop actin' the fool and come down here? We won't lay a hand on 'ee. Come down and watch and you might learn something.'

'Bugger off,' Billy said. 'I know what you'm going to do to the badgers.'

Dunning started up the slope towards him and lost his footing to crash down on his back. The spade and the shovel continued to open the sett.

'Old fatty Dunning's used to this, idn' he?' Billy sneered. 'Cuttin' up sheep and cows and pigs all week in Lansworthy slaughter-house then watchin' bloody dogs tear badgers to bits at the weekend. You're like bleedin' Nazis, all of you.'

'Here,' Small cried. 'Who the bleddy hell are you callin' a German? I fought them buggers while you was still in your nappies.'

Billy lifted two rigid fingers of scorn and defiance. Jackdaws rattled their cries into the hubbub of the loomeries and Eric Rapson advanced purposefully up the side of the goyal.

'Get out of here, Drew,' he grated. 'Get out before I kick your ass all the way back to Mary's Haven. No more lip, now. Understand? Understand?' His voice rose to a yell. 'One more word and I'll let you have it. Get home and find out who's in bed with your old lady.'

'You bastard,' Billy sobbed and he threw himself at the man but Rapson hit him across the face with the flat of his hand and the boy slid on his chest towards the stream. Then Eric Rapson caught him savagely by the belt of his mac and jerked him to his feet. Twisting like a ferret Billy kicked him on the kneecap.

'You little sod,' Rapson hissed, white with rage; and he hit Billy about the head until Strawberry intervened.

'Leave it, Eric,' he said. 'We're into the sett. Get the tongs, Charlie, and show Billy what it's like being in at the kill.'

'For Christ's sake, mister,' Billy sobbed, blood and snot creeping from both nostrils.

'Don't let him go, Eric. He's out guest.'

Billy's guts churned to nausea and he suddenly felt weak at the knees.

'Dad,' he wailed. 'Dad, help me.'

'Shut up,' Eric Rapson said through clenched teeth. Billy's arm was twisted until he bent double and for him reality juddered from the general to the particular. Through his anguish he saw with startling clarity the tiny green buds on the thorn waiting to break into bullen blossom. At his feet was the discarded feather of a buzzard, and miraculously, the larks were singing. Lifting his gaze he saw through the bloom of alder catkins the sun-streaked hillsides.

The terriers were barking and leaping out to the full extent of their leashes.

'I'm sorry, mister,' he choked. 'I'll never bother you again. Can't you let the badger go, just this once? Please. For God's sake, please, please.'

'That idn' possible, boy,' Eric Rapson whispered in his ear. 'They old brocks is pests. Farmer wants them out the way.'

'Please,' from sobbing that racked Billy's body.

'Stop bloody bawling,' Rapson growled, tightening his grip on the boy's arm.

'You're breaking it, you bleedin' coward,' Billy cried.

'Shut up, then, and stand still.'

The tongs dragged the badger from the sett and Dunning leaned hard on the handles to clamp the creature to the ground. The boar grunted and turned his body in an attempt to bite the implement.

'Let's have him down on the beach in among the rocks,' said Strawberry.

Billy shook his head.

They scrambled down the bank beside the waterfall onto the pebbles. Dunning held the badger by the tail and swung it into a corner against the cliff face and watched it fluff out.

A flock of fieldfares landed in the elms and fixed Billy with their manic stare. Then the badger vanished beneath the terriers but every once in a while he shook off the dogs despite his illness and broke free. It was now obvious that he was sick. Billy shut his eyes but the vision remained and the noises would not be denied.

When it was all over Dunning said: 'You can have the carcass, Billy.' He held up the body. 'They make good shaving brushes out of the hair.'

'You wait,' Billy wept. 'You wait, you cruel sods.'

Eric Rapson released him and he stood over the dead animal, trying to knead the pain out of his arm.

'I'll get a gun and shoot you, the bloody lot of you. If my dad was here he'd fill you in, no trouble, because you're – you're just a load of dogshit.'

'Get your old lady to send for the US marines,' Dunning chuckled. 'I reckon her knew half the American army.'

Billy knelt and stroked the badger. He was shaking so badly his teeth rattled. The boar's eyes were open but they were no longer bright. Looking up through his tears the boy met the fieldfare's gaze. Now there was something grotesque about the snow and the buried primroses and the endless lark song. The chill in his stomach came from the heart.

Sheena could offer no words of comfort but her anger smouldered as painfully as his own. In silence they used slates from the beach to dig a shallow grave in the goyal under the elms. Then they laid the badger to rest and covered him with earth before building a cairn of large pebbles over the grave. A

151

fighter plane flew low over the sea to make an explosive entrance into the çalm.

'Maybe we ought to say a prayer,' Sheena said, washing her hands in the stream.

'I said one while we were covering him,' Billy muttered. 'It's only words, anyway. I said lots of prayers for my dad but it didn't bring him home.

Sheena pressed her lips together until they whitened.

When Garrison got back at the end of the week he went to the police; but the Badger Club denied everything and Billy's word was not enough.

'I got a bad record,' he admitted. 'Still, it don't matter. I'll get even with the Rapsons.'

The snow had long since turned to rain but there was enough sun between each heavy downpour to keep everyone happy.

'What happened when you told your mum?' Garrison said.

'She called him a lyin' little bleeder and belted him,' Sheena said.

'And she wouldn't let me keep the rabbits,' said the boy.

Garrison threw another shovelful of coal on the fire.

'So I've got 'em,' said Sheena. 'My old girl played up but she'll get used to 'em.'

'I've been in touch with the RSPCA at Abbot's Quay,' Garrison said. 'But there's nothing they can do except try to nail Strawberry and Co., for cruelty to their dogs.

'That's bleedin' rich!' Sheena cried.

'It idn' the dogs' fault,' said Billy. 'I feel sorry for them. Some get killed by the badgers.'

'Serves 'em right,' said Sheena.

Garrison looked at the clock on the mantelpiece and said: 'Lucy Ordish will be here in about half an hour. Do you two want to stay and have a chat? We're going to try to sort out a campaign to stop Strawberry raiding our setts.'

'I got to fetch some coal from the goods yard,' said Sheena.

152

'Billy helps me. We got this big old pram.'

Skyhook was at his station five hundred feet above Bullen Down, and beyond the drift of waders and duck he saw the man leave the cottage on the cliffs. Garrison took a deep breath of sea air. A blackbird sang from the highest tamarisk and Garrison wondered if he had ever heard anything so beautiful. Strolling to the top of Woodash Down he looked across to Hay Tor, the noblest of Dartmoor's outcrops, where it stood on the horizon to the north-west. That glimpse of the distant wilderness made him aware of the world beyond the South Devon coast. It was like the view of the mountains from Ann's window.

Evening hazed to dusk and out to sea the lights of ships conferred a poignancy on the approaching night. He carried the loveliness which the close of day can lift from a landscape to the fireside and drank scotch. A knock at the door brought him hurriedly to his feet.

'It's open,' he called. 'Please come in.'

Lucy was not at all what he had imagined. Perhaps it was the combination of the large eyes, the smile and the alertness which suggested a keen intelligence that sent Garrison's mind flying back again to those days in Paris. Ann in the radiant cotton frock, everything before them and what they shared leaving them dry-mouthed with excitement.

After the introductions he sat her by the fire and gave her a glass of cider.

'From Woodash Farm,' he said.

'I thought it was familiar,' Lucy smiled. 'We keep some at Fishacre.'

In a little while he was telling her about Billy's ordeal.

'Alas, the police couldn't do anything,' he finished. 'Billy's a bit of a romancer, as they say in Devon, and he's always in trouble. Baiting, of course, isn't illegal.'

'It is on our land,' she said indignantly. 'Putting a child through that trauma is beyond belief. Grandmother and I like Billy and Sheena as much as we detest Rapson.'

153

She was studying the cello at a college of music near Totnes, not too seriously, she admitted, 'being somewhat light on talent'. The tiny red indentations high up each side of her nose hinted at glasses.

Their conversation resolved very little. A closer watch would be kept on the setts when the new farm bailiff was installed. Meanwhile they would have to rely on the children's vigilance and Garrison's availability. It was a far from satisfactory situation.

'Trespass is so tricky in law,' Lucy said, blinking repeatedly. 'Rapson and Co. can always pretend they are exercising their animals. Then all we can do is ask them to leave the estate by the quickest route.'

'Maybe if we keep getting up their noses they'll clear off for good,' Garrison said.

'And dig badgers elsewhere,' she observed.

Garrison nodded. 'We can only do so much. Barbarism is universal but perhaps Fishacre could become an important bastion against it. When the war ended I was naive enough to believe the whole world would turn life into a sort of continual celebration. After all the dying you'd think no one would want to kill another living thing ever again.'

Seeing Lucy close her eyes tightly from a shudder he apologized and said: 'All this chinwagging won't solve anything.'

'My father thought we were a pretty imperfect lot,' she said. 'Despite being a non-churchgoer and a sceptic he put it down to Original Sin. I'm certainly guilty of it. When my cousins come to stay I get hot under the collar about fox-hunting. They're mad about it.'

'And you dislike it?'

'No, not really. I don't suppose I've given it a lot of thought, not on moral grounds, anyway. It's just that I'm useless at riding. I'm not very athletic although I traipse round in jodhpurs; and I'm short-sighted. What you said about the celebration of life is a bit special. You see things clearly don't you, Mr Garrison?'

154

'David, please. I'm not that ancient.'

Her eyes were watering badly.

'I left my glasses on the train coming back from Bath and I'm afraid my eyes are playing up.'

'The wood-smoke can't be helping matters,' he smiled. 'Or is it my cigar?'

'No, no, please,' she said, wrapping both hands round her glass. 'Until I found out about baiting I hadn't realized what killing animals for sport meant. You're right, the war hasn't shocked us into becoming better human beings. Children are still ill-treated and for a nation that's supposed to love animals we have dozens of societies and organizations devoted to their welfare.'

He topped up his scotch but she refused a refill.

'D'you know, Lucy,' he said. 'Even as a child I never felt at ease watching animals performing in a circus or standing around looking bored in cages at the zoo. Organizing nature for our amusement seems almost as bad as deliberately pushing a creature through misery into death for similar reasons.'

There was a moment's silence. The driftwood crackled and hissed from its bed of hot coals.

'I suppose Billy's made me aware of something I've always felt in my bones,' he went on. 'Animals aren't things or toys or distractions. They live under our mercy, and that's a hell of a responsibility.'

Again silence stood between them until she asked if he was working on a picture. Then he was glad to leave their intensity among the ash on the hearth and show her the studio. It was an even greater relief when she departed, determined to walk back alone over the fields.

He pulled on a sweater and went outside, yawning. The night was full of stars and silence. Yet behind nature, Garrison thought, was humanity. Wordsworth was right.

Chapter 19

Lights

Another curious theft at Warren Fishacre coincided with the disappearance of certain equipment and materials from the building site behind Bullen Down. Five life-size lead otters were taken from the two ponds in Fishacre's higher garden. After hearing about it from Lucy, Garrison wasn't surprised to receive a visit from PC Tapley of Mary's Haven. There were the usual questions about strangers on the cliffs and a request for him to 'keep his eyes open'. During the conversation Garrison casually mentioned the badger baiting and Rapson's persistent trespass and was told no formal complaint had been made by Mrs Ordish. The constable was a quiet-spoken young man with a level gaze and pleasant manner.

'Old Mrs Ordish is a bit of a law to herself,' he said. 'And trespass isn't the easiest of things to prove. I'd like to spend more time out here but work keeps me in town.'

'What about the baiting in Rapson's yard?' Garrison said, and the policeman looked puzzled.

'Couldn't we get them for cruelty to the dogs?' Garrison added.

Tapley puffed out his cheeks. 'Even with RSPCA support it would be difficult to hang that sort of charge on them. The yard's private property and a lot of respectable men belong to the Badger Club.'

'Do you like what they do, officer?' Garrison said.

'No,' the constable replied. 'But I'm paid to enforce the law, impartially.'

'All those thefts of metal and things,' Garrison said. 'Don't they suggest an obvious connection?'

'Rapson has never been in trouble,' the constable said. 'And I had a good look round his yard just in case he'd been sold something on the list of stolen property. To be frank, he was most helpful and from what I saw he seems to be running a straight business. There's a lot of money in scrap metal, Mr Garrison.'

Garrison sighed. 'God knows I don't want to blacken the man's name but after what he did to Billy Drew I could willingly throttle him.'

'Billy's a bit of a handful, sir,' Tapley grinned. 'He's had more than his fair share of scrapes.'

'The Rapsons hate him.'

'Without proof we're helpless to act,' said the constable. 'And Billy's tongue doesn't help. He's his own worst enemy.'

Alone once more Garrison recalled his last conversation with Ann. 'I'd like to keep chickens, David – laying hens. There's something delightful about fowls scratching round in the garden. Perhaps it's because I'm so homesick. To be honest, I miss the little things I used to take for granted...'

Garrison buttered a Ryvita and spooned some pickle onto his plate, swamping the cheese. The song of the blackbird from the overgrown tamarisk filled the evening. He built up the fire, finished his snack, put the guard in place and went out for a walk. On the marsh the mallard drakes were pursuing the ducks with a ferocity that startled him. To the north St Mary's Head Light was flashing.

*

'There's the light behind the hills in the bottom of the sky,' Aspen said.

'It's never as bright as the one across the sea,' said Hawscrag, nodding towards Start Point.

'What do they mean?' Aspen said, looking first in one direction, then the other.

Hawscrag sighed and shook her head. A typical response to mystery, Aspen thought. How often Nightworld left them inarticulate as though its beauty could only be interpreted with the senses. She gazed out to sea. The mussel reefs around Dragon Rock were exposed to the moonlight and the white water of the advancing tide. Like the disant lights coming on and off there were truths beyond the reach of thought.

The old sow was brimful of night.

'I saw Earth Mother once,' Aspen said. 'Saw her face.'

'In Sunworld?' said Hawscrag.

'No, in the Bluebell Radiance on the great steeps. She was the Radiance.'

'The dream,' Hawscrag murmured.

And isn't this a dream? thought Aspen. The night vanishes but the stone wall and the thorns remain.

Venus, the star of the evening and the morning, blazed among the shift of the constellations and dimmer stars. The two lighthouses continued to flash and Nightworld was lapped by the whisper of the sea. The small lights winking in the meadow above Old Spanish Cove were ignored by the sows.

'She speaks through the life of things,' Aspen continued.

Feeling the presence behind thought the badgers stood motionless. The gut-constricting excitement of being alive on such a night took their breath away. Mother and daughter turned and smiled at each other but the beauty had saddened Hawscrag.

'In the end,' she sighed. 'What can we give each other?'

'Comfort,' said Aspen, rubbing her snout against her dam's muzzle.

While the other sett-dwellers quietly came and went through the long hours of darkness Hawscrag and Aspen sat motionless on Froward Point. At last the new day was ready to dawn and the tide was ebbing. Waders and gulls congregated on the reefs, filling the air with their piping and clanging cries. A thousand beaks probed and levered, greedying amongst the seaweed, turning over the shellfish.

The badger sows might have been asleep sitting upright, eyes closed. Then they shook themselves, raked at their fleas, visited the scratching tree and trotted off to forage as the stragglers returned to the sett. Swiftly the last of night clouded over and the rabbits were running in all directions through the bracken. Down in Ramsons Dip the kestrel alighting on the alder branch shook free the pollen dust from the catkins. Three or four migrant wheatears pattered down and roosted in the thorn. Then a yellowhammer began to sing and the sows raised their snouts to find the light swelling grey around them. Hawscrag licked off a cluster of ladybirds from the joint of branch and twig. Aspen's nose twitched. The winteriness in the air seemed to have come from inside her and all at once she sensed danger. Among the scrub willows stood the unknown boar. He was staring down the slope over their heads out to sea and his loneliness moved Aspen. Without warning he rolled in the bracken and pawed his head and moaned.

'Come on,' Hawscrag said, butting her daughter's rump. 'Leave him be.'

'He's more pitiful than frightening,' Aspen said.

They trotted through the oaks and conifers of Warren Fishacre to drink in the stream. Impending sunrise made them uneasy but they knew the sett below the steeps was at hand. It was many-holed and ancient with tunnels and galleries running in all directions.

Before retiring they ate woodlice and dug in the shrubberies for worms. Beneath the new foxglove leaves there were also snails and bettles; but when the sun began to show the sows were safely underground in the empty sett. Before they could curl up together Birdcherry burst in.

'D-dogs,- she gasped, clambering over Hawscrag to the back of the chamber. 'Big, l-long-legged dogs. They're everywhere. One ran me d-down – knocked me off my feet and would have c-caught me if I hadn't rolled into the brambles.'

'How many are there?' Aspen asked.

'This many,' Birdcherry raised her paw despite the opaque dark of underearth. 'Five'.

The smell of dog filtered through the musk of her fear.

'Long-legs aren't yap-dogs,' Aspen said briskly. 'They can't get at us. We're quite safe here till they go away.'

'Are y-you sure?'

'Nothing's certain,' said Hawscrag. 'I'll doze until this sorts itself out one way or other.'

'Wait here and try to calm down, Birdcherry,' Aspen said. 'I'm going to have a look round.'

The first two passages ended in chambers but the third took her steeply down before it shot upwards again to an opening that framed the sky. Poking her head cautiously into the wind she found herself staring across the sea from the top of the crag. The badger path ran southwards about three feet below the clifftop before rising to the steeps in a patch of brambles. Badgers had used the path recently despite its spectacular situation high above the water; but it was hardly wide enough to take a large animal. From the overhanging clifftop the 'terrace' was invisible. Hearing men's voices and the whine of dogs Aspen turned and retreated underground.

Eric Rapson and two of his friends, the Gurney brothers, were out lamping rabbits on the downs above Hellweather Point. The sport was good although most of the rabbits taken by the lurchers were young. Throughout the night the lamps had caught startled creatures in their beams and the dogs sprinting over the turf did the rest. Every so often a scream signalled the death of a hare.

Lying tight against the straw rick by Garrowcombe Barn Cowtail's ears pricked and she swallowed nervously. The unborn cubs she carried were more than a physical burden. Against the stars the white owls drifted and Cowtail's mind sailed back to her dead mate while her loneliness grew.

Towards dawn the lamping gang climbed the side of Blackbottle Cove and the lurchers ranging ahead surprised Birdcherry who had trailed her mother and sister all the way from Froward. She came thumping down to the sett with the two dogs breathing on her rear unable to use their speed because of the thorns and bramble snarls. They were amiable creatures with no real interest in the badger.

'Pity us didn' bring a Jack,' one of the youths said.

Eric looked at his watch.

'You and the dogs stay here, Ted,' he said. 'And I'll go for dad and the terriers. We've got plenty of time. Mum'll give us a good breakfast when this is over.'

'Leave your fags,' the other Gurney said. 'And fill the flask. I'm bloody dyin' for a cup of tea.'

The sun had been up for half an hour when Eric and his father appeared. Strawberry wore one of his broadest grins.

'Talk about sly buggers,' he said, dumping the sack of digging tools and unscrewing the top of the flask. 'So you've got an old brock trapped below, have you boys? Well, a bit of spadework will warm you up. We'll have a fag and put in Jimmy.'

'We brought the van right down the cart track and tucked it away behind the old linhay,' said Eric. 'So you haven't got far to walk.'

'Get me a badger and I'll buy you half a gallon of the best back at the Ship,' Strawberry chuckled.

He was really happy. The Gurneys were good boys. They'd make excellent club members providing he could persuade them to buy a couple of Jacks to go with their lurchers. More than one dog fight had taken place on board their fishing boat off St Mary's Head. There was a lot of sporting blood in the Gurney family.

Below ground the sows were alert.

'Yap-dogs,' Birdcherry whispered and she shuddered.

For once Hawscrag had nothing to say.

'Stay put,' Aspen said and she wedged herself in the approach tunnel.

Birdcherry gave a little cry and Hawscrag said, 'Hush. We're with you.'

Jimmy came down the tunnel on his belly but at the junction he took the upward passage and as he wriggled through the darkness an idea came to Aspen. Shuffling forward she turned and faced the chamber. The shaft to her left climbed to the empty chamber the dog was approaching.

'Make a noise,' she whispered to her companions.

'But h-he'll hear us,' said Birdcherry.

'Do as I say,' Aspen said sharply.

Birdcherry needed no encouragement to sob out her fear but Hawscrag's grunted irritation made it difficult for Aspen to check her giggling despite the seriousness of the situation.

Slithering down the tunnel came the terrier and at the entrance to the sow's chamber he began to bark. But Hawscrag barred his way and snarled her challenge, forcing him to back off and lift his voice. Then Aspen sank her teeth in his rump and the startled animal loosed a squeal of pain. He would have darted back up the shaft but Aspen threw him off balance and he was pushed in the opposite direction, still yelping. Down the tunnel he ran, ricocheting off the walls in his eagerness to escape the badger's fangs in an environment where his speed and nimbleness were useless.

The sudden upward swing and the circle of light racing to meet him were baffling. Digging in his claws he scrambled clear of the sett to be confronted by the abyss. Far below him was the sea. Whimpering now Jimmy struggled to retain his balance but charging up behind, Aspen hit him with all her weight and he somersaulted into space. The cries died in his throat and he spun down into the sea. For a moment he was underwater, choking and spitting. Then he surfaced and beat at the sea with his paws. The swells lifted him gently against the crag, sliding over his head as he barked out his terror. Eventually he swam to a rock some twenty yards off-shore and clambered onto it to shake himself, run up and down, and howl.

'Quick,' Aspen called to her companions. 'Follow me, and be brave, Birdcherry.'

'What happened t-to the yap-dog?'

'He went for a swim.'

Confronted by the path across the precipice Birdcherry groaned.

'You really are more rabbit than badger,' Hawscrag said angrily. 'Aspen will lead, you go next and I'll bring up the rear. Don't look down and don't stop. The alternative is to hole up and wait to be killed.

At a steady pace Aspen walked along the path, talking all the while to her sister. Keeping her eyes fixed on Aspen's tail Birdcherry came trembling after her, wincing every time Hawscrag's snout nudged her rear. Around the buttress of mica and shale the path curved, eighty feet above the sea, until it slanted into a steep gully choked with mallow stumps and withered thrift. Birdcherry breathed a sigh of relief and scampered up into the brambles and on across steeps hidden by gorse and thorn.

The three sows did not stop running until they were on the slopes south of Warren Fishacre.

'Earth Mother certainly looks after you, Aspen,' Birdcherry panted.

Aspen smiled. Cattle were belving from the fields behind them and back towards Effords a tractor was growling into life.

After all the muffled commotion underground Jimmy's clear yelp of terror shook Strawberry.

'You don't think the crazy little heller's having a go at the bugger, do you?' he said to Eric. 'He's got enough guts to take on a bull.'

'If he fights Old Brock underground he's a goner,' Eric said.

'That last yell didn' come from the burry,' said Ted Gurney. 'I bet your dog's out, Mr Rapson. The badger must've bolted from some hole us haven't been watching and Jimmy's after him. What's that howling?' he added.

'It came from somewhere near the cliff,' said his brother. 'Look at Mitch and Fang. They can hear something.'

The lurchers were staring intently towards the sea and whining. The distant howling lifted into the hush.

'Jesus Christ,' Strawberry grated, hurrying to the edge of the cliff. The others joined him and saw Jimmy sitting on the rock below, head thrown back as he vented his misery. Lying flat on his stomach Eric parted the grass on the brink of the precipice and located the path. The fresh badger tracks told the whole story.

'There was three or four of 'em,' he said. 'They must have knocked Jimmy off the path. It's a miracle he's survived that fall.'

'Jimmy's a Rapson terrier,' said Strawberry from the ghost of a smile. 'Get down in the cove and call him, son.'

'He's one hell of a dog, Mr Rapson,' Les Gurney said. 'It's around a hundred foot sheer to the sea.'

'And he took on a whole pack of badgers,' Ted grinned.

Strawberry passed round the cigarettes and licked his lips before letting the smile light up his pug face. Failure had turned to a kind of triumph. Once it did the pub circuit of Mary's Haven and Lansworthy the story of Jimmy's underground battle and fall would assume epic proportions. The value of the Jack Russell as a stud animal would increase with his legend.

'The little devil won't come,' Eric called up to them. Reluctantly he tugged off his boots and trousers.

'It's a bit cold for a dip, idn' it boy?' Les Gurney cried and Strawberry's smile became huge. It was amazing, he thought how so much family status could be salvaged out of apparent disaster.

'You boys ought to invest in a good terrier,' he said cheerfully. 'I know someone who's got a couple of dogs that would suit you down to the ground.'

'How much, Mr Rapson?' Ted Gurney said.

'We'll talk about it over breakfast,' Strawberry smiled, placing the palms of his hands one upon the other and rubbing them gently together.

Chapter 20

Wild Daffodils

A blackbird sang in the pouring rain above the linhay where Billy was sheltering. The shower swept out to sea. Around him the young wheat glittered and the downs were washed with light. Across the next field the heifers walked to greet him and he stood among them. All along the hedges blackthorn was flowering. Walking on he put up a lark whose song seemed to spill from its feathers. Billy raised his face to the sky. Spring was a week or so away and the hedge bottoms were splashed with dandelion gold. Rooks flew to the nests at Woodash carrying sticks in their beaks.

On his tour of the setts Billy had missed very little. The courtship flight of lapwings led him to the scrapes in the meadows where they would lay their eggs. In the marshy goyal at Ramsons Dip he picked a bunch of pussy-willow for Garrison. Everywhere colour and scent were emerging from winter's drabness and the sun shining through the red-tinted elm buds was warm.

'Bleedin' hell,' he whispered. 'Bleedin' hell.'

The sea cliffs were the most fabulous place in the world, and he remembered his dad saying Devon rhymed with Heaven. Billy laughed, feeling the closeness of that special human being who had filled corners of his past with love and kindness. Clenching his teeth he was raising a fist to the sky when a strange tom-cat screech pulled him up sharp. In the grass next to the steeps a couple of jack hares were fighting. Their ears were flattened and they snarled so fiercely Billy had to smile. They tangled, kicking and biting, before separating to circle each other until the next clash sent them rolling over and over, legs blurred with the fury of the raking and kicking. And still the larks sang, Billy noted, crying with laughter. Maybe birds had no sense of humour.

On the promontory at Blackbottle Cove he found evidence that the sett had been visited by men although it had not been dug. Matches, cigarette butts and an empty Woodbine packet brought Strawberry Rapson to mind. The dog excrement, footprints and paw marks on the mound of clay confirmed his suspicions but it did not look as if badgers had been taken.

He departed puzzled, and made his way to Coastguard Cottage.

'I'll kill Strawberry one day.'
The cold certainty in the boy's voice disturbed Garrison. He had completed an abstract but felt the picture lacked something and was still angry with himself when Billy arrived.

A moment later Sheena joined them, also taking refuge from domestic anonymity, Garrison decided, coming out of himself. The sight of the girl fussing over Billy was touching. She did it without putting his dignity at risk.

Garrison sat back and let her make the tea while Billy toasted the buns over the fire.

'Everyone thinks them didakais is thievin' things like Lucy's lead otters,' Sheena said. 'I ain't so sure now. Old Strawberry's walkin' round like the bleedin' cat wot got the cream. I had a look in his yard the uvver night but everyfing's straight. He's so bleedin' foxy – a right spiv.'

167

She folded her arms and stared into the fire before continuing.

'What puzzles me is why nuffin's happened to you, Mister Garrison. Old Strawberry is capable of anyfing. So why ain't you copped one?'

'He probably doesn't regard me as a threat,' Garrison smiled. 'I'm not exactly a hard case like Billy.'

'Billy!' she snorted.

'I'll get him,' the boy said.

'You chuck another brick through his window and he'll get you – for good,' Sheena said.

Again the look on Billy's face left Garrison uneasy. His memories of childhood certainly weren't furnished with kids like him and Sheena. The boys at his school had played games and waved flags and acted like embryo patriots and respectable adults. There was something anarchic about the pair.

'Old Muvver Ordish ain't really with us,' Sheena announced. 'She's a toff and toffs are crazy about killin' animals for fun.'

'I think you're wrong about Mrs Ordish,' Garrison said. 'And a lot of toffs who hunt, shoot and fish care a great deal about animals. I knew a man who rode to hounds as often as he could and kept a houseful of cats and dogs, and he was mad about bird watching.'

'It don't make him much better than Strawberry, though,' said Billy. 'Animals idn' there to be killed because we're bored or need a bit of exercise or just like doin' it. It's wrong whether you're a toff or a bumhead like Strawberry.'

The following Saturday he took them out in the dinghy and watched them fish for pollock off December Rocks.

'Don't you fish, mister?' Billy asked.

'No, Billy. I don't want to kill anything. I suppose the war did that to me.'

Seeing the guilt flush Billy's cheeks Sheena said: 'Have you got any kids, mister?'

'I had a son,' he smiled. 'Neil. He was killed in 1945.'

'Bleedin' war,' Sheena said, and Billy fixed his eyes on Garrison as the rod bent and he reeled in a great hank of kelp. They all laughed.

After lunch Billy decided to take them on a tour of the setts between December Point and Froward. Garrison had shed some weight but was still blowing after the climb up Garrowcombe Head. The trio sat on a bank among the primroses, taking in the scene. Using his field-glasses Garrison located practically the entire guillemot colony of Hellweather Point out at sea, about half a mile offshore. Nearly a hundred birds dotted the surface. Even further out in the Channel gannets plunged from the sky in their fishing dives.

Billy was fascinated when it was his turn to hold the world in the binocular window.

'Crikey!' he murmured. 'It's as if you can touch them birds.'

'You haven't got binoculars, then, Billy? Garrison said.

'Leave off,' the boy grinned. 'Old Washbrook don't get things like this in his junk shop.'

'Or Billy would've nicked 'em,' Sheena laughed.

'Borrow them any time you go out on your sett-watch,' Garrison said.

'Honest, mister?'

'Honest, Billy?'

Halfway into the coombe at the back of Parson's Cove they were overtaken by a stranger who came up very soft-footed. He was a tall, bare-headed man in his mid-forties with a pleasant face and grey moustache. He wore overalls, an old tweed jacket and wellingtons. His accent was pure Devon and at his heels was a mean-eyed collie that growled when Sheena tried to stroke it.

'Do you know you'm trespassin'?' the man said. 'This is Warren Fishacre land.'

Then Garrison explained and the stranger introduced

himself as John Kerslake, the new farm bailiff. Walking with him down to the stream Garrison was relieved to discover they had a new ally. Kerslake was a farmer who cared about the countryside and wildlife. Lucy Ordish had chosen him from over twenty applicants for the job and listening to him air his opinions Garrison could understand why. Lucy was obviously taking everything seriously but he suspected Mrs Ordish of being more concerned with the sanctity of property than the fate of a few badgers.

By the time Froward was reached much of his gloom had lifted. Billy and Sheena were their usual chirpy selves, reminding him of Ann and Neil back in the twenties.

During the next couple of days he could not bring himself to start another picture. The thought of all the hard work and concentration was so unattractive he used every possible excuse to postpone the moment of standing before the bare canvas. Cooking occupied a lot of his time and he found a vegetable stew could be spiced up into something tasty by adding Madras curry powder. Then there was the exercise – the running and hard walking along the switchback of the clifftops in tennis shoes, cords and sweater. He also loved to idle over the downs with a picture taking shape in his thoughts and the need to get paint onto canvas becoming a compulsion. Away from houses and people he could really use his eyes. Farmwork was never intrusive. The man-made country was on one side, the wild country on the other. And they lent each other something which as an artist he found pleasing.

In the large ploughed field above Garrowcombe Barn the zigzag harrow was raising the dust, and towards Woodash a cloud of black-headed gulls followed the drill for loose grains. Everything was moving towards spring. Garrison closed his eyes on his happiness. Ann would be home when the landscape was at its best.

Blackthorn blossom covered most hedges as he wandered inland. The lane was full of South Devons driven by a boy with a stick and two work dogs. The stink of hungry-gap kale masked the fields below the big house at the head of the coombe. The hush was broken by the squeal of pigs and the crowing of cocks. Garrison climbed the hedge and dropped into one of those old neglected cider apple orchards common to the area. Walking among the mossy trunks, he tried to imagine what the place would be like in late April under all the blossom and bird song. He lit a cigarette and saw the wild daffodils. They grew each side of the stream that glided through the orchard.

Garrison sat on a fallen tree and finished his cigarette while the flowers bowed and trembled in the breeze.

Chapter 21

Billy the Kid

The grey wagtails beside the stream in Ramsons Dip had breasts the colour of wild daffodils. The birds flirted their tails and hopped from stone to stone. The day faded and an hour or so after dimpsey the badgers left the sett at Froward. On the south-facing slopes bluebell leaves were pushing through the dead bracken with spurrey and shepherd's purse. The buds of the wild hyacinth were beginning to show as hard little spear points on stubby stems. Aspen put her nose to some but lifted it again to sift through the random scents hooding the steeps. The air flowed cool around her as Nightworld exhaled its scent. Now and then she dropped her snout to sniff the rocks which were patched with moss and lichen or splashed with gull droppings. Greybob ambled on ahead, content in their relationship and his own position as sett-master. The scents pleased him and he swung his head in a way that reminded Aspen poignantly of old Cragbriar.

Winter was drawing to a close and the wind was freshening to the first gales of the spring equinox. Sow and boar touched muzzles and went into the bracken at the top of the steeps as the clouds cleared. When the animals emerged by the fence they were covered in tiny white stars of bullen blossom.

All along the edge of the pasture were corners and tunnels where night fumed. Flopped back on their haunches Aspen and Greybob scratched, holding their small, neat heads motionless with pleasure. Afterwards they scent-marked and Greybob spoke in the purring voice he reserved for her alone. Beyond his rolling haunches she could see the back of his head and the white tufts on his ears. There was something reassuring about his shape and smell and his concern for her. Beneath her pads and claws the mud gave a little but the earthy smell and vegetable stink came from the nearby field of kale. Flattening her back she followed Greybob under the lowest strand of wire and was soon munching kale stalks.

Halfway through the forage her scent told Greybob she was ready for mating.

The easterlies of early spring kept the weather fine if cool. Everywhere along the coast from St Mary's Head to the Marl estuary badgers were busy. The sea was wild and surf boiled around Dragon Rock and the gull cries seemed shriller. But after dark the steeps were of those creatures that trod Nightworld on the edge of peril.

Cowtail had given birth to three cubs in a chamber rarely used by the kin group. She did not go far from the sett and was as cautious as any sow badger with young. Fingo found her behaviour amusing.

'She's around and about like a ferret in a rabbit bury,' he grinned. 'Not so long ago it was difficult to stop her talking. Now you're lucky to get a word out of her.'

There was pollen on the cat's face and he sneezed and jabbed at his nose with a paw. The windy night and the moon breaking from the clouds made the countryside shiver and gleam. Fingo could not cope with all the movement. It excited and disturbed him and for a moment he forgot the sows as he pounced first on a blade of grass then on a leaf and finally chased his own tail in a frenzied circle that baffled Aspen and Birdcherry.

'Is it m-moon madness?' Birdcherry laughed when the cat had departed.

'Foxes are very much the same whenever it's blowing up,' Aspen said.

They rooted for bluebell bulbs on a bank thick with long shiny leaves. Then the wandering brought them to Ramsons Dip and the sight of Guelder pacing nervously among the stumps of mallow for fresh grass bedding.

'How are the cubs?' Aspen said.

'Beautiful,' came the hurried reply. 'Come and see.'

They followed her below ground and bumping along the tunnel Guelder gave a strange little double-noted cry. Eager to suckle, the cubs began to yap and soon they were struggling through Guelder's warmth to get at her teats.

Feeling like intruders Aspen and Birdcherry retreated.

'I envy her,' Birdcherry confessed, sniffing the darkness before leaving the sett.

'I told you you'll have cubs of your own – many and often,' Aspen smiled.

'Do you really see it in the y-yet-to-come?' Birdcherry whispered.

'Yes, and I feel it in my heart.'

She led her sister up the steeps and the wind blowing strong off the sea lifted hanks of their fur and pushed it back the wrong way. The surf was roaring but not loud enough to muffle the chattering cry of the boar. And it was answered by a loud screech so close the sows were startled. Ashblacken charged over the turf on the edge of Down End and threw himself at the pale stranger.

The skirmish was brief and furious. The boars locked together and cart-wheeled down the slope before they separated. Picking himself up Ashblacken ran off, shaking and staggering a little. Catching their scent the stranger turned and stared at the sows from a look of distraction. Then he cried

174

and rubbed his head on the grass as if he were trying to rid himself of something. On impulse Aspen called to him but he trotted away.

'W-what do you make of him?' Birdcherry asked.

'He's very unhappy,' said Aspen.

Wool spiked on the fence fluttered in the moonlight and the wire strands vibrated. Catching the stink of man the sows ran across the steeps and disappeared into a gorse thicket as Eric Rapson and Ted Gurney came clumsily down the slope to fish for bass from the cove below.

'No dogs,' Aspen breathed. The wind in the gorse was a soft rushing sound. Beside her Birdcherry was panting.

'There's nothing to fear,' Aspen said gently.

'There's always s-something to fear,' came the low reply.

But night held no terror for Billy Drew. He had climbed down the wash-house roof below his bedroom window while his mother, another woman and two men were playing cards in the parlour. Leaving the town he had walked the lanes to Woodash with the wind roaring in the trees and moonlight swimming over the fields. The badgers would be out treading their paths and reading the smell of the sea as he read it with dilated nostrils. His hand strayed to the handle of the sheath knife hanging from his belt, then to the catapult in his back pocket. The night was wild and it brought a grin of joy to his face.

Sometimes he identified individual smells: the unpleasant reek of the kale, the scent of primroses, fox musk. Standing on the third bar of the gate he could see the Channel holding the moonlight. Jumping down he began to run, whooping softly in the back of his throat but the sight of Rapson's van drawn up onto the grassy verge at the bend by the lane leading down to Garrowcombe halted him. Crouching he searched the darkness under the hedge for any sign of life. In the short silences between gusts he heard the creak of metal contracting and venturing forward he put his hand on the bonnet. It was slightly warm. Billy frowned and climbed onto the hedge-bank. The small dark shapes in the fields leading to the sea were sheep. Nothing moved except the light racing over the countryside to lose itself in the brilliance of the water. Satisfied he took out his knife and went around the van slashing and stabbing the tyres. The sudden sharp hiss of escaping air left his face hard and blank. He recalled the badger cowering against the cliff and the look on Strawberry's face, and his blows became more savage.

Eventually the knife was sheathed and Billy picked up a large stone and began breaking the headlamps and windows, sobbing with anger. The noise woke the farm dogs at Woodash. Lights came on in the house and Billy took to the fields and made for home. He was crowing now.

The party was still in progress and the couples were dancing to a tune from the gramophone. Silhouettes moved on the curtains. Billy washed his wellingtons in the galvanized iron bath full of rainwater before climbing up to his bedroom. Moments later he was under the blankets reliving the pleasure of wrecking the van as sleep took him.

'Have you been up to your bloody tricks?' grated the familiar voice. 'Have you? Have you?'

His mother was shaking him but his thoughts were in disarray. The badger's black and white face was pressed against his own. Its breath came in short gasps.

'Bloody have you?'

Mrs Drew had him by the front of his pyjama jacket. A wing of blonde hair had fallen over one eye and she was pale with temper in the candlelight. Billy groaned.

'The police are downstairs and me in this state,' she said, flinging him back onto the mattress. 'They want to know if you had anything to do with Rapson's van.'

'What van?'

The flat of her hand caught him across the mouth and her wedding ring drew blood.

'It was you, wasn't it? No one else would be mazed enough to do a thing like that. I hope they bang you away in reform school.'

176

'The Rapsons kill badgers,' Billy said.

'So what?' She pulled her dressing gown across her bosom and lit a cigarette. 'Bloody badgers! They're only animals. The world's full of human beings. You don't give a damn about your own mother or anyone else except that little cockney tart.'

He gazed at the ceiling where her shadow swayed.

'Was it you, Billy?'

'Yes,' he said. 'You know they made me watch them kill a badger the other day.'

'You open your mouth to the law and I'll kill you. Now get dressed and come downstairs. You weren't out last night. Understand?'

'Yes.' He looked at her and blurted: 'If dad was here he'd bleedin' slaughter the Rapsons and them blokes you had in the parlour.'

'They were just friends,' she said, averting her eyes as the colour rose in her cheeks. 'Anyway, your dad idn' here. I'm on me own and you're no help – you thievin' little swine.'

Her voice broke and she pushed her fingers up through her hair. Billy closed his eyes. He heard the door click and her footsteps on the stairs then voices from below. He swung his legs over the edge of the bed and began to pull on his clothes.

'It was PC Tapley,' he told Sheena and Garrison at Coast-guard Cottage that afternoon. 'He idn' a bad bloke.'

'You didn't own up, did you?' Sheena said.

''Course not. I idn' daft.'

'You're jokin'! What you done last night was crazy. Old Strawberry will skin you alive.'

'The police believed mum,' Billy said, eyeing Garrison.

The man had little to say. He recognized a code of behaviour which was to him as alien as it was baffling. Considering Rapson's activities it was probably poetic justice, but it alarmed him to think a ten-year-old capable of pursuing such a ruthless vendetta.

'You don't get on with people, do you, Billy?' he said,

thinking it was probably the biggest understatement of his life.

'You sound like mum,' the boy said sullenly.

'Come on, Bill,' Sheena said. 'Mr Garrison's on our side.'

'Bleedin' people,' Billy growled. 'Bleedin' Japs. Bleedin' Yanks. Animals don't hurt you. They love you when you're kind to 'em.'

'So do people, Billy,' Garrison said. 'Perhaps you ought to give your mum a chance. It can't be easy for her living alone.'

'She idn' alone,' Billy sneered. 'She's never alone.'

'And they got a down on him at school,' said Sheena.

'But it's nothing to do with him, is it?' Garrison pressed. 'Only fools go round asking for trouble.'

The children exchanged glances.

'If you keep misbehaving in class and giving teachers hell you aren't going to be very popular,' Garrison said, and feeling he had gone far enough he suddenly clapped his hands and added: 'Look, why don't I make you two a jug of cider shandy and let you take me on a nature ramble.'

Billy sniffed and drew his sleeve across his nose.

'Thanks, Mr Garrison,' Sheena said. 'We'll have the cider but the ramble's out 'cos I got my paper round to do and Billy helps.'

'Yes, of course; I keep forgetting,' Garrison smiled.

'You are growing a beard,' Sheena grinned.

Garrison set his fingertips dancing self-consciously over his stubble and nodded.

Chapter 22

Dragon Rock

The easterly gales were followed by settled weather, and the last days of March were so still and sunny the dog fox kennelling beneath the sycamores was reluctant to get up to urinate. The animal's name was Moonscritch. He lay, nose to tail, in a circle of drowsiness hoping the ache in his bladder would go away. Then a cry stiffened his ears, but it was far off and left him undisturbed.

Billy shouted again.

'You're a noisy devil,' Sheena said. 'Why d'you keep on bawlin'?'

'I feel good,' he said and he threw back his head and roared again.

'Blimey! What d'you do when you feel bad?'

'Leave off,' Billy said, feathering the oars and narrowing his eyes against the glare of the sea.

'Where we going?' Sheena said. She leaned back and draped her arms over the stern of the dinghy to trail her fingers in the water.

'Dragon Rock.'

'You promised Mr Garrison we wouldn't go too far. Garrowcombe and back, you said.'

'Dragon Rock idn' too far – not on a day like this.'

'Ain't the sky big,' Sheena whispered.

Billy pulled on the oars and made no reply. It was the most perfect Sunday afternoon he could remember and they were going to try for congers in the water around Dragon Rock where many ships had come to grief. Old Garrison was a great bloke, Billy thought; dad would have liked him a lot. He wasn't teetotal and he always kept his word and no other grown-up cared as much about the badgers.

The blades broke the surface with twin 'cloops' and the dinghy surged forward on the ebb tide.

'We can use the boat to come out for gulls' eggs,' Billy said. 'Dragon Rock's like a bloody great hen house in May. We'll get baskets of 'em and make a bleedin' fortune.'

'What d'you want to be when you grow up, Billy?'

'An outlaw,' he said. 'Robin Hood – or an Indian chief.'

'Not Tarzan?'

'No. I don't like his American accent. It idn' right.'

'Johnny Weismuller can't half swim.'

'So could my dad,' said Billy. 'He could have been Olympic champion. He could've beat bleedin' Johnny Weismuller.'

'My dad couldn't have,' she said, lidding her eyes against the glare. 'My dad has a pot and can't swim a stroke.'

Out of the shelter of the headland the calm was broken into bottle-glass swells.

'Are you really going to marry me, Bill?' she said, eyes wide open.

''Course,' he murmured with absolute sincerity. 'We'll live in a tree house on Froward Point.'

Staring into the water Sheena saw her facsimile broken on the surface and waited for the calm to reassemble the jigsaw. Landward the headlands and points were printed on haze, wonderfully insubstantial. Light fed on light. The sea threw back the light of the sky only to receive it again. A luminosity prevailed which even the brightest winter day could never rival.

'D'you ever think about old Strawberry?' Billy said, apropos of nothing at all.

'Yeah,' said Sheena. 'I think he's a bleedin' rat.'

'No, I don't mean like that. D'you ever think what makes him do them 'orrible things to badgers?'

Sheena shook her head.

'I don't get it. He loves his dogs but he can do in badgers like they – they –'

'What's that bird?' Sheena said, coaxing him away from crisis.

'Razorbill,' Billy said. 'He's got a bill like a pair of secateurs. Have a gander through the bins.'

It was nearly teatime when they reached the leeward side of Dragon Rock and made a landing carrying the fishing tackle and the rucksack full of picnic ingredients. The tide was still dropping and Billy made sure the mooring rope had plenty of slack. Seabirds exploded in an angry mass to circle and scream as the children clambered onto the broad ledge that was littered with cormorants' nests.

'It's ruddy creepy,' Sheena said.

Billy sniffed and climbed steadily to the top of the taller of the two rock towers. It was guano-caked and smelt of dead fish.

'Is it safe, Bill?' Sheena cried.

'Safe as houses,' he said. 'Pretend you're climbing the stairs like a monkey. Come on. The other side's great.'

'All this bird shit don't half pong.'

Out of the shadows on the summit she felt safer. The sun was losing its warmth but the late afternoon was bright.

'We'll go back soon,' Billy said.

She looked at him. 'Not in the dark.'

'No – it's light for ages now, not like winter.'

'What you goin' to do wive the congers?'

181

'Flog 'em to the chip shop in Market Street. They cut 'em up, dip 'em in batter and pretend it's cod.'

'You're havin' me on.'

He grinned. 'They say you can catch really big ones off here. There's these deep holes between the rocks where giants bigger than pythons lie waitin' for dead sailors and fishermen.'

'Don't,' she shuddered.

The seaward slopes were more hospitable. Broad ledges of rock and soil and bird droppings, hackled with salt grass and mallow, fell to a massive, barnacle-encrusted terrace. Between the base of the rock and the nearest reef was a black stretch of water.

'I don't like it here, Billy,' Sheena said.

'Well I do,' he growled. 'Follow me down and get out the grub. You'll feel OK with some bread and strawberry jam inside you. And I got a tin of condensed milk.'

The current was running hard in the Rips, swirling and whirlpooling over the skerries.

'It's too creepy for words,' Sheena whispered.

But she unpacked the food and drink while he sorted out the hand-lines and baited the hooks. Around the stacks and pinnacles the gulls yelled their protest. The sky was full of wings.

'Them birds,' Sheena said.

'They'll quiet down,' Billy grinned; but it was a long time before any sort of peace returned.

He threw the weighted line and watched the bait vanish into the depths. Driftwood was scattered along the terrace and Sheena began to gather it as if she had read his mind.

'We'll have a fire,' he said. 'And toast the buns.'

Oystercatchers settled on the exposed reefs below the two large stacks known as the Manacles. Watching Billy fish Sheena cheered up. The late afternoon was golden and the tide was about to turn. Across Marlham Bay the sun was huge and blood-red over the South Hams. Out to sea the sprat boats were heading home. Further out, beyond the scallop dredgers, the big steam trawlers returning from the Scilly Isles were laying their smoke on the horizon. A rock pipit fluttered above the Rips towards the mainland.

'On a desert island,' Sheena said and Billy looked up into her smile.

'We could live out here,' he said. 'I could build a hut.'

A seal barked and the sound carried along the surface of the water.

'There he is,' Billy cried, pointing. 'Amongst the tangle by the big rock over there. See his head?'

Sheena adjusted the binoculars and nodded.

'The water's dripping from his whiskers,' she said. 'He ain't half lovely.'

A sense of spiritual well-being gripped Billy. They were hidden from the mainland by the lie of the rock, and the sea and sky seemed forever. He was conscious of the endlessness of things.

'Shall I light the fire?' Sheena said.

'Not yet. Let's have one of they cheese and pickle sandwiches.'

The sun was lower now and Sheena thought of the long row back to Hard Sands. When she voiced her anxiety Billy told her the tide would be with them. He didn't want to put a full stop to the day. Catching congers didn't matter. It was something else.

They heard the chugging of a crab boat in the Rips and glanced up as the gulls took to the air again.

'They old black-backs don't sound like birds,' he said. 'They'm more dog than gull.'

'I'm going to light the fire,' said Sheena. 'When it goes out we're leaving.'

The evening was unbelievably calm. Built on a base of dried grass the fire burnt with a lot of smoke. Birds settled and the piping of oystercatchers was soft and liquid against the increasing noise of the Rips where currents were meeting.

'The tide's turned,' Billy said. 'I'd better take in a bit of slack on the mooring rope.'

'How long are we stayin' here?' Sheena said.

183

'Just till the sun goes down,' he replied, clambering up the ledges.

'You're worse than Robinson bleedin' Crusoe.'

Hauling over the flat summit Billy looked down and saw the mooring rope trailing free in the tide race. The boat had gone and the chill in his stomach grew as he scanned the waters towards Hellweather Point. Half a mile away the dinghy was turning broadside to the current and drifting swiftly out to sea. Off Old Spanish Cove a crabber was making for Mary's Haven. Billy waved and shouted and the figures in the stern waved back.

'Bring up the bins, Sheena,' Billy cried. 'Quick.'

'What's up?' she gasped, passing over the case.

'The bleedin' boat's broke loose. It's out there.'

He focused the binoculars. The three fishermen gathered round the wheelhouse of the crab boat were still waving but it was difficult to tell who they were with their sou'westers pulled down tight on their heads. Sacks covered the name on the stern.

'I bet it's the bleedin' Gurneys,' Billy said in a stony voice. 'Their boat's that colour. Them and Eric Rapson.'

Pulling in the rope he found it had been cut.

'The bleedin' swines,' Sheena whispered. 'What are we goin' to do, Billy?'

'Light a fire up here – wave and shout. Someone'll see us. There's a lot of boats about.'

The sea was creaming over the reefs but the scene was no longer romantic and beautiful. The sun had gone and above the afterglow the evening star was hardening to brilliance. Start Point lighthouse began to flash, and on the lift of panic Billy searched the approaches for vessels with dusk gathering off the Channel and ships' lights showing.

'It'll be dark soon,' Sheena said.

'They'll come lookin' for us,' said Billy. 'Mr Garrison will put things right. Come on, help build up the fire.'

Putting his own unease aside he wrapped an arm round her shoulders. She was shivering.

184

'Sheen,' he said. 'Nothing's goin' to happen to us. Someone will see the fire.'

'What about Mr Garrison's boat?'

'Forget it. He won't mind so long as we're safe.'

It became darker. More stars appeared and lights twinkled across the water. The fire burnt down and soon it was too dark to search for wood.

'What we goin' to do?' Sheena said.

'Wait for them to come,' said Billy. 'Let's get down under and have some condensed milk.'

'Ain't you afraid, Bill?'

'What of?'

'Them congers and fings?'

'No,' he said. 'I got me sheath knife. I wish I'd brought a torch.'

Froward Point was black and the Monterey pines against the sky were even blacker. The cold brought the children together in a huddle. The evening star had dimmed but the pole star burnt brightly amongst the haze of constellations, and Start Light continued to throw out its beam. Other lights speckled the sea but none came close to Dragon Rock. Almost drowned by the rumble of the Rips the gulls cried as they fidgeted on their roosts.

'They ain't goin' to find us tonight,' Sheena said from a spasm of shivering. 'Crikey – I'm bloody freezin'.'

'That's odd,' Billy said, gazing intently out to sea. 'Them lights are goin' out.'

One by one the lights of the passing ships were fading and disappearing. Then Start Light flashed, dimmed and vanished.

'Bleedin' heck!' Sheena whispered.

'Fog,' Billy said, clenching his teeth in an effort to stop them chattering.

'They'll never find us now,' Sheena said in more of a whimper than a voice.

The gulls had fallen silent. Billy and Sheena stared out to sea, the hair stiffening on the back of their necks. A faintly

185

luminous bank of mist was advancing over the Channel, and Start Point's fog warning began to boom. A solitary light remained for a moment bobbing on the bay but that, too, was engulfed.

Now the cold had an eerie texture and the fog spread until it spilled around Dragon Rock, rolled over it and flowed on to billow up the cliffs.

'Billy,' Sheena sobbed.

On all sides foghorns sounded, some close at hand. The ghostly greyness was total. It carried the damp mouldy reek of the ocean.

'It's like sitting in a cloud,' Billy said and Sheena pressed her face to the front of his pullover, too cold and miserable to speak.

Presently the tops of Dragon Rock's twin towers emerged and the children were looking over a vast silver fleece. Landward it was still climbing the steeps.

Sheena lifted her face to the stars.

'Billy, we're in the sky. We're on top of the clouds.'

The tide race continued to roar and the foghorns sang out to each other. The stars seemed closer now. Gazing up at them Billy was unafraid. Start Lighthouse droned.

Towards midnight the Mary's Haven lifeboat returned to the fishing port with the dinghy in tow. Sheena's foster parents and Billy's mother stood apart from Garrison on the outer harbour slipway, barely visible in the mist, and Constable Tapley shuttled between the little groups and the solitary figure. There were no recriminations; children and boats were integral to Mary's Haven life, and the sea was forever leaving gaps in the community.

The constable stood before Garrison, his face yellow in the light of his lamp.

'The rope was cut,' he said simply.

'Cut?'

'With a knife.'

186

'And the children?'

'The boat was empty.'

'Oh Christ.'

'We mustn't think the worst, Mr Garrison. Billy's got more lives than a cat.'

'How's his mother taking it?'

'Bad. She's a strange woman.'

'In what way?'

Behind the conversation were the bow lights and masthead lamps of departing trawlers, blurred by the fog. It was a curious backdrop, hinting callously at the unfeeling continuity of nature.

'She loves Billy but can't cope with him.'

'Things might have been different if her husband had survived the war,' said Garrison.

'Drew was a gambler, Mr Garrison. He didn't spend much time with his family and she had a lot to put up with by all accounts. He neglected her and she didn' know from one week to the next where the housekeeping was coming from.'

'I see,' Garrison said.

He walked Mrs Drew home along the mist-wreathed streets.

'They idn' drowned,' she said and the certainty in her voice saddened him.

'I'm sure you're right,' he said.

'I mean it,' she went on, detecting an unwelcome hollowness in his words.

'I idn' no angel but Billy gives me a hard time.'

Their footsteps beat against the silence of the houses.

'He blames me for his dad's death. It's not fair. Harry never really loved anyone but his bloody self. He preferred his mates and his beer and the horses to us. I was just a convenience – like the armchair when he was drunk.'

'I'm sorry,' Garrison said.

'Are you?' she said coldly. 'Why? Can you put it right? Billy loves his rabbits and the Nelson girl and nature. I'm not even

187

on the list. I love him but that idn' enough. I wish he'd never been born.'

She was weeping when she broke away from Garrison and ran off into the darkness. He let her go, contemplating the walk back to Coastguard Cottage with dismay. It was not just the fog and his weariness but the sense of loss like an illness. How could the children vanish like that? He tried to puzzle it out as he stumbled and slithered along the cliff path. They couldn't have gone swimming. Even Billy would have found the water too cold. Perhaps they had been picked up out to sea by a foreign trawler; but why was the rope cut?

At home he fed driftwood to the fire. His clothes and hair were grey with fog as if he had walked through cobwebs. The cold had got into him but the scotch gave the coffee a kick and the flames leaping up the chimney were pleasant enough. Then on a heart-chilling lurch of misery he saw Billy and Sheena crouching at the hearth, and beyond them other ghosts – Neil, young Ann, boyish faces in the landing craft driving onto the Normandy beach. Beyond them all were the trawler lights dimming in the fog and the sound of Mrs Drew's high heels clicking on the cobbles.

He glanced at his watch and yawned. Four o'clock. He opened the door and sniffed at the fog. Out on the Channel vessels were sounding their horns. Garrison lit a cigarette and buttoned himself into his reefer again before setting off for Froward Point. It was nearly low tide and he was determined to search all the coves and beaches. God! – he'd kill the little devils if he found them curled up beside a fire in one of Billy's secret places. The thought made him smile. That would be typical of Billy. But the cut rope? Maybe they'd run away and the rope and the drifting boat were part of the cover-up.

Shortly after dawn the fog began to lift and thin. Sunrise was amazing with headlands and rocks bursting from greyness.

The horizon remained invisible but between the land and the next fogbank lying stationary on the water, the sea gleamed. Garrison trudged up through the trees of Warren Fishacre and came over the fields to the meadow below King Arthur's Tower.

Mist was still streaming off the sea as he stepped out of the pines onto Froward Point and stood on the sloping turf above the blackthorns. The incoming tide was pouring over the reefs and Dragon Rock rose dark and jagged in the morning light. Around it a great flock of gulls wheeled and screamed, and something else was moving on the nearer of the two towers. Shading his eyes Garrison saw the little figure waving both arms. Beside it was another figure in a plum-coloured sweater standing motionless and holding something to its face.

The sweater was enough to set Garrison jumping up and down and yelling. Sheena would have him in the binoculars and sure enough when he had controlled himself he saw her waving too. Towards the horizon the lifeboat cruised along the edge of the second fogbank. No other vessel was in sight.

Garrison turned into the trees and began to run.

Chapter 23

Showers

Billy and Sheena were brought back to Mary's Haven in a Greenaway crab boat to become local celebrities. Their picture and story were in the national press but police enquiries were again unsuccessful and the severed rope remained a mystery despite obvious links with the Gurneys and the Rapsons. Garrison was disturbed by the depths of malice surrounding the affair but the excitement was short-lived as the April sun brought the bloom back to the coast.

Near the top of the crag under Hellweather Copse the buzzards were at their bulky nest. Day after day they quartered the countryside, drifting on thermals and crying their cat-calls. Sometimes Hebog descended to nail a young rabbit to the turf.

Foraging in the deep coombes the sett-dwellers of Froward carried feelers of goose grass on their coats and starlight in their eyes. Hawscrag accompanied Aspen and Birdcherry, and all three sows paused beneath the hedgerow saplings to place their snouts to the coltsfoot which a fox had watered.

'And Fingo has been this way,' Aspen said, crinkling her nose at the pungent odour of tom cat.

She was first through the hedge where the nettles stood taller than the dandelions. Clouds passed over the stars and rain fell in big heavy drops which holed the dust on the edge of the wheat. The sows had almost reached the other side of the field when they detected the scent of Ashblacken. The rain stopped and moments later they met the creature himself in one of his bumptious moods. He was unable to forget his disastrous skirmish with the pale stranger and thought the Froward animals were secretly laughing at him.

'I've just seen off a couple of big old boars,' he huffed. 'Talk about a fight.'

'Seen off?' said Hawscrag in her most mordant tone.

'Yes. They won't cross my path again in a hurry,' Ashblacken said.

Hawscrag walked round him, her nostrils dilating and contracting.

'How odd!' she said. 'You can't smell them.'

'Perhaps they were scentless,' Aspen said innocently.

'It was some time ago,' Ashblacken said, and he glared at her. 'They weren't eager to get to grips.'

'And how is Guelder?' Hawscrag enquired.

'The twins should be above ground soon,' he said, answering her real question.

'Cowtail has three cubs,' said Birdcherry.

'That fox,' Ashblacken said. 'I wouldn't have her stinking out my sett.'

'She's a good friend,' said Aspen.

'She smells,' he said.

'So did Cragbriar, come the end,' said Hawscrag.

'But he was a badger,' said Ashblacken.

'A badger who smelt like a ripe sheep,' Hawscrag said as unwilling as ever to be cheated of the last word.

Boar and sows parted company on less than friendly terms.

'Pompous fool!' Hawscrag growled. She tried to keep up

191

with her daughters on the steep flanks of Garrowcombe. 'Ashblacken takes himself much too seriously. He really is a rabbit brain who would run a mile if he met anything with sharp teeth.'

'Guelder's cubs are l-lovely,' said Birdcherry.

'All cubs are lovely,' said Aspen.

'Ashblacken wasn't lovely when he was a cub,' said Hawscrag. 'He was a podgy little whelp forever grizzling round his mother's paps.'

Another scent lay on the grass close to the fence on Woodash Down. It was a cold scent, like fear, Birdcherry thought. The badger musk had soured to something the sows were reluctant to recognize. Trotting forward Aspen saw the lifeless body in the snare. The frenzy of terror had tightened the noose round the creature's neck and left her horribly twisted on the lowest strand of barbed wire. She had dug in vain and had left her claw marks on the fence post before perishing.

'Briarfrost,' Aspen said sadly. 'Not long dead.'

'Oh dear,' said Birdcherry. 'She w-was so young.'

'With Earth Mother now, and neither young nor old,' said Hawscrag.

But life that is ended so easily is so precious, though Aspen. To breathe the scents of Nightworld and run free is the great joy. What is to come will look after itself.

The snare was fixed to the barbed wire so there was no stake to dig free, and Briarfrost had to remain with the snarl of agony of her face while the sows paraded slowly up and down before her, heads bowed, moaning their lament. Another shower fell, pattering on leaves and grasses. Then the cloud drifted seawards and the badgers lifted their muzzles and saw the stars blazing above them.

The dead sow was found by Mrs Ordish whose after-lunch stroll was her first since her return from the Caribbean. Rabbits were vanishing into the thickets on the steeps as she

192

crouched and contemplated the tragedy. The afternoon was warm and butterflies were in frantic flight over the bracken.

'Now that is shameful,' the old lady whispered to herself, and she was white-lipped with anger by the time she had walked to Coastguard Cottage.

'It's not just the poor creature,' she explained to Garrison. 'The thought of those louts tramping over my land while I'm asleep makes my flesh crawl.'

Mrs Ordish took coffee and departed lamenting the stupidity of the law which regarded trespass as a civil matter. The loose hasp on the door rattled as the wind lifted off the sea to clear the clouds from the sky. He made a fresh cup of Camp coffee although the taste was an unpleasant reminder of the superiority of the real stuff he drank whenever he was in Switzerland.

A ship's morse was bleeping across the music on the wireless. The day was warm enough for him to sit outside under the tamarisks where the blackbird had nested. The male bird was singing his refrain from the top of the clothes-pole. Smoke from ships blotted the horizon and gulls came and went on a flash of white wings. But behind the sheer physical presence of the place and the season was the image of the dead badger in the snare. Yet he was acutely conscious of the natural forces embracing life, and, above all, the greenness pushing through the ruin of winter. There was also the enigma of the inextinguishable which Ann's voice whispered in her letters.

Garrison lit a cigarette. How barren everything would be without her. He squinted against the eye-tiring glare of the sea. The picture would have to wait. It was one of those irresistible days of early April. He got up lazily and stretched. Small waves were crisping on the beach and he came down to the water's edge and pulled off his shoes and socks. The coldness was a shock but he let the water fizz around his ankles. The sand below the shingle banks had been left flawless by the outgoing tide. It was littered with empty cockle shells.

By the time he had paddled up and down the length of Hard Sands Garrison's feet were numb and he hobbled painfully up the rough stone track to the cottage. The tall slim girl from Warren Fishacre was on the lawn tossing bread to the birds. She wore a blue, polka dot, cotton skirt and a white blouse, and her legs were bare. Unaware of Garrison standing close by she dipped into her bag and continued to scatter the pieces across the lawn while the gulls wheeled and the blackbird refused to be interrupted.

Alive with all the urgency of youth, Garrison thought.

He smiled, but the tight sinus pain warned him he was close to tears. Again the ghost of the young Ann came noiselessly to mind.

'Lucy,' he said but for a moment it was Ann who turned and swung through the grass. Then his head dropped and he waited for reality to reassemble around him.

The girl had buried the snared badger. Sitting in deckchairs they talked about the 'Rapson problem' and the tide turned with clouds massing out to sea and the air cooling. An hour or so later he walked her along the cliffs as far as Garrowcombe and watched her run down the hillside. Clouds covered the sun and he slipped into his reefer jacket. Lucy was climbing the far side of the coombe and she did not look back. Garrison strolled over to the barn and stood under the straw rick waiting for the shower to fall. The elms were gathering the wind in their top branches and the gulls were crying as they always did before rain. Garrison reached for his cigarettes but changed his mind and kept his hands in his pockets. Big drops smacked onto the rick and became a downpour. Half the landscape was in shadow, the rest in sunlight. A rainbow sprang from Hellweather Point to Firebeacon Point, and the shower was drifting on, leaving the fields of young wheat glistening. Garrison drew a deep breath of primrose scent and the darker fragrance of rain-soaked leaves and grasses. It reminded him of the smell of Ann's hair when they had come in wet off the rainswept Paris streets straight into the love-making.

Ewes and their lambs moved out from the shelter of the hedges and he walked among them, trying to recall the music that would bring the episode alive. One of his back teeth began to ache and he closed his mouth and breathed through his nose. Stepping out of the barn Fingo ran towards him, mewing, his tail upright and curled at the tip.

'Come here, puss,' Garrison said, stooping and holding out his hands, but the cat would only come so far, and whenever Garrison reached for him Fingo retreated with flattened ears.

'See you tonight at the door,' Garrison smiled, 'unless you're getting better cuisine at Fishacre.'

Another shower threatened. The man turned up his coat collar and headed for home, wondering if he would find the energy to drag himself off to the pub after dinner to stop the loneliness developing into one of his black moods.

Fingo studied Garrison's departures before sniffing the wet grass and licking his lips. The elms murmured and the cat's ears pricked forward and he loped along the cattle-creep to the path at the top of the steeps. Ahead of him the young rabbits were slow to bolt and he pursued a couple out of sheer devilment. Rain slanted across the sun again and when Fingo blinked the drops out of his eyes he missed the first house martins winging in from the sea at the end of their migration flight.

Where the bramble and blackthorn gave way to turf the thrift was showing small pink flowers that twitched in the breeze. Some ewes and lamps had found a gap in the fence and were grazing the lower slopes. Fingo ran on, trying to decide which farm to visit for the favours of the promiscuous shes. Leaving the path he cut over Down End and took the track up to the old army camp. High above the downs Skyhook saw the tiny dark shape running between the nissen huts. The peregrine tiercel also noted in awesome detail oystercatchers flying low over the water, the gulls and fulmars above Garrowcombe Head and the house martins flickering around the roofs of Effords farmhouse. Dropping with a hiss of pinions Skyhook took one of the house martins and carried it lifeless back to the eyrie in Old Spanish Cove. Here the falcon was sitting at the scrape on four red-brown eggs and she screamed as her mate brought in the food. Then Skyhook flapped up to his look-out rock on the crag.

Lying in the bracken opposite the nesting ledge Tony Rapson lit a cigarette and waited for the hen bird to stretch her wings and take a short exercise flight. The boy had already planned his route from the beach to the scrape. The climb did not look difficult but the rock was crumbly in places and there was a bit of an overhang at the top.

When he had finished the cigarette he scampered up the steeps keeping a wary eye open for adders. At the fence Kerslake nearly had him but the boy was quick and darted into the trees of Warren Fishacre before he could be collared.

'Don't come back,' Kerslake shouted. 'I know who you are, so keep off this land unless you want trouble.'

'Silly old bugger,' Tony bawled, fishing out another cigarette.

The peregrines were climbing together and calling their raw, grating cries. Kerslake came down to the stream as the rain pattered through the conifers. The crackle of undergrowth told him the boy was still running, but Kerslake was in no hurry. He walked up the stream to the pond below the terraced gardens and the house. The martins were hawking the water and closing their beaks on winged insects. Cello music drifted across the lawns from one of the downstairs windows.

The shower died and he came up the drive past the farm and out-buildings to the lane and the farmhouse. All above the nests under the eaves martins swooped and darted; and standing in the middle of the lane chattering his teeth at them was Fingo.

'Get on out of it,' Kerslake cried, clapping his hands. Stray cats took chickens and ducklings and urinated on the sacks in the barn.

Fingo laid back his ears, made as if to scramble up the hedge-bank, changed his mind and ran up the lane. Next time I do the rounds, Kerslake thought, I'll carry the gun.

On Froward Point Fingo was safe. The wet blackthorn blossom was mounded white against the deep blue of the Channel. He wormed his way through it and entered Big Sett, his nose working to separate Aspen's scent from the smell of the others.

At last he found her curled beside Greybob in one of the upper chambers. The cat was tired but felt in need of company. Furthermore he was puzzled.

'Are you asleep, Aspen?' he whispered.

'No,' she said. 'But Greybob is so please speak quietly.'

'I can't work them out,' said the cat. 'Men, I mean. Some speak softly with kindness in their voices, like him down by the sea. Others shout with death in their words. It's odd. Anyway,' he sniffed as he lay down and began grooming his forepaws, 'I thought you might know.'

'I don't Fingo,' said Aspen. 'Sometimes I'm just as puzzled as you.'

'Do you suppose there's a place somewhere just for cats and badgers and other animals, and no men?'

Again Aspen could not answer him.

Dimpsey darkened to twilight and the evening star burnt hard between clouds. The sett-dwellers emerged and took the paths to forage. The pines were shivering when Aspen and Greybob stepped from under them onto the steeps. Bats quartered the night for moths and through the stillness the badgers could hear the grunts of hedgehogs and the drumming of rabbits. After lifting their muzzles the boars and sows dug out bluebell bulbs and bracken rhizomes which were devoured with gusto.

Suddenly Greybob's hackles lifted and he said: 'He's back.'

The pale stranger was on the slope against the fence. He was shaking his head and moaning. Greybob started forward and growled but the intruder turned and ambled away.

197

'I'm sure we could find room for him in Big Sett,' Aspen said.

'Perhaps,' said Greybob, 'but he would have to take his place with the other boars and acknowledge my position.'

'Of course,' Aspen said solemnly.

'What c-can be wrong with him?' said Birdcherry.

'He's touched,' Greybob said in a gruff voice. 'Moon-mad, crazy – call it what you like. If he keeps creeping up on us like that I'll have to finish him.'

'That would be a pity,' said Aspen, and she met his gaze without flinching.

'Remember Aspen is m-moonborn,' Birdcherry said placatingly. 'She has the wisdom.'

'She is also a sow,' Greybob said from the remains of a growl.

Sunrise was close when Aspen's companions disappeared into the sett, but she sat for a while on the lawn at the end of the Point. Start Light was flashing and as usual other lights moved slowly across the sea. No other creature stood between herself and the night whose beauty seemed to speak directly to her spirit. The solitude reached up into something profound and it was glorious to be there under the stars for like all animals Aspen never took the living world for granted. The solitude was more than a place at peace. It was another lifetime walled in with sky and scent. So, the wonder she felt and the beauty of the sea were a reflection of the wonder of creation.

'What does Nightworld s-say to you, Aspen?' said Birdcherry's voice.

'It says nothing,' Aspen replied.

'B-but you are moonborn,' Birdcherry persisted. 'You've seen Earth Mother's face.'

'That is her face,' Aspen said, nodding at the starry sky. 'My face is her face and so is yours. So are the trees and fields and cliffs.'

'Where are we going?' Birdcherry said miserably.

Aspen turned and licked her sister's muzzle.

'Isn't this enough?'

'I don't understand,' Birdcherry sighed.

'You don't need to understand. Look and listen, hold the smell of it all in your nostrils, feel the wind in your fur and the coolness of night on your eyes. Breathe it, open your heart to it, accept it and whatever it brings you. That is the badger way, the way of all animals. Can't you feel it?'

'Y-yes, yes,' Birdcherry said quickly. 'And is this w-what life is all about? – belonging to a place and the seasons?'

'Yes, and the loving of it all and the gratitude for it.'

Birdcherry nodded, saddened a little by the simplicity of the notion.

'She is Earth Mother and we are Earthborn, not Moonborn. The moon is up there with the stars. We are here,' and Aspen brought a forepaw down hard on the turf. 'The sett-dwellers tend to make too much of this moonborn stuff.'

'And what of Sunworld?' said Birdcherry.

'It's like any dream place you visit in sleep, but Sunworld is the dream you never wake from.'

'Ah, yes,' Birdcherry breathed. 'I can s-see that. I'm beginning to understand.'

'Good,' Aspen smiled.

Chapter 24

The Eyrie

The people at Woodash sympathized with the baiters. Garrison knew it even though Steer would not be trapped into voicing an opinion. The farmer saw the efforts to protect badgers as an erosion of rural traditions and privileges by interfering townees.

'So he won't be sprinting down here to warn us when Strawberry crosses his land to get at the setts,' Garrison told Billy and Sheena.

They stood under the horse chestnut candles while the wind shook the raindrops from the trees and the shower faded.

'Old Steer's got a sly face,' said Sheena. 'Like a bleedin' weasel. He's anuvver of them tight-fisted yokels I'd like to strangle.'

The boy and girl were such creatures of extremes Garrison had to smile despite his toothache. They had never been given any moral compass bearings. He glanced at Billy. The hard little face was expressionless. Its owner, Garrison decided, was the most self-serving human being he had ever met, but the same fingers which lifted someone else's milk money off the doorstep could gently free the butterfly from the spider's web and part the nettles to reveal the wild flower.

They heard a bicycle rattling down the lane behind them and saw Constable Tapley wobbling to a halt. There had been another series of thefts from several big gardens including Warren Fishacre.

'Garden ornaments, lawn-mowers, stuff like that,' the policeman said.

'The work of some sort of lunatic?' said Garrison.

'We're dealing with a gang, sir,' said Tapley. 'And they aren't fools. Those lead statues and the mowing machines are worth a bob or two.'

'It's got to be Strawberry,' Sheena said.

'In my business it would be easy to put two and two together and get five,' said Tapley. 'If I didn't think Billy had turned over a new leaf I might be tempted to think him and you, Sheena, were responsible for this morning's thefts of money left out for the milkman.'

'It wadn' me, mister,' Billy shrilled.

'Whoever it was can rest assured they'll get copped and put away.'

The policeman wanted to know if Garrison had seen anything suspicious on the cliffs. The children celebrated his departure with broad grins. A lark was singing as sunlight swelled. Garrison probed his bad tooth with the tip of his tongue thinking again of Ann. Sheena was chattering away although for a while he heard only the larksong.

'Ain't it, Mr Garrison,' Sheena said, tugging at his sleeve. 'Ain't it.'

He lifted his eyebrows and smiled at her enquiringly.

'Ain't it awful.'

'Ain't what awful, Sheena?'

'Piles, mister. Old man Rowden's piles. Do everybody get 'em when they're old?'

'I hope not,' Garrison laughed.

'Old man Rowden has to sit on a cushion,' Sheena

continued. 'And he reads the paper at breakfast and tea. Holds it right up to his face and just grunts when she talks to him. That makes me want to scream.'

'Tell him about the dumpling,' Billy grinned.

Sheena chuckled. 'The other day we had stew. We have it so bleedin' often I'm beginning to look like a bloody turnip. Anyway, there was old Rowden behind his *Chronicle* and she was yappin' away non-stop and he was oinkin' like the old pig he is. So I got this dumplin' on the end of me fork and sort of twanged it at him. It went through the front page and hit him right in the eye before slidin' down the front of his waistcoat.'

Billy's belly laughs were infectious. They staggered helplessly up the path to Coastguard Cottage. Sticking out of the letter-box was an envelope with a Swiss stamp on it.

'Come on, let's go along the cliffs as far as Froward, Bill,' Sheena said, seeing the sudden glow of happiness appear on Garrison's face.

'Shouldn't you two be at school?' Garrison said absently.

'Yes,' Billy said.

'They'll put you in one of those reform schools for bad kids,' Garrison said.

Billy shrugged. 'They haven't built the jail that can hold me, mister.'

'He got that from an American film,' Sheena said.

'You'd miss all this, Billy,' Garrison said.

'Oh leave him go, mister,' Sheena said. 'He's a big-headed little bleeder.'

The children climbed the stone wall and walked together up the hillside.

'Is Mrs Garrison goin' to die?' Billy said.

'People wiv TB usually do,' said Sheena.

'Not all of 'em,' he said sharply. 'But I wish Strawberry would catch it – 'im and the rest of that bleedin' club. Why don't God dish out something rotten to the rotten devils? Why didn' the Japs get hold of Strawberry instead of – instead of –'

'Don't keep thinkin' about the war and fings, Billy.'

He shook his head, swallowing hard and repeatedly.

'What d'you want to play?' she said. 'Robin Hood?'

'Doctors and nurses,' he chuckled and pawed at his eyes. 'Or mothers and fathers.'

'Come off it,' Sheena snapped. 'I don't like rude games.'

'OK,' he sniffed. 'Indians. I have to be a Navajo brave and you have to be my squaw. The white men are after us and we have to hide and ambush them with out bows and arrows.'

'We ain't got no bows and arrows.'

'Pretend bows and arrows,' Billy said patiently. 'Come on.' And he set off at the trot along the path of mud and pink and silver shillets.

At Garrowcombe they stopped for a moment to tie handkerchiefs round their heads and stick in some gull's feathers.

'You look like a proper indian,' Sheena said, adjusting his headband.

'A brave,' Billy said, hearing the thunder of buffalo in the coombe.

Tony Rapson had his mother's dark hair and moon face and his father's small features. He had also acquired his brother's love of tobacco and was never without cigarettes. At primary school he had gained a reputation as an egg collector although his climbing on the gulleries of St Mary's Head was outshone by the sons of fishermen like the legendary Ginger Gurney and Billy who was in a class by himself. Gull's eggs were gathered every spring for the table but most of the boys had collections of local bird's eggs and the lucky few like Tony Rapson could trade in rarities. Unlike most of the others, though, he took complete clutches because that was the way professional collectors operated.

Sitting on the stone wall of what had once been a small open-air swimming pool on the beach of Old Spanish Cove he carefully wiped the soles of his black gym shoes. The crag rose vertically in three short pitches to the eyrie. Sunlight slanted across the slabs of shale and mica. On her ledge the falcon was crying and Skyhook at the look-out on his rock above answered her screams. Tony blew on the tip of his cigarette before grinding it under his heel and bending to tighten his shoelaces. The gas-mask box was slung over one shoulder and across his back. Stepping forward he set hand to rock and began to climb.

Both peregrines took to the air rattling out cries which always sent a shiver down Billy's spine. Sheena joined him on the grass above the gorse thicket overlooking the cove.

'What's upset them?' she frowned.

'Ravens, fox – a stoat maybe,' Billy speculated.

The birds were diving and climbing again with a terrific din and Billy began to run down through the trees to the cove. At the top of the steps leading to the beach he paused and looked across at the eyrie. No one was there but the birds were still frantic. He was halfway down the steps when Sheena saw Tony Rapson clawing his way up the opposite cliff.

'He's got the eggs,' Billy grated. 'Wait here in case he doubles back.'

'Then what?' said Sheena.

'Stop him,' Billy said. The colour had left his face and he was trembling.

'Don't do nuffin' daft,' Sheena cried after him but Billy was already lost to the world.

Rapson came sobbing and panting through the final clump of bracken and was crawling under the barbed wire into the field when Billy vaulted the fence and caught up with him. The white moon face swung and the eyes widened. Billy clenched his fists.

'The eggs, Rapson,' he said in a low menacing voice.

'What eggs?'

'Give me that bloody box or I'll knock out your teeth.'

'Wait till my brother hears about this,' Rapson said but he was wriggling free of the gas-mask case. Then in a changed voice he said: 'I got nine fags. You can have 'em if you leave the eggs.'

'OK,' Billy said. 'Give us them.'

He stuck the packet in his shirt pocket and snapped his fingers.

'Now the eggs – and don't drop the box. Set it down careful and bugger off.'

'That's stealin',' Rapson croaked. 'Them eggs are mine. I climbed for 'em. And the fags belonged to Eric. He'll bloody brain you, Drew – you thievin' little fart.'

Billy took two steps towards him and the boy retreated hurriedly on his heels.

'Drew,' he gasped. 'You're askin' for it.'

Billy landed a right hook to the head and the moon face crumpled behind a howl of pain. Then Rapson fled clutching a swollen ear and Billy knelt and undid the case. Four rust-brown eggs lay on a bed of cotton wool. They were still warm.

'Bleedin' hell,' Billy whispered, closing the top. Thoughts buzzed through his mind. Maybe the birds wouldn't even know the eggs had gone. He glanced across at the eyrie crag. One bird was on the rock above it. The other was airborne but silent now.

Billy shouldered the case and made a quick return to the steeps.

'He took all four.'

Sheena looked at him then at the gas-mask case.

'I'll put them back,' Billy said.

'And it'll be OK?'

He shrugged.

The climbing was easy and he was dismayed by the peregrines' lack of cunning. The eyrie could not have been in a more vulnerable position. He hauled onto the ledge and carefully returned the eggs to the scrape. The birds were screaming once more and he wondered if they would attack him as he made the trickier descent.

'You're like a monkey,' Sheena grinned.

'Let's go over the other side of the cove and see if she settles,' Billy said.

'Did you bash Rapson?'

205

'I only gave him a tap on the ear.'

'His brother won't like it.'

'His brother can drop dead. I'm having one of they eyasses when they've fledged. I'll train him for the fist.'

'One of them wot?'

'Eyasses – young falcons.'

'You didn't want an egg, then?'

'I got a peregrine's. Bleedin' Rapson took all four.'

They sat among the sea pinks opposite the eyrie, hidden by blackthorn and sycamore saplings. After a while the falcon returned to the ledge and presently she began to rearrange the eggs with her bill. Then she covered them with her body and fidgeted into stillness.

'Will they be all right, Billy?' Sheena said.

'More than likely.'

'Your mum won't let you have a hawk in the house.'

'It idn' a hawk; it's a falcon.'

'Whatever it is she won't have it.'

He stared at her although Sheena felt he was looking at something else beyond her.

'Wouldn't it be better to leave the birds alone, Billy? I don't like the thought of one of them endin' up in your back shed.'

He nodded and trailed his fingers through the pinks.

'Billy.'

'All right – I won't take one.'

Sheena caught hold of the nearest blackthorn bough and gently shook it. The blossom drifted down to star her hair.

'I love bullen blossom,' Billy said and her eyes were still open when he kissed her awkwardly, his hands on her shoulders.

The sun had set by the time they reached the Marl estuary, exploring all the coves, inlets and promontories on the way. Dusk turned distances blue and Start's flashing light was hypnotic above the water where sea and river met. All the stars of spring firmed to cold brilliance and the children sat on the pine needles gazing through their separate daydreams while the light greyed.

'I'm cold, Billy,' Sheena said in a quick little whisper.

He put an arm around her but she could not stop shivering.

'We'd better get home,' she said. 'They'll start worryin'.'

'I like this place,' he said. 'When I grow up I'm goin' to live here like a Red Indian.'

'What about me?' she said, getting to her feet and brushing the needles off her frock.

'It's always you and me, Sheen.'

'And you won't ever stop lovin' me?'

''Course I won't.'

'Promise?'

'God's honour.'

They trod the badger path to the Monterey pines of Froward Point. A breeze had risen from the sea to whisper in the treetops.

'Let's take some cones back for Mr Garrison's fire,' Billy said. 'They'll burn smashing – like fireworks.'

'What'll we carry 'em in?'

He took off his pullover and tied the bottom tightly with his headband and said: 'You put 'em in the neck and use the arms as rucksack slings.'

'Crikey, Bill – you ain't half smart.'

They were on all fours when he laid a hand on her arm and lifted a finger to his lips.

'Down there,' he whispered.

Two badgers had emerged from the scrub thorn below the trees. Hesitantly they swung their black and white faces as they read the air; but the wind held nothing save the smell of the sea and sea things. Together the animals plodded up the slope as others stepped from the undergrowth.

'Don't move,' Billy whispered.

Four large adult badgers walked in single file less than twenty yards below the kneeling boy and girl, grunting and snuffling as they went. Then Billy heard a noise behind him and turned to see the pale badger boar staring at him from a snarl. The creature seemed totally unafraid and Billy who had watched many badgers was surprised to find it so close and holding its ground. The thick neck, broad face and fluffed-out body hair lent it a startling ferocity. Then without warning it gave a loud wailing screech and threw back its head.

'God!' Sheena choked and the sett-dwellers were scattering to vanish into the thicket. Only the pale boar remained and continued to scream.

'Let's get out of here,' Billy cried.

'Don't leave me, Billy,' Sheena yelled.

'Catch hold of my hand – quick,' and they hurtled down the zigzags and up onto the fields of Back Ways to sprawl breathless in the wheat.

'I've never seen a badger like that,' Billy panted. 'Never.'

'Perhaps it was a ghost badger,' said Sheena.

'Don't be bleedin' daft.'

'I'm not. I mean it. He didn't look real – and that cry!'

'He was only warning the others.'

'Sez you! I reckon he would've had us.'

'Badgers aren't like that. They don't hurt anything unless they're attacked.'

He sat up and looked back towards the Point.

'It was bleedin' creepy under them trees,' Sheena said, and in a gentler tone: 'We'd best get home, Bill. Your mum will wallop you if you stay out any longer.'

'She'll wallop me anyway. I left my pullover on the Point.'

'We could go back for it.'

'Tomorrow maybe,' he said unconvincingly.

Kerslake had placed a scarecrow twenty paces down from King Arthur's Tower. It had no face. Crumpled onto the blank turnip head was an old broad-rimmed hat. The long coat lifted gently in the wind and Billy stood before it, his knees turning to mush.

'That old dawbake,' he murmured. 'He knows. He bleedin' well knows.'

Chapter 25

Ashblacken's Courage

She could hear the low bleating of the ewes and the more urgent cries of their lambs. The steeps were silent and the sky starry. From the water on the landward side of Dragon Rock a seal barked. The badger sow ambled under the blackthorn and flowering ash with scent rising from everything living and the barn owl adding his silence to the darkness. Aspen glanced up. Something large and white eclipsed the stars as it passed overhead. Then she caught the drift of the pale stranger's musk and on an impulse called out to him but received no answer. His cries were harrowing.

'Who are you?' Aspen demanded.

He was there on the edge of the pines, his fur alive with moonlight although the night was moonless.

'Join us,' Aspen pleaded.

But he lumbered off.

'Fingo says he's seen the stranger leaving the little sett on the edge of the cliffs where we escaped the dogs,' she told Birdcherry later on in the friendly darkness of underearth. The other animals gathered in the large chamber were wide awake. They were all sows, for the boars were still at forage.

'Greybob will kill him,' said one of the yearlings.

'He won't,' Hawscrag grunted.

'B-but why not?' Birdcherry asked. 'He c-can't keep on h-hanging about scaring us and r-raising Greybob's hackles.'

'Something's always there between him and us,' Aspen said.

'Oh don't make a mystery of it,' Hawscrag said impatiently. 'The creature is touched. He'll end up in a wire or under the yap-dogs. There's no place for him in Nightworld.'

The discussion continued but Aspen's mind was elsewhere. The mystery was waiting beyond the moment and she wanted to clutch it gently with her teeth as if it were a cub. You come up the steeps into the sunrise, said the voice, and you walk into it. If you don't feel awake don't worry. The dark will close in behind you until you stand in the bottom of the sky. What you have left behind will vanish like your breath. Ahead the dream materialized into a great elegy of light and emotion to swamp the senses.

Outside the night was singing. Sauntering northwards Aspen was hardly aware of her companions. While they ate beetles and beetle larva she sat wrinkling her nose to the smells which were the invisible fabric of Nightworld.

Every so often she lifted herself on her haunches and swung her muzzle. A cold wind got up and blew from the north. Clouds drove in and by the time the badgers had reached Down End a shower of snow fell. For a while the sows puzzled over the cold whiteness. They had forgotten winter and did not associate primrose scent and the fall of blossom with snow.

It was one of those 'Blackthorn Winters' which even a South Devon spring can muster. In the hedges elderberry, thorn and ash creaked and rustled. Stars appeared and vanished, then the sky was clear from horizon to horizon and the star dance was brilliant in the clear, cold air. Small shapes passed overhead as wheatears, warblers and chiff chaffs arrived at the end of their migration flight. To the north the sky was lit up at regular intervals by St Mary's Head light. Aspen sighed and Birdcherry who was constantly reading her every mood asked if anything was wrong. Aspen shook her head. Snow was melting on her coat.

A little later they met Ashblacken. He had eaten young rabbits and was coughing up a fur ball. Hawscrag wished to avoid him but the boar was thick-skinned and oblivious of her sarcasm. Soon the sows became amused by his bragging. It exceeded the normal boar proclamation of warriorhood which was apparently necessary to the life of the sett; but Ashblacken's self-glorifying mythology fooled no one although his stories were so fantastic they compelled attention.

'There were these two giant dogs,' he said after the preliminaries had made it difficult for the sows to suppress their giggling.

'As big as – as –'

'Bullocks?' Hawscrag offered drily, arching her bony old body.

'Well, almost,' he said. 'I don't want to exaggerate.'

'Of course not,' Hawscrag agreed, and she looked first at Aspen then at Birdcherry who had to push her snout into the grass and grunt to conceal her laughter.

'They jumped me up on the cart-track and there was a fight I wouldn't wish on my worst enemy.'

'But miracle of miracles,' Hawscrag said, 'you're unscathed. There's not a scratch on you.'

'I had to be quick on my feet,' Ashblacken admitted. 'Dodging and leaping about like a stoat, and all the time slashing and biting those horrible killer dogs.'

'I thank Earth Mother you saw them off,' said Hawscrag, 'What would have happened to us if we'd met them!'

'I shudder to think,' said Ashblacken solemnly. 'In the end they just turned tail and ran.'

'Wait till I tell them back at Big Sett,' said Hawscrag. 'Maybe Aspen will sing Ashblacken's saga once the full magnitude of your deed has sunk in.'

211

'She could do worse,' the boar nodded, and he grinned at Aspen whose eyes were watering with the effort of controlling herself.

When he had gone the sows rolled about kicking the air and hugging each other, their bodies shaking with laughter.

'The great bone-headed fool,' Hawscrag sobbed. 'He must think we're cubs – him and his stories. Ashblacken would make scats if a mouse squeaked at him.'

'But Guelder took him for a mate,' said Aspen.

'She's just as bad,' Hawscrag said.

Yet Ashblacken's boasting turned out to be almost prophetic. He rooted around the steeps and pastures until it was time to go below ground in a small sett that had been recently excavated by two maiden sows. The single chamber held some of their scent and he curled happily into it and was soon asleep. His dreaming was pleasant and he was reluctant to open his eyes, but the noises brought him irritably back to consciousness. And suddenly Ashblacken was frightened. Something hard was crunching into the roof of the sett and there was a yap-dog in the tunnel. Then he heard other dogs and men's voices and spades ringing on shillets. Ashblacken whimpered and pressed back against the wall of the chamber. Earth pattered down on his head and he snarled up at the gap that let in the light and the stink of man. With a crash the roof fell and as he struggled to free himself from the debris Ashblacken was taken. A light blow on the nose left him dazed and unaware of being dumped in the sack. When he came to he was half-suffocated by the stench of men and dogs.

Strawberry Rapson had decided to hold the baiting in the disused quarry on the northern flanks of Garrowcombe. It was a small tree-choked hole in the hillside with a natural arena of long grass under rowans and elms. Here Ashblacken was tumbled out of the sack and gripped by the tail while his hindlegs were chained together.

'He looks like a seal, don't he,' Charlie Dunning said, lighting an own-roll. 'It's the way he drags his back legs.'

''As anyone ever baited seals?' Stike asked.

No one knew but the spectators thought the idea interesting. Strawberry told Tony Rapson to go up in the trees and keep watch. Meanwhile Ashblacken shuffled backwards until his rump was against rock. He gazed short-sightedly from figure to figure, shivering now in spasms and resigned to what was about to happen. Gritt and Jimmy were dancing and choking on their leashes and the other terriers were yelping. Ashblacken's forelegs were numb and he flopped over.

'Here,' Dunning laughed. 'The bugger's been on the scrumpy. 'He's drunk.'

He dug a foot into Ashblacken and the badger grunted.

'The dogs will wake him up,' Strawberry smiled, and the terriers were released.

Five animals fell on Ashblacken and he struggled to rise and shake them off using his teeth as anger blazed and released him from terror. His response surprised even himself. Holding his ground he slashed the bodies covering him and with a heave of the shoulders shook them off. One of Stike's bitches came too close and was gripped by the throat. Her scream of pain sent the rest of the pack scuttling out of range. The smell of blood and the bitch lying motionless left the dogs uncertain. Throwing back his head Ashblacken gave the high-pitched cry of his kind, a cry of triumph and defiance – tinged with sorrow.

Before he could be stopped Stike swung the iron bar and put Ashblacken beyond further suffering.

'You damned fool,' Strawberry said. 'That brock was special. He would have really tested Gritt and Jimmy.'

'But my Lassie, Frank –' Stike began.

'A rubbish animal who got what she deserved.' Strawberry's voice was thick with rage. 'Gritt and Jimmy would have done the sod and it would've been a baiting to remember.'

'Sorry, Frank.' Stike said slowly. 'I just saw red when he –'

'Shut up,' Strawberry said. 'You'll be before the committee

213

over this. No one buggers up a baitin' in my club.'

Tony Rapson slid down the bank and tugged at his father's arm.

'Kerslake's coming,' he said. 'The posh girl and Old Mother Ordish are with him.'

Strawberry nodded and his fingers lifted self-consciously to the birthmark, his mind still computing the degrees of resistance the badger might have offered if Stike hadn't blundered.

'Take the chain off the animal and put the tools in the bag and hide them in the rocks. Do it good, Charlie.'

'What about Lassie?' Stike said.

'Leave her,' Strawberry said. 'If she strayed onto Fishacre land and died fightin' a brock it wasn't your fault. How far off is Kerslake and the old lady, Tone?'

'They're by the stream but coming this way, dad.'

Strawberry nodded and licked his lips.

From the bottom of the coombe the quarry trees screened the approach to the hedge at the top of the field. Strawberry was glad the sunshine was crisping the remains of the snowfall to vapour. The men scrambled onto the downs and Stike wanted to keep going up over to the lane and the vans.

'Have a look ahead, Tony,' Strawberry said.

The gang crouched under the hedge and waited for the boy to return.

'Garrison and a copper,' he panted. 'Coming towards us. They're in the next field but one.'

'Then we'd better get back to the vans sharpish,' said Dunning.

'Don't be a fool, Charlie,' Strawberry said. 'There'll be a copper waiting for us and we'll look as guilty as hell. We go down and meet the old girl.'

'Are you mad, Frank?' said Stike.

'No – I'm a law-abiding bloke exercising my dogs on Hard Sands with some mates when suddenly the poor animals take off after a fox. So we chase after 'em on Ordish land because us don't want them upsettin' the sheep or the badgers.'

214

Charlie Dunning chuckled.

'Let your dogs go,' said Strawberry. 'And make sure they follow Gritt and Jimmy.'

He caught his terriers by the collar and led them to a gap in the hedge.

'Run, my beauties,' he cried. 'Go on, Jim, Gritt – run.'

And the terriers set off barking down the hillside pursued by Dunning's smooth-haired bitch and Small's rough-haired dog. They were playing the exercise game. Halfway between the quarry and the stream they met Mrs Ordish, Lucy and Kerslake and bounded around them with wagging stumps and ears cocked. Kerslake's mean-eyed collie became a snarling lunatic, gnashing her teeth and fighting the lead in an effort to attack the lot.

'Now,' Strawberry cried and he came through the hedge with his cronies at his heels. 'Call your dogs, boys. They naughty little animals are trespassing.'

Mrs Ordish was taken aback by the dramatic entrance of the terriers and their owners. Strawberry was breathless and apologetic, smiling directly into the old lady's face as he poured out his story.

'First they was all over the cliffs,' he concluded. 'Then they were off across the fields and down here. We're sorry, ma'am. Of course I'll pay for any damage they've done.'

Mrs Ordish looked at him coldly. Up on the skyline Garrison and PC Tapley appeared.

'You're a nasty little man, Rapson,' Mrs Ordish said. 'Men like you are always up to no good.'

Strawberry lifted his shoulders and his hands, palms upwards, and let them fall again; his smile grew broader. When Garrison and the policeman arrived he repeated his story.

'Us parked in the lane by Woodash and came down to Hard Sands to exercise the dogs. Sometimes a rabbit or two can be picked up in the bank by the marsh. Mr Steer don't mind us taking a few.'

The rest of the tale sounded plausible enough and PC

215

Tapley noted the absence of digging tools.

'Right,' he said. 'Leash your dogs and take the quickest way off the lady's land.'

'I'll shoot any dog I catch running loose here in the lambing season,' Kerslake added and his collie growled.

Strawberry's smile became frostier and he narrowed his eyes at the bailiff.

'Did you believe him, constable?' Mrs Ordish said as the gang departed in the direction of Garrowcombe barn.

'They didn't have any spades or picks,' Tapley said.

'They could have hidden them,' Lucy said.

Coulds and ifs, the policeman thought but he managed a smile and said: 'Yes, miss.'

'Rapson was after badgers,' said Mrs Ordish. 'The man's got shifty eyes. Oh the law is remarkably stupid! I can have him prosecuted for poaching rabbits on my land but not for digging badgers. It really is infuriating.'

'But at least we foiled him, grandmama,' said Lucy.

'The man's incorrigible,' Mrs Ordish snapped. 'He continues to trespass despite everything.'

'If I catch him setting wires, ma'am, I'll put an end to his games,' Kerslake said.

Garrison searched his pockets for his cigarettes and remembered Sheena's words about Rapson and the rules. He stroked the grey-streaked hairs of his new beard. The pain of the rotten molar had become a dull, fiery ache and he knew he could postpone the visit to the dentist no longer.

Greybob and Furzebright nosed-out Ashblacken's body. It gave off the faint tincture of death that both scared and saddened the boars. In the quarry the wind dwindled to silence and night contained all the smells the badgers loathed – nicotine, human body odour, the stink of yap-dog.

Ashblacken lay in the grass on his side, his eyes dull. In front of him was the dead terrier. Gingerly the boars placed their noses to the two carcasses, sniffing at the wounds and

216

hoping Ashblacken would breathe again.

'The dew was like rain on his coat,' Furzebright told the sett-dwellers. 'And the blood of the dog was on his lips.'

'S-so he was a hero,' said Birdcherry. 'A real hero.'

'Few boars kill a yap-dog in combat,' said Greybob.

'And you gave him back to Earth Mother?' Hawscrag said.

'We covered him with grass and leaves,' Furzebright nodded.

Hawscrag released a long shuddering sigh and said: 'I can't remember a worse time of troubles and misery. Ashblacken irritated me but I'd rather have him as a live fool than a dead victim of the yap-dogs, hero or no hero.'

They had congregated on the lawn at Froward with the night sky clear and the sea calm. Sensing the mood of the sett-dwellers Cowtail silenced her cubs who were playing with a gull's wing nearby. The dew pressed cold on her pads and her breath hung on the air. So Ashblacken was dead. So? The father of her cubs was dead too. Dying was part of it all.

She sniffed and inclined her head to lick the nearest cub. The badgers mystified her. Sometimes their behaviour had her itching. The lone life was the best – coming and going, never staying too long in one place, never settling for a particular earth. When the leaves fell she would move on. Yes, south towards the land where the light flashed at night. Sitting upright she could see the blink of Start Light and despite the cubs yearned for the wandering.

It was left to Aspen and Birdcherry to break the news of Ashblacken's death to Guelder, and she took it badly. The death of a mate never failed to leave a sow with cubs feeling vulnerable and lost. For some time she paced around in a circle of misery, head bowed, moaning to herself and quite beyond the reach of kind words. Aspen and Birdcherry stood by helplessly. Then, when she came to a halt and raised her muzzle they approached and licked her face. Automatically

217

she began to gather fresh bedding for the nest and they helped her.

The darkness underground was wholesome with the scent of the cubs, and their squealing brought Guelder back from despair; but she could not speak and Aspen made sure Birdcherry held her tongue. The sisters lay at the entrance to the nursery chamber listening to the cubs sucking milk from Guelder's body.

Chapter 26

The Pale Fire

A few nights later Furzebright became Guelder's mate to the surprise and chagrin of Birdcherry and the young sow Thornsong. Since Ashblacken's death Guelder was a much quieter, less bossy animal, and Furzebright lodged comfortably in her sett. But at the centre of Guelder's world were the twins who would soon be ready to go above ground. Furzebright provided extra protection for the cubs. Ashblacken was still mourned but the twins were everything and Guelder fussed over them in a way that impressed even Hawscrag.

Early spring was releasing some of its beauty into Nightworld. Aspen and Greybob sauntered among the wood sorrel and young vetches under the ash trees. Every once in a while moths bumped against their muzzles and they snapped at them and felt stupid and giggled. All about Ramsons Dip the dark green leaves of the wild garlic were clustered but the white flowers had yet to appear.

Boar and sow scent-marked and shared the forage until their snouts were muddy and they had eaten their fill of earthworms and beetles. Then it was fine to walk through the darkness with bats on the wing and the sea murmuring.

Men had topped swedes above Down End and the fields at either hand were alive with young wheat. The badgers stopped every twenty paces or so to sniff the air or put their noses to the nettles and leaves of the cuckoo pints. Over the hedge-banks ran the paths of rabbits, fox and badger. Sheep coughed and shifted in their sleep as Aspen and Greybob negotiated the side of Garrowcombe to drink at the stream beneath the gone-wild hedge of hazel, ash and elm. Further down they could hear water rattling over pebbles and rocks to meet the sea. On the bank above the cove were primroses, celandines and thrift. The tide was rising and swells spread with a crunch and a lisp over the shingle. Between the wave-break was the sound of the waterfall higher up the beach.

Aspen rounded her nostrils to the salty, half-rotten smell of kelp.

They ranged up the bluebell slopes of Garrowcombe Head to find new grass and leafing elder scrub. On the drystone wall were the fleshy green leaves of pennywort and the mutes of song-birds and some of the freshness left behind by the evening's showers.

Both sow and boar crunched any bury beetles they discovered on the sheepwalk. They were among the gorse and bramble now and crossed a very narrow stream that ghosted over the cliffs. Spring was in the animals. Occasionally they paused and groomed each other while the moonlight dappled the crags and slabs of shale.

Returning to the downs they scrambled up a slope dense with celandines whose star-shaped flowers shook in the sea breeze.

The following evening Aspen foraged with Birdcherry and Thornsong. All the sows were aware of the earth coming alive again beneath their feet. At times they were moved to thrust their snouts into it and grunt and snuffle. Dog violets and dandelions were blooming and, as each cloud passed, bands of moonlight spread across the Channel. Although the brightness left them wary the sows felt uplifted. Everything seemed to combine in a moment of pure rapture – the life of creatures and things, and the life of the universe which was the stars.

The countryside blazed with pale fire, more lovely than hoar-frost. Out to sea the lights of the sprat boats were bobbing. Again there was no telling where the world ended and the sky began.

Slowly at first then with increasing strength the wind lifted from the sea. At once the moonlight was full of small pieces of dead grass and bracken. They whirled around the badgers snagging in their guard hairs and making them blink and bow their heads. Now the steeps were hissing and undulating to the horizon as if they were alive. Soon great swells were peaking to waves in the Channel and the force of the wind was such that the animals had difficulty keeping their feet. Birdcherry called to Aspen but her words were snatched away. The sows stood facing the storm with winter's debris sailing past them to vanish over the farmland. But behind the noise Aspen heard the whispering voice and although the words ran together the meaning was clear. It was the voice of the sow badger addressing her young while they lay asleep in the nest unaware of the world.

The giddy dance separated her from her senses and the ground slipped from under her so that she seemed to be flying with the scraps of winter fern to spin weightlessly among the stars.

'Aspen,' said Bullenspur, but Aspen kept her eyes closed.

'Aspen.' This time it was the voice of Ashblacken, a voice so tranquil Aspen smiled with the pleasure of it.

Then once more 'Aspen' and she opened her eyes to find Birdcherry's face held close to her own. The night was still and she was lying in the dog violets.

'Y-you fainted,' said Birdcherry.

'I'm all right now,' Aspen whispered, but she was reluctant

221

to get up. The earth smelt so sweet and she was pleasantly drowsy.

'You c-c-can't stay here all night.'

'Why not?'

'Yap-dogs might find you.'

Aspen smiled and raised herself. After a final shake along the whole length of her body she had a good scratch and gazed at her companions; but if they expected an explanation they were disappointed.

Three nights later Guelder brought her cubs out of the sett onto the steeps but not before Furzebright had stood at the entrance testing the air with his snout. Guelder joined him and when at length she was satisfied no danger threatened the twins were permitted to step through the grass well away from the clifftops. This was followed by a further spell of scratching and more scenting and listening. Eventually the sows of Big Sett gathered at Furzebright's invitation to inspect the youngsters whose charm would have been hard to resist even if the onlookers had not been badgers.

At first the twins strode slowly about together suddenly breaking apart to sniff at a blade of grass or a leaf. They uttered yelps with Guelder in close attendance constantly scenting the air. The twins were snub-nosed, fluffy creatures who amused the onlookers by their slow and solemn appraisal of Nightworld. Guelder walked behind them, her dignity forgotten for once. It was the darkest night for weeks and the threat of rain was in the air. Forsaking their mother the cubs struggled to read the dark until one began to dig. She was bolder and more adventurous than her brother. The quieter cub rose on his haunches and licked his mother's ear. Guelder promptly tumbled him onto his rump and took the opportunity to run her teeth like clippers through the soft belly fur in search of body bugs. The cub squirmed and threw himself about and even attacked Guelder's snout. Hawscrag laughed and the other cub sprang to her mother's defence. But while the scuffling took place Guelder nipped the parasites out of his rump.

222

'W-was I like that?' Birdcherry chuckled.

'No,' said Hawscrag. 'You were a little oddling – never without a cold or a headache. We thought you wouldn't survive the summer. I saw you through some bad times. In fact, I nearly ate you once.'

'B-b-b-but why?'

'Dogs. They got into the sett and killed one of your brothers. I thought they'd get you and Aspen but your father drove off the dog or you'd be bothering Earth Mother now with your endless questions.'

'Why d-do I talk like this?' Birdcherry asked.

'The dogs frightened you, and so did I. I suppose you sensed my intentions.'

The cubs ascended the steeps with a nervous curiosity which the watching sows found delightful. Everything the small creatures did was deliberate and excessively cautious because Nightworld seemed so huge after the underground nests. Its scents were overwhelming and the twins were forever swaying back and forth, heads tilted at the sky. And the onlookers began to feel conscious not only of their age but of a heaviness in themselves that was not entirely physical.

Eventually the rain which had been threatening fell heavily, hissing as it penetrated the undergrowth. The young took it hard on the snout and sneezed. The sow cub tried to pat the downpour with a paw and fell over. Guelder smiled and shepherded them underground.

Hawscrag gave a toss of the head and scattered the raindrops from her face.

'Well,' she said. 'Ashblacken lives in that pair.'

The shower did not disturb the sows and its passing left the sky clear except for a cloud or two over the sea. The rain had released the cool fragrance of the steeps and the badgers held it in their nostrils like a drug. On its heels came the musk of a boar and Aspen and her companions turned to mark the stranger's presence on the darkness.

'What is he up to,' growled Hawscrag. It was not a question. 'Old mope-about. Always there but never here, coming and

223

going like the wind.'

They could hear the stranger moaning.

'It isn't the behaviour of a sett-dweller,' Hawscrag grumbled. 'He's like that Cowtail – farting about and talking to himself and scaring the hell out of everyone.'

'He certainly gives m-me the j-jitters,' said Birdcherry.

The sows wandered off and when they took to the sheep-walk they separated into single file behind Hawscrag, hindquarters swaying and heads held low.

'What are you thinking about, Birdcherry?' Aspen asked, butting her sister's rump.

'C-cubs,' said Birdcherry.

At dawn the last shower swept over the coast catching Strawberry Rapson as he returned to his van, this time at the toll-house on the Mary's Haven – Greenaway Road. He turned up the collar of his mackintosh and licked his lips and tapped his pocket. The notebook was safe and he had added the sites of five more setts to his coastal map.

Chapter 27

Dialogues

It was impossible for Garrison to ignore the badgers. Their paths were everywhere and on a clear night he expected to see a black and white face peering out of the undergrowth on December Point. He was out of doors early or at dusk and his face was sun-flushed. The beard had gone because he could not stand the itching. Studying himself in the shaving mirror he wondered what Ann would make of him. Why did one's hair thin on top, only to grow bushy on the back of the head?

Painting took him out of himself but he loved being between pictures. Whenever the weather was fine he was on the steeps or clifftops with his sketchbook although he needed no excuse to get out into the fresh air. At times he regretted the springs he had lived through unaware of what was going on beyond the studio window or pub door.

Bees droned around the white dead nettles in the bottom of the hedge by the marsh and there were pale blue flowers of speedwell on his garden wall. Walking onto Froward he considered how easy it had been to cross the countryside with his eyes open and yet be blind to what nature and the seasons had to offer. At times he spoke out loud to Ann or simply repeated her name over and over as though it were a spell against bad luck. Yet there was a sinister presence on the coastline and Strawberry Rapson was never far from his thoughts. Despite the promise of April Garrison occasionally turned a bend or came over a hill with a sinking feeling in his guts, wondering what he would find. Often he expected to stumble on a badger in a snare or a badger shot to death. Maybe Rapson was deliberately leaving reminders of his destructive energy on the clifftops in an attempt to bludgeon him into throwing in the towel. Once or twice the temptation to get away to a new place was strong. Then he thought of Ann's enduring courage.

'Rapson,' he grunted, smacking his fist hard into the palm of his left hand.

Froward Point was a splendid place. He sat on the grass between the pines and the blackthorn thicket, watching the play of light on the sea and the gulls speckling the air around Dragon Rock. He was happy and the morning was warm. The network of narrow paths once again brought the badgers to mind. Perhaps one day they would be left alone to live their lives in peace. Maybe the dark side of man's nature would vanish as part of some miraculous evolution of the spirit.

The tide turned. Water moved over the reefs and the Rips were noisy. He lay back and closed his eyes. It really was like summer. Behind him the pines were whispering. Then he heard the first cuckoo and sat up to see mares' tails in the sky to the east and swallows flying low over scrub thorn.

That afternoon he went for a long run along the edge of the steeps determined to make it to the top of Down End without stopping, but the severity of Garrowcombe Head defeated him as it always did and he returned to the cottage drenched in sweat. A splash in the tub and a brisk rub down left him feeling twenty years younger and ready to work. Now the prospect of the large blank canvas was unbelievably exciting and he set to at once. Colour met colour in contrasts both sensuous and startling.

Pausing to light a cigarette he saw Lucy at the studio window and went outside to greet her. She had caught the sun and had that bloom on her flesh which is the exclusive property of the young. Self-consciously Garrison ran his fingers through his hair, meeting little resistance.

'You've shaved off your beard,' she smiled. 'What a pity. I'd grown used to it.'

'I was beginning to look like a biblical prophet,' he said.

'Rubbish! You looked distinguished.'

'You'll be calling me "sir" next!'

Lucy laughed and Garrison felt his tension easing. She was a girl who saw him as nothing more than a friend and ally. Anything else was the product of his ego. Toasting teacakes in front of the fire he tried to imagine her consternation had he acted the fool and made a pass. My God! he thought, as if she could ever see me as an attractive male! He smiled to himself, glad it was only a week before his next trip to Switzerland.

It was too chilly to eat outside. Going to the door he was startled to discover a motionless landscape. Not a breath of air disturbed the afternoon's close. The swallows were flying so low he might have caught them if he'd had better reflexes. Not the dinosaur reflexes of middle age when a kick up the arse takes four seconds to register!

'How about some gramophone music?' he said cheerfully. 'Classical music?'

'So long as it's not piano sonatas and stuff like that,' she said, pulling a face.

'Brahms's Concerto for Cello and Violin. Bruch's Violin Concerto.'

'I love the Bruch,' Lucy said. 'But I don't know the Brahms.'

'We'll play that first,' he said. 'It should go well with the time of day. It's got the feel of evening about it.'

But the cello and violin singing out to each other was like a

227

dialogue between two lovers and before he put on the Bruch he was pining for Ann. She had a habit of sweeping into his thoughts to bring the past alive, especially at dusk. Company was the last thing he wanted and when Lucy had gone he resented the arrival of Billy and Sheena. Fortunately it was a brief visit and Billy's news was encouraging.

'They got cubs in the sett at Ramsons Dip,' he said.

'Have you seen them?' asked Garrison.

'No, but there's tiny droppings in one of the pits where they go toilet,' Billy said.

'You don't miss much, do you?' Garrison said, impressed yet again by the boy's ability in the field.

'There ain't no flies on him,' said Sheena.

'Were you two at school today?' Garrison asked.

'Yes, mister,' Billy groaned.

'I hope you were,' Garrison said, 'or you'll be in the other school where there's no running off to see badgers or peregrines.'

'They've got four chicks,' Billy said quickly. 'Eyasses they'm called. I had a look at 'em this morning.'

'From the classroom window?' Garrison said.

Billy coloured. 'Before we went to school.'

Garrison gave them a shilling each and they ran off laughing and joking. He threw some driftwood on the fire and took a scotch out into the garden. Light was fading and long shadows were reaching across the down. The sun set and dusk thickened. Then the tawny owls of Woodash began to call. The hooting was sad and beautiful and continued long after twilight had deepened to night. Then a blackcap sang from the tamarisks and Garrison returned to the fireside to write Ann a love letter.

On Saturday morning Mrs Drew called, looking drawn and blousy. Her peroxide hair was dark at the roots and her face had sagged since Garrison had last seen her, but her coat and shoes were new and she carried herself with a kind of buoyant defiance.

'You got a moment, Mr Garrison?' she began as he opened the door and looked past her at a mackerel sky. 'It's Billy. It's never anything else but bloody Billy.'

He sat her on the settee and offered her a cup of tea which she declined.

'What's he been up to?'

'Mitching school mostly – that and thieving.'

'Milk money?'

'No. That's finished by the look of things. The police put the wind up him and he idn' stupid. Him and the Nelson girl nicked a fiver from Old Man Rowden.'

'Sheena's foster-father?'

'Yes, that tight old devil. Soon as I found out I gave it him back but he'd already gone to the law. If Sheena hadn't said she borrowed it – borrowed it! Christ that's rich! Anyway, she saved Billy's bacon but the police weren't amused. Billy's been mitchin' school something rotten. The bloody school inspector actually follows him up the road now on his bike most mornings. So Billy goes in the front of the building and over the wall at the back, cool as a cucumber. Caning don't bother him.'

She lit a cigarette. 'He's out of control and wearing me to a bloody shadow. So maybe I ought to give up on him and let them stick him away somewhere. It'd serve him right. I'm just a skivvy in our house. Billy's never got a kind word for me. It's bloody badgers this and badgers that and Mr Garrison this and Mr Garrison that. He thinks the sun sun shines out your behind.'

The colour rose in Garrison's face. 'I don't encourage him or Sheena to play truant. Quite the contrary. In fact I warned him only a few days ago that he'd land in hot water if he didn't knuckle down.'

'He's such a wilful little sod,' Mrs Drew growled. 'You tell him one thing and he does the exact opposite. I thought we could sort him out together. Otherwise –'

She shrugged and blew smoke at the ceiling. 'I can't keep tanning him.'

Garrison promised his full support but as the woman prepared to leave he wondered what was expected of him.

It was raining when he set off to walk the cliffs and consider the problem. How could he confront the little anarchists with anything resembling social consciousness? Billy was as self-serving as a feral tom. The rain drove into him but it lacked winter's sting and he rejoiced in his fitness. He strode along Woodash Down, swishing through the plantain that Billy called 'chimney sweepers' after the swarthy flowers. By the time Warren Fishacre was reached he had put together some sort of scheme although he was pessimistic about its chances of success. Billy could spit in the world's face without thinking but Garrison hoped the boy respected him sufficiently to at least meet him halfway. It would all hinge, he thought, on the badgers.

On Monday he would be en route to Switzerland and Riedlinger had told him not to worry. Ann would soon be well enough to come home. Soon. Two months? Three? Doubt churned up the coldness in his stomach. Yes, he thought grimly, Billy couldn't be allowed to have his own way at the expense of everyone else. So he wrote the sort of letter Billy would understand but it was Mrs Drew who opened it at the breakfast table and read it aloud while the boy sat staring at his porridge.

'Billy, If you play truant again I'm afraid you will be banned from Coastguard Cottage and the Warren Fishacre Estate. Mr Kerslake has orders to chase you off Ordish land if he receives word from me that you have failed to pull your socks up.

'Do not call at my place unless you're invited and this goes for Sheena as well. When you stop mitching and stealing you will both be welcome at the cottage as my friends.'

'From Mr Garrison,' said Billy's mother.

'Silly old fart,' Billy rasped.

'You don't mean that,' said Mrs Drew. 'You know you like him.'

He glared at her. 'I bet you put him up to this. You told on me.'

'I don't know why I bother,' she sighed, folding her hands around the teacup. 'You're such a selfish, hateful little devil.'

'Is it all right if I go to the cliffs today?' he said sarcastically. 'I mean, Saturday's OK, is it? Is it?'

'Yes – go,' she exploded, tears of anger prickling her nose. 'Go and break your grubby little neck for all I care.'

Moments later the front door slammed and she cried: 'Billy, I didn't mean it. Billy.' Then, in a desolate whisper: 'What the hell have I done to deserve this?'

Hot with temper Billy ran across the fields to Froward Point, stopping briefly to cut an ash sapling and make a spear of it. Creeping out of the pines he saw the Channel gleaming and heard the seabird din rising from Dragon Rock. A green woodpecker yaffled from the other side of the Point. At the thorn-scrub Billy knelt and examined the gaps where the badger paths entered the thicket. Snags of coarse grey hairs on the bullen spines calmed his anxiety. He got to his feet with a picture of his mother filling his mind. Her eyes were lowered and she was shaking her head in the sort of bleak misery he could not comprehend.

'Well,' he gasped. 'Well,' suddenly wanting her arms around him.

Grunting with anger and remorse he hurled the spear across the fading blackthorn blossom and heard it rattling through the massed branches. Then he sat back against one of the pines and stretched out his legs. The tree swayed slightly and a few needles fell. Swinging up and over Froward Point the kestrel held its wings stiff to the air current and hovered.

'Kee-kee,' Billy whispered, imitating the bird's cry. 'Kee-kee.'

Out on the Channel the wind moved in dark patches across the water. Light had transfigured the morning. The mica of

231

Dragon Rock was ablaze with it but the sea was pure light. It shifted in all directions, dilating and contracting.

Chapter 28

Near Effords Farm

Then the wind blew grey with drizzle from the east sending the rain in gusts across the bare fallow and the hay meadows. Billy hated the weather because he wanted to sleep out on Froward Point but at least the rain was an excuse for giving the sea cliffs a miss and on Monday morning he was at his desk in school. By afternoon the drizzle died but it remained cloudy and leaving Big Sett early Aspen and Birdcherry hesitated on the edge of the pines catching a suggestion of Billy's scent among the darker and richer scents of the trees. Their nostrils crinkled and they walked on.

The sows found Fingo playing with Cowtail's cubs on the steeps overlooking Wrangle Bay. The vixen lay close by grooming herself. As her ears pricked forward she said: 'Why is everyone out so early this evening? There ain't nothing special on is there? Is there?'

'Only your cubs,' Aspen smiled and she playfully bowled over one of the youngsters with her snout. 'They really are pretty little things, Cowtail.'

'Meaning they don't take after their mother,' said Fingo mischievously.

'B-but they are C-cowtail exactly,' said Birdcherry.

The fox grinned and the pupils of her eyes became thin vertical elipses and her sigh was of pure delight. Inching forward on her belly she pounced on the nearest whelp and licked its head. The sisters foraged up the steeps onto the pasture where sheep were standing around waiting for darkness to bring them into sleep. Aspen read the air. From the paddock under Effords Farm drifted the faint whinnying of work horses which had been loosed from their gears to run free. Cautiously the sows fed on beetles...

The wind bent the ash whips and willows in Ramsons Dip and Guelder's twins came wide-eyed to stare at the darkness that wouldn't stand still. They romped together with soft, yickering cries. Nipping each other's tails seemed a favourite game with playfulness developing into scuffles which bordered on the serious skirmishes of adult boars. Every so often they would roll down the slope together yelping and growling and Guelder would suddenly take hold of one and groom it while it squirmed and grizzled.

The night had brightened when Aspen and Birdcherry walked down into Ramsons Dip. Under the willow scrub by the stream Guelder lay holding a cub in close embrace as its brother gently licked out her ear.

'What are their names?' Birdcherry asked.

'Whitethorn and Maple.'

'Maple,' Birdcherry smiled.

She and Aspen laid their snouts on the tiny creatures and smelt all Guelder's motherhood. Aspen shivered and her sister glanced at her but did not speak until they had returned to the pastures.

'W-what did you see in the cubs?'

'There was no seeing, just a rawness round my heart.'

'Is s-something b-b-bad going to happen?'

Aspen sighed. 'I can't say but the ache was strong.'

They walked around the body of a dead ewe. Between clouds the moon shone. In the next field they smelled the faint milkiness of cows' udders and some of the milking shed dust on the underparts of the cattle. Curious horned heads were lowered to sniff them and the sisters responded with raised muzzles until they caught a whiff of vixen. Cowtail was panting.

'Dogs,' she gasped. 'Dogs everywhere. Big dogs with long legs and long teeth. They put the wind up me, I can tell you. Lucky I gave 'em the slip.'

'Outfoxed them,' Aspen smiled.

'Yes, foxy – that's me,' Cowtail chuckled.

'W-what were you doing?'

'Having a look at the chicken house,' the vixen grinned. 'Mouth-watering pullets, plump hens, chubby little chicks.'

'And the farmer heard the clatter and set his dogs loose,' said Aspen. 'Trying for hen house fowls when you've got young to look after is asking for trouble.'

'I know, I know,' the fox protested. 'But I just fancied one of them birds. Couldn't resist it. Anyway, that's that. I won't do it again.'

'You'd better not or you'll p-put Big Sett in d-danger,' said Birdcherry.

The work horses were stamping the turf and breathing their contact calls through their nostrils. In the calm Aspen sensed danger.

'Run, Birdcherry,' she cried and galloped across the pasture towards the hedge with her sister close behind. Cowtail had vanished. From the bullock yard of Effords burst four collie-crosses, their fangs gleaming. Birdcherry heard them and swallowed a sob of fear. The brambles held her and for an awful moment she thrashed about in panic unable to move backwards or forwards. Aspen bit through the main feeler and catching her sister by the loose shoulder flesh tugged her free. Birdcherry screamed but was able to worm through the tangle

235

and drop into the wheat field. Bramble spines drove into her back.

'Aspen,' she gasped.

'Keep moving,' came the low urgent reply. 'They're coming.'

'We'll never make it,' Birdcherry sobbed.

'Then turn and fight,' Aspen growled, fluffing out her guard hairs.

'Is that w-what you saw when we were w-with Guelder and the cubs?'

'I don't know. Does it matter?' Aspen said sharply and seeing her sister's head drop added in a softer tone. 'Please, Birdcherry. We need each other. Few dogs are a match for a pair of badgers.'

'But Aspen,' and Aspen licked Birdcherry's muzzle aware of her own heart thumping away.

The dogs struggled out of the bramble snarls and standing beside Aspen Birdcherry doubted the wisdom of holding ground. Her throat was dry. Her limbs shook and she was completely helpless. Down came the dogs to dance and bark and circle the sows with a confidence that was half-playful. They were secure in their strength and the badgers not only looked cowed but they were females. The boldest dog leapt in and crouched and snapped and waited for his comrades' approval before he rose on his hindlegs and jumped over the sows. Aspen and Birdcherry huddled together and waited for the play to become the killing business. At least Birdcherry isn't alone, Aspen thought, listening to her sister's panting. Sharp spasms of shivering convulsed Birdcherry's body as the dogs circled them with raised hackles. They were not large animals although to the sows they seemed enormous in the dim light. Their breath smelt of boiled rabbit and their coats carried the sickening stench of diesel for they had been lying under Kerslake's machinery in the open shed.

Lifting her head Aspen screamed the badger cry and set her teeth in a snarl. One of the dogs instantly dashed forward and tried to seize her by the hindlegs but she twisted and slashed his muzzle. His high-pitched yelp brought the game to an end. Lowering their bellies to the ground the dogs slowly advanced growling in chorus.

Beyond King Arthur's Tower Cowtail met Greybob and Furzebright at forage.

'Quick,' she gasped. 'Dogs have got Aspen and Birdcherry trapped by the hedge near the farm.

'Yap-dogs?' Greybob asked.

'No – long legs, nasties. Hurry, hurry.'

'How many?' Greybob shouted over his shoulder as he ran.

'Lots,' came Cowtail's reply.

The boars went up the field under Effords homing in on the barking of the dogs. Greybob was faster than his companion and more determined. His charge scattered the dogs and his teeth found a leg but before his jaw could close he was bowled over by Furzebright. Aspen immediately sprang to their aid leaving Birdcherry crouching with her face hidden in the wheat. Although wary of the badgers' teeth the dogs were brave and strong. Unlike terriers they were prepared to move in regardless to deliver a wound and spring out again before the badgers could retaliate. In the end Aspen knew she and the others would be broken by the tactics. The only thing to do was run and fight.

'Birdcherry,' she cried. 'We've got to go or we're finished.'

'I c-can't,' Birdcherry sobbed.

'Yes you can,' Aspen growled and she bit her sister's rump. Up sprang Birdcherry and Furzebright sent her staggering with another of his mis-timed attacks.

'Trot ahead of us,' Greybob said, dodging from side to side to block the assaults on the sows.

'It's no use,' Birdcherry panted. The life threatened to leave her limbs again.

'OK, would you prefer to stay here?' Aspen said and she winced as teeth cut into her haunches. 'Could you face this alone?'

237

Birdcherry shook her head and set off at an unsteady trot.

'Good,' Aspen cried. 'Keep going.'

'B-but we're a long way from B-Big Sett.'

There was no time for further chat. The dogs brought them to a halt in the middle of the field by the scarecrow. For a moment Furzebright was buried under three animals and Greybob had great difficulty freeing him. There was no respite for the boars and Aspen was constantly harassed as she attempted to get Birdcherry moving again. Between clouds half a moon flooded the farmland with its dim light. The badgers stood together, turning to meet each fresh attack but now Aspen felt anxiety where anger had once burnt strong. Furzebright was weakening and it was obvious Birdcherry had resigned herself to her fate. Only Greybob carried himself with a conviction of a sett-master for whom defeat was inconceivable. But we are finished Aspen thought. Behind the unreal Nightworld of pain and noise and fear she saw Guelder's cubs and everything that was life and badger.

Then from her dream she heard the eerie challenge of a boar. It was a cry unlike the shriek of naked aggression Greybob delivered every now and then to confirm his unflagging power. The dogs froze and laid back their ears and growled softly. All the animals stared into the darkness, their nostrils rounded with expectancy. The moon came out again and there like a trick of light was the great pale badger boar, every hair on his body stiff with fury and his musk so strong even Birdcherry lifted her head. It was an arrogant statement of potency that demanded recognition. And all at once the stranger charged, his cry ending as his jaws closed on the nearest dog. The crack and crunch of breaking bone was followed by the keening of the crippled animal.

Greybob and Furzebright promptly fell on the others before the effects of the stranger's assault could wear off. The dogs fled, howling and whining with the pale boar lumbering after them screaming his challenge. From the farmyard Kerslake called his animals by name and ran across the cow field to meet them, his torch flashing and his tethered house dog going mad in the kitchen.

'Get up and run, Birdcherry,' Aspen said and the hardness of her tone persuaded Birdcherry to do so without argument.

'Are you coming with us?' Greybob called to the stranger but he was trotting off towards the trees of Warren Fishacre.

'Come with us,' Furzebright cried. Again there was no response.

'Leave him and get out of here,' Greybob said.

They ran into the Monterey pines and hurried under the blackthorn to the lawn on Froward Point where they flopped down and licked their wounds.

'He saved us,' said Aspen. 'But who is he and why is he so sad?'

'Sad?' Greybob growled as his cuts and bruises began to ache.

'I f-felt he was too,' said Birdcherry.

'You!' Greybob exclaimed. 'Your gutlessness nearly got us killed. I don't need your opinion. Your words have less value than a cub squeaking or one of Hawscrag's farts.'

'I c-can't help being afraid,' she said miserably. 'I w-wanted to help b-but I was numb. I couldn't move.'

'But you can t-talk,' Greybob said, mockingly. 'Those dogs would have chopped us because of your cowardice. Aspen did her best but you –'

He snorted and turned his back on her.

'Aspen is Aspen,' Birdcherry said quietly. 'I am m-me and I'm always afraid. She knew s-something bad was going to happen.'

'The amazing *moonborn* sow,' Greybob sneered and Aspen wondered why she was out of favour.

Greybob had not finished. 'Perhaps,' he said. 'Earth Mother sends the ghost boar to fetch her favourite daughter.'

'That boar was real enough,' said Furzebright. 'If he hadn't come to our rescue this conversation wouldn't be taking place.'

'Then why's he so unsociable?' Greybob grumbled. 'He knows he'd be welcome in Big Sett.'

'On your terms, of course,' said Furzebright.

The healing qualities of his tongue found their way into his cuts.

Greybob glared at him and said: 'Any time you'd care to challenge my authority you'll find me only too willing to oblige.'

Aspen looked at her mate and no longer felt close to him. Instead of licking his wounds and permitting him to groom her she went to Birdcherry whose unhappiness was pitiful.

'D-did you see the d-dogs in your daydream, Aspen?'

'No – that wasn't what I saw.'

'Was it something to do with G-Guelder's cubs?'

'Perhaps.I can't tell. It was a feeling.'

'A bad feeling?'

Aspen nodded and Birdcherry sighed.

Chapter 29

Spring Frost

The pasture was dotted with ewes and lambs listening to the cuckoo repeat his double notes from the copse halfway up Garrowcombe. A few cirrus clouds were sketched on an otherwise cloudless sky and the mist gathering on the sea foretold fine weather. In the flooded ditch were tadpoles and frog spawn and clusters of marsh marigolds. The bracken croziers stood as high as Aspen's shoulder in the sheltered places. The badgers were motionless and uncertain in a world that was not completely dark. Hawscrag had mustered the sows of Big Sett and led them through sundown to Garrowcombe Head.

'The badger is early afield who hears the cuckoo,' chuckled the old sow.

Aspen, Birdcherry, Thornsong and two young maiden sows exchanged glances. Evening was fading rapidly to dusk.

With eyes sparkling Birdcherry and the maiden sows walked solemnly around Aspen, nudging her with their snouts and uttering small cries like cubs. The stars stood still and Aspen's musk wafted across the night masking all other

241

scents. Down on the beach the sea was silent between tides.

'Tell us about Big Sett, mother,' Birdcherry said.

They sat beneath the elms on the clifftop in a half-circle before Hawscrag who nodded and smiled benignly. Her grey muzzle was held a little to the left as was her habit. One eye was half-closed. She cleared her throat.

'And the sett was Cragbriar's and before him
it was Ironpate's and Brokenclaw's
and Gorsedagger's and Wildvine's
and Stonecob's and Baldrump's
and Brackenbold's.
The sett is as it was and the Great Boars
are alive in Sunworld.
What they were lies in the earth.
Now the sett is Greybob's
but tomorrow he will belong to the sett.'

Aspen was tired and the forage had yet to be made although she was not hungry. For no reason at all she thought of the stranger and his loneliness. A lost animal, yes, but what had he lost?

She looked at Birdcherry and smiled. The fog rolled in.

The street lamps of Mary's Haven burnt with a low throaty chuckle of gas in the sea mist.

'This weather makes my hair go all frizzy,' complained Mrs Rapson taking the arm of Charlie Dunning's wife and climbing the stairs to the upstairs room of the Ship.

Strawberry smiled. His club jacket was deliberately open to reveal his new waistcoat. He smelt of shaving soap and cigar smoke. Dunning and Stike idly watched Small who was attending to the drinks at the bar. There were few customers in the saloon for it was the middle of the week and most of the fishermen were at sea.

The Mary's Haven Badger Club was holding its spring Ladies' Night with a fish supper and housey-housey, but Strawberry had to broach the serious business first.

'I've been thinking about the twenty-five years do,' he said. 'And I reckon I've come up with somethin' appropriate.' He tapped his jacket pockets. 'Bloody fags! I'm always losing them.'

'Us wondered why you asked Archie Stoneman and his missis,' Dunning said.

Strawberry smiled, nodded and tapped the side of his nose with a forefinger. Small stuck a pint pot in his fist. The Stonemans sat woodenly in a corner, he with his brown-split and Wills Whiffs, she, rouged and impassive before a large port and lemon. Strawberry caught Stoneman's eye and the big morose man got up and came across the bar with the creak of new leather shoes. Pleasantries were exchanged but the small talk was kept to a minimum. Stoneman sensed something in the offing. Through his lashes he focused on the bright red birthmark which always made him feel Strawberry had emerged from battle. The pug face, smile and the tongue sliding across the lower lip created a disturbing spectacle – disturbing and hypnotic. He's like an old snake, Stoneman thought.

'A grand baiting, Arch,' Strawberry said. 'No messin' about. Your Lansworthy dogs and our dogs and something in the kitty for blokes prepared to put their money where their mouth is.'

'What sort of stakes?' Stoneman asked over the rim of his sleever.

'Fifty quid in the middle – twenty-five from each club. Winners take all.'

'Agreed,' Stoneman said. 'And a private side bet? Your best pair and mine, say a fiver?'

'Make it ten,' Strawberry grinned, and they shook hands.

'Toss for territory,' said Dunning and when the half-crown had come to rest against the fender Stoneman had called wrong.

'So it's tails our place,' Strawberry purred. 'My yard at a date to be fixed.'

'And you'll supply the badgers?' said Stoneman.

243

'Of course – eight good animals, two pairs and four singles, six dogs to a pair and four to a single. My Gritt and Jimmy and your animals should give the best sport of the meet.'

'Suits me,' said Stoneman. Again the men shook hands and lowered the level of their ale.

'I hear Mrs Ordish and that artist bloke are giving you a bad time,' Stoneman went on as they sauntered across to the counter.

'They're making things a bit awkward,' Strawberry confessed. 'But they'll have to get up early to bugger me around.'

'Is that Billy Drew still playing up?'

'Him,' Strawberry whispered. 'Oh no, Archie. Billy Drew idn' trouble. He's a fly buzzin' on the window. One day I'm going to crush him under my thumb.'

'He done your van I hear.'

'Someone done the van,' Strawberry smiled, accepting a cigarette from the landlady.

Towards midnight Dunning, Stike and Small joined Strawberry and Eric in the Rapson's living room for a final light ale.

'That Stoneman's a cocky bugger,' Dunning scowled.

The heavy clock on the mantelpiece ticked among the clutter Strawberry had brought back from his service days in the Far East: dolls with oriental faces and gaudy kimonos, a pair of bronze-type cobra candlesticks, cheap china figurines and fairground bric-a-brac.

'He won't be laughin' when I lift his cash,' Strawberry said.

Mrs Dunning placed the dish of ham-off-the-bone, cheese and pickles on the table and said good night. The terriers sat at Strawberry's feet gazing up at him expectantly. He beamed and fed them slices of meat.

'Where are we going to dig, Frank?' Stike said. 'Perce Hannaford says there's three or four big buries over Aish way, on the river.'

'We got our own buries,' said Strawberry. 'One old woman,

244

a couple of bloody kids and a half-baked artist won't stop me digging the Fishacre buries. Kerslake idn' exactly the sharpest bloke in the world and the rest of them can't be out and about all hours, all over the place. They won't beat me – no sir.'

He unfolded the map on which he had marked the clifftop setts.

'Eric and the Durney boys can get along and see which buries are in use. Then we'll need four digging teams and a couple of vans out before dawn to start work at first light and be away with the goods before Garrison's awake.'

'Will you keep 'em all in the shed down the yard?' Small asked. 'Eight badgers in there . . .' he shook his head.

'Some will be bagged,' said Strawberry. 'And us'll hobble the others.'

'What if they kick up a racket?' Dunning said.

'They don't,' Strawberry smiled. 'The buggers always bide quiet as if they make up their minds they're in for the chop. Then, when the dogs are put to 'em –'

'All hell breaks loose,' Dunning chuckled.

Strawberry drank and forked cheese and pickles into his mouth.

'Yes,' he mumbled. 'The dogs have a knack of bringing the buggers to life.'

Gritt whined from the centre of a huge yawn and began to scratch. His bottom lip had been ripped away by a badger and had never healed properly.

'Stoneman's got a new pair of Jacks,' Dunning added.

'I don't care if he's got a cross between a wheelbarrow and a donkey,' said Strawberry. 'There idn' no animals like my Gritt and Jimmy. If you want to make a couple of quid on the side bet on those little devils.'

The Jack Russells' stumpy tails quivered and their eyes became round and bright. They scrummaged to lick the hand Strawberry extended.

The steeps were leafing and the wild cherry on Down End was

ready to blossom. In Ramsons Dip the flowers of golden saxifrage had suddenly appeared, but nights could still be very cold as Guelder discovered after frost had lent a hard edge to twilight. She nosed confidently up into the farmland, her mind elsewhere in a daydream of happiness. The twins were a constant source of delight. She sighed and considered the prospect of forage. Whatever wind there was came off the sea but the frost had killed scent. Vaguely she was aware of a huge dark shape blotting out the stars to her left and instantly her senses were alert and she was turning towards the fence when the white and red light flared. Then the explosion and the pain swelled and receded together leaving a numbness and giddiness she could not understand. She fell down and got up and staggered through the gap to roll down the steeps in a flurry of legs. The pain hit her again and persisted. Disorientated she lifted her muzzle and began to walk around in a circle of bewilderment, like an animal preparing for sleep. Every so often she keeled over unaware of the blood leaking from the shotgun wound in her neck.

Soon it became difficult to breathe but she padded on blindly, wanting nothing save the sett and the warmth of her cubs. The instinct which had never betrayed her in the past brought her not to her young but to the Monterey pines where she sat swinging her head, frightened, dizzy and totally baffled. It was here that Fingo found her and guided her to the main hole of Big Sett. When the badgers gathered around her they knew she was dying.

'Oh Guelder,' Aspen whispered and the other sows gently licked the creature who was already lost to their world.

Guelder lay down and the faint smell of earth breaking free of frost filled her nostrils. The stars were sailing slowly away, leaving a darkness that was comforting. She closed her eyes and as her last breath faded opened them again. And there were Dogrose, Bullenspur and Briarfrost and all those who had gone before her, calling her by name. Then a voice of infinite kindness began to speak and Guelder knew the perfect happiness.

246

'She is gone,' Hawscrag said, hoarse with grief and bitterness.

Sows and boars sat around the motionless body and Aspen spoke.

'Then I am animal,
After sundown I walk from the sett
Through the mercy of She
who is Ageless.
Cool moon-silver glory of grass,
Softness of wind,
Sea whispering.
I am animal.
I am the seasons, indestructable.'

Hawscrag nodded her approval and said: 'She belongs to the earth. Let us give her back to it.'

The sea was whispering, with the reefs bare at low water and small waves lapping at Dragon Rock. Guelder was buried in the wild lawn between the blackthorn while the pines murmured and the owls called as if Nightworld was still complete. That, thought Aspen, is the saddest thing.

'And now', said Hawscrag when it was all over, 'the twins must be brought here. Life must go on.'

Aspen turned startled eyes on her mother and received a sad smile. Yes, Aspen thought, the old dam can look into my heart as I looked into this moment many dusks ago and felt the ache of it all.

Birdcherry picked up the thread as they trotted along the path.

'This was your b-bad feeling, wasn't it?'

'Yes, but please don't go on about it.'

'Guelder's death c-could have b-been more unpleasant,' said Birdcherry in the small voice which told Aspen she was concerned about herself. 'At least she wasn't alone.'

'Nothing's going to happen to you,' Aspen said sharply.

The cubs were hungry and irritable when the sows found them in the nursery chamber.

'Fortunately they're weaned,' Aspen said. 'Although I think there's a milky sow on the bluebell steeps. Take Maple, Birdcherry, and I'll grab this little misery.'

They closed their jaws on the scruff of each cub's neck and carried them into the darkness, ignoring the squeals and growls of complaint. All that remained of Guelder was a faint suggestion of her musk at the entrance to the sett. Again Aspen's heart faltered. She was beginning to share Birdcherry's belief that some evil force had come to the coast determined to wipe out all the badgers of Big Sett and the outlying dens. Hawscrag had never known such persistent persecution. She could remember seasons when the steeps were never visited by men with yap-dogs.

An aeroplane droned across the sky and the cubs hung limp and silent in the mouths of the sows. Outside Big Sett Hawscrag was waiting.

'You must be brave, my little ones,' she said tenderly. 'Your mother is dead but now you have many mothers.'

'Where is she?' Maple asked in a puzzled voice.

'With Earth Mother.'

'But why?' said Whitethorn.

'She was called and had to go. But she leaves you her love and all of us love you.'

The cubs' heads drooped and they whimpered.

'D-don't be sad,' said Birdcherry.

'Oh be quiet!' Hawscrag snapped. 'You can't tell an animal not to be sad or happy. Use your head.'

Then the cubs were led underground and comforted by Thornscrag and the maiden sows. Hawscrag turned to the cat who had patiently remained silent from beginning to end of the affair.

'You are a good and loyal friend, Fingo,' she said. 'Big Sett is your sett. Please regard it as your home.'

'In the winter I may take you up on that,' the cat smiled. 'In the meantime I like my own company.'

'Hawscrag speaks for us all,' said Greybob, and Fingo

248

bowed his head in recognition of the honour.

Aspen walked with him up under the pines whose music was comforting.

'I've never seen Earth Mother,' the cat confessed. 'I've always felt something there behind things but I've never seen her. Maybe it's because my mother was a pet. Perhaps that's why I still go to people and expect to be treated well.'

Aspen was sorrowing for Guelder and did not wish to chat. Fingo spoke his thoughts at great length, trampling on some of Aspen's old doubts. So it was quite a relief to meet Cowtail and listen to the vixen's bragging.

Chapter 30

Sycamore

The turnip head on Efford's scarecrow had rotted away and was replaced with an equally featureless mangel. Travelling foxes left their cards on the faded, insect-crawling coat, and rooks and crows used the broom handle arms as perches. Often as he ran with a curious stiff-legged gait a little faster than walking pace, Fingo stopped in the wheat field to sniff at the scarecrow whose attire carried pungent information. Kerslake was aware of the feral tom and after Cowtail had made a successful raid on his fowls the bailiff laid the blame at Fingo's door.

Among the work dogs at Effords was the surly collie, Candy. She was feared by every dog in the neighbourhood. Once she had fought and killed a mongrel stray she had caught worrying sheep. Her eyes were pale blue and her gaze unwavering.

On his return from Switzerland Garrison met Candy on Hellweather Point lying sunning herself; but the animal growled when he approached and her bared fangs warned him to back off. The man was in high spirits. Ann really was looking better and he'd begun to believe the doctors who assured him that she would be home that summer.

Climbing the steeps to avoid Candy, Garrison thought of his wife's splendid, self-effacing humanity, cheerfulness and broadness of spirit. Then he wanted her beside him in the sunlight of the English spring in that most heavenly part of England. The wild cherry among the stumps of the felled beeches on Down End was flowering and the sight of the snow-white blossom had Garrison sucking in his breath.

Although he was not religious in the orthodox sense he wanted to sing one of the hymns of his childhood, 'How Great Thou Art', but could only remember the first verse.

'"Oh Lord my God when I in awesome wonder
Consider all the works thy hands hath made
I see the stars, I hear the mighty thunder
Thy power throughout the universe displayed."'

He sat on the old drystone wall and looked over the water. Three Mary's Haven trawlers were steaming south for the Lizard and the Irish sea. Gulls swooped and cried and further along the steeps a kestrel hovered. A long way out to sea gannets were diving and he held them in the binocular window until a fly settled on his lower lip and he spat it off with a little gasp of disgust. The acceleration of greenness during his absence was startling. The bracken crooks were knee high and among the clumps of bramble and briar were dark-green masses of bluebell leaves.

He clenched his fists and tapped the knuckles together. The sky was blue, the sun shone and turtle doves were crooning on the roof of Down End barn. Along the sheep-walk loped the collie and Garrison made a mental note to inform Kerslake his dog was on the loose. House martins lifted from the crags below and hawked the slopes of thrift and mallow, but Candy stared straight ahead growling softly.

All day the collie traversed the steeps, back and forth with a restlessness she could not allay. A glimpse of Fingo rapidly climbing the opposite side of one of the deep, sea-filled inlets did not help sweeten her temper. She galloped after Fingo but he had long vanished into the gorse when she arrived. Cats angered Candy. Their smell and appearance and cries left her breathless with the lust to savage them into silence and stillness. At length she settled down and slept for a while and on waking found dusk turning to twilight. Waves of scent washed over her and she was aware of the insect chirr and tick in the grass where her muzzle rested. Something soft and light bumped against her head and whirred away but she snapped her jaws at it before getting to her feet, shaking herself and stretching. Then she left the sheep-walk and took to the badger path that traversed it to cut across the lower slopes. The sea was speaking in whispers and its smell had a coolness and cleanness which Candy disliked. She preferred meaty, dark-textured scents but the sudden musk of badger brought her to a halt. Slowly her hackles stiffened and she growled.

Aspen who was foraging ahead of Greybob smelt the dog before she heard the growl. Immediately she dived into the brambles and crouched low among the shadows but Greybob was taken by surprise. He had stopped to probe the wayside humus with his snout and Candy was on him before he could move. The charge swept him off his feet and the dog's teeth ripped open one of his ears. He cried out and Aspen ran to his assistance only to be knocked down and bitten on the face. Shocked by the onslaught Greybob was slow to turn and the next attack left the flesh on his right foreleg open to the bone in a long gash. Candy's momentum sent Aspen flying as she too struggled to rise.

With a paw pressed to Greybob's neck the dog delivered three slashing blows to the shoulder before Aspen closed and forced a retreat. By now both badgers knew they had met no ordinary long-legged dog. This creature had cunning as well as bulk and she was quick and nimble. Greybob's screech left her unmoved and although the badgers tried to get into the brambles Candy caught them again, scoring with her teeth on the hindleg Greybob kicked out as he rolled away.

The noise the animals were making startled the sheep on the pasture above and brought Billy cautiously to the steeps. He had been trying to take hens' eggs from Effords but Kerslake had scared him off. Instead of running for home along the lanes Billy had doubled back over the fields to Backways, intending to go the long way and call in on Garrison. The growling and barking and weird screaming brought him to the fence. And a few yards down the steeps the sight of a black and white striped face told him it was badgers – badgers and a dog. He crouched like an animal and sniffed the air. It was free of tobacco smoke, so it wasn't one of Strawberry's efforts.

Billy squatted in the bracken. The dim light made it hard to tell what was happening. Then he sensed another presence and held himself perfectly still. Crashing through the dead cow parsley and brambles the pale boar ran grunting onto the steeps. A swift turn of the head and a snarl and he was slithering through the bluebell leaves to crash down on the dog. His jaws gaped as he screamed his battle cry.

Candy staggered and Aspen's claws raked the dog's nose to fetch up a yelp of surprise and pain. Before she could recover the stranger hit her again, cracking one of her ribs as he knocked the wind out of her to choke off the howl of pain. Aspen took the opportunity to nip the dog's tail and the badgers regarded her hasty retreat. Greybob was badly hurt and had lost interest in the proceedings. He lay on his side pawing at his ruined ear between licking the wounds he could reach. The stranger stood rocking and moaning and swinging his muzzle.

'Please, what is wrong?' Aspen whispered but he continued shaking his head.

'Leave him,' Greybob gasped. 'Can't you see? He's mad. He'll attack you.'

'But he saved us,' Aspen said.

'I doubt if he knows it,' Greybob said.

Aspen paced slowly up the stranger and licked his face.

253

'Are you hurt?' she asked, glad he hadn't pulled away.

'There's ice in my head,' he groaned. 'Ice. Brain numb. Can't think. Can't sleep. Always numb or aching.'

'Ice?' Aspen said and despite his injuries Greybob laughed.

'And the claw pain in the back of my head. It comes and goes.'

The stranger began to whimper and rub his snout in the leaf mould at the wayside.

Greybob was on his feet swaying, but he could still raise his muzzle and laugh again.

'Leave Old Ice Head alone, Aspen,' he said, letting a little menace into his voice. 'Let him follow his own path and you come back with me to Big Sett.'

'He saved your life,' Aspen said passionately.

'Well, he's got my thanks. Now let's go before the dog comes back with more dogs.'

'You go,' Aspen said.

'Very well,' said Greybob. 'But don't bring Old Ice Head to my sett.'

He went and Aspen turned back to the stranger. He had not moved but his snout still beat the rhythm of his misery.

'What's your name?' she said.

At the end of a long wavering moan he murmured: 'Saltsycamore.'

'That's a bit of a mouthful,' Aspen smiled. 'I'll call you Sycamore.'

'Now the pain,' Sycamore sighed. 'It drives deep into my head.'

'Is there something there?' Aspen said.

'How should I know?' he growled and was instantly remorseful. 'Sorry – sorry. The cold numbness and then the pain make talking difficult, too painful most of the time. Usually I want to run off and bang my head against a tree.'

'Let me look at the back of your head.'

'There's nothing to see,' he said, the words rising to a snarl as the pain corkscrewed in his brain.

254

'Let me look,' Aspen persisted and she licked his snout and eyes.

'Were you wounded in a fight?'

'No, never,' he said, closing his eyes. 'Now the ice, the deadness.'

'And you haven't banged your head on anything?'

'No, no, nothing, never. Once, I can't remember when, there was the blinding flash in the dark and the loud noise.'

'When, Sycamore?'

'Long ago or yesterday,' and he laughed. 'Flash! Bang! It knocked me down but I got up and ran. Then I went to sleep and woke up dizzy. Couldn't walk straight. After that ice-in-head or the hot pain that stabs and twists.'

'Let me look – please.'

He bowed his head and the tip of Aspen's tongue located the small bald patch and scar behind Sycamore's right ear. Beneath it was a hard little lump.

'Have you got ice head now?' she demanded.

'Yes yes yes! Can't feel a thing. Nothing. Dead head.'

So Aspen bit into the skin and laid bare a patch of Sycamore's skull. Lodged in the bone was the sort of heavy shotgun pellet men used to kill deer. Aspen's teeth closed on it and gently worked it free. Then she licked the wound. Eventually Sycamore shook his head and sighed.

'I'm giddy,' he said.

'And is there still ice in your head?'

'Not so much and it doesn't feel as if my brain is being crushed between two rocks. What did you do?'

Aspen told him and he sniffed at the lead slug.

'Something so small,' he said in a puzzled voice.

Aspen laughed and continued to clean the wound with her tongue.

'You're very kind,' Sycamore said and groaned as the ice closed briefly inside his skull only to recede again. 'What's your name?'

'Aspen, daughter of Hawscrag. The pain and numbness will go.'

'Forever?'

'Yes.'

He stared dreamily at the sky. 'The stars are going round and round but my head no longer feels heavy or on fire or frozen.'

'Come to our sett,' Aspen said.

'But you have a mate.'

'No. I am moonborn. Sometimes I can ignore the sett laws. In any case, I'm not really fond of Greybob.'

'Who is he?'

'You just saved his life,' Aspen smiled. 'Don't you remember the dog and the fight?'

'I only remember your voice and kindness, Aspen the moonborn.'

They laughed and Sycamore wobbled but did not fall. From his hiding place on the steeps Billy watched them depart. He got up shivering and clambered blindly back to the fence. The stars were bright and close and inevitably rabbits were panicking along the edge of the pasture.

'Where are you, dad?' Billy cried.

The stars blinked back at him and he let the sobs go as he began to run. But he couldn't remain unhappy for long. Moths ricocheted off his head, brambles spiked his legs, his gym shoes were sodden and by the time he had crossed the Garrow Brook Billy was giggling. Sheena would be waiting outside the chip shop, her hands stuffed in her raincoat pockets and her mouth full of bad language. Sheena had big eyes and she loved him.

He ran over Woodash Down crowing like a cockerel. The lights were on in Coastguard Cottage. Billy ran hard, stampeding the sheep and hurtling down the hillside with arms raised like a triumphant boxer.

Answering the knock at the front door Garrison found the boy standing, hands on hips, taking great gulps of air and grinning between each gasp.

'I saw a big pale badger, mister. He beat up a dog. There

were three badgers. The big pale one went off with a little sow. That old boy put the wind up me.'

'Why, Billy?'

'I dunno. He was kind of spooky, I suppose – not like a real badger.'

'Would you like something to eat?'

'No thanks. I gotta get home to supper.'

'How are things at home now, Billy?'

'OK,' and Billy coloured. 'My mum's a terrific cook.'

Garrison smiled. It was the first time he had heard the boy speak kindly of Mrs Drew. Maybe the letter had achieved something but he never expected Billy to mention it.

Chapter 31

Gulls' Eggs

On the bare ground between the pines and the blackthorn scrub Greybob and the other sett-dwellers were waiting. Aspen stepped from the shadows followed closely by Sycamore.

'No further,' Greybob growled and the ripples of hair along his spine told everyone he was angry.

'Aspen is of my tribe,' said Hawscrag.

'Our sister,' chimed the sows.

The yearling boars and Furzebright kept quiet.

'She lives in Big Sett because I say so,' said Greybob. 'The stranger is welcome providing he knows who is sett-master.'

'I'm not here to cause trouble,' Sycamore said amiably.

'Good,' Greybob barked. 'Remember, I defeated you in combat.'

'Did you?' Sycamore said. 'The trouble is I can't remember.'

'He was shot in the head,' Aspen explained. 'I took out the little hard thing that usually brings death.'

Then she set her tongue once more to Sycamore's wound and licked it in a manner which Greybob disliked.

'You're my mate, Aspen,' he said, his eyes fiery with accusation.

'Listen,' Sycamore said. 'You are sett-master but if necessary I'll fight you for this sow.'

Greybob's upper lip twitched. 'She is of no importance to me,' he sneered. 'Take her. She's stuffed full of dreams like her ga-ga old mother. I can have any sow I want.'

His wounds were still smarting and his legs were weak, and something about the pale stranger worried him. Sycamore might prove a rough rival with his craziness healed. Greybob was the established sett-master and it would be incredibly stupid to jeopardize his position by fighting a boar who was fit and strong. The confrontation was avoided without loss of face. It was satisfactory. Snuffling and grunting Greybob retired to the sett to sleep. The rest of the tribe gathered around the newcomer and Guelder's twins crept forward to sniff his forepaws. Then the play of sows and cubs was a celebration of all the badgers held dear – starlight and the events of Nightworld and the life that is lived without terror. They rolled together in the dew, laughing and calling to each other until Sycamore and the other boars had to join in. Only Hawscrag remained aloof. She sat smiling and nodding her approval as the animals romped and the lights of ships ran along the bottom of the sky.

Furzebright and Thornsong did not remain long in Big Sett but when Greybob took Birdcherry for a mate everyone except Hawscrag was surprised. She had known boars like Greybob before. They thundered bristling from cubhood to old age as if the living world was a threat and their dignity had to be maintained at all costs. A sett-master without a mate or several sows would be open to ridicule.

'Greybob looks at the world and sees only himself,' she told Aspen. 'But such vanity is good for the tribe and Birdcherry will give us good cubs providing she doesn't die of sheer gratitude.'

'Greybob has changed,' Aspen said sadly.

Behind everything, thought Hawscrag, is the sisterhood of the sows, serving life which is Earth Mother. There were times, she conceded, when dream and reality became one, leaving her in a daze. Then she heard all the voices of the past and walked the long tunnel between sett-life and Sunworld.

The gentle breathing of the cubs was reassuring. Leaving the chamber she came bumping and puffing onto the Point to find the wind freshening and waves showing white on the Rips. The easterly had left the sky clear with a scimitar moon and every star blazing wherever she swung her muzzle.

'Never alone,' she whispered. The wind furrowed her coat and the Point was all movement and noise. In the sky behind her Monterey pines roared and rocked and Fingo crossing the wheat field had one of his fits, pouncing on blades of corn as they bent and twitched. The soil was hard and dusty. It lifted in a cloud as the wind that brought the smell of the sea also sent the fragrance of bluebells wafting across the farmland. It was the first thing Billy and Sheena smelt early next morning when they walked the stony cart track over Down End towards Hellweather Point. It was the time of the gull egging and Garrison had promised to meet them later on Garrowcombe Sands. Like many Mary's Haven boys Billy visited the gulleries and loomeries along the cliffs each spring for the seabird eggs which had been part of the town's economy for centuries. The tradition was dying hard, partly because of the actual adventure of climbing but mostly due to the rich taste of gulls' egg omelettes.

'Always omelettes,' Billy said. 'You can't boil the egg 'cos they might have young in 'em and it's awful when you crack the shell and see a tiny beak and a little eye lookin' back at you.'

'Blimey!' Sheena shuddered. 'Bleedin' old fishy eggs with bits of bird in 'em. You lot are like animals.'

'Tarzan probably ate stacks of birds' eggs raw,' Billy said. 'And so did the Red Indians.'

'Only 'cos they had to. I bet they'd rather have had a spam sandwich with sweet pickle or beans on toast.'

'I like 'em,' he said.

'Bleedin' liar. You've never had a raw egg.'

'I've had hundreds,' Billy declared, breaking away from her.

Sheena pushed her fingers up through her curls and sighed, but the matter was not pursued.

The waysides were full of lady's lace, bluebells and campion. Glimpsed from gateways the fields curved down into Garrowcombe. Larks trilled and beyond the headland the sea rushed to the horizon.

'Nearly there,' Billy said in a conciliatory tone. It was his place but he wanted her to be part of it. Sheena remained silent.

They climbed the last gate into a meadow pitted with rabbit burrows and scarred with runs. Rabbits departed hurriedly and a wheatear flew long the top of the gorse that grew between the cultivated land and the steeps. Billy forgot his companion. The afternoon was perfect and the sea cliffs were waiting for him.

'We don't have to do no dangerous climbin' do we?' Sheena asked.

'No, silly,' he grinned. 'We just walk round the bottom of the cliffs and get the easy ones today. There won't be many, any rate.'

'I wish the bluebells was out proper,' Sheena said. 'I love bluebells.'

They picked a route through the chin-deep gorse and emerged hot and scratched on the steeps. The jabber of kittiwakes lofted from Hellweather Point. Wherever bracken gave way to turf there was thrift, yellow vetch and sea campion. Gulls dived at them and slanted sharply down under the cliff tops.

'Bleedin' old shite hawks,' Billy said, and he tightened the straps of his small army back-pack.

'You ain't going down them cliffs,' Sheena said.

261

'There's a path,' he said. 'It goes down to the rocks. Anglers use it. Come as far as the big grassy bit and wait for me.'

'OK, and remember, Billy – I got the grub.' She tapped the satchel.

Soon he was at the base of the cliffs picking up eggs but leaving the nests with doubles and threes untouched. Singles meant fresh lays.

The climbing was easy even on the vertical slabs and Billy moved with the confidence of a cat. Inching round a rock buttress or promontory he sometimes found himself below the loomeries of guillemots and razorbills or the nesting ledges of kittiwakes and fulmars. The birds made a terrific din, and the air was full of wings and beaks and bright eyes. In places the shale was wet and slippery with seaweed but almost every cleft and hollow above the high water mark had its nest of plaited grass holding the beautifully mottled eggs of the herring gull.

Eventually Billy reached Garrowcombe Sands with his pack half-full and climbed the head to trot back to Sheena.

'Hungry?' she smiled, seeing the joy on his face.

'Thirsty,' he panted and she gave him the bottle of dandelion and burdock.

'It's warm,' he said but drank nevertheless in noisy gulps. Then he belched.

'Pig,' she said. 'Have you finished gettin' them bleedin' eggs?'

'Not yet. We'll go the other side of Hellweather and you can come down this time. My gran could do that bit.'

'I don't like heights,' she said.

'You have to be Jane and I'm Tarzan,' he said.

'Weedy little Tarzan!'

'Well, Tarzan had to be a boy once, didn't he?'

Among the boulder jumbles under the cliffs pickings were good and Sheena cheered up. Billy showed her the house martins' nests in the roof of the sea cave and the great broken slab a fox had zigzagged up one unforgettable autumn evening during the war.

'Don't go so high,' Sheena mewled as he showed her exactly what the fox had done. 'Please, Billy. It makes me feel all queer in my belly.'

He shook his head, unable to comprehend her distress.

'I'm going home if you don't come down, Billy.' And then in a shout: 'Billy!'

The turf on the slopes of the deep inlet was littered with the skulls of seabirds, rabbit bones and grubbed-out bluebell bulbs. All the narrow paths converged on the sett behind the salt-withered elderberry on the promontory. Fresh bedding lay in the main hole and the spoil heap was as high as the mound of clay the bracken was trying to hide. The children met the sun amongst the cushions of thrift.

'You can get out the food now,' Billy said, unslinging his pack.

'Won't them eggs break in there?' she asked.

'They're wrapped in newspaper and grass,' he said. 'We always do it this way.'

'Who's we? It's just you, Bill. You ain't got no pals except me and I'm your sweetheart.'

He went red. 'Yes, well, you can dish out the sandwiches and stuff now. I'll just have a peep at the ledges down over before I tuck in.'

'Bleedin' eggs! I don't fink Tarzan would've done anything so daft.'

'Yes he would,' Billy said. 'He'd have gone after crocodile's eggs or something. Tarzan liked climbing trees and swinging about and divin' into rivers.'

'Crocs don't nest in trees.'

He left her sitting with her legs drawn up and her chin on her knees staring out over the Channel.

'If you ain't back soon I'm off,' she called as he arrived at the tip of the promontory.

'You wouldn't leave me.'

'I would, Bill. I bloody would.'

Gulls rose in a mass and screamed at him.

'Bloody old shite hawks,' he grated through clenched teeth.

Then he lowered himself down the vertical rock to make a hair-raising trip along the ledges eighty feet above the sea. In the cool shadows he hummed 'Rule Britannia' but the tension of climbing over crumbling rock that was smeared with gull mutes had his whole body quivering. Sheena, he reflected, resting precariously for a moment, would have fainted at the sight of him perched on the dark rock face surrounded by birds.

Then his shirt front was full and he climbed directly up to surface into sunlight again behind Sheena.

'You mad bleeder,' she squawked as he crept up on her and tumbled her over.

The great black-backed gulls boomed and flapped up to hang on the wind and register their anger.

'Come on,' Billy said. 'I'll show you where they nest. It's OK, Sheen – honest. Follow me.'

They slid on their behinds down the bluebells steeps and sat together overlooking a stac. A large group of great black-backs took to the air.

'They give me the creeps,' Sheena said. 'I hope you ain't even thinking of gettin' onto that rock. Just you try and I won't only go home, I'll never see you again.'

'Then who will you go to the pictures with on Saturday mornings?'

'Aw, don't be so bloody silly. Come and eat the picnic and stop assing about.'

They ate and lay side by side in the thrift watching the gulls flash across the sky.

'Whatja thinkin' about, Bill?'

'The sun makes me happy,' he murmured, staring into the blue through his lashes. 'The place makes me happy. Sometimes it's like what I feel for you.'

He raised himself on his elbows and looked across the pink heads of the flowers. Sheena caught hold of his hand.

'Have you got enough of them old eggs?'

He nodded and yawned.

Walking back up the cart-track that evening they met Mrs Ordish and Lucy. Billy spoke about the egging and the old lady smiled and patted his head and gave him sixpence.

'He really is a wicked little chap,' she said when the children had ran on. 'A little tike.'

Lucy gazed at her. She had met a young man at the music school who seemed to possess virtues she had never imagined could be housed in one human being.

'David Garrison is worried about him,' said the girl. 'He's in and out of trouble and only goes to school when he wants to.'

'A proper boy,' Mrs Ordish laughed.

'But it's no joke for his mother,' said Lucy.

'These people tend to fuss a bit, Lucy, but they always cope. The working class is remarkably resilient.'

Leaving her grandmother on Hellweather Point Lucy walked to Coastguard Cottage and was pleased to see Garrison in his garden as she came down the hillside. The wind had built up the surf and the spray was flying; but Garrison was full of his new picture.

In the studio was a six feet by three and a half feet canvas on two heavy easels. A small section in the top left-hand corner showed signs of what Garrison called 'intense activity'.

'I've never seen green like yours,' Lucy said. 'And it's full of other greens. What about the rest of the picture?'

He shrugged. 'It'll grow. I've an idea of what's coming next but nothing's really positive or fixed. The other day I saw the drag-fold below Bullen Down.'

'Drag-fold?'

'Different sorts of rock in layers set one above the other in a cliff face,' Garrison explained. 'I'm going to take my time with this. I want to indulge myself. When Ann comes home it'll be done – and I know it'll be good. I can feel it.'

'In your heart?' she smiled.

'In my bowels,' he laughed. 'A gut reaction.'

'Have you stopped drawing badgers?'

He went to the table and opened a folder. It was packed with ink, charcoal and pencil studies of animals and birds.

'They're superb,' Lucy murmured and her eyelashes fluttered down. Then, at that moment, Garrison knew why the girl kept bringing Ann alive. She had his wife's habit of slowly lidding her eyes when she was pleased or happy.

He was pouring the sherry when he heard her little cry of surprise from the living room.

'What is it?' he called.

'The cat on the bird table.'

Garrison joined her at the window. 'That's Himself,' he said. 'He that walks alone and comes and goes when he chooses. He trots round with the badgers.'

'Of course!' Lucy exclaimed. 'The one who fetched you when the little sow was in the trap. He visits us, too.'

'Himself.'

But the next moment a dog was scrabbling on the side of the bird table and Himself was gone.

'It's Kerslake's Candy,' Garrison said. 'She's a menace.'

They burst into the garden and the bitch dropped down on her belly and rested her chin on her forepaws and gazed at them.

'She bites,' Lucy warned.

'Where's the cat?' said Garrison.

'Gone – no! There he is.'

Fingo was up one of the tamarisks.

'Shall I get rid of Candy?' said Lucy. 'She isn't too bad with me.'

'I'll get you some cord,' Garrison said. 'Sure you can manage?'

'Yes, no trouble. And in any case I have to get back to Fishacre.'

The crisis passed. Twilight faded and Garrison stood in the porch and lit a cigar. The wind had slackened but the surf was still thudding onto the shore. Fingo had gone with fish in his belly and a swagger that had made Garrison chuckle. The loose hasp was rattling and firelight played on the living room ceiling and walls. Presently loneliness soured to one of his black moods and he went into the studio, lit the lamp and contemplated the picture. The windows shook as the wind gusted strong again and brought the first flights of swifts in over the water. They came screaming through the starlight and the badgers leaving Froward Point for the forage raised their heads. Even the noise of the breakers hitting Dragon Rock could not drown those high, thin cries of joy. Below the zigzags the sycamores swayed and thrashed about. The night was a shifting ocean of scents. Rising from the steeps the fragrances and smells tingled in Aspen's nostrils. All the gorse and thorn, bracken, bramble and grass was alive and singing. She gazed through the vault of twigs and leaves that beat against the sky. Her comrades were also rapt. Sycamore stood motionless beneath the elderberry tree and Birdcherry, Hawscrag and Thornsong sat on the clifftop turf where the thrift grew, pointing their muzzles at the sky.

Turning towards the sea Aspen breathed the heavy odour of guano from the loomeries of Dragon Rock. It was veined with the wet scent of honeysuckle leaves and flowers. The roar of the sea was answered by the roar of the pines.

Chapter 32

Skirmishes

At dawn the wind fell to a whisper and the stillness framed the sort of sunrise that even calmed the gulls. Skyhook was aloft early hanging at his station nearly a thousand feet above Hellweather Point. His large, yellow-ringed eyes focused on the small dark cloud drifting in from the Channel. The migrating butterflies settled on the undergrowth of Garrowcombe Head with a patter that woke Fingo. He stretched, yawned and ignored the exhausted red admirals clinging to the bracken fronds and bramble leaves after their journey across the water.

Before long the adders were coming out to sunbathe. Between naps the cat heard their slitherings. Young rabbits were also on the move in the bracken but Fingo had eaten too much fish at Coastguard Cottage and had been sick twice. He lay listening to the swish of waves and the kittiwake babble. Every so often jackdaws rose from the headland crags to descend again in vertical dives, fanning their wings to brake suddenly and vanish into their nesting holes. The cat unsheathed his claws and sank them in the roots of a hawthorn which had fallen many winters before. Then dogs began to bark along the steeps to the south, far off but in an excited clamour.

The Gurneys walking up from Shippen Cove after an all-night fishing expedition had unleashed their lurchers to kill one of Cowtail's cubs. The little dog fox had been slow to get underground when his mother had called her warning. His death was swift but Cowtail's distress surprised and moved the badgers. For most of the day she lay beside the body, nudging it gently with her nose and whimpering, but whenever crows flapped about in the sycamores she leapt up gnashing her teeth. After dusk Aspen and Birdcherry approached her cautiously but her mourning was over although the pain of loss was with her for days.

'W-was it the dogs?' Birdcherry asked.

'Long-legs, big long-legs,' Cowtail snarled. 'My little one was asleep. He answered my call too late.'

She flashed them a hard, critical glance and added: 'Don't give me the Earth Mother stuff. Don't tell me about the good places and safe earths and warm days with no dogs or men to make the bad things happen. I want my little one – that's all I want. If Earth Mother is so good why did she take him from me? Why did I carry him inside me? Why? – bloody why? No,' she barked, seeing Birdcherry preparing to speak, 'I don't want words. Words won't make the pain go away.'

'Is it s-safe to let the twins come out?' Birdcherry asked Aspen as Cowtail padded off.

'Yes. There's nothing bad on the air.'

Like the vixen Aspen had no desire to spend half the forage in idle conversation. Obviously Greybob had not curbed Birdcherry's talkativeness. Aspen was glad to move on alone and join up with Sycamore where the flowering mallow stood at the top of the gully above Wrangle Bay. A large aeroplane droned overhead and all along the steeps spread the scent of bluebells. Boar and sow walked into it, absolutely content to be together.

Occasionally Sycamore suffered from an attack of what he called 'ice-brain' but the bouts did not last long and he often went several nights without being troubled. Now the forage was really good with larva, beetles and earthworms and bluebell bulbs to satisfy all the sett-dwellers from Froward Point to St Mary's Head.

Wherever the badgers lived and were raising cubs the sows were out collecting fresh bedding and the boars were ranging across the nearby fields whose hedges had been sculpted by the prevailing winds. It was a beautiful spring night. The evening star blazed and Vega, Arcturus and Antares were brilliant in the moonless sky. Light glinted on bluebell leaves and shillet while boar and sow walked the ancient trails, sometimes traversing steep crags but generally keeping to the steeps. Now and then they stopped for mutual grooming or long luxurious scratching.

Back on the bracken slopes below the zigzags the cubs were amusing Hawscrag and the other sows. They kept attacking Thornsong and were either clinging to her tail or her ears, but the young sow was a patient and loving creature capable of shrugging off most things with a smile. Instinctively she rolled the whelps over every so often and sent her teeth chattering through their belly fur. Hawscrag approved and even joined in the play. On their return to Big Sett, Aspen and Sycamore sat with Greybob and Furzebright as the twins became more boisterous, kicking up a racket that brought Fingo out of the pines to see what was going on. Then the cubs rolled around the cat, nipping his tail or getting under his feet. The sweet musk of gorse spilled off the steeps.

The startling rise of sap continued to transform the coast. Grass was growing steadily and the green of the pasture where the stirks and heifers grazed was so vivid it appeared artificial. In the hedges hawthorn was breaking into blossom and the gorse was flowering wherever it grew on the steeps. These great furze thickets were full of linnets, chaffinches and yellowhammers, and low down in the branches of one bush Billy found a stonechat's nest. The little black song-bird had cried its 'whit-chat, what-chat' with the crisp intonation of two pebbles being knocked together and Billy had seen the white patches of its wings, neck and upper tail and the dark red breast. The nest was a little masterpiece of interwoven grass and moss, lined with hair and feathers. Sheena knelt reverently before it. For most of the morning she had been an unwilling spectator while Billy swarmed over the crags from Hellweather Point to Blackbottle Cove, doing what he called his Cheeta impersonation and lifting gull's eggs to sell to local hotels.

'I'll be glad when the bleedin' birds stop laying,' she said after one particularly hair-raising exhibition.

'Aw come off it, Sheena,' he smiled. 'When I flog these' – he tapped the rucksack – 'we'll have enough to go to the pictures tonight and have ice cream and chips afterwards.'

'Not if you finish up in hospital or pushin' up daisies.'

'Have you ever seen someone who's dead?'

'My gran, when I was little. She was an 'orrible yellow colour.'

'When I was little I wanted to be a grave robber,' Billy said.

'You bleedin' liar,' Sheena scowled. 'You'd run a mile if you saw a dead bloke.'

'I saw a ghost once. It was in St Mary's churchyard and it didn' have a head. It spoke to me.'

'How could it have if it didn't have no head?'

'Ghosts don't need heads to talk.'

'All right. So what did it say?'

Billy cleared his throat. 'It's a secret. I had to cross my heart and promise on God's honour not to tell or the ghost would come and get me when I was asleep.'

'You and your bleedin' whoppers,' Sheena said hotly, and she got up and brushed down her frock and walked away from him.

'Wait for us, Sheen,' he called, shouldering the rucksack.

271

'Why? – are you afraid you'll bump into another 'eadless ghost?'

'There are ghosts, though,' he said, trotting beside her until the path narrowed on the approach to Parson's Cove. Here the moon daisies sprang out of strands of cow parsley and thistle.

'Shut up, Billy,' Sheena said and he knew it would be unwise to continue.

They crossed the hay field to the furze thicket above Warren Fishacre and Old Spanish Cove and Billy took out the binoculars. The peregrine falcon was flying back and forth across the cliff face screaming her alarm. The male bird was nowhere to be seen.

'What's up?' Sheena said.

'Could be anything,' but his heart was beating fast as the falcon's agitation reached out to him. 'You go down to the steps at the top of the cove. Take the rucksack.'

'What you goin' to do?'

'Look over the cliff into the eyrie and see if everything's all right.'

'That's all?'

He nodded and grinned and she knew he was lying. But it was no use arguing so she set off for the steps.

The gorse made his descent a penance although Billy had the knack of wriggling under things like a fox. Hot and itchy he eventually scrambled onto the clifftop, crawled to the edge and looked over. There were three chicks in the peregrine's scrape thirty feet below. Less than half that distance from the ledge Tony Rapson and another boy were negotiating a tricky little overhang.

Billy studied the situation. To his right was a vertical crack bounded with flakes of rock and jug-handle holds which from the bottom of the cliff were invisible. Getting down into the crack was the most difficult part of the exercise, and watching him through the binoculars Sheena's heart turned to ice.

A small buttress concealed Billy from the intruders but as

272

Rapson hauled up the last few feet to the ledge Billy swung around the bulge to his left.

'Bleedin' little bumhead,' Billy growled. 'I'll bash you in the gob, Rapson. Them chicks would die if you took 'em. You haven't got a clue and you don't care, do you?'

Rapson tried to retreat but his friend had lost his nerve and was squealing at him to climb on.

'You do and you'll get this.' Billy balled his fist and stepped onto the ledge.

Both birds were in the air now below the eyrie.

'If they desert I'll kill you,' he said.

'Let me up,' Tony Rapson cried. 'Let me up or my brother Eric will cripple you.'

'Jump,' Billy said. 'The tide's in and you can swim.'

'Eric'll get you, Drew. You wait. You wait.'

Billy grinned and lifted two rigid fingers of scorn.

Twelve feet from the bottom of the crag Rapson missed his footing and his downward slide over earth and loose shale dislodged his companion. They fell with an enormous splash into the sea.

'What's it like, Tone?' Billy crowed. 'Show us your breast stroke and watch out for sharks.'

The shock took Rapson's breath away but he was soon swimming for shore, bawling threats and insults. Billy saluted him with several more V-signs.

'I think Kerslake got 'em when they went through Fishacre,' Sheena said when they were reunited under the trees. 'I heard a man shouting and one of the little bleeders yell out as if he'd copped one round the ear.'

Billy's grin was huge. He took the binoculars and settled down to wait and see if the birds returned to the eyrie.

Before long the falcon was back on the scrape covering the eyasses with her warmth. Billy breathed a sigh of relief.

'Lucky it's a sunny day,' he said, 'or them little birds would be dead of cold.'

'That Tony Rapson's a rat,' said Sheena. 'But old

273

Strawberry will really have you this time, Bill. You could've killed him.'

Billy shrugged. 'He should leave the peregrines alone. I warned him.'

'Seriously, you'd better watch out.'

But Billy soon forgot the incident. The weather and the climbing took over his life. Then one hot cloudless day the thought of school left him weak with misery so he persuaded Sheena to 'mitch' with him. On the road to St Mary's Head they passed Eric Rapson and Bob Gurney, and Sheena was disturbed by the look they were given.

'We didn't oughta go to the cliffs today,' she said after voicing her fears. 'Let's go round the other way to Lansworthy and have a go on the slot machines down the Olympia.'

'Just because Eric Rapson gave you a funny look,' Billy sneered. 'He's another bumhead.'

'And you're plain bloody cuckoo,' Sheena grated.

'If you don't like what I do you can go home.'

'That's what Tarzan would say to Jane, is it – dopey?'

'Jane wouldn' care about the Rapsons.'

On Bullen Down cock linnets were singing from the gorse, their crimson crowns catching the sun in a warm blaze of colour. The children ran down to Coastguard Cottage but Garrison was out so they continued along the cliffs as far as Garrow Sands.

'It's too hot for walking,' Sheena said, collapsing on the gritty sand at the top of the beach.

'Look at them poppies,' said Billy and he pointed at the yellow flowers which were growing on the shingle banks behind them.

'They ain't poppies,' Sheena frowned. 'Poppies is red.'

'They're yellow-horned poppies,' Billy said. 'There's a picture of them in my flower book.'

'D'you want to be a bloke who studies flowers when you grow up? What d'you call 'em, Bill?'

'Botinists.'

'Funny name, ain't it? Botinist Bill, the flower bloke.'

He smiled and began unpacking the rucksack. Footsteps crunched over the shingle and Sheena turned, shading her eyes against the glare. 'Run, Bill,' she cried. 'For God's sake! – it's Eric Rapson and the Gurneys.'

But there was nowhere to run. Strawberry, Stike and a couple of others were clambering down the rocks beside the waterfall to block the opposite end of the beach. Billy looked up at the crags. They were low but smooth and overhanging.

'Give it a try,' Eric Rapson said perceptively. 'By the time you made it to the top I'd be waitin' for you.'

Tony Rapson and a short pale boy with carrot-coloured hair brought up the rear. Billy stooped and grabbed a pebble.

'OK,' he said. 'The first one to have a go at me gets this in the gob.'

His voice shook and the Gurneys laughed.

'Put the stone down, Drew,' Strawberry said. 'Ginger wants a word with you. Ginger's Tony's pal. He don't like what you did to my boy on the cliffs, but you don't care about people do you, Drew? All you care about is hawks and badgers and rubbish like that. Little animals like you need to be shown who's boss. You need a sharp lesson, boy.'

'Yes,' Eric hissed. 'You can't go around smashin' up people's vans.'

The men formed a circle around Billy and Stike caught hold of Sheena.

'Leave him alone you bleedin' bullies,' she screamed.

'We aren't goin' to touch him,' Strawberry smiled. 'Young Ginger has a score to settle, that's all. Him and Drew, a straight scrap.'

Billy knew Ginger Gurney only by reputation. Their paths rarely crossed for the older boy went to the secondary modern and spent most of his free time on the trawlers. He was about Bill's height and had the cold gull eye of someone unacquainted with fear.

'Ginger has never lost a playground scrap,' Eric Rapson

275

told Billy. 'He's a real little ferret and he don't like you, Drew.'

Billy swallowed and his shoulders sagged.

'I'll tell the police,' Sheena cried.

'Tell them what?' said Strawberry. 'That a couple of lads had a set-to on the beach? Why should that interest the law?'

Billy was trembling now and his sunburnt face had lost its flush. Ginger Gurney swayed forward and planted a crisp punch on his nose. Like a stoat playing with a rabbit, was Strawberry's description of the fight in the pub that evening. Billy tried to defend himself but he could not match Ginger's cold fury. His knees buckled as he took a flurry of punches to the head. Then Ginger worked on his body until Billy dropped to his knees and dizzily watched the blood splat from his nose onto the pebbles.

'Leave him alone,' Sheena sobbed. 'Leave him.'

'That's enough, Ginger,' said Strawberry. 'Maybe you've knocked some sense into that big head. No more pranks, hey, Billy? No more treadin' on my toes – understand?'

'Yes,' Billy croaked.

'You bleedin' wait,' Sheena said from a kind of high, animal cry of passion. 'You rotten sods.'

'Little cockney tart,' Eric said savagely. 'Watch your lip or you'll get what Drew got.'

Sheena was so full of emotion she could only sob. When the gang had gone she sat on the beach with her arms around Billy. It was some time before he could control himself. Then he had the hiccups and they ended up giggling.

'Your face,' Sheena gasped. 'You look as if you've gone fifteen rounds wiv King Kong. It's all red and puffy and lumpy.'

Billy gently fingered the damage and sighed.

Garrison was also taken aback by the state of Billy's face. Even at this late stage in his dealings with Strawberry Rapson he could still be shocked by the depths of hatred in the back-streets of Mary's Haven. It was violent, unforgiving and tribal in the worst possible sense. Yet Billy could not be persuaded to go to the police. He saw his fight with Ginger Gurney as something honourable to be kept under the wraps of the taboos and rituals of his class.

'You people really mystify me,' Garrison said.

He was walking Billy and Sheena home through the lanes into the top of Mary's Haven.

'There's nothing honourable about letting a gang of thugs hammer you senseless.'

'I'll get Ginger in my own time, in my own way,' said Billy.

'Meaning a brick through his back room window one tea-time,' said Sheena. ''Course, the Gurneys won't guess who done it.'

'Ginger's got a bike,' Billy said mysteriously and Garrison did not want to hear any more but Mrs Drew paled when she saw her son on the front doorstep.

'Christ Almighty,' she breathed halfway through Garrison's explanation. 'I swear I'll swing for the Rapsons and the rest of the big brave men.'

She grabbed her coat off the hall stand and pushed past them.

'Where you going, mum?' Billy cried.

'Down the Ship to straighten Strawberry out once and for all.'

'You can't,' Billy said desperately. 'He'll –'

'He'll do sod all,' Mrs Drew interjected. 'No one's going to attack my son and get away with it.'

'Mum,' Billy piped. 'It was a fair fight.'

'Fair my ass! I'll give them fair fight.'

'Let her be,' Sheena said. 'Strawberry's got it comin' to him.'

'But they'll call me a mamma's boy,' Billy said. 'I don't want her fightin' for me.'

'She ain't going to do Ginger Gurney,' Sheena said. 'Old Strawberry's a bloke. Blokes don't count. Come on,' and she grabbed his arm and dragged him along.

'Is your mother serious?' Garrison asked, unsure of what

277

they expected of him but wanting him to be part of it all.

'I hope Strawberry idn' in the pub,' Billy snuffled but he was and the children stood in the doorway as Mrs Drew went into action.

For the rest of his life Garrison would recall in minute detail the events of the next five minutes. First there were the expressions on the faces of Billy and Sheena – almost identical, frozen between rapture and alarm. Then there were the looks on the faces of Strawberry and his cronies – Strawberry's smile falling apart at the sight of Mrs Drew storming across the bar, Stike's guilty sideways glance and descending eyelids, Dunning's lower jaw hanging slack. The other anonymous faces were merely curious or puzzled but the landlady's was a picture of amazement.

'I doan want –' she began and stopped aghast as Mrs Drew knocked the pint pot out of Strawberry's hand and sent it flying into the hearth. The crash of breaking glass silenced the bar; but Strawberry was struggling to reassemble his smile when he was hit. It was one of those upward blows delivered from the elbow with the flat of the hand. A fingernail split one of Strawberry's nostrils and as his head jerked away he sneezed and Sheena and Billy snorted with laughter. The smear of blood on Strawberry's jowl seemed to goad Mrs Drew to more extravagant violence. Her next swing caught Strawberry in the mouth and he backed off, palms raised is a most uncharacteristic manner Garrison thought. Now it was Stike's turn but he did not expect the toe of Mrs Drew's shoe raking his shins. Charlie Dunning closed to forestall his own humiliation and the landlady ran out from behind the counter to assist him. Lulled into a false sense of security Dunning released the woman and took a kneecap in the genitals. Billy's mother had learned this defence during the war when American servicemen 'got too physical' as she called it.

'Right,' the landlady said. 'Out you go, madam.'

'Those buggers ought to be behind bars,' Mrs Drew said, folding her arms defiantly. 'Come here, Billy.' She swung

278

round and seeing Billy hesitate repeated in a softer tone: 'Come here.'

Billy made a sheepish entrance but his mother took him by the hand and addressing no one in particular said: 'Look at his face. Strawberry bloody Rapson did that. Him and his cronies set it up and the Gurney's youngest did the damage, but Rapson's behind it. And d'you know why? Because Billy is trying to stop them killing badgers. And what are they killin' them for? For bloody fun. Christ Almighty! – didn't the war teach you anything?'

It was magnificent, Garrison reflected – the speech, her exit and the embarrassed silence she left behind. He bought a double rum and sipped it on the edge of marvellous elation. The shits of the world rarely got their come-uppance, but to see justice done in public was good for the soul.

Small and Stike was sympathizing with Strawberry and the landlady was going to great lengths to blacken whatever remained of Mrs Drew's reputation; and all at once the atmosphere in the Ship was suffocating. He drank up and brushed past Rapson on his way to the door.

'Garrison,' said a soft voice. 'You watch how you go.'

The door clicked behind him but no footsteps pursued him up the road towards St Mary's Head. He walked hard until he was on Bullen Down within sight of home. The spring twilight and the bare muscular countryside rolling down to the sea were refreshing. Seabird cries crept out of distances lost in the blue haze he loved and often captured in his watercolours.

Sitting on the dew-wet turf he tried to determine what nature had given him. Hope, yes, even after Neil's death and Ann's illness – hope and belief in something death could not destroy. Wonder, certainly, and self-knowledge. It was a simple credo. Neil had once said after reading Wordsworth that to turn away from nature was to turn away from truth. Well, the bluebells on December Point were ravishing. If only Ann had been there to share it – the bluebells, the sea and sky, the hills darkening to silhouette. He thought then of the badgers creeping out of their holes all along the cliffs to walk through the night. It was soul-numbing to consider the power man had to molest those creatures. Billy sprang to mind. What a strange little chap, self-loving, amoral, a kind of fallen cherub who possessed an intense vision of the living world. Or was that place merely a refuge of convenience for crippled spirits?

The hedges below Woodash were alive with glow-worms. Dor beetles blundered heavily across the marsh. Was Richard Jefferies right when he wrote: 'The hills purify those who walk on them'? Did Billy understand through instinct and the senses things he couldn't perceive? Garrison smiled. Billy the seer!

At the cottage he lit the lamp, brought the cider jar to the table and tried to read while the gramophone gave him Mozart's 'Prague' symphony. The fire blazed and moths thudded softly against the windows.

Chapter 33

The Bluebell Slope

The moth-haunted night brought out the Froward tribe. The boars were on the slopes first, pushing confidently under the thorn vault which almost entirely hid the sky now except for the odd gap in the leaves. Then the sows and cubs took to the paths and climbed the stone wall and came through the barbed wire tangle onto the turf. Here they dispersed for forage – mated pairs, maiden sows, sows and young. In the old cider apple orchard between Effords and Warren Fishacre, a nightjar was pouring out his whirring rattle of a song and trotting through the wheat Aspen heard Cowtail calling her cubs and the answering yaps. Something flitted past her head uttering high-pitched squeaks. She snapped her teeth and Sycamore looked up enquiringly before lowering his muzzle to eat some violet ground beetles. The scent of blackthorn blossom and gorse filled the darkness. An owl spoke, a sheep coughed, small creatures whispered through the corn.

Aspen and Sycamore were uneasy about walking too close to the scarecrow. Although it had no life-smell it was obviously a man-thing and was therefore regarded with suspicion. They foraged for earthworms and young rabbits until a strong emission of Aspen's musk led to the mating both animals desired. Afterwards the grooming was an expression of tenderness and the forage continued with slugs, mice and bulbs.

Slowly Aspen's inner consciousness took over as it shaped spent feelings into a waking dream. Then she could not tell what was reality – the dream of walking the fields or the sad dream beauty of Sunworld with the creatures she recognized and loved. The stars shone and the moon came up and the countryside fell silent. Heavy fragrances eddied around her. Then there was a curious blending of sensations and a weightless drift through brilliance. Aspen could recall during cubhood the long walk into darkness that held nothing but horror and fear. A long walk through darkness into darkness then a bang, a rasp and the whimper of frightened animals. Moonlight flooded the moment. She was chin-deep in buttercups now and aware of the patient, noiseless growth of things around her but not the place itself. The nightjar continued to utter his strange cry and Sycamore was grunting quietly as his snout worked among the grass stems.

They passed beneath horse chestnut trees into the lane that ran from Effords farmyard to the gate of the pasture where sheep had been put to graze and keep down the ragwort. Glow-worms lit the hedge bottoms all the way to the cliffs and the fields were breathing the warm smell of animals.

At length the badgers reached Ramsons Dip. The tinkle of the stream running beneath vegetation barely broke the hush. Both sides of the coombe were thick with wild garlic or ramsons as they were called by country folk. The dark stink delighted Aspen and Sycamore and they rolled among the leaves and tight white flowers, taking the smell on their coats. Then they followed the stream down onto the steeps near Guelder's old sett and heard the waves and saw the lights on the ocean. Gorse musk filled their nostrils and the stars trembled within the deep silence above. The coats of both animals were dew-spiked. They lumbered to the clifftop and lay in the thrift and sea campion.

It was a beautiful time of year. The wild crab above Old Spanish Cove and the cider apple trees of Woodash were in blossom. Cowslips clotted the meadow from Efforts to Bullen Down and evenings were flooded with the scent of flowering hawthorn and bluebell. Horse chestnut candles were shaken by the wind and broke apart to litter the waysides; and the leaves of the oaks were more gold than green. The cuckoo called across mornings of mist and sunlight, swifts screamed on the wing and the steeps were loud with songbirds. Evenings faded through a haze into dusk and twilight, but the swifts continued to screech long after the stars had firmed to brilliance and the badgers had left their setts.

Late one evening Cowtail and her cubs lay in the grass close to Froward Point listening to the activity of the squirrels in the top of the pines. Every so often the 'chuck-chuck' cries were broken by screeches of alarm. Cowtail laid back her ears and licked her lips. Another sound sprang from the hush. It was a funny, pronounced hiccupping noise that brought a smile to Cowtail's face. Fingo was sicking up a fur ball. Raising herself she saw the cat crouching rigid on the pine needles, mouth gaping, neck extending and withdrawing and extending again as the spasms racked his body and sent him shuffling backwards in an attempt to escape the misery. By the time it was over Fingo found Cowtail crying with laughter.

'What's up?' asked the cat.

'It's what you brought up and how you did it.' said Cowtail. Fingo smiled for he was a good-natured animal. Cat and fox sat side by side in the fading light, at peace with themselves. Soon the ghost moths were dancing all along the slope, hardly shifting their positions in the air. The din of seabirds on Dragon Rock subsided to a few solo cries and the tide began to flood with a muted roar over the skerries. The animals' ears pricked whenever a closer noise was detected: the rustle of tortoiseshell caterpillars on the undersides of nettle leaves behind them; the whisper of a beetle through the grasses; a vole sneezing. Nightworld was transparent to their senses, but the stars which had no scent and never made a sound were the frontiers of mystery. At times it was good to enter that mystery and dream.

Through the night Fingo trod his hunting trails, meeting the occasional travelling fox, stoat and weasel, all of whom loitered with intent wherever there were rabbit runs and burrows. Cries rising from the darkness were quickly ended as life passed to life. Sinking back on his haunches to clean himself the cat wondered why he hadn't met any badgers on the steeps. Their absence left him uneasy. He sat in the hay field above Old Spanish Cove and birds began to sing although the pale light on the horizon was hardly noticeable. Presently Fingo's ears caught a familiar sound – the snuffling and grunting of badgers, and across the field came more sett-dwellers than the cat had ever seen together before. A line of boars with Greybob prominent and Sycamore at his heels marched in front of the sows and cubs, heads lowered and haunches rolling purposefully. Among the sows was Aspen and Fingo loped along beside her.

'Where are you all going?' he said.

'To the Bluebell Radiance,' she said.

'What's that?'

'A badger happening,' came the mysterious reply.

'Can I come?'

'N-no,' said Birdcherry, appearing at the other side of Fingo.

There was something even in Birdcherry's demeanour that impressed the cat, and he stopped and watched the badgers hurry on into the strengthening light.

On the way to Hellweather Point the kin group and their relatives were joined by other badgers from as far afield as St Mary's Head. The sett-masters circled each other, the hair on their backs rippling and their noses busy. Sows exchanged greetings and the cubs pressed inquisitive snouts to inquisitive snouts. The sun was rising when the gathering assembled above the copse on Garrowcombe Head but the animals turned their backs on it. For once the brightness swelling every moment did not alarm them. The broad flank of the headland glided up into the sky where the moon was still a complete, if pale, disc. Warmth stole through Aspen's body and she knew the sun had risen from the sea. Light crept past her up the steeps which were one huge carpet of bluebells. The light spread until the whole headland was radiant blue. Every badger head was raised and the blueness became so intense it drew a chorus of gasps from the assembly. Colour pulsed and released the thin fragrance which the animals loved. From the nearby gorse thicket the linnets began to sing.

'In the very beginning,' said Hawscrag's voice, 'the first sow came to the place between the sun and the moon. She was heavy with cub and close to her time. Among the flowers she roamed at peace with the place and herself. Then she lay down and gave birth to all badger kind which multiplied with the seasons. Now under the hill lie the greatest boars. In the earth sleep yesterday's sows. Their life that was is in the Blue Radiance and we are the shapes of those that were. In the seasons of plenty the Blue Radiance breathes its scent into Nightworld lest we forget the shadows of things gone and the way things were and she whose heart is open to all mystery.'

The rock doves of Garrowcombe Head clattered across the hush behind Hawscrag's voice and the bird cries from the loomeries suddenly rose to a tremendous din. The wind looping up off the water cut dark swathes in the bluebells and sent the colour rioting all the way to the sky.

Then Greybob ascended the hillside a short distance to stand apart from the crowd. His muzzle pointed at the sky where the moon had faded almost to invisibility.

'By the great boar's strength,' he cried, 'the sett is ruled.'

'By the great boar's strength,' answered the other sett-masters in chorus, 'strength prevails and all are safe in underearth and in Nightworld.'

'Through Earth Mother's truth and love,' Hawscrag sang out, 'the green seasons provide all – warmth, plenty, young to fill tomorrow. Tooth and claw are less than the cub's mewl. At the reckoning the boar is weaker than the cub.'

Greybob's head dropped and he growled and shook but did not voice his dissent. The sows blew gently through their nostrils, resenting his intrusion. Even the radiance could not douse his aggressiveness but a remarkable compassion united the sisterhood.

'We are walking with the wind and cannot go against it,' Hawscrag continued, 'but the walk through darkness is not forever. Many dimpseys ago this hillside was winter. Now it is the Radiance.'

Yet it seemed to Aspen that the dam was still groping for something beneath the outpouring of wisdom. Stepping from a rush of dreams the phantom badgers revealed nothing except a sublime happiness. Earth Mother provided wonders beyond reason as a kind of forage for the soul. Hawscrag was speaking again but her words blurred to a monotonous drone in Aspen's ears. The bluebell scent was everything. Turning away she found Birdcherry's bright gaze on her.

'Please d-don't abandon me, Aspen.'

'How could I? We are sisters. But what of Greybob?'

Birdcherry's head dropped. 'Already he f-favours one of the maiden sows, B-Bellbind.'

All about them badgers were dispersing. The kin group of Big Sett were plodding back towards Froward. For Birdcherry, Aspen reflected, woe piled on woe. And once more the distraction of wonder was over. The Bluebell Radiance had dimmed and the brightness of the sky was making most of the animals anxious. Sycamore trotted up to the sows and gently nuzzled Birdcherry's face before licking her ears.

'I'm tired,' he yawned, gazing kindly on the sisters. 'The

brightness hurts my eyes. I can hardly keep them open.' He smiled. 'Do you think Earth Mother takes any notice of our gatherings?'

'Yes,' said Aspen. 'Gatherings, mating, forage, births, deaths, sleeping – all are one to her.'

But to explain would have meant talking at great length with an intensity she wasn't prepared to summon up from her own fatigue. She glanced at Sycamore, loving his strength and honesty and aching to have his cubs.

They scent-marked beneath the wild cherry, crushing the fallen blossom and running their snouts repeatedly through the fragrance. Then Aspen's nostrils rounded to identify the smell of Fingo. The cat was a shadow with almond-shaped eyes in the furze tangle.

Aspen separated herself from her companions and waited for the cat to join her. Birdcherry had also stayed behind.

'This is a bit unusual,' Fingo said. 'Every one of you out and about after sun-up.'

'It's a special occasion,' said Aspen.

'The B-Bluebell Radiance,' Birdcherry added.

'Flowers?' the cat sniffed.

'Flowers and other things,' Aspen smiled, warming to the down-to-earth little animal.

Fingo yawned and nodded. The badgers were no longer capable of surprising him.

Chapter 34

To Save a Cat

The cubs were awake and underearth at dimpsey, fretting to taste the excitement of Nightworld. The maiden sows were finding it difficult to amuse them and Hawscrag was becoming bad-tempered. She wanted a good scratch but there was little space in the nursery chamber. The strong smell of recently dug soil failed to soothe her.

'Come up above ground, you pair of body bugs,' she growled. 'Come up and I'll tell you a story.'

The other sows sighed with relief as the youngsters tumbled into the passage behind Hawscrag and followed her out onto the steeps. It had been raining in one of those showers of late spring which rarely amount to much, but the air was sweet and all the scents stamped themselves keenly on the cubs who swung their muzzles to read the dusk.

After Hawscrag had visited the scratching tree and had done with raking away at her own coat she settled briskly to groom the cubs using hard, long strokes of the tongue which knocked the youngsters off balance, much to the amusement of Aspen and Sycamore who had also left the sett early.

Hawscrag's licking was typical of an old sow's reactions with co-ordination difficult and the practice of cub care a distant memory.

'Tell us a story, grand-dam,' said Maple.

'A special story,' Whitethorn added.

'I'll tell you the one about Moonwise the boar and how he came to this place and began Big Sett,' said Hawscrag. 'How Moonwise met Starborn the first sow and how they made the kin group in the long ago seasons of Before Man.'

'I like that one,' said Sycamore and Hawscrag gave him a cold sideways look which meant 'keep quiet'.

'In a long ago spring,' she began, 'on the great rock out there where the seabirds nest and the storm waves break there once lived three great boars. Since the first stars were lit in the sky these brothers had been content to dwell on the rock contemplating the beauty of Nightworld and –'

'What is contemplating?' asked Whitethorn.

'Do not interrupt again,' Hawscrag said severely. 'To contemplate simply means to consider, to think deeply about something. So,' and she frowned at the cubs, 'so there they were contemplating the beauty, happy that the rock supplied all their needs – good forage, rainwater, a sett, peace. The great spirit who is Earth Mother had dropped them as cubs in a den among the mallow and they grew up asking for nothing save what they had.'

The cubs fidgeted and Maple coughed.

'Moonwise had a friend, a seal called Delver who sometimes came to the rock and sang to Moonwise. Everything was perfect for the three boars until one day they came upon a dying seagull and were saddened and worried by what they saw. They knew then that life was not forever. "One day we will die like this bird," said Moonwise. "And there will be no badgers in the world and Earth Mother's heart will break for she loves us above the rest of creation." Moonclaw and Moontag, his brothers, cried out in their grief but Earth Mother did not hear them. And that night she sent Moonwise the dream of the young sow, Starborn, who told Moonwise of the love between boar and sow that can bring forth cubs.'

'Us,' Maple giggled.

Hawscrag narrowed her eyes and Maple quailed.

'Where is this young sow?' Moonwise asked in his dream and Earth Mother told him she was here where we are sitting, and she was waiting for whichever brother reached the mainland first.

'Now Moonwise was a true heart and told his brothers of the dream. Looking towards the crags they saw Starborn on the steeps and smelt her scent. So together at low water they walked the skerries and swam between the outlying reefs until they were halted by the fast-flowing Narrows. At once Moonwise sensed danger. The water was deep and had an invisible strength which could carry off the strongest badger. But Moontag was foolish and entered the sea and was swept away never to be seen again in this life.

'The remaining brothers did not know what to do. Then a great silver-scaled fish with eyes of red fire and golden teeth appeared and told them to climb onto its back and it would take them to the shore. Moonwise, however, didn't trust the fish but Mooncdaw stepped eagerly onto its back. Instantly the fish rolled over and as Mooncdaw struggled in the water he was eaten.

'Moonwise considered the problem –'

'Contemplated it,' Maple smiled.

'Considered the problem,' Hawscrag growled. 'But felt defeated until his friend the seal appeared and asked him what he was doing. Moonwise explained and Delver dived to reappear a little later with many others of his kind. They formed a chain, nose to tail, across the Narrows and Moonwise was able to run over them to the shore, thanking his friend and praising Mother Earth. At the top of the cliff the beautiful Starborn was waiting. Soon they had made musk together and mated. Then they dug the first tunnel and the first chamber of the first sett. Today we call it Big Sett, and where we find comfort together the remains of Moonwise and Starborn sleep in the earth and what they are is elsewhere and yet they are here in you, Maple and Whitethorn. Do you understand?'

The cubs nodded, desperate to be at the forage as the rest of the sett-dwellers came noisily along the passages. Hawscrag smiled. When they had heard the story twenty times the twins really would understand.

Aspen and Sycamore walked slowly through the twilight together with Birdcherry a few paces behind.

'Were you told the Moonwise story in your sett when you were a cub?' Aspen asked her mate.

'Yes,' he smiled. 'Through it we learnt that the weak and foolish or reckless do not last long in Nightworld, and that mating creates all the tribe's tomorrows. It is a good story.'

'Aspen has the vision,' said Birdcherry.

'The gift few possess,' Sycamore nodded. 'And then always sows.'

Beside the stream in Ramsons Dip they found Fingo crouched in a posture of agony. Birdcherry immediately thought the worst and could not resist a small cry of anguish.

'Is he – is he –' There was no need to finish the question.

'Fingo,' Aspen touched the cat gently with her snout. He was breathing in feeble little gasps and for a while was quite incapable of replying.

Aspen sat beside him and waited for him to gather his strength.

'What is it, little friend?' whispered the badger.

'Runny scats, thirsty, stomach on fire. Thirsty but can't drink.'

He sighed and winced and screwed up his face.

The badgers looked at each other, understanding now and sympathizing.

'Gut-burn,' said Sycamore and he walked out of earshot. Aspen joined him. 'There's nothing we can do. It's Earth Mother's decision now. He lives or dies.'

291

'And gut-burn usually kills,' said Aspen sadly. 'It is such a shame. Fingo and I are very close. He saved my life once.'

'How?' asked Sycamore and Aspen explained.

'W-we can't fetch the man who h-helped you, Aspen,' said Birdcherry. 'The c-cat is used to humans. He can c-come and g-go between Nightworld and their w-world. We can't.'

'But the man with the kind voice often walks this way,' said Aspen. 'Some dimpseys I find his smell on the air. I shall sit by Fingo and attract the man's attention.'

'You c-c-can't!' exclaimed Birdcherry.

'Of course not,' said Sycamore. 'We must help Fingo to the man's house.'

'He's too weak,' said Aspen.

'He must try or he's doomed,' said Sycamore.

'W-wait a moment,' said Birdcherry. 'He's always on about v-visits to the h-house in the trees j-just over the fields. Someone th-there feeds him.'

'Yes, Birdcherry,' Aspen said. 'I think you're right.'

They put it to the cat and he nodded miserably. 'I'll have a go. Could you stay with me part of the way, Aspen?'

'All of the way. Lead on at your pace. We won't leave you.'

'If anything is to happen,' the cat groaned, 'I'd rather be alone at the end.'

'We understand. Do your best. It isn't far to the house.'

But for a sick cat it was a long and arduous journey. Every few steps he crouched and panted and retched. Then he tried to make scats but succeeded only in dribbling a foul-smelling liquid.

The darkness deepened. Clouds crossed the sky and rain fell with a soft ticking on the leaves. Then the stars shone again and the animals came slowly through the trees into Warren Fishacre. The cat brought them up the path towards the house. At the rose garden Birdcherry would go no further and was left to nervously sniff the shadows and jump whenever some large animal crashed through the undergrowth.

Aspen and Sycamore plodded behind Fingo up onto the

terrace lawns by the ornamental pond and the stone otters. Rectangles of light from the open French windows fell across the grass. In the drawing room Mrs Ordish was reading while Lucy and a young man sat talking quietly beside the gramophone. The strange music made the badgers' ears twitch. Boar and sow exchanged glances but Fingo was on his side in the grass breathing faintly. The ghost moths fluttered in hovering dance and the scent of roses wafted up from the pergola.

'Now what?' said Sycamore.

They sat together in the yellow light blinking uncertainly. Then the music ended and on impulse Aspen uttered her eerie cry.

'Aspen,' Sycamore growled and the hair rippled in the tell-tale wave along his back.

But once more Aspen screamed and saw the shapes move in the room full of light that hurt her eyes and frightened her. She lowered her head. The shapes were coming towards her over the lawn and Sycamore was already running. A human voice called out and Aspen's nerve broke. She too came tumbling after Sycamore down the rockery and galloped up through the shrubbery into the Warren Fishacre pines where Birdcherry was waiting.

'What w-will they do to Fingo?'

'Fingo says they are kind humans,' said Aspen. 'Fingo will die if he isn't helped.'

'I think we should leave,' said Sycamore. 'I smell dog.'

The three occupants of the drawing room heard the unearthly scream and turning towards the windows saw the badgers' black and white faces on the lawn. Lucy immediately cried 'Badgers' in a voice full of delight and surprise. Mrs Ordish and the young man were at her heels as she came out into the garden to witness the animals' exit. Then she saw the small dark shape lying in the grass and ran forward thinking it was a cub.

'A cat,' she breathed, stooping over Fingo. 'And it's the

little stray David and I are feeding. David Garrison,' she smiled seeing the enquiry on the young mans face. 'You'll have to meet him, Paul.'

She knelt and stroked Fingo but he did not respond.

'The poor little chap's ill,' said Mrs Ordish.

Lucy picked him up with one hand clutching the scruff of his neck and the other supporting his rump.

'There are no marks or wounds on him,' she said. 'Could he have been knocked down by a car?'

'I don't think so,' Mrs Ordish said, making a swift examination. 'He wouldn't have walked here if a car had got him. Judging by the state of the fur under his tail I'd say he's got chronic diarrhoea and that means a stomach disorder or something really bad, like poisoning.'

'Kerslake's fowls and the rat poison?' Lucy said.

'Hardly likely. Bring him in and I'll phone the vet.'

'At this time of night?' Lucy smiled.

'These people like to think they're earning their money,' said Mrs Ordish.

The boyfriend shook his head. For a horse or a dog, he thought – but a stray tom! He slipped an arm around Lucy's waist and she planted a kiss on his cheek and whispered: 'The eccentric Ordishes.'

'The lovely Lucy Ordish,' he said seriously.

When word reached Garrison of the sick cat at Warren Fishacre he brought Billy and Sheena on a visit.

'Why ain't you got a car, mister?' Sheena asked.

'I'm a bit of a Luddite when it comes to machines,' he said.

'A bit of a wot?'

'It doesn't matter. I simply don't like cars. Anyway, it would just rust up at Hard Sands, and driving it up and down the lane would be the equivalent of taking it regularly over a tank training ground.'

Fingo was recovering. They were giving him warm milk to

combat his thirst and dehydration, and the vet had injected him with something to help cure the enteritis.

'It was touch and go,' said Lucy and she told them about the badgers.

'One was a big handsome silvery fellow. The other was a lovely little thing with the neatest head imaginable.'

'The spooky old boy,' Billy said. 'Me and Sheena saw him on Froward. So he's got a mate. That's good.'

Fingo was curled up purring in the cat basket outside the french windows in the sun.

'Cats are born sybarites,' said Mrs Ordish. 'They also know how to milk a situation.'

Billy and Sheena dropped their heads and looked sideways at each other.

'Come with me, you two rascals,' the old lady went on. 'Into the kitchen now for something nice. What about tinned pears and cream?'

'And a glass of sherry, mum,' Billy said.

'How do you know there's sherry in the kitchen?' Mrs Ordish chuckled.

Billy coloured and brushed back his hair. Sheena glared at him.

'It's only cooking sherry but you're welcome to a thimbleful.'

Garrison hid his face in his handkerchief and pretended to blow his nose, but Lucy was laughing outright and only the young man looked puzzled.

'Billy's light-fingered,' Lucy explained. 'Paul, that boy is the reincarnation of the Artful Dodger.'

'With a fair bit of Gilbert White, Thoreau and Richard Jefferies chucked in,' said Garrison.

'Grandmother thinks he's special,' Lucy said.

'There's no denying that,' Garrison said. 'Billy and the cat have a hell of a lot in common.'

Eventually the conversation touched on Garrison's latest picture and he let his enthusiasm show.

'Perhaps I could see it sometime, sir,' said the boyfriend. He was tall, fair, well-fleshed and youthful in a Nordic way that made Garrison feel suddenly older than his fifty years. Being a distinguished artist, he decided, wasn't much fun. It was better to be young and on the edge of everything life could promise.

He went outside and crouched over Fingo's basket. The cat looked up at him, its nostrils working. Then it went back to sleep and Garrison strolled across the lawn breathing the scent of the roses but thinking now of Ann. How often moral beauty or inner beauty weren't reflected in physical beauty yet occasionally had the power to outshine it. He came to the pond and sat smoking a cigarette while the dragonflies whizzed into their amazing right-angled turns to stand on the air with whirring wings. Billy came almost noiselessly to his side smelling of sherry.

'They old dragonflies is busy, mister,' the boy said and he squatted at the edge of the water.

'The strong always muscle in to mess up paradise, don't they, Billy?'

'I like dragonflies,' Billy murmured, and the gaudy insects tacked around his head in pursuit of prey. 'They didn' ask to be dragonflies, did they?'

Chapter 35

Loose Rock

Fingo's recovery was steady but even in the groggy stage when he at last found his feet he cringed from the outstretched hand. Lucy and the children found it impossible to pet him. He would lay back his ears and make himself small in the basket, quivering in every muscle. Then one night as he lay dozing out on the terrace half-aware of the ghost moths and the cries of the tawny owls someone called him. Opening his eyes he saw Aspen and Sycamore on the lawn waiting for him. The household was asleep so he uncurled, stretched and yawned and walked through the dew to join them.

'How was it?' asked Sycamore.

'It was warm milk and warm doss and warm voices,' the cat said. 'This is a good place. This place and the place down by the sea are good places.'

'Are you better?' said Aspen.

'Much. My stomach isn't on fire any more,' Fingo said. 'And I make proper scats. I'm all right thanks to you.'

'Were you tempted to stay?' said Aspen. 'I mean, being a cat –'

'There is only the wild,' Fingo said. 'The rest isn't real. The wild is freedom.'

The badgers nodded solemnly. On the edge of the fields the cat left them and walked alone under the stars with some of his old panache. Aspen and Sycamore smiled at each other and went to forage.

Sitting with his back to King Arthur's Tower Strawberry Rapson saw the great pale boar and his mate chesting the corn. He had come alone to watch for badgers and the sight of Aspen and Sycamore brought a smile to his face.

'A big old silver brock,' he told his cronies the following lunch time in the Ship. 'True as I stand here, Charlie – a silver badger. The Ordish land is crawlin' with big animals. Talk about sport! Some of they brocks would eat Stoneman's dogs.'

He drank and licked his lips and let his fingertips trail slowly down the livid birthmark that wasn't so conspicuous with his face tanned.

'I reckon Froward's crawlin' with the rubbish.'

Again the tip of his tongue traced the outline of his lower lip.

'There must be a way of gettin' at that bury.'

'A fire on a foggy night wouldn't be seen,' Stike said.

'Too risky,' Strawberry said. 'If a spark hit the pines they'd go up like an atom bomb.'

'We could have another go at cuttin' through,' Dunning offered. 'A gang of blokes working with hooks and cleavers could open up that thorn tangle like it wadn' there.'

'And if Mrs Ordish found out who did it we'd be in the dock for all sorts of things I don't even want to think about. Leave this to me.'

By late afternoon he had joined the Gurneys in their boat on a fishing trip to Dragon Rock and even as Froward Point came into view lit by the sun he felt he had solved the problem.

They dropped anchor in the lee of the rock and baited the hooks for pollock but Strawberry was content to sit in the stern and turn his binoculars on the point. Two entrances were visible where the sett met the clifftop, and Strawberry smiled.

'The crafty little devils,' he whispered following the sweep of thorn to the Monterey pines. Then he took his rod and fished until dusk, enjoying the slap of asphyxiating pollock on the deck and the gentle rise and fall of the boat as the tide changed. The moon rose over the Channel and Start Light was flashing. Strawberry sat in the stern once more and glassed the Point. In the binocular window vague and ghostly was the face of a badger. Strawberry goose-pimpled. The animal seemed to be staring down at him. Then, the glasses misted over with the heat of his excitement and sweat trickled into his eyes. By the time he had cleaned the optics the badger had gone.

Strawberry waited until all the members had brought their beer to the upstairs room. Pint pots lined the mantelpiece below the badger mask. The babble of conversation and the laughter always gave club evenings an atmosphere that left Strawberry feeling well-disposed to the human race. Stike was telling one of his interminable shaggy dogs stories, the Gurneys were fussing over Gritt and Jimmy and everyone was contributing to the din and smoke.

Ted Gurney swaggered up to him, glass in hand, Woodbine clamped in his smile.

''Ere, Mr Rapson,' he said and the cigarette hung from his lower lip as he nodded at the badger's head. 'That old brock don't say much, do 'ee?'

Strawberry laughed. He was glad the youngster was part of everything he valued most – the dogs, the digging, the sport and the socializing.

Eventually the meeting was called to order and Strawberry revealed his plan.

'This hasn't got anything to do with the twenty-fifth anniversary,' he said. 'But I know you're all interested in the Froward sett. Well, boys – I'm certain we can open up the place from the sea by going up the cliffs.'

'You're joking,' said Dunning. 'You won't get me on them cliffs. The bloody rock's rotten for a start and no one's ever got through they overhangs.'

'Don't fret, Charlie,' Strawberry chuckled. 'I idn' askin' you to turn into a mountain goat and drag that beer belly of yours up anything steeper than the stairs to bed. Some of us could do it, though, if a real climber got to the top first and lowered a couple of ropes and a couple of rope ladders. Try to look at it like this. The climber gets to the top with a cord tied to his belt. Then he pulls up a bag with the rope ladders and stuff in it, and fastens one end of 'em to a tree. Then up we go, followed by the digging tools in another sack.'

'What about the dogs?' asked Small.

'Eric's gettin' a few of they bags the terrier man uses at foxhunts to carry his dog in.'

Stike grinned.

'It would be one up on Old Mother Ordish and Garrison.' Strawberry continued and he knew in his blood they were rising to the bait. 'A military operation, Charlie – like a commando raid.'

'I was on a few of those,' Small said. 'They weren't picnics.'

'But this one will be,' Strawberry smiled. 'And if old silver brock is up there we'll have him for the big baiting.'

'Who's the climber?' said Dunning.

'My youngest brother, Ginger,' said Ted Gurney. 'He could climb an iceberg in daps.'

'I've promised him a couple of quid when he pulls it off,' said Strawberry. 'Me and Eric and the two Gurneys here will be on his heels. Is anyone else willing? We need a biggish digging team.' Stike and Small raised reluctant hands and Strawberry beamed.

'Charlie can look after the gear and the boat,' he added.

'Beach master,' Stike chuckled. 'When do we do it, Frank?'

'Sunday morning – if the sea lets us. Meet on the fish quay at three-thirty, sharp. And not a word to anyone outside this room.' He glanced up at the badger's head, unsure whether the mask was snarling or smiling.

It was still dark when the Gurney's crab boat *Tango* left Mary's Haven to chug south along the coast beyond St Mary's Head. A heavy storm had broken during the night with thunder and lightning but the morning was fine and the sea calm. Tony Rapson and Ginger were in the bows and the club members sat amidships, smoking and chattering. The bow waves creamed away as they cruised past Firebeacon Point and the landslips of Bullen Down to December Point. Garrowcombe Head loomed large and as the *Tango* rounded Hellweather Point porpoises swam alongside her and the men regretted leaving their guns behind.

Strawberry's timing was perfect. Ploughing through the slack water at high tide they were approaching the reef under Froward when the sun lifted from the haze of settled weather and the crags stood out in finely chiselled definition. The overhangs appeared to be more soil and shillet than rock and Charlie Dunning felt the queasiness lift in his stomach. But Ginger was laughing and joking with his brothers and Strawberry wore an expression of calm expectancy. He was thinking of the silver badger and all the others sleeping in the sett ready to be winkled out. Already he regarded it as a personal triumph. The Gurneys were good boys, yes, as gutsy as his dogs, and Strawberry stooped to murmur the endearments his terriers loved. His swarthy face was radiant under the thatch of tight curls.

They moored the boat and landed the gear. Ginger stood, hands on hips, looking up at the cliffs and choosing his route. Then he tested the rock face and sat down to take off his black gym shoes and socks. The shoes were put on again and laced tight before the socks were pulled over them.

'Rock's a bit greasy,' he said. The carrot hair picked up the sunlight that was bringing a glow to the pinks and oranges in the cliff. Bob Gurney tied the cord to the boys belt and slapped him on the back.

At the spot chosen the crag rose a little less than a hundred feet above the sea. It was a vertical composition of slabs and flakes below a series of overhangs which were divided by cracks and a narrow chimney of more broken, suspect rock. To begin with Ginger climbed easily, flowing up the face on good holds. Then as he approached the overhangs he traversed to his right where the chimney offered some sort of protection from the exposure. But the chimney was damp and the rock had a looseness that surprised the boy. He felt around in the shadowy cleft, limbs quivering.

'Heads,' he bawled and a lump the size of a small loaf spun down to shatter on the terrace below. The men scattered.

Ginger grunted and swung out of the chimney. A new diagonal line was suddenly apparent. He found purchase for his toes and reached up for a solid-looking flake. It was a move of delicacy performed without effort. For a moment he hung, one-handed, searching for a hold to accommodate both feet. Then the top of the flake snapped off and Ginger was falling backwards in a lazy somersault. Strawberry saw him land on his feet and heard the crack and crunch of the breaking bone followed by the scream that ended abruptly. The force of the fall sent the unconscious boy sliding on his back towards the sea but Charlie Dunning was waiting to stop him. Strawberry swung his own horrified gaze around to look into the ashen faces of the Gurneys. The air was alive now with screaming gulls. Tony Rapson began to wail.

'For God's sake,' Bob Gurney cried, rushing forward. 'He can't be dead. He can't be. He bloody can't be.'

Dunning put an ear to Ginger's chest. 'His heart's still beating, Bob, but his legs are broke and Christ knows what else has gone.'

'Get him to the boat,' Bob said. He cut the cord on Ginger's belt and reached down to lift the boy.

'Careful,' Strawberry said, restraining Ted Gurney. 'He may be hurt inside. Link arms beneath him and do it gentle.'

Ted Gurney was sobbing. 'Who's goin' to tell mum, hey,

Bob? I idn' and that's for sure. Christ! She'll kill us.'

'Ginger idn' goin' to die,' Stike said. 'He's a tough little bugger.'

'Look at his legs,' Ted groaned. 'The bones are sticking out white.'

'Shut up and get him in the boat,' Bob grated. 'We'll put you ashore and you can have the ambulance waiting at Greenaway.

'Mum'll kill us, Bob. Look at the bloody mess Ginger's in.'

Strawberry bent to comfort Tony who was sobbing through the fingers covering his face.

'I'll murder you, Ted, if you don't stop whining,' Bob said. He stared at Strawberry as they lowered Ginger onto the deck. 'Soddin, badgers,' he snarled. 'Soddin' animals.'

'It's that big, pale old brock,' Strawberry said. 'I'm buggered if he don't lift the hair on the back of my neck. One day, though, we'll have his head on the club room wall.'

Ginger was regaining consciousness and moaning. Tony caught hold of his hand.

'The poor kid must be in agony,' Small said.

'You bloody wait,' Bob Gurney said through clenched teeth. 'We'll have the pale bugger stuffed and mounted. I swear I won't rest till we've dug Froward bury.'

Strawberry wrapped an arm round his shoulders and tried to console him.

'It wadn' your fault, Mr Rapson,' Bob continued. 'Rock climbing's in Ginger's blood. He's mazed about it.'

'He's got guts,' Strawberry said. 'I think I can persuade the committee to make him an associate member till he's old enough to drink and become a full member.'

'He's lucky to be alive,' Small said.

Dunning agreed. 'There's something about Froward I can't fathom,' he said. 'Maybe we ought to leave that sett be. There's a bloody jinx on the place.'

'We'll give it a rest for the time being, anyway,' said Strawberry, glancing back at the Point and Dragon Rock with its screaming gulls. He had chalked up another failure but the bloody badgers would come unstuck in the end. The big celebration baiting would put him back on top and by Christ, he thought, he'd make those badgers jump one way or another.

Chapter 36

Playing by the Rules

'There were men on the cliffs under your sett this morning,' Fingo said.

Aspen and Birdcherry had met him below the pines chattering his teeth at the squirrels which were moving less frantically in the trees as the light faded.

'Something bad happened. One of them screamed like a rabbit under the claws and fangs. I've never heard a man give a cry like that before.'

'Do you think they suffer as we do?' Birdcherry asked.

'Yes,' said the cat. 'I was over the other side of the zigzags towards the little coombe with the strong smell when I saw and heard them. They came and went by boat.'

'To dig out Big Sett,' Birdcherry said.

'Don't worry,' said Aspen. 'Big Sett will never be dug out by men. It is one of Earth Mother's own places. Moonwise and Starborn lived there and we are their children, aren't we?'

'You're right,' Fingo said emphatically. 'They won't be back. I told you something bad happened to one of them. Try to cheer up, Birdcherry.'

'Why d-don't they leave us alone?'

'Why don't we leave the rabbits alone?' said the cat. 'Why don't I leave the birds alone? Why don't the dogs leave me alone? Life's a great big Why. Why did the girl at the house in the trees save me from gut-burn? Why did the man by the beach save Aspen? Why do the men with yap-dogs want to kill you?'

The air was warm and heavy and full of the threat of thunder. Twilight was clouding over and quite suddenly the temperature dropped and it began to rain. A clap of thunder was followed by a flash of lightning. Fingo shivered.

'Curl into me, little friend,' said Aspen. 'It's only a noise in the sky. It can't hurt you.'

The boom and flare and deluge closed around the Point and the animals pressed together and waited. At length the storm passed out to sea leaving the sky clear and the air cool. Great fields of stars blazed in a darkness that was almost luminous. Raindrops pattered though the branches onto the carpet of needles; but the animals had managed to keep quite dry under the trees.

'May I come with you?' the cat said. 'I'll probably pay a visit to the man at the beach. He's good for sardine or kipper.'

'And gut-burn,' Aspen smiled.

'True,' Fingo growled. 'All I have to do is sniff at the fish and walk around him, brushing his legs with my body and off he goes to get me something else. Humans learn quickly. Cats are usually welcome in their homes.'

Sycamore caught up with them in Ramsons Dip and they foraged and ambled on to the hay field between Old Spanish Cove and Parson's Cove. Here the light from the half-moon ran in waves before the wind. Grass heads danced above the animals and all the light and movement made them playful. Soon they were rolling around together with the world shut out, and the scent of the meadow was all the sweeter for its drenching.

Other badgers were enjoying the deep wet grass and before

306

long Aspen came face to face with Hawscrag. Close at hand were the twins. They were burly little creatures now, not much smaller than the old sow. Their play was violent and noisy and Hawscrag was forever calling them as they strayed to the edge of the steeps.

'You're in good voice, mother,' Aspen said. 'Are they too much for you?'

'Of course not,' Hawscrag snapped. 'The virgin sows look after them most of the time and I let them forage with me every once in a while. They seem to like it.'

Sycamore and Birdcherry came grunting softly through the massed stems.

'Are you and my daughter well mated?' Hawscrag asked the pale boar.

'Very well mated,' he smiled. There were grass seeds on his face and his snout smelt of sap.

'No more fits and tantrums?' Hawscrag went on.

'Hopefully not,' Sycamore replied in his amiable voice. Hawscrag sniffed and turned to Birdcherry. 'Whatever will become of you, my little oddling?'

'N-nothing, I hope,' Birdcherry said. The grass whispered around her and the field was a moving tangle of dark scribbles printed on the sky.

'Greybob has at last settled down with a mate – a little thing barely old enough to conceive cubs,' Hawscrag said.

'Is her n-name Bellbind, mother?'

'Yes,' Hawscrag said bluntly. 'Bellbind. That beauty has brought the great sett-master to heel. He's mooning about with eyes as big as wagon wheels.'

Hawscrag could still be a cruel old creature, Aspen thought, licking Birdcherry's ear and catching the tail-end of a sigh. She began to rake at the grass and soil and soon Birdcherry joined in, digging for the sheer love of it. Then the sisters scratched and Sycamore regarded them from a smile. Walking to the top of the field the two sows and the boar sat on the hedge-bank and inhaled the fragrance of the night. The half-moon filled the countryside with its dim radiance and the animals delighted in the beauty. Over them stretched the canopy of stars. Sycamore looked at Aspen. The light in her eyes came partly from within and partly from the sky.

The seal swam the slack water of the Rips and hung for a while over the reef before sliding down into the depths to vanish. Eric Rapson waited to see if the animal would show again but soon lost interest. He had the prison look of a man who had recently been the victim of a brutal short back and sides. He stood in his overalls and ex-war department boots on the edge of the cliffs at Parson's Cove while Ted Gurney answered nature's call behind the gorse. Presently Gurney joined him, adjusting his braces and grinning self-consciously.

'Mum and Bob went to see Ginger yesterday,' he said. 'The kid's bucking up a bit but his legs are in a hell of a mess. He won't walk straight again. Thank Christ he didn't do his spine.'

'It was a miracle he survived the fall, Ted,' said Rapson.

'Gurney's luck,' his companion said, offering his cigarettes.

'I had a full packet of twenty last night,' Eric said. 'This morning six were gone. It's bloody Tony. He's aways knocking off dad's cigs and now he's into mine. His fingers are brown. I'll hammer him if he keeps it up.'

'Ten's a bit young to be smoking, any rate,' said Bob. 'Does he inhale?'

Eric Rapson shrugged. 'I dunno. I did at that age.' And he grinned. 'And I was always nickin' dad's fags.'

They walked the badger path to the sett on the promontory at Blackbottle Cove and poked around for signs of activity. Two of the holes were packed with grass and bracken and there were fresh droppings in the latrine pits.

'They'm here all right,' said Eric. He crouched with forearms on knees and his hands dangling loose. 'I bet this bury's crawlin' with 'em.'

Gurney agreed. 'It's handy for the lane by Down End barn,'

he said. 'Us could whip in and out before them at Fishacre could brush their teeth.'

By mid-morning Eric was reporting to his father who was 'doing his horses'.

'You and Bob are good boys,' he smiled. 'No one saw you, did they, son?'

'No one,' Eric affirmed.

Strawberry scribbled on the betting slip and folded it carefully.

'There's some stuff to shift before we fetch that load from Lansworthy,' he said. 'Him over Marlham dropped off a bit of heavy just after breakfast.'

'Do you trust him?' said Eric.

Strawberry nodded. 'He'll keep quiet. The Allens idn' blabbermouths and Perce needs the cash. His missis has got to have an operation.'

'What for?'

'Something to do with her insides.'

They went into the scrapyard.

'Tony's lifting my fags, dad,' Eric said awkwardly.

'And mine keep disappearing,' said Strawberry but his smile broadened. 'The little rascal. I bet he's swapping them at school for sweet coupons and stuff. He's always been smart when it comes to business. The answer is – don't leave 'em lying around. Make it difficult for him and see how he gets on. If you catch him give him a thick ear.'

The lead was wrapped in sacking.

'We'll need the crane,' Strawberry said.

'Where did Allen get this lot?' Eric asked.

'That big house across the river has gone empty and judging by the amount of heavy we've got here the roof's goin' to leak like hell after the next shower.'

At playtime Sheena ran down the back road past Rapson's yard from Mary's Haven Primary to buy a couple of doughnuts from the corner shop. She heard the crane start up and saw the arm swinging through the sunshine above the high brick wall. Purely on impulse she shinned up the lamp post that stood beside one of the pillars supporting the big double gates and parted the valerian on top of the wall. The rusted-out body of a car was dangling in the sling and Strawberry was steering it away from the pile of car doors, bicycle frames, prams and assorted scrap. Then Eric lowered the arm and cut the engine as his father unhitched the hook from the sling. Working at speed the Rapsons cleared a gap in the junk until Sheena could see a tarpaulin. When Strawberry folded back a corner the girl had a glimpse of several bulky bundles. Eric re-started the crane and his father attached the sling and the hook to something which was obviously very heavy; but the sacking remained in place throughout the operation.

After the load was dumped and the tarpaulin pulled over it the scrap metal was thrown back again and the car body once more placed on top. Sheena slid down the lamp post and padded on to the shop hoping her sandals really weren't as noisy as they sounded.

'But it could be anything legitimate,' Garrison said after she had poured out her story.

'It's heavy and it's crooked,' Sheena persisted, wondering why people like Garrison were so blind and wet. 'Strawberry wouldn't go to all that trouble if it wasn't bent. He's a real villain.'

Garrison walked up and down the lane searching for the right words.

'You can't expect the police to barge in on private property just because you think someone is hiding something.'

'You're playin' by the rules again, mister,' Sheena said with quiet contempt. 'You'll let Strawberry bash you on the head with his bloody cricket bat again before you do anything. It's so stupid. Pigs like 'im only understand this,' and she lifted a fist.

'If I keep going to the police with cock-and-bull stories they'll think I'm barmy. Harassing Strawberry like that amount's to persecution.'

310

'So what? He bleedin' well needs persecution. He's persecutin' the badgers and Billy, ain't he?'

'It's not that simple.'

'Yes it bloody is,' said Billy. 'My mum gave it to Strawberry just like dad gave it to the Japs.'

And Neil gave it to the Germans, Garrison thought. Someone always has to give it to someone else and at that moment he didn't want to even think of violence or crime or the darker side of human nature. The Ordishes had invited him to dinner and in an hour or so he would be using their telephone to speak long distant to Ann. The Rapsons and everything they stood for had left a nasty taste in his mouth – a taste he couldn't spit out. In the end a kind of spiritual fatigue set in, he reflected. Then you just want to pack a rucksack and clear off to fresh horizons leaving the mess behind you for someone else to sweep up. His mind flew back to his service days in the Great War and juggled for a moment with images which brought the sweat to his face.

Walking through the lanes to Warren Fishacre in the evening sunlight the problem surfaced again. He had always prided himself on being a man of action but it was turning out to be self-deceit. He was an artist dealing in easy realities and self-gratification under the grandiose pretence of serving humanity. Neil hadn't turned his back on grim reality and that fine young spirit had been snuffed out along with hundreds of thousands of others. So many small flames which had come together to create a blaze that had burnt away Hitler's darkness.

From Woodash all the way to Warren Fishacre the hedges were hung with dog-roses and honeysuckle which was beginning to bloom. Larks sang over wheat, and the great elms swayed in the breeze. Three buzzards slowly circled Effords Farm. A more heavenly English scene was difficult to imagine. Garrison slung the jacket of his suit over his shoulder and loosened his tie. The hedge-bank was a mass of moon daisies and wild orchids. 'No negative thoughts, Garrison,' he breathed through his teeth. The figure in khaki waving from

311

the train window faded and there were two white butterflies mating on a foxglove leaf. Something for a Pre-Raphaelite to draw. The sort of minutiae Holman Hunt relished.

The lane was deep with the top leaves of ash and hazel caught in the last of the sunlight. Every so often hovering blackflies attached themselves to his face and he brushed them off. In the end it was impossible to look beyond love or to exist as a complete human being without it.

He arrived famished at the house and after the usual pleasantries the Ordishes left him alone to speak to Ann. Listening to her he saw the sanatorium roof again among the pines on the mountainside below white peaks and blue sky. They spoke like a couple of love-sick teenagers.

'And I'll collect you from that place next Wednesday,' he concluded.

'You sound uncertain,' Ann said and he knew she was smiling.

'No delays or last minute hitches?'

'I'll be with you soon darling – really.'

'Really really?'

'Yes. Now you'd better hang up. This call is costing you a fortune.

'I can afford it,' Garrison said. 'You'll love it here. It's paradise. Devon – God! I can't put it into words.'

At dinner he spent far too long talking about his wife but the Ordishes understood and found his enthusiasm refreshing after so many dull occasions of polite, verbal ping-pong across each course. Towards the end of the evening the subject of the badgers and Rapson was raised by Mrs Ordish.

'Kerslake told me a boy from Mary's Haven fell whilst trying to climb Froward,' she said. 'It seems Rapson and a whole boatload of his cronies were intent on getting up the cliff to the sett.'

'The boy's one of the Gurney's,' said Lucy. 'Both his legs were broken.'

'Rapson ought to be shot,' Mrs Ordish said and her jaw

312

jutted. 'My late husband or your poor father Lucy would have horse-whipped the rogue. Violence is all imbeciles like him understand. His sort looted and burnt Rome.'

'Sheena's sentiments.' Garrison said with a ghost of a smile.

The French windows were open again and the aeroplane droning across the stars was a poignant reminder of Normandy. Flying north the bomber passed over Mary's Haven and returning to the bar across the beer garden from the urinal Strawberry looked up.

'Got a match, Frank?' Charlie Dunning called.

Once the cigarettes were lit the two men stood for a moment gazing at the sky.

'Them brocks will be out and about, Charlie,' Strawberry murmured. 'Poppin' out of their buries and galloping over the fields as bold as brass.'

'But tomorrow mornin' some of them are goin' to get a shock, idn' they Frank? Tomorrow mornin' some of them will be in the bag.'

Strawberry's pug face picked up the glow from his cigarette.

'I hope we get old silver,' he said. 'I don't want no rubbish at the anniversary do.'

'Stoneman reckons his new dogs will see off Gritt and Jimmy.'

'The day after tomorrow that big mouth will be light of a few quid,' Strawberry smiled. 'And Warren Fishacre will be light of some of their precious bloody brocks.'

He raised a hand to his face and rubbed the birth mark with his fingertips.

Chapter 37

The Bright Spirits

The misty morning suited the diggers. Two vanloads left Mary's Haven at first light and took the Greenaway road before cruising down the lanes towards the coast. Les Small brought his gang over the fields from Garrowcombe Barn and Strawberry and the others followed the cart track onto Down End.

'This bit of fog won't last,' said Stike. 'It'll be blazing hot around breakfast time.'

'But it'll suit us,' Strawberry said.

Some of the men carried sacks and there were three rough-haired and five smooth terriers, a few leaping about on the leash, choking with the effort to break free but the majority content to walk quietly beside their masters. The diggers wore overalls and old tweed jackets. Strawberry was whistling softly. The pug face held an expression which might have been considered angelic if it hadn't been for the birth-mark and the dead eyes.

Hawthorn hedges climbed out of the mist and to the men's right the corn stood silent and still. Ahead invisible seabirds were crying and at either hand larks gushed the music Dunning hated because it drilled into his brain. Beyond the last gate onto the headland the babble of the loomeries seemed to have been turned up like a wireless. The mist shifted, billowed and rolled around the men. Behind it they could feel the sun's warmth. Small birds cried across the bracken and brambles.

The gang took one of the sheep-walks onto Hellweather Point and met the complaint of daws and gulls. Every time a rabbit got up and bolted the dogs fought the leash and barked. Eventually the mound of clay and shillets appeared. It was conspicuous despite the new bracken growth. Here the men took two maiden sows called Damson and Holly, the sisters of Bellbind. Dazed, injured and terrified they were hobbled and bagged and carried away.

The next stop was the slope overlooking Shippen Cove but the sett was empty. The sun was visible now with the mist thinning. Grey drifted across the silver disc and Strawberry squinted at it and lit a cigarette. The lump in one of the sacks at his feet moved and he prodded it with the toe of his boot.

'Sows,' he said pensively. 'Still, they can be hellers once the dogs get to 'em. But we need boars if we're going to make an occasion of it.'

A perfectly defined badger path brought the diggers along the clifftops to Blackbottle Cove and a small sett which was served by two main holes with three tunnels running to two chambers. Fresh dung in the latrine pits and the recent unearthing of bluebell bulbs convinced everybody the place was occupied. Stike even claimed he could smell badger.

'Boar badger,' he sniffed.

'Put in your dog,' Strawberry smiled and Stike caught his Jack Russell, Sam, by the scruff of the neck and tail-stump and thrust him into one of the holes. Then he knelt and listened and pointed out the direction to Eric Rapson and Bob Gurney who took up positions on the slopes in line with each other and about five yards apart. Each had a pick and they were on their knees with ears close to the ground. Sam's muffled snarls and barks soon established the underground site of the chamber where the badgers were trapped.

'Dig away,' Strawberry said, and Eric and Bob Gurney drove the picks through the thrift into the top soil. Every so often they paused and listened and Sam continued to bark as he crouched in the tunnel holding the badgers prisoner.

Dunning and Stike got to work with the spades, and the dogs were whining and yelping in their eagerness to be part of the action.

'Bide still,' Strawberry said. 'Bide still, you little rascals.'

The mist was ghosting up the steeps in streamers and the sun burst through in a hot flood. The sweat dropped in beads off Dunning's face. Every time he drove home the spade he grunted but the animals in the sleeping chamber heard only the sound of metal cutting through compacted earth and stones, and the barking of dogs.

'I knew we should have gone b-back to Big Sett,' Birdcherry gasped, unable to believe it was happening.

Aspen and Sycamore were also frightened but the dog was becoming more daring by the moment and had to be confronted.

'Is is to be here and now?' Sycamore whispered. He gently licked Aspen's muzzle, conscious with a swelling of heartache that she was shivering.

'Perhaps,' came the low reply.

Sycamore turned and taking Sam by surprise savaged the dog. Howling all the way Sam retreated backwards and was hauled out of the sett by the stump. Another dog pushed warily along the tunnel to meet the badger snarl with his own snarl. Then the roof caved in and the muddy terrier was grabbed by Stike. Sycamore raised his snout and bared his teeth, blinking in the harsh light. The stink of Dunning's body caught in his throat. The blurred giant shape stood in the sky and the tongs descended and caught Sycamore by the hide in the middle of the back. He growled and writhed but the clamp

316

held firm. Dunning straightened and as Sycamore was lifted clear of the sett Stike's dogs flew at him and had to be dragged off.

'The big silver bugger,' Strawberry whispered and he nodded his approval as Eric rapped Sycamore on the snout. Before he could recover the boar's hindlegs were chained together and he was thrown into a sack which was tied at the neck.

Birdcherry burrowed into the nest of grass and bracken. Her mouth was gaping and her eyes closed. More of the roof came down and she was half-aware of voices and the stench of dogs. Then Aspen was advancing behind a long drawn-out snarl. The tongs fumbled, connected and bit into her shoulder. She squealed and thrashed about.

'Come up out of it, you little sod,' Dunning grunted and she was squirming in mid-air with the pain jolting through her body. By the time she was dumped on the ground she was numb with terror but the snarl on her face had not been dislodged.

Before the men could act she wounded one of Dunning's bitches and the animal backed off howling. Dunning sucked the mucus up his nose into his throat and spat phlegm. Then he closed the tongs with all his strength and Aspen groaned and the terriers pranced on their hindlegs to whine and bark. When she was lifted again she screamed but twisting she managed to close her jaws on another of Dunning's terriers and rip off half its ear. Dunning blasphemed and thumped her down so hard the breath left her body in an explosive cough.

Something hard and cold chewed through the hide and flesh on her hindlegs and she was hoisted by the tail and dropped in the sack. The mist continued to peel away, gold flushed, with patches of blue showing above the steeps. Sycamore caught the smell of his mate's fear and tried to reach her but Stike kicked him and he lay still.

'The sow's a fighter,' Strawberry said. 'Open the bag, Charlie, and put a bit of red wool on her chain.'

317

'I know what I'd like to do to her,' Dunning grated. He dabbed iodine on the terrier's torn ear and held him while the animal whimpered and tried to paw at the wound.

'You'd be up before the committee,' Stike chuckled.

'Hang on,' cried Bob Gurney. 'There's another one in here.'

The dogs' staccato yapping drew Fingo to the edge of the steeps and he stared down through the last of the mist. Dunning applied some more iodine to his terrier's ear and the burn of pain made the dog bite his hand. The fat man lashed out and the whimpering lifted to wild yelps. But the tongs reached into the sett and Birdcherry did not resist. She was hauled motionless into the sunlight and her hindlegs were chained before the sack received her.

It had happened with brutal swiftness. The badgers were asleep one moment and plunged into trauma the next. But it was always like that, Aspen reflected. The joyful run would end in the wire or gin; reverie would be shattered by a blast from a gun; dogs would suddenly appear and life would end in surprise and disbelief. Perhaps it was Earth Mother's way of easing the departure from Nightworld and all the badgers held dear. In her confusion the old dream of cubhood unwound; the long dark tunnel, the bang and rasp of metal on metal; bewilderment. The sack in which she lay was swung onto a human back and born away. Reality fragmented. The long jolting journey ended when she was slammed down on something hard. Sycamore and Birdcherry were close by, for she could smell them. Then the floor moved and vibrated and Birdcherry was crying out in fear. Sometimes the floor tilted or suddenly swung to the left or right so that Aspen was flung off balance and smashed against the metal wall.

'Help me, Aspen,' Birdcherry whimpered. 'Help me.'

'Try to stay calm,' Aspen said.

'But this is the n-n-nightmare. We are in the nightmare now – Hawscrag's n-nightmare.'

Her voice became a shrill of hysteria.

'Birdcherry,' Aspen said. 'We're with you. Nothing can

happen to you for my dream of your motherhood and the cubs yet to come was as clear as all my other glimpses of tomorrow.'

'Y-you aren't j-just making it up to comfort me?'

'Three cubs, the Bluebell Radiance and Birdcherry singing in the moonlight.'

The van hit a pothole and bucked. Sacks and badgers ended in a heap together and Birdcherry was sick. Petrol fumes and cigarette smoke added to the animals' distress but at last the vehicle came to a halt. The bundles were removed and carried a short distance before being thrown into a place with an even harder floor. There was a short conversation between the men then a door was slammed and the bolt shot with a rasp and a click. Aspen sighed. The bang and the rasp of metal on metal. She lay and considered the situation, slowly becoming aware that she and her companions were not alone.

'I am Aspen,' she whispered, pushing her snout against the sack.

'Aspen – is it really you?' demanded Furzebright's voice. 'There are so many offensive smells here it's difficult to shape your musk.'

'Sycamore and Birdcherry are with me,' said Aspen. 'Did the men capture any more of our kin group.'

'Me, Thornsong,' said the young sow, close to tears.

'Speak out all who are here,' Sycamore commanded.

'Holly and Damson,' chimed the maiden sows and after a pause a sad voice whispered: 'And Mulberry.'

'Eight of us,' said Aspen and her heart sank. Words failed her. To take so many bright spirits from Nightworld in one sweep. All around her fear was darkening to something else. For a wild creature there is no terror equal to the terror of losing liberty and being held captive in a confined space. Though the badgers were used to the crowded atmosphere of underearth they were overcome by despair and soon the shed in Rapson's yard was full of soft, piteous cries. Behind her misery Aspen could hear the voice chanting. Oh my sisters and brothers, oh the life that is so fine and precious. She

319

became alert and listened carefully. The sack stank of bruised metal, oil and industrial grime. Was it the wind crying or the long, wavering call of a seabird? Beside her she could sense Birdcherry's absolute resignation. Her sister was not only weak with fear but numb and unresponsive. Time passed and all save Birdcherry tried to find solace in Sycamore's fortitude and Furzebright's sullen defiance. When the boars spoke in voices that quaked the sows struggled to get close to them.

'I don't hold with defeatist talk,' said Sycamore. 'We're not finished yet. I for one intend showing the yap-dogs who is master when it comes to fighting. Earth Mother would have it so. We are badgers, not rabbits.'

Furzebright added his growl of assent. 'Claw and fang,' he said. 'Claw and fang,' the sows whispered dutifully.

Throughout the day men came and went and the shed door opened and shut many times. On each occasion the badgers expected the worst and by nightfall the mood of defiance had been replaced by despair. The silence outside served only to intensify their loneliness, and before long the sows were sobbing again.

Aspen who was in control of her own misery could hear them twisting and turning in the sacks and all of a sudden said: 'Bite through the end of the bag where it's tied. Do it now and stop acting like cubs.'

At once there was an urgent champing of jaws and the sound of rough material yielding and ripping. It was not long before the badgers had chewed their way to freedom. But Birdcherry remained in the bag until Furzebright and Sycamore broke the cord and coaxed her out. Then Aspen and Sycamore comforted each other in the dark. She licked his ears and eyes and for a little while the tenderness excluded everything else.

'This isn't enough,' Sycamore said coming back into himself and shaking his head.

Aspen could feel his smile and smell his breath.

'I'll get the bonds off your back legs.'

320

'It's not a bramble feeler or a vine,' she said as he chewed at the chain. Although he tried to be gentle the biting and tugging worked the metal deeper into her flesh and she cried out.

'It's no use, Sycamore. No badger can bite through the rabbit wire or the barbed wire. We must try to dig our way out of here as we are and take our chances.'

The sett-dwellers chose their corners but the stone floor would not yield and the shed walls were of thick corrugated iron nailed to wooden uprights.

Sycamore licked his broken claws and groaned. Placing her muzzle to his snout Aspen smelt and tasted the blood. He had cut his gums on her hobble chain.

'That's it,' he whispered and the young sows were sobbing again.

'Come close together, everyone,' said Aspen, and they gathered around her to sprawl in a mass. Then despite everything there was warmth and love and the badgers slept.

As soon as her eyes closed Aspen sank into a dream. Love of life was the ache which took the shape of hills rolling to the sea and the starry sky. Again the Bluebell Radiance and the steeps of summer with their myriad scents. The stream sang, the wind blew softly through the grasses and leaves and Hawscrag was playing with Guelder's cubs in the meadow where the ghost moths danced. The stars were huge and Nightworld immense and friendly. Lights moved across the ocean and the moon shone behind the tower in the wheat field. All about her on the hill sows and boars and cubs lifted their heads to scent the presence. Then Aspen woke and fetched up a sob only Sycamore heard.

Chapter 38

To Bait a Badger

Rapson's Yard had once been a stone quarry in the high part of Mary's Haven near the church. It was bounded on the street side and at the bottom by walls, with the old quarry face on the other side and the back of Strawberry's house at the top. Across the narrow back street were a coal yard, derelict stables, three low sandstone cottages and a corner shop. Rapson's premises were a self-contained island in a sprawling working-class area of allotments, terraced houses and pubs where the town spilled into farmland. Red and white valerian lined the top of the walls which were sooty with the grime of bonfires.

The yard was full of scrap – old engines in the process of being dismantled, bicycle frames, mangles, baths, pots and pans, iron and steel and more precious metals. The baiting ring was in reality a horseshoe of corrugated sheets held in place by wooden stakes. It backed onto the quarry wall. Pervading everything was the smell of smouldering metal from the bonfire that was never quite extinguished. It was the first thing Aspen smelt when she woke. The stink brought her out of a deep sleep to find daylight filtering through the cracks in the door and her metabolism complaining. Then the horror of her predicament returned in a gush of panic. Gulls' feet scratched on the shed roof, a fly buzzed against the corrugated above her, sparrows twittered and Aspen began to pick up other smells – badgers' scats, the musk of her companions' fear, the sour stench of human sweat that produced the first quaking of nausea in her stomach.

Beyond the door the light grew brighter but the badgers rarely spoke although all were now awake. Crouching beside her was Birdcherry, inconsolable, snout pressed between front paws in blind terror. Sycamore was struggling to hide his own distress. Occasionally an animal shifted and dragged its useless hind legs in an attempt to ease cramped limbs.

'Oh Earth Mother, save us,' Thornsong whispered.

The alien sounds and smells were fuel for the sett-dwellers' anxiety. Someone crossed the yard whistling and terriers came to the door and cocked their legs and growled and scratched. Then the bolt was drawn and the door opened just wide enough to admit Tony Rapson and his friend Colin, one of Charlie Dunning's nephews. The badgers huddled together in the corner.

'Don't touch 'em,' Tony warned. 'They bite like hell. One of 'em had your uncle's hand backalong and he needed eleven stitches.'

Colin shook his head and said 'wow' in a low voice. He accepted the Woodbine and let Tony light it but his heart was no more in the smoking than it was in the baiting. A small black and white striped face lifted as the match flared and the boy felt a pang of pity. His cigarette was puffed but not inhaled for he had swallowed a mouthful of smoke once and had spent half a Christmas Eve vomiting.

'Are they goin' to kill all these?' he asked.

Tony grinned and sucked on his own cigarette before breathing a 'yes'.

'What for?'

'They'm pests. In any case, it's sport.'

'But don't it hurt the badgers?'

'No,' Tony laughed. 'They don't feel a thing. They'm all bone and muscle. You hit one on the head and it just growls at you.'

'Aren't they animals, then?' Colin said.

''Course they are, stupid.'

'Well, when I tread on our cat's paw she yells. She feels pain.'

'Badgers idn' like cats, honest, Col, you can't hurt 'em. But they can put paid to a dog.'

Colin was unconvinced but kept quiet. Then one of the badgers tried to run for the door only to be checked by its hobble chain.

'Get back,' Tony snarled and he kicked Furzebright between the eyes. The boar stopped and gazed up at him. Then he moaned and returned to the corner.

'I don't like it in here,' Colin said and he pushed past Tony into the sunlit yard.

The bolt was slammed home.

'Killing they brocks with dogs idn' my idea of sport,' Colin went on. 'My dad thinks it's bleddy cruel.'

Tony's lip curled. 'You have to be born to it,' he said. 'My dad idn' cruel. He knows what it's all about.'

Colin gazed sulkily down at his feet and dropped the cigarette.

'There's cider in the kitchen,' Tony confided, feeling the friendship foundering. 'Sweet and rough – loads of it.'

'Dad won't let me drink scrumpy,' Colin said without lifting his head. 'I had some at Christmas and it got me puggled. I kept fallin' down all over the place.'

'And you don't like it?'

'I love it.' Colin looked up and grinned and the boys laughed.

'When the fun starts we'll have a few glasses in the house. Mum and the girls have gone shopping in Abbot's Quay. Tell

324

you what, Col – I'm goin' to get puggled today. Today's special.'

'Like Christmas Eve?'

'Not that special,' Tony had to admit. 'But Thelma Trant's coming round later on.'

Colin grimaced. Thelma was a large eleven-year-old, all puppy fat, freckles and sexual precociousness.

'We're going to play mothers and fathers,' Tony said peering furtively around him. 'Thelma likes cider and' – he paused to gather breath before blurting – 'I promised to show her my willie.'

Colin giggled. 'That Thelma!'

Final preparations for the baiting gave the Badger Club members plenty to do. Midway through the morning a trestle table was placed close to the baiting pen and the men began to lay it. Strawberry revelled in it all. He had shaved, and was wearing clean overalls under his club jacket. The Brylcream he had rubbed into his hair had only succeeded in making his curls sit tighter to his scalp. His tan had faded a little and the birth mark was its old livid self. The early haze had lifted and the sun shone from a blue sky, slanting across the top of the quarry face. Strawberry smiled upon the bustle to which he was central. Stoneman would be impressed. The Lansworthy club approved of the niceties. Riff-raff could dig brocks and kill them on the spot before opening time on a Saturday but only a club like the Mary's Haven could incorporate some sort of gracious living with sport.

Charlie Dunning and Eric had been left to organize the spread but Strawberry was at hand to inspect the items and the layout as it progressed. He was not a heavy drinker but could sink more than most on the odd occasion. So when Eric opened a bottle of Symons' Royal Excelsior, 'the champagne of ciders', he needed no persuasion to swig away at a half-pint. As well as the Imperial Cyder from the fruit mills of Totnes, there was an extravagant display of Henley's Devonshire Cyder purchased direct from the mills at Newton Abbot.

325

Gold Label, Extra Quality, Green Label, bottles and jars of medium sweet and dry were displayed with an array of pint and half-pint pots and sleevers. Under the table were casks of farmhouse rough – the sort of cider that burns the stomach lining and loosens the teeth before sending a man berserk.

It was satisfactory, Strawberry reflected while the food came out on tin trays: pasties, pies, bowls of pickled onions, pickled cabbage, wedges of cheese, bread and dry biscuits, all under muslin cloths.

High above the yard swifts were on the wing and screaming and even higher a pair of ravens croaked to each other as they swung lazily towards the sea cliffs. Strawberry took another glass of the Imperial with Archie Stoneman who had honoured his host by wearing his best bowler hat and a collar and tie. He held his terriers on a tight double leash. The smooth dog and bitch were impressively calm. Elsewhere as the men gathered and the noise of conversation and laughter swelled to a din dogs were getting in each other's way and there was a lot of barking and snapping and tangled leads. Strawberry grinned. He loved the apparent chaos. The activity of the dogs and the feast and the sport yet to come left him parched with excitement.

'This champagne cider is the tops, Frank,' said Stoneman.

'It's a champagne do, Arch,' Strawberry said and his guest promptly called for order. Sweat beaded his heavy red face and Strawberry wondered how long the collar would stay buttoned.

'Gentlemen,' Stoneman said in his mellow, after-dinner voice and Devon accent. 'I give you the Mary's Haven Club and their guiding light on this their twenty-fifth anniversary. May the sport be good and the dogs courageous. Long life and God bless.'

Then the drinking and betting really began with Small acting as bookmaker. After he had parted with his money Stoneman loosened his collar. The smiling pug face and its hideous splash of what looked like red ink down one cheek was an unpleasant apparition. Already the alcohol was heightening Stoneman's awareness. Yet he had complete confidence in his new pair of Jack Russells, Skipper and Jill. He declined another drink but ate one of the homemade pasties. Strawberry refilled his own glass and the guests gathered expectantly around him.

'We've got eight brocks, boys,' he smiled. 'And hardly any rubbish among 'em.' The tip of his tongue skated over his lower lip as the alcohol working rapidly through his system left him feeling wonderfully light-headed. The potent Henley's Gold Label was as smooth as Symons' Excelsior. Raising his eyes to the top of the quarry he found the stone had taken on the colour of cider.

'Keep the refreshments flowing, Eric,' he added. 'I don't want to see no glum faces at this do. Keep the glasses full and I promise you some rare sport.'

'Soon, I hope,' said Stoneman. Behind his friendly smile was an impatience to get on with the baiting. The stink of the bonfire smouldering in the corner made it difficult to enjoy the food. Out of the corner of his eye he saw Tony Rapson take a couple of bottles of the best stuff off the table and run towards the house. He also noted that a few of his own club members were already 'half shot away'.

'Let's have one of the brocks in, Frank,' he pressed, recalling other 'special occasions' which had ended in drunken shambles.

'I've got a little sow who'll give your dogs a rough ride,' Strawberry smiled. 'She'll do for starters.'

'I don't like the idea of my dogs going up against a sow,' Stoneman said. 'It wouldn't be much of a contest and over Lansworthy us usually kick off with a gutsy old boar.'

Stoneman's refinement surprised Strawberry who prided himself on his knowledge of tradition and etiquette.

'It's our way, Arch,' he said. 'We've discovered over the years that some sows can give as much sport as the best boars.'

Stoneman nodded, unconvinced, and looked at his mates.

'A brock's a brock,' Strawberry smiled.

'But not for the ten quid, Frank.'

'Certainly not. Just to warm up the dogs for the big one with the silver brock.'

'I bet you ten bob no sow can go twenty minutes with my animals,' Stoneman said.

'Done,' Strawberry smiled and the men raised their glasses to each other.

The sun sprang across the rooftops of Mary's Haven into the yard. The air was full of the manic wailing of gulls and the screams of the swifts.

'Go and get the little sow with the red wool on her hobble,' Strawberry told Eric. 'The one who ripped the ear of Stike's mongrel. It's time us got down to business.'

Tony was at Dunning's side, tugging at his sleeve. 'Can me and Col have a drop of cider, Uncle Charlie?'

'Course you can, my boodies,' and Dunning filled the tumblers with medium sweet.

Tony winked at Colin and giggled. They stood behind the table until it was possible to grab another bottle, this time of Henley's Extra Quality. On the way back to the house Tony fell down but the bottle did not break and both boys eventually staggered through the kitchen door crying with laughter.

'Here,' Colin slurred. 'What happened to Thelma?'

'Dunno,' Tony grinned as the floor lifted and fell under him. He fought the bottle top, opened it, lost his balance and sat down on his rump. The cider fizzed out onto his lap and Colin was braying with laughter again.

'I want a fag,' Tony said. 'Come on, come on – let's take the scrumpy upstairs. If dad catches me smokin' and drinkin' he'll knock my head off.'

'Mine's been knocked off,' Colin tried to say but the words came out in an unintelligible mess.

'Here,' he added, crawling up the stairs behind Tony. 'Doan drink all tha' yourself.'

328

They collapsed in a heap on the landing and Tony clawed at his pocket for the cigarettes, but Colin was too far gone to participate any further. The lighted Woodbine slipped from his fingers onto the mat. He tried to retrieve it but gave up and made for the nearest bedroom on hands and knees with Tony hooting behind him. United in nausea they climbed into bed and with the ceiling spinning pulled the counterpane over their heads and sank through giddiness into unconsciousness.

Down in the yard the sportsmen gathered at the baiting pen and the dogs were voicing their intentions. Eric banged open the shed door and several startled black and white faces lifted as Bob Gurney separated the animals with his boot.

'The one with the red bit of wool on her chin,' Eric said.

Sycamore and Furzebright started forward but kicks to the snout left them senseless. The sows cowered together against the far wall.

'There she is,' Eric breathed and Aspen was gripped by the tail and swung out into the bright morning with all its terrible smells and noises. She had a brief, blurred upside down vision of scrap metal, men and dogs before she was dumped heavily in the pen and her legs were unchained. Dazed, she walked slowly along the corrugated iron fence to the quarry wall and stood up on her back legs to sniff the air. Someone flicked a cigarette end at her but she was buried beneath an emotion which for a while eclipsed everything the outside world could conjure up. Then the dream reality lurched into another harsh reality with all its painful vibrations. 'Must it be now?' She dropped onto all fours and turned towards the giant, dark shapes which moved and roared and expelled smoke.

The human stench, the acrid smell of burning tobacco and the cider fumes filled her with terror and confusion. The light was too bright and the din unbearable. Something awful was about to happen and she moaned and pressed into the shadows under the corrugated but Stike prodded her savagely with his stick and she staggered into the sun again.

'Put in the dogs,' said Strawberry.

*

329

Mrs Drew had opened the doors and windows of the Railway Hotel's public bar and was contemplating a quiet morning when a sunburnt little man came in for some tobacco and cigarette papers. He had a couple of Jack Russells on leashes and looked peeved.

'Lost the rent money, love?' Mrs Drew grinned.

'Lost my bloody way,' the little man said. 'The others took off without me. I was ten bloody minutes late and they couldn' hang on so I came over on the bus. Pour us a small Guinness, dear.'

He glared at her and worked loose a sliver of skin from his peeling nose.

'Where you going, anyway?' said Mrs Drew.

'Rapson's yard,' he said and she gave him a steady look and angled the glass to pour the Guinness.

'It's the Mary's Haven Badgers Club anniversary do. Is that clock right?'

'Ten minutes fast,' she said.

'I'll kill Archie Stoneman if they start without me,' he continued.

'You haven't got far to go, love,' said Mrs Drew. 'Turn right and it's the third turning left past the butcher's.'

He thanked her and downed his drink.

'If it's started I'll hear the dogs, anyway,' was his parting remark.

Mrs Drew took off her apron and called the landlord.

'Got to pop out for five minutes, love,' she said and he knew better than to object.

'Five minutes,' he reminded her. 'I got a business to run, Amy.'

Her face was set hard in an expression that boded ill for someone. She stalked up the road to Garlic Street Primary and found the playground full of children. Sheena saw her at the gate and fetched Billy. The boy was cringing with embarrassment.

'Your dad used to look like that when I bawled him out in

the pub,' Mrs Drew said. 'It was his Saturday lunchtime leave-me-alone-look. Well, Mr Big Man, I reckon your mate Strawberry is havin' one of his badger things down the yard and it must be big because blokes have come over from Lansworthy.'

'Now?' Billy said.

His mother nodded and said: 'Are you goin' to just stand there yappin' or are you goin' to let Mr Garrison know?'

'But how –' Billy started.

'It don't matter how I know. Let's go.'

'I wish I had a bike, mum,' Billy said, trotting beside her into the back street.

'Well, you haven't got one and I can't afford one and you'd better not nick one.'

The whining and barking of the terriers confirmed everything long before Billy had climbed the gate to peer into the yard.

'Have they started?' Sheena said when he dropped back into the road.

'Not yet. Crikey! – there's hundreds of 'em.'

'They must have a lot of badgers,' Sheena said. 'Bleedin' heck, Billy – let's get old Garrison.'

'But it'll take ages to run there and back.'

'Here's four bob,' said Mrs Drew. 'Get a taxi.'

Billy took the money and jumped up and hung for a moment from her neck while she kissed him.

'Cupboard love,' she smiled. 'Go on – and hurry. I've got to get back to the pub or I'll lose my job.'

The taxi driver was reluctant to take his cab down the stony lane to Hard Sands until Billy told him he could have two shillings and another florin if he waited at the cottage and brought them back. Garrison was in the studio and immediately abandoned everything to join them.

'We'll phone the Ordishes,' he said, 'and see if they can drum up some support.'

'And I'll get the police,' said Sheena.

'They won't be able to help,' Garrison said.

'They will when they hear what's under Strawberry's junk,' Sheena said. 'It's worth a try, mister.'

Crawling back up the lane the taxi broke down and the driver spent valuable time trying to re-start it before admitting defeat.

'I should never have brought it down here in the first place,' he grumbled but Garrison cheered him up with a pound note and the promise to meet the garage bill. Then he followed the children through the hedge into the field.

'The quickest way back to Mary's Haven,' Sheena said and she clapped her hands to stampede the heifers.

'Will we be in time?' Garrison asked.

'Even if we save half the animals it'll be something,' Billy said.

Garrison clambered over the gate to drop into the next field.

'What a bloody caper,' he grated. 'So-called civilized men allowed to kill innocent creatures for amusement in the middle of an English town in the twentieth century.'

'Two more fields to go,' Billy shouted over his shoulder.

'Then what?' Garrison panted.

'Then the road into High Town and Rapson's Yard.'

'Is there a phone box on the way?'

'Yes,' Billy cried, wading through the stinging nettles to climb another hedge-bank.

The terriers sprang at Aspen and fastened onto various parts of her body before she was aware of what was happening. Then the hair lifted and ran in waves along her spine and the rest of her coat was alive. Heaving her shoulders she shook off Skipper and Jill and turned to dislodge Gritt and Jimmy. By now her every hair had stiffened and she had become an awesome opponent. Jill tried to bite her cheek but she was bowled over and had her side raked by Aspen's claws. The sow's nostrils were clogged with the stink of dog – a strange, unclean stony smell. The sun got in her eyes and she blinked,

332

and Gritt and Jimmy were on her, tearing and slashing while Stoneman's dogs pranced stiff-legged around her.

'Yours know how to dance, Arch,' Strawberry laughed. 'Where d'you get 'em – the ballet school?'

'I'll have another ten bob on 'em both,' Stoneman retaliated and Strawberry drank some more and sent Eric off for refills.

Again Gritt and Jimmy tore into Aspen from the front and avoiding her swinging head, left their mark. She tottered and reeled as Stoneman's terriers hung from her hindquarters.

'She's a tough little brock,' Strawberry slurred.

'But not as tough as my dogs,' said Stoneman.

Strawberry draped an arm around the big man's shoulders and chuckled. His eyelids drooped and his tongue flickered.

'You always were a bit of an old woman, Archie. You ought to keep poodles, boy. That'd be right up your street.'

'And you always were a stroppy little shit, Rapson' Stoneman said, ducking out of Strawberry's grip.

'No offence intended,' Strawberry smiled. 'No need to get personal, boy. It's just that where fightin' dogs are concerned you don't know your ass from your elbow.'

Stoneman turned away. Aspen was struggling to rise but the dogs were tenacious. They were in and out, snarling and snapping, urged on by the yelps of the other terriers and the cries of the men whose thirst for blood seemed as insatiable as their thirst for cider. The jars continued to do the rounds and the dogs in the pen hit Aspen in a concerted rush, leaving her bleeding from the head. She raised her muzzle but the smooth-haired bitch had an ear badly torn when she threw caution to the wind. Her screams brought the attack to a halt and Aspen went on the offensive. Now her head was held low and she made a series of furious sorties. Jimmy was thrown so hard against the corrugated he was too winded to cry out. In Aspen the former numbness of spirit had become a wonderful vigour. She saw off the three active dogs before turning on Jimmy again to take him off-guard. Sharp teeth and claws did the rest. Wedged between the sow and the corrugated he craned his neck and sought one of the white-fringed ears. A downward sweep of Aspen's teeth lacerated the artery in his throat.

Strawberry stared through his alcoholic haze in astonishment and grief as the badger crouched to gather strength. 'Jimmy,' he cried and the sleever slipped from his grasp. He swung a leg over the corrugated and Eric and the Gurneys restrained him, but he continued to struggle and call for his dog as Jimmy's kicks became feebler and the animal's tongue protruded from crimson froth.

'Leave 'em be,' Stoneman thundered. 'What sort of do is this, hey? The dog's copped it, fair and square and my animals will finish the job.'

'Your animals,' Strawberry growled. 'Those bleddy mongrels idn' fit to eat Jimmy's shit.'

'Jimmy's dead,' Stoneman observed coldly and Strawberry balled a fist in his face while Eric clung to his father's arms.

'You're pissed, Rapson,' said one of Stoneman's men.

'Order!' Dunning roared. 'The baiting's still in progress. Let's have a bit of decorum. Come on now, Frank.'

Aspen had been badly mauled despite her show of aggression. She sank back in the shade panting and licking her wounds while the dogs paced up and down before her with that bristling gait the spectators loved.

'Go to, go to,' Strawberry said, salvaging what was left of his pride. The tears ran down his face and streaked the birthmark. Stoneman caught his hand and the men wordlessly acknowledged something they could not label. Lunging swiftly from the rear Gritt tore at the slack flesh behind one of Aspen's ears and the sow had to somersault to free herself. In the process her underfur was exposed and Stoneman's terriers drew more blood, but not without hurt to themselves.

Aspen gazed desperately about her, shaking dark red drops from her muzzle. She was one throb of pain and felt the first spirals of dizziness which she knew would whirlpool to the blackout from which there was no waking. The smooth-haired

334

bitch taunted her, moving stiffly sideways, and she snarled at the animal. Then with mounting despair she lifted her head and her mouth gaped.

Chapter 39

Smoke Shadows

Garrison was stoking up his anger as he ran, and the children had never seen him looking so grim. The thought of what was happening to the badgers in Rapson's Yard sparked off a whole chain of images and sensations. He saw Ann weeping over the telegram that had announced Neil's death and the loneliness he had felt when she had gone to Switzerland pulsed coldly beneath the other emotions.

They pushed him through the final hedge onto the road and he let his bitterness colour everything. There was a night where the human soul was put in quarantine. All the devices used to suppress the spirit were paraded in those shadows, century after century, without shame.

He swung open the door of the telephone kiosk, pumped in the coins and spoke to Lucy Ordish. His words came out in a gabble and he slammed down the receiver and was running again, his thoughts out of focus now. Sheena had gone and Billy was on the top of some faded blue gates. Garrison hoisted himself up after the boy into sunlight that flashed and winked on metal and dappled the quarry wall. Faces were distorted and wobbling in the reflected heat. El Greco figures, he mused, trying to re-shuffle the images against the barking of the dogs and the shrilling of the swifts. And all at once the yard roared into life and clarity. Weaving through the junk he saw men lurch to meet him and smelled the stink of the bonfire and heard the cries. Willow herb rocked among the twisted heaps of metal then a faint scream lifted above the other noises. For Garrison it was the distillation of all the misery of a life coming to an end in squalor, bewilderment and fear. It was neither human nor animal but an abstract proclamation of despair. He saw Billy vanish into the crowd of men and heard him yelling. The face with the hideous red birthmark came sailing out of the heat-dance and the voices blended to a snarl. He fell sprawling over a dog and got up and charged the mass of drinkers. Strawberry was gone and he was shrugging off the hands and vaulting the sheet of corrugated iron into the pen. The dogs worrying the grey lump against the quarry wall were too busy to spare him a glance. Garrison kicked them apart and was bitten on the ankle. Eric Rapson flung himself over the side of the pen and landed awkwardly, but Garrison had seen the black and white head lift and the small round eyes open to stare up at him and close again. He gathered Aspen in his arms and stood with his back to the quarry wall. Eric Rapson's eyes were glazed but he advanced half-crouching and snapping his fingers like a fairground wrestler. Strawberry's cronies thought this funny but Stoneman was appalled. Calling off his dogs he gestured to the Lansworthy Club members. The badger stirred against Garrison and he laid her down gently close to the wall. At that moment Billy wriggled out of Stike's grip and was in the pen before he could be stopped. His dive took Eric Rapson at knee height and brought him crashing down.

The cider had goaded Rapson to a rage that amazed Garrison. The young man was trembling as he caught Billy by the hair and smacked him across the face with the knuckles of his free hand. Billy grunted and stood there rocking to and fro, his head bowed. The Gurneys closed on Garrison and held him, the badger forgotten and Strawberry lurching over to begin the new baiting.

Stoneman protested when the first blow was struck.

'For the love of God, Rapson,' he cried. 'Leave the man and boy alone. Can't you see, this has got out of hand? Pack it in – now, or they'll throw the book at you and I'll help them.'

'Bugger off,' Strawberry growled. 'This is my property and they broke in and are gettin' what they deserve.'

'You're mad,' Stoneman said. 'It's got to be the bleddy drink talking. Still, it's your funeral, mate.'

Strawberry smiled and lifted two stiff fingers, but the Gurneys released Garrison and he was allowed to dab at Billy's nose with a handkerchief.

'You've broken it,' he said, staring in disgust at Eric Rapson.

'He attacked me,' came the unrepentant reply.

'A ten-year-old boy attacked you! That'll sound great in court – and that's where this is going to end, believe me. The police will be here soon.'

The welter of violence had left him drained. One of his eyes was closing and he was beginning to shake.

'Kick Drew out of here,' Strawberry said and before the gates clattered behind the Lansworthy men Billy was hustled into the street.

'Is Mr Garrison OK?' Stoneman asked.

Billy sniffed and nodded, holding the red-stained hand-kerchief to his nose.

'Best get home, boy,' Stoneman said but Billy shook his head and sat on the kerb. Every so often he hawked up blood and spat into the gutter. A gull glided down off the roof and stood beside him. Billy looked up the street. Smoke was uncurling slowly from the top side window of Rapson's house. Mystified the boy walked up the road for a closer look. The gull flapped after him, its feet trailing over the paving stones . . .

'Are you going to keep me here against my will?' Garrison said.

'As if we'd do that,' Strawberry smiled. 'Me and the boys wouldn' want to break the law.'

Eric and the Gurneys chuckled and passed the jar of farmhouse rough.

'Tell you what,' Strawberry continued. 'You're welcome to watch the rest of the sport. We've got a shed full of brocks.'

Garrison glanced at Aspen who was lying motionless in the sun.

'I thought they'd got rid of all you bastards at Nuremberg, Rapson,' he said.

'Help the gentleman out of the ring, Eric,' Strawberry said, taking the cider jar in both hands and rocking on his heels. 'Then fetch us a fresh brock – the big silver bugger.'

'What about the one who killed Jimmy?'

'I'll deal with her in a minute – what's left of her, anyway.'

The jar was tilted and cider dribbled down his chin. Dunning and Small exchanged looks of dismay but the Gurneys reached for Garrison's arms. He brushed them aside. Horror and anger had faded to helplessness. Where the hell was Lucy Ordish and Sheena and the police? He gave the small grey body pressed against the wall another glance and his legs buckled.

'Here, mate,' Eric Rapson crowed. 'I hope you haven't been on the scrump.'

The Gurneys laughed and the swifts went on screaming as they hurtled through the sky. The valerian waved in the heat and Garrison wanted to be sick.

'Fire,' Billy yelled, straddling the top of the gates. 'Your house is on fire, Rapson, and I'm bloody glad.'

'You never give up, do you, Drew?' Eric Rapson sneered.

'God's honour it is,' Billy cried. He jumped into the yard and ran over to them. 'You can beat me if it idn'. There's smoke comin' out the landin' window.'

The light easterly wind had kept the smoke out of the yard

339

and out of sight, and the place was already hazed in smoke from the bonfire. Strawberry pushed forward and would have hit the boy if Garrison hadn't stepped between them.

'That's it, Rapson,' he said. 'It's easier to punch someone else's head than use your own. Why not go out in the street and have a look. We're not going anywhere.'

'If this is another of your tricks, Drew,' Strawberry said menacingly.

'I can smell it, Frank,' Dunning said. 'Something's burning and I don't mean the bonfire.'

'It's that bloody kid,' Strawberry slurred and he rested his buttocks on the top of the corrugated sheet and tried to stay awake.

Billy led the rest of the men out of the gate and up the street.

'There,' he shouted and pointed. 'The window and all along the edge of the roof.'

The smoke was yellowish grey. It seeped from under the guttering and through the half-open landing window.

'Jesus,' Eric whispered. 'Where's Tony?'

'And Colin,' Dunning said.

Glass tinkled down as the landing window shattered in the heat. Behind the smoke was a red glow.

Garrison dragged himself over the wall and dropped into the yard. A moment later Eric Rapson and Bob Gurney were at his side. Garrison pushed open the back door. There was very little smoke in the kitchen but the hall was full of it. Thick smoke flowed down the stairs and the men could hear the crackle of the fire above. Eric and Gurney made a frantic search of the lower rooms but drew blanks. The horror stood out in Eric's eyes when he turned to Garrison.

'Get a ladder up at the bedroom window,' Garrison said. 'You know where your brother sleeps.'

'Do it, Bob,' Eric said. 'The one above the front door.'

The top of the stairs was ablaze but Garrison took the steps two at a time. A sudden gust of heat singed his hair and sent him staggering against the wall. Flames licked around him and

340

the smoke was in his eyes and lungs. Under the palm of his hand the wallpaper was bubbling. He coughed and beat at his trouser leg. Through the smoke the bedroom door was hardly visible. Eric pushed past him and kicked it open. A furnace blast of heat sucked them into the room.

'On the bed,' Garrison gasped.

The two heaps under the counterpane were the boys and they could not be woken. Then part of the landing collapsed and flames licked across the bedroom floor. But the top of the ladder appeared on the window sill and someone was breaking the glass.

Eric passed Tony to Charlie Dunning and Colin soon followed. By now a crowd had gathered and the Mary's Haven fire engine was speeding into High Town. A billowing column of smoke climbed the sky before the wind spread it over the neighbourhood. Garrison came down the ladder as part of the roof caved in and held it while Eric made his descent. The two men faced each other unsmiling in the small garden.

'Thanks,' Eric said, but he did not offer his hand.

The badger club members tried to organize a chain of buckets but it was too late and the back street provided unexpected problems for the firemen. By the time hoses were run in from the main road Rapson's house was gutted.

While Garrison and Eric talked to the police, Strawberry returned to the yard and found PC Tapley and Sheena standing together just inside the gates. The scrap merchant was sobering rapidly but the sight of the pair left his knees dead. What had occurred was inconceivable. He looked at the smoking ruin and back at the girl. She was pointing at the car body then the wall. Everything in Strawberry's world had turned sour. Maybe Charlie Dunning was right. Maybe there was a jinx. Down in the baiting pen Billy and Lucy Ordish were kneeling before Aspen. Strawberry swung a leg over the corrugated and shuffled past them to Jimmy's body. The

341

terrier might have been sleeping, only his eyes were open and dull.

Strawberry bent to stroke him but could not keep his balance and sat down in the dirt.

'Poor little fella,' he murmured. 'Poor little Jimmy.' And he laid his hands on the dog and gently brushed the dust off its face.

The hot, smoke-darkened day was brewing its chaos and Strawberry recognized within it elements of his own destruction. The house wasn't insured, the baiting had come to nothing, he had lost a dog and Tapley was heaving aside the scrap above the hoard of stolen lead, garden machinery and building materials.

'Mr Rapson,' the constable called. 'Can I have a word with you.'

At breakfast time he had been reasonably well off, commanding respect in the working-class community. By noon he was ruined, without a home and under arrest facing a custodial sentence for theft and receiving. Eric Rapson had also been charged, among other things, with ABH on Billy.

The Mary Haven's Badger Club ceased to exist.

Billy snuffled through his broken nose and stroked the badger sow with such exaggerated tenderness Lucy had to smile. Mrs Drew had arrived but the look on Billy's face kept her at arm's length. She took a light off Garrison's cigarette and remembered other occasions when her son's face had been transfigured. Then her exclusion from the source of his enchantment had left her bitter – Billy crooning to his rabbits in the back yard; Billy trying to stick a feather back in the tail of an injured pigeon; Billy and the sparrow he had retrieved from the cat's mouth, opening his hands to release the bird into the sunshine. The dried blood was caked round his nose and his hair was a mess but bent over the badger he was radiant.

The sow's breathing was soft and irregular and Lucy's heart

342

sank. Before long she was weeping and Garrison could not comfort her.

'Don't cry,' Billy said, looking up in surprise. 'She idn' going to die.'

'How do you know, Billy?' said Garrison.

'He knows,' Sheena said fiercely. Her haggard, old-young face glared at them. 'He knows, mister.'

And Mrs Drew nodded.

'Where's Paul, Lucy?' Garrison said.

'He took Rapson and the boys to hospital. The ambulance was out on a call. He shouldn't be long.'

Behind them the police were sifting through some of the items recovered from under the tarpaulin.

'You'd better get them animals out of the shed, mister,' Billy said. 'Us doan know how long they've been there without food and water. I can look after this one for a while.'

It was PC Tapley who pushed open the door. Three or four black and white faces surfaced from the scrum of badgers in the corner. The stench of excrement and urine, and the heat and stuffiness made the policeman turn away for a moment. Standing on the threshold Garrison heard the low moaning of the sows and the panting of creatures half-crazy with thirst.

'There's six or seven of them,' Tapley said. 'Could you get a bowl of water from one of the houses down the street?'

'I'll go,' said Mrs Drew.

Then Tapley added in a voice thick with emotion. 'The bastards have chained their back legs. I'd better call a vet.'

'And I'll see if I can remove the chains,' Garrison said.

One of the badgers still had the strength to resist. He was a big pale animal that shuffled back against the wall and bared his teeth.

Presently Lucy came to the door nursing Aspen with her boyfriend in close attendance.

'Oh how dreadful,' she whispered, averting her eyes. 'How could they do it!'

Garrison had the reply on his tongue but did not voice it.

343

Smoke drifted from the ruins of the house and the swifts continued to shrill.

As soon as it was possible the badgers were bagged once more and ferried to Paul's car. The ride to the sea cliffs was the final part of their trauma, yet so great had been their mental suffering the sett-dwellers were hardly conscious of the journey. Then, as each was carried across the lawn at Coastguard Cottage, they recognized the sound of waves breaking on the shore and heard oystercatchers piping and smelled the keen, salty tang of the ocean. Their senses became instantly receptive to everything the day could offer.

One by one they were released onto Woodash Down, and began to run, stopping every twenty or so paces to push their snouts through the clustered scents.

'Have we won, David?' Lucy asked, watching Birdcherry's progress towards the steeps.

'I hope so,' and he smiled at the children.

'What about the little sow, mister?' Sheena said. 'Will you make her well again?'

'With the vet's help – yes.'

'Mr Garrison will do it,' Billy said solemnly.

He tugged a grass head, collected the seeds on his palm and blew them away.

Evening became dusk and Garrison was tired. His face ached from Strawberry's blow and his legs and ankles had been slightly burnt. He needed a bath and bed.

The vet called but was pessimistic about Aspen's chances of recovering. Her injuries and the shock had been substantial, and she had lost a lost of blood.

'She'll survive,' Garrison said.

'You sound so positive,' the vet frowned.

'Billy said so,' Garrison explained. 'And Billy knows his animals.'

Waiting for the pans to boil for his bath Garrison sat in the rocking chair, loving the way it clacked across his drowsiness while the loose hasp rattled and Aspen sighed in her sleep and the blackbird sang from the darkness.

344

The badger lay wrapped in a blanket before the fire and Garrison smiled as her muzzle twitched and she kicked out with her hindlegs. He had forgotten what it was like to be in the gentle company of animals. Putting a match to a cigar he considered Strawberry's downfall. For men like that it had to be a squalid full stop to a squalid pursuit; nothing to make the front pages of the nationals. It had to be something appropriately petty, enacted in a small provincial courtroom – a way of life reduced to something unpleasant rather than shocking; a whiff of dental decay rather than the stink of brimstone. But it was always enough to keep society's compassion on ice.

Chapter 40

Moonrise at Froward

The badgers assembled on the steeps of December Point, subdued and a little dazed after their ordeal. But Nightworld gradually coaxed them back into themselves and they spent a long time grooming and scratching. Then Birdcherry asked the question that weighed heavily on all their minds: 'Where is Aspen?'

Sycamore hung his head and whispered. 'They took her and gave her to the dogs. I heard her cry out.'

'She c-can't be dead,' said Birdcherry. 'N-not the moon-born.'

Sycamore licked her face and caught her tears on his tongue. The words of comfort he wanted to say balled in his throat. The maiden sows were weeping quietly as he led the sett-dwellers back towards Froward. The moon was not yet full and the sky was hazy. Sometimes the badgers stopped and rolled in the thick vegetation, leaving the metallic, sappy smell of crushed bracken stems behind them. Up and down the hillsides they went, nursing their sorrow. Too distressed to forage they came at last to the point and scented Hawscrag.

346

She was sitting on the lawn close to the sett listening to the incoming tide roaring over the skerries.

'So, it has happened,' she whispered when Sycamore broke the news. 'The one who was so full of life has gone from us.'

She looked at them. 'Go below ground and rest. I shall stay here and think of her.'

'May I stay w-with you, mother?' asked Birdcherry.

'No. Go with Sycamore. Sleep, and grow strong again.'

Then her grief swelled. It had been a cruel spring but there would be other springs and summers and young sows full of the beauty of life. Alone, Hawscrag stared up at the stars and let the dream lift her out of misery.

A few miles away at Coastguard Cottage Aspen's fraility puzzled Garrison. She was losing weight and would not take food. Her movements were sluggish and even Billy was scared by her total lack of interest in what was going on. At times she would leave the fireside and totter into a corner, delivering a strange bird-like cry. Picking her up Garrison noticed for the first time the mark of the gin trap on her leg.

'So it's you,' he whispered, but he knew that the mind behind the eyes staring up at him was elsewhere.

It was not a physical problem.

'She's simply lost her will to live,' he told Billy.

The boy sat with the badger on his lap, stroking her head and crooning things which on another occasion might have made Garrison smile. Billy's presence always produced some sort of response in the creature and she seemed to anticipate his visits. Her head would rise when he came to the door and the bond made Garrison a little jealous. Most of the time she slept and dreamed. Nightworld was waiting almost as soon as her eyes closed and those who were dead and those she believed to be dead gambolled in the moonlight: Guelder and Ashblacken, Bullenspur, Dogrose and Briarfrost; Sycamore, Furzebright, Thornsong and Birdcherry. Dear Sycamore and poor mouse-like Birdcherry. Guelder's cubs came romping through the dream to drive sadness away. Why had she alone survived? The nightmare cast its shadow and drew her into it – the barking that hurt her mind, the blood and agony and terror, the white, searing sun and the giddy fall through darkness. Darkness and human scent and the smell of burning. Then the curious, bumpy flight out of the dark and the return to self. 'Oh Sycamore,' she whispered. 'Sycamore.' But a voice was calling her and an image was forming to eclipse the others. It was not as she first supposed Earth Mother. The voice was familiar and the black and white face greying with age was unmistakably Hawscrag's. On the Point below the pines with stars in the sky and the sea and Nightworld full of the season's sweetness.

She sighed in her sleep and her muzzle twitched.

'Bless her,' Sheena said.

'Don't touch her, Sheen,' said Billy. 'Let her rest.'

'She ain't goin' to die, is she?'

Billy shrugged. 'I didn' think so but now I'm not so sure. Animals sometimes just lie down and go to sleep and never wake up.'

'But why?' Sheena whispered.

'I don't know.'

Garrison brought in the mugs of cocoa and the biscuits.

'You ain't half got a shiner, mister,' Sheena chuckled, and Garrison rubbed his eye.

'Bleedin' Strawberry only tried to blame Billy for the fire,' Sheena continued, sitting on the hearth beside Aspen. 'He got that rat Tony to say he saw Bill on the stairs lighting a newspaper. The police came and took Billy down the station.'

'Then what happened?' Garrison asked although he had already heard the story from Tapley.

'Colin Brewer owned up,' Billy said. 'He told the police him and Tony had been smoking and he'd dropped a fag on the landing.'

'Pity you didn't let the little rat roast, Mr Garrison,' said Sheena.

'You don't mean that, Sheena,' Garrison smiled.

348

'Well, they should be grateful he's still alive. Fancy tryin' to drop Billy in it after what you done.'

'I don't get why they had all the stolen stuff in the yard,' said Billy. 'That was askin' for trouble.'

'Every two or three months Strawberry hired a big lorry,' Garrison said. 'That was how long it took him to get enough stolen gear together. Then he would drive the stuff to Bristol and sell it. The junk piled on top was a clever trick. No one would bother to look underneath to see what he was hiding. It was simple but Strawberry's scrap runs to Bristol have been going on for years.'

'How long will he get?' Sheena said.

'At least twelve months – father and son. Apart from the raids on places like Warren Fishacre they also stole from farms, including Woodash. Tapley thinks they're finished locally. Poor Mrs Rapson and the children have already moved to relatives in Okehampton.'

'I ain't sorry for her,' Sheena said. 'The bleedin' Rapsons not only murdered stacks of badgers, they give Billy hell.'

The following morning the vet called and admitted he was mystified.

'Her wounds are healing nicely,' he said, 'but she seems to be sinking, David. And I can't put my finger on it. Maybe there's some sort of internal damage.'

'But there's no blood in her droppings,' said Garrison.

The vet shrugged and patted Aspen's head.

'She drinks from her bowl,' Garrison continued. 'But she won't eat.'

The sorrow in the badger's eyes grieved him. Waking from a daydream of Sunworld she wondered why Sycamore, Birdcherry and the others taken by the baiting were absent. Her obvious distress dismayed Garrison. She uttered the faint, chirping cry, gazed about her and struggled to her feet only to collapse again. He knew then she had no desire to live. Curled up at the fireside her eyes remained half-open and feeling the approach of one of his black moods Garrison poured himself a whisky and returned to his picture. It was Friday and on Monday he would be on his way to Switzerland and Ann.

The studio was unbearably warm so he flung open the windows. The month was certainly living up to its reputation. Flaming June! When Ann was part of it, it would have relevance. Everything would have relevance. If only he could pull the badger through. That would tie up things neatly for once. Why did so many episodes of one's life end in a mess? He stepped back and looked at the abstract. The colours were singing. Well, he thought, perhaps it wasn't an abstract. Perhaps it was simply an emotion made visual.

Billy and Sheena called after tea but the picture was finished and he felt he had nothing left of himself to share with anyone for a while. So he left them to nurse Aspen and went for a walk over the cliffs to Garrowcombe Head. The sea was flat, the horizon lost in a pearly haze and the seabirds swung through the warmth with a gracefulness that was soothing.

Back at the cottage a strange scent coaxed Aspen out of sleep. It was like the scent of flowers in the gardens of the big house in the trees. She opened her eyes and looked up into the face of the woman whose smile held a sadness the sow could feel in her own heart. She also felt the warmth and kindness. Then Fingo was butting her head firmly with his own and purring his delight.

'I'm not dreaming you, am I?' Aspen said.

'If you are then I'm dreaming you,' Fingo smiled. 'Everyone at the sett thinks you're dead. Sycamore is pining away and Birdcherry goes around splashing everyone with her tears.'

'Sycamore, Birdcherry?' Aspen whispered. 'I don't understand. Are they alive?'

'Sort of,' Fingo said. 'But like the others, Furzebright and the rest, they're grieving for you. They think you got the chop. I've never seen Cowtail so upset.'

'They're all alive and well? Honestly, Fingo?'

'Alive and glum. You'll have to come back as soon as possible and cheer them up. Wait till I tell them.'

Aspen sighed and closed her eyes again and through her sleepiness paraded the sett-dwellers she had believed lost to Nightworld. Then she ached for the steeps and the old life.

Garrison struck inland to come back along the lanes past Woodash Farm. In the bottom of the valley behind Hard Sands the hedges were full of honeysuckle. He was still breathing the scent on the lawn as dusk greyed to twilight. Even the smell of wood-smoke from the cottage chimney could not erase the memory. He lifted the latch and stepped into the living room and saw Ann. She was smiling up from the fireside where the badger lay sleeping.

Garrison was dumbfounded. It was the vision that had haunted him and he could not believe she was real.

'David,' she murmured, rising and holding out her arms. She was tall, thin and pale with grey-streaked chestnut hair falling to the shoulders. Her lined face was still lovely, Garrison thought, holding her close. Slowly her lashes descended and she kissed him but he was too moved to respond. So they stood hugging each other and laughing through the tears while the driftwood spat and crackled and the oystercatchers fluted across the hush outside.

He sat her in the rocking chair and crouched before her.

'I wanted to surprise you,' he said. 'This was planned weeks ago. Peter from the gallery met the boat train and drove me down. Billy and Sheena were here when I arrived. I didn't have to introduce myself. They seemed to know who I was. The little girl made me laugh. She said she thought I'd be younger. What on earth have you been telling them about me?'

'Only the truth – that you're lovely.'

She cupped his face in her hands and kissed him on the forehead.

'Strawberry gave you the black eye?'

351

He nodded and began to tell her about the baiting but she pressed her fingers to his lips.

'The children gave me a very vivid account,' she smiled. 'It's all over now, darling. And I'm home.'

'I've got some bubbly in the studio,' Garrison said. 'Wait here and I'll open it.'

'I'd rather have a cup of tea,' Ann said.

They went into the kitchen and he filled the kettle.

'By the way,' she continued. 'As the children left, in shot a scruffy little black cat.'

'Himself,' Garrison grinned 'The badger's friend.'

'Yes, it was extraordinary. He rushed right up and made a fuss of her, purring his head off and licking every square inch of her face.'

'You know, Ann,' Garrison said, holding her in his arms again. 'There's a kind of magic about this place and this stretch of coast.'

'And it's in your work. The picture's stunning.'

'I knew you'd like it.'

Returning to the fireside they were delighted to find Aspen crouching at her bowl drinking milk.

'Let's see if she'll take some cereal and honey,' Garrison said, and before long Aspen was crunching the cereal. Then she groomed herself and had a long pensive scratch before curling up again on the blanket.

'She's like me,' Ann said. 'A bit tottery, but on the mend.'

'Are you well enough to take a walk?'

'Yes, David. I'm not an invalid. Before I came home I was walking from the sanatorium to the village and back.'

He took her first to the lane with its hedges of honeysuckle and then to Hard Sands. Glancing back as they came bare-footed down to the water's edge he saw with a pang of heartache the double line of footprints along the shore.

The days passed and the ripening grass on Bullen Down took on a purplish sheen. Watching Ann and the badger play on the

352

lawn Garrison wondered whether he would be able to cope with the happiness of having her there occupying his every moment. Mrs Ordish and Lucy had called expecting to meet a film star but finding instead a charming lady with a smile and lovely eyes who was just beginning to lose the pallor of illness. Now, in the twilight, as she pretended to hide behind the cane chair, teasing Aspen so that the sow darted in to bite the hem of her frock or nip an ankle, the past rose again. He set down the tray of drinks and smiled as Aspen ragged Ann.

'She's ready to go back to the wilds, Ann,' he said. Aspen was galloping across the garden, inviting pursuit. Her chattering cries made Ann laugh.

'Perhaps she doesn't want to go,' she said. 'Oh, she's such a sweet little thing, David.'

'But she's not a pet,' he smiled.

'No, of course she isn't. It was stupid and selfish of me to want her to stay. I suppose I'm used to having her around.'

They linked arms and watched her rolling and kicking in the dew.

'When?' Ann added.

'Now,' he said and gathered up Aspen in his arms. Her eyes brimmed with trust and her nostrils rounded and crinkled to inhale his scent.

Although he could have released her sooner he carried her to the top of Woodash Down before lowering her to the turf. At once her muzzle went up and she cast about among the clover. They thought she was going but instead she ran quickly back to Ann and Garrison and uttered a low cry unlike any she had delivered in their presence. Then she trotted off, head and haunches swaying, stopped for a second to test the air and was gone.

'To Froward Point,' Garrison said.

'The place in your letters,' Ann murmured. 'Can't we go there, David?'

'Right this moment? It's quite a long way.'

'We've got all night, darling.'

She dragged at his hand but he had no intention of refusing her.

Aspen trotted along the edge of the farmland with the steeps to her left and the hills rolling into the sky before her. Ghost moths were on the wing and all the scents of Nightworld eddied around her. It was her place and she was happy in it. Up the sheep-littered slopes above Parson's Cove she plodded and flattened her back to crawl under the stile into the hay field which was criss-crossed with animal trails. Now she was walking through plantain and grasses, under swaying heads and the whisper of wind.

She was well into the field when a drift of musk brought her to a halt. It was Sycamore's scent laced with the less distinctive smells of Birdcherry and Hawscrag. Uttering their chirping cries the badgers met and the mated boar and sow rubbed snouts and sniffed at each other's coats. Their joy went deep but Hawscrag and Birdcherry were permitted to romp with them until they were all covered in grass seeds and pollen.

'Fingo told us,' Hawscrag said at last. 'We thought we'd lost you, Aspen.'

Aspen shook her head, unable to speak.

Leaving the meadow the badgers walked up into the bean fields, stopping every so often to gaze at the silvery glow that was creeping into the sky beyond Froward.

Slowly the moon edged up from the trees and raising their muzzles to breathe the scent of the pines Aspen and Sycamore climbed the zigzags onto the Point and waited for Birdcherry to join them. The animals were dew-spiked and their eyes were full of brightness.